THE PERFECT GIRL

ALSO BY ANDY MASLEN

Detective Kat Ballantyne:

The Seventh Girl

The Unseen Sister

The Silent Wife

The Lying Man

The Rebel Son

Detective Ford:

Shallow Ground

Land Rites

Plain Dead

DI Stella Cole:

Hit and Run

Hit Back Harder

Hit and Done

Let the Bones Be Charred

Weep, Willow, Weep

A Beautiful Breed of Evil

Death Wears a Golden Cloak

See the Dead Birds Fly

Playing the Devil's Music

Gabriel Wolfe Thrillers:

Trigger Point

Reversal of Fortune

Blind Impact

Condor

First Casualty

Fury

Rattlesnake

Minefield

No Further

Torpedo

Three Kingdoms

Ivory Nation

Crooked Shadow

Brass Vows

Seven Seconds

Peacemaker

Edged Weapon

Other Fiction:

Blood Loss – A Vampire Story

Purity Kills

You're Always With Me

Green-Eyed Mobster

THE PERFECT GIRL

A DETECTIVE KAT BALLANTYNE THRILLER

ANDY MASLEN

Published by Thomas & Mercer, Seattle

www.apub.com

EU Product Safety Contact:
Amazon Media EU S.à r.l.
38, avenue John F. Kennedy, L-1855 Luxembourg
amazonpublishing-gpsr@amazon.com

ISBN-13: 9781662530678
eISBN: 9781662530661

Cover photography and design by Dominic Forbes

Printed in the United States of America

For Jo. My perfect girl.

It is only through shadows that one comes to know the light.

—St Catherine of Siena

Chapter One

Lena normally opened up Blooming Miracles at 9.00 a.m., but this particular Tuesday, she was in at 6.30 a.m. to prepare the order for a big corporate event. Nobody about this early. Just her and her flowers.

The shop was a girlhood dream, now realised thanks to the divorce settlement Lena had achieved over the vociferous but ultimately futile objections of her sociopathic ex-husband.

Spring had come late to Middlehampton this year, and the cherry trees on Five Cups Lane still bore their blossom. As she stripped leaves from the long-stemmed roses, she glanced out of the shop window, enjoying the way the sun crested the rooflines of the houses opposite the shop.

The shop was in what everyone called the Old Town. Part of a quiet little neighbourhood away from the traffic and the noise of the town centre. Lots of lovely little two-up-two-down terraced houses with front doors opening on to the street, and a few businesses steadily making their way, like fish swimming upstream against a strong but manageable current. A cafe, an Italian restaurant, a Turkish barber, a convenience store, a vintage clothes 'emporium' and Lena's florist's shop.

She put the finishing touches to another arrangement and decided she'd earned a break. She made herself a coffee and took it outside, standing beneath the sturdy metal canopy above the shopfront. She lit a cigarette, frowning at a fallen gerbera on the pavement, crushed beneath someone's heel. There were plenty more in the shop, but she hated to see even one dead before its time.

The coffee was too hot, but the cigarette was perfect. She drew the smoke deep into her lungs and let it out with a sigh. She allowed herself a few more minutes, but those roses wouldn't prepare themselves, would they? She smiled and turned to go back inside.

The body hit the pavement right in front of her with a flat, wet crunch. Lena screamed and dropped her coffee mug, which shattered on the pavement. She was rooted to the spot, hyperventilating.

The dead girl – poor little thing couldn't have been out of her teens – lay right by the front door, arms splayed, legs at angles Lena just knew meant they were broken. The girl's face was scratched and bloody, her long blonde hair every which way.

Lena dragged her phone out of her jeans pocket and with a shaking finger summoned help.

'Emergency. Which service do you require?'

She gasped out her location, the 'nature of her emergency', and her name.

Lena ended the call, even though the lady on the other end asked her to stay on the line. And with her back to the plate-glass window, through which she could see a dozen smooth-stemmed roses lying ready on her table – *must remember to take off the guard petals, people think they're mouldy* – she slid down until her bottom bumped on to the pavement.

'Don't worry, lovely,' she said to the dead girl. 'Help's on its way.'

Chapter Two

Inside the cordon, crackly blue nylon booties over her shoes, DS Kat Ballantyne stared down at the dead girl. The poor thing couldn't be more than twenty.

Her nose had been pushed to one side, her lips were split and bloody. No make-up, smooth skin already beginning to lose its lustre and mottle in the building heat of the unseasonably warm spring day. Beneath the scrapes and cuts, she had the well-scrubbed look of a girl who took care of herself.

She wore a baby-blue corduroy jacket with a sheepskin lining over a thick crocheted tank top, a white vest, and the baggy jeans girls favoured these days. Her outfit as a whole suggested a student. Young female workers in Middlehampton went for trousers or skirts from H&M or Primark. Wore more make-up, too. And would probably have taken the eyebrow ring out for work.

One sneaker. The other foot was bare. Toenails painted bright green. Kat looked around. Where was the other shoe?

Her bagman, DC Tom Gray, sighed.

'Tell me what you see, Tomski,' she said.

'Female. White. Young. Eighteen? A year or two older?'

'How about the injuries?'

'Multiple broken bones. I mean, badly broken. Abrasions, lacerations and contusions to face and hands. Broken nose.'

'Foul play?'

'I'm not seeing much blood. Certainly no spatter. No obvious penetration wounds. Not stabbed, shot or bludgeoned. Looks like she was hit by a car . . . or a truck.' He turned, looked up and down the road. 'A hit-and-run? The collision threw her up on to the awning?'

Kat nodded. Not because she agreed with the fast-track DC. Because she was thinking. She tugged on her earlobes, a habit she'd developed in school when trying to unscramble a difficult problem. Why was the dead girl so warmly dressed? The jacket could have been a fashion statement, but Kat reckoned she'd put it on because she knew she'd be cold. She must have come out the previous night.

'Five Cups Lane's hardly a main route through town, though, is it, Tomski? Have you ever come down here at night?'

'Nope.'

'I have. It's dead. None of the businesses would need a delivery from a truck. And look.' She pointed at a wasp-waist in the road twenty yards further up, where the kerbs converged to slow down cars. 'Traffic-calming. How could you get up enough speed to throw a body ten feet into the air?'

'OK, so you don't like my theory,' Tom said huffily. 'What's yours?'

There it was again. Always just below the surface these days, and occasionally breaking through – the irritated tone Tom used whenever anyone contradicted him.

When he'd arrived in the Major Crimes Unit, he'd had a sharp mind – and still did – and an even-keel approach to investigation. But since recovering from a coma after they'd been bushwhacked by a murder suspect, he'd undergone a decided personality shift, acquiring a short fuse and a temper to match.

Kat was determined to bring him back to the right side of the fence. That meant keeping him close by for now, even if he did bridle at being on such a short rein. Ignoring his short-tempered response, Kat looked up. Looming above the florist's was a multistorey car park.

'She came from up there.'

He sighed. 'That would be the second suicide since I arrived in Middlehampton. Last year, a girl threw herself off a bridge.'

'Who said anything about suicide?'

He frowned. 'Well, *you* did.'

'I said she might have *come* from up there. I didn't say she *jumped* from up there. She could have been mucking around with friends and fell. Or someone could have pushed her. Might not even have meant to kill her, you know, just kids messing about.'

'Yeah, Kat, but the most likely explanation is she went up there and jumped, don't you think? Look, she even wrapped up warm so she wouldn't mistake shivering from cold for fear.'

Kat had a fourteen-year-old son at home. Riley could transform from well-mannered boy who'd offer to lay the table, share details of his dates with girlfriend Millie, and hug his mum spontaneously, to a roaring bull of a boy whose door-slams were the stuff of legend in the Ballantyne household. So she was quite able to deal with the impatience of an ambitious DC who felt his career had somehow been put on hold.

'I think the most likely explanation for *how* this girl ended up looking the way she does is she fell from a great height on to something hard.' She paused, looking at the steel canopy. 'As to *why* she fell, I'm keeping an open mind. You should, too.'

'You're the boss.'

'That I am, Tomski.' She looked around. A CSI with a digital camera was standing by the white forensics van parked a little way down the street, just beyond the cordon. She went over. 'Have you finished taking photos?'

The CSI nodded. 'All done.'

Kat went back and knelt beside the body. An ID would make life simpler. She pulled on nitrile gloves and lifted the girl's jacket aside. It had an inside pocket fastened with a press stud. She un-popped it and gently felt inside. Her fingers closed on a thin, firm rectangle. She extracted it: a slender credit-card wallet in bubblegum-pink nylon, scuffed and emblazoned with a band sticker. She pulled out a white plastic card – struck gold. The girl's student ID.

'Her name is Rosie Duggan. Date of birth, 19th June 2007. Just eighteen, poor love. Can you track down next of kin?'

'Of course. But we'll do the death-knock together, boss, yes?'

'Don't worry, Tomski. I'm not letting you out of my sight.'

But as Tom made a note, Kat felt a disorientating sense of vertigo and had to reach out a hand to steady herself on the shop's plate-glass window. Rosie was eighteen, the same age Kat's best friend, Liv, had been when she'd vanished – apparently the victim of a serial killer. Decades later, it turned out that Liv's disappearance had been of her own making, and now Kat was the only other person who knew the full story. But Rosie Duggan's time on this earth was over for good. There would be no resurrection for her.

Kat's mentor DS – and now DI – Molly Steadman had once told an inexperienced DC Kathryn Ballantyne that their job was to rule homicide *out*, not in. On acquiring her own bagman, she'd told him the same thing. So, what had happened to Rosie Duggan? Could she find evidence of foul play?

She inhaled deeply, dragging sweet-scented spring air deep into her lungs, and stepped away from the window. She squatted beside the body again. If someone had attacked Rosie, coming at her brandishing a knife, there'd likely be defensive wounds on her hands or forearms.

Kat inspected the girl's left hand. The heel was scraped, but the palm and fingers were devoid of even a shallow cut, let alone the deep incisions murder victims often sustained when fighting to ward off a knife attack.

She looked at the right hand. The fingers were curled lightly against the palm as if holding something special. Nails painted green to match her toes. One was missing. Torn off at the quick, exposing angry red flesh beneath. Kat winced. The others were clogged with fragments of what looked like wood. Paint flecks, too. A bright blue.

A missing shoe. A missing nail. The shoe could have flown off on impact, although she'd leave it to the search team to find where it had landed. Could it be up there – she craned her neck – on the top storey of the car park?

But it took a lot of force to rip a nail out at the bed. Had Rosie tried to fight off an assailant? Lost her nail when it snagged on their clothing? No, because that didn't account for the splinters and the blue paint. A bat? A length of wood torn from a pallet?

The bell labelled 'homicide' was ringing loudly.

The clanging became deafening when she couldn't find Rosie's phone.

Chapter Three

A familiar smell insinuated itself into Kat's nostrils. A subtle, expensive aftershave a million miles away from that of her boss, DI Stuart 'Carve-up' Carver, who she'd been expecting to arrive on the scene at any moment.

Carve-up favoured Aramis, which Kat suspected he did only because her father – Carve-up's paymaster – used it. This was a woody, spicy fragrance and it signalled the arrival, at her shoulder, of the pathologist Dr Jack Beale.

He knelt beside her. The smell intensified. Kat felt a not altogether unpleasant squirming low in her belly. She tried to stay focused on the dead girl's face. Turning towards Jack would bring their faces far too close for comfort. But standing up would be awkward.

'Morning, Jack.'

'Morning, Kat. Want to tell me what we've got?'

'I think she fell – or, more accurately, was pushed – from the roof of the car park. It looks like she landed on the canopy over the shop doorway. I think she lay there all night before something changed, maybe as rigor mortis set in, and she rolled off on to the pavement.'

Jack nodded. He reached out a gloved hand and encircled the dead girl's left wrist. Tried to lift it. He'd rolled his shirtsleeves up. Kat watched the muscles and tendons under the skin of his forearm moving.

'Rigor's well developed. You could be right. If she was finely balanced, small shifts over a few hours could have changed the weight distribution just enough for her to fall. I'm assuming you want a full forensic post-mortem?'

'When could you do it?'

He turned his head. Locked eyes with her.

'For my favourite DS I want to say this morning. But sadly, I can't.'

There it was again. That flirtatious tone he'd directed her way since the very first time they'd met. She batted him away every single time. But she had to admit, it was nice to know at least one man other than her husband, Ivan, noticed her in that way.

Mind you, even Van had been a bit less forthcoming with the compliments the last week or two. Just overworked, she supposed. The small businesses whose IT he ran – and the bigger ones too, sometimes – seemed to think that by paying Van's invoices they'd bought him body and soul, and not just for the day or two a month he was contracted.

'When can you? This afternoon?'

'Sorry, Kat, I'm snowed under. The arson cases your other two DCs are working have me and Ashleigh at the table all day every day. Five dead of extensive burns. Let's just say it's not pretty and it's not easy work.'

'When *could* you do it for me, Jack?'

'It's Tuesday today. Friday morning, first thing? Say 8.00 a.m.?'

'You can't do it sooner?'

He tilted his head, his lips quirking into a half-smile. 'I could do it *later*.'

She huffed out a breath. 'Fine. Friday then.'

'It's a date.'

'Can you give me an estimate for time of death?'

'Based on the rigor and a couple of other signs, the films over the corneas, I'd say six to eight hours.'

'Thanks, Jack. I can probably narrow that down once I've spoken to the lady who called it in. And, I know what you're going to say, but what's your best guess on cause of death? Did she break her neck?'

He peered at Rosie Duggan's head, palpated the skin of her neck, frowning as he looked away and closed his eyes.

'I can't be sure it's what killed her. But the neck's definitely broken.'

'Thanks, Jack.'

Kat straightened, her knees popping, and went over to Tom who was making notes and sketching the scene.

'PM's on Friday morning. Eight. Be there or be square.'

He nodded. Made a note.

'I tried speaking to the woman who called it in. I think she's in shock.'

Kat turned her head. 'Which one's she?'

'Sitting on the wall over there with the takeaway cup.'

Kat wandered over to where a woman in her early forties was sitting on a low metal railing, cradling a Starbucks cup in both hands. She seemed oblivious to the uniforms, CSIs and assorted police personnel filling the narrow lane outside her shop.

Kat sat next to her on the narrow iron rail.

'Hello. My name's Kat. I'm a detective. What's yours?'

The woman's head jerked round.

'Lena. Ralston . . .' She frowned. 'I mean Lena Ferry. She's dead, isn't she?'

'I'm afraid so. I understand you found her, is that right?'

Lena shook her head. It looked to Kat as though she was having to remember how to operate her body from the inside. An unwilling passenger in a machine sent deep into foreign and inhospitable territory. And had she forgotten her own name?

She looked at the woman's left hand. An indent on the ring finger. Recently divorced, then. Still getting used to using her maiden name again.

'I only went out for a cigarette.'

She sniffed and a tear tracked down her cheek. Kat offered her a tissue from a cellophane-wrapped packet. The woman blew her nose and then clutched the sodden tissue against the coffee cup.

'Can you tell me what happened, Lena? Take your time.'

She sniffed again. Tears began rolling freely. Kat handed her the packet of tissues.

'Keep it.'

'Thanks. I didn't *find* her. That makes it sound like one of those people on the news. You know, they're always saying it. "The body was found by a man walking his dog." Aren't they?'

'They do. It happened to a friend of mine.'

This was not a well-intentioned lie to keep a witness talking. Kat's dog-walking friend Barrie Price – an ex-copper himself – had discovered a dead woman on Bowman's Common a couple of years back.

'Well, this was a lot worse. I was having a coffee and a cigarette and then she . . . she . . .'

A loud sob escaped her. She brought the coffee cup to her lips between both hands, which were shaking, and took a hasty gulp. She cleared her throat before she shook her head sharply from side to side.

'She fell on to the ground right in front of me. I called 999 and then I just sat here, waiting. Making sure nobody, you know, tried to touch her, or take pictures.'

'*Did* anyone?'

'No. It was too early. This part of town's pretty quiet until the shops open.'

'Can you tell me what time it was? When she fell?'

'About seven-fifteen. I know because I checked the time before I went out with my coffee and cigarettes.' She checked her watch. 'I ought to go. I've got a big order to fill.'

'You're sure you'll be all right?'

'No. But I have bills to pay like everyone else.'

Kat fished a spare pair of booties out of her murder bag. 'Put these on to cross the pavement. I'll square it with the crime scene manager. But once you're inside, can you stay there until all this lot' – Kat waved an arm to encompass the CSIs – 'have left?'

Lena nodded.

'Actually, Lena . . . one more thing. You haven't got a stepladder, have you?'

Lena nodded. She slipped the booties over her shoes and crossed the narrow street and entered her shop. Kat signalled to the CSI who held up a hand to stop Lena that it was OK. Lena reappeared a few minutes later with an extending aluminium stepladder.

Kat took it from her, erected it against the front of the metal canopy and climbed up. Once she got a look at the upper surface, the narrative of Rosie Duggan's last moments revealed itself.

Two-thirds of the way along the canopy was a patch of congealed blood in which blonde hairs were stuck, waving gently from side to side in the light breeze that had sprung up. A trail of blood ran down the slope and into the preformed gutter along the edge, where Kat found Rosie's missing sneaker.

Kat looked up. Rosie had fallen or been pushed from the car park roof, losing a fingernail in the process, presumably as she scrabbled for grip on a railing designed to prevent people falling, or at least give them pause before climbing over.

She'd fallen five floors before she hit the steel canopy, opening a laceration on her head and breaking her neck. Jack would tell Kat whether that was the fatal injury on Friday. Either way, she'd died there and lain, undisturbed, until around 7.15 a.m. Then, owing to temperature changes, a minute shift in weight distribution as her body settled, or the sheet metal expanding in the warmth of the sun, she'd fallen the remaining eight or nine feet to the pavement.

Kat took the steps back down to ground level.

'There's blood and hair up there, and her missing sneaker,' she said to the closest CSI.

Then she went over to where Tom was talking to the crime scene manager.

'Tomski. Let's go and take a look at the car park.'

From the uncovered top storey, they had an uninterrupted view across the town centre. Market traders were dealing with their first customers of the day, and the traffic on the major arteries was building steadily.

Kat led Tom across the open area: shoppers and commuters were still filling the lower floors and hadn't reached the rooftop yet. She held up a hand once they were within twenty yards of the spot where Kat estimated Rosie must have been standing just before her fatal fall. She donned a fresh pair of booties and motioned for Tom to do the same. Gloves followed.

She headed for the railing – blue paint weathered away in patches to reveal wood – and worked her way along towards the spot directly above Blooming Miracles.

Leaning out, Kat looked straight down, the acute angle foreshortening the CSIs and uniformed cops into heads and shoulders, long shadows spearing out westwards from each figure. Jesus, it was a long way down. The backs of her knees trembled and ached. She told herself she wasn't frightened of heights. It was just a natural reaction to a dangerous situation. *Yeah, right.*

Several scratches in the paint ran across the narrow wooden railing. She squatted and checked the ground beneath it. In the corner between the tarmac and a low concrete lip she saw a flash of bright green. An artificial nail, the front edge broken, the rear stippled with blood.

'Can you hand me an evidence bag, Tomski?'

He passed her a small plastic baggie. She dropped the torn-off nail inside and sealed it.

She stood up.

'I think someone brought her up here and then, possibly when her back was turned, pushed her off. She flung her arms out to try and save herself and managed to grab the railing. But she was already going over and all she managed to do was tear her nail out.'

Tom nodded. 'Or she climbed over and held on, intending to kill herself. Started to fall and then changed her mind at the last minute. Same story from then on.'

'If we find evidence that definitively points to suicide then we can look at that theory, but for now I'm treating it as murder.'

'I'm looking for a note, then?'

'Yes. Or evidence of mental health problems. Addiction issues. Money problems. But honestly, Tomski, and I'm sad to say this, I know more about young girls killing themselves than I want to, and this doesn't look like that. It's too brutal. You know the most common methods, don't you?'

'Hanging-slash-asphyxiation, followed by drugs. For both sexes.'

'Exactly. And when it comes to the more, you know, extravagant methods – shotguns, jumping in front of trains, cutting your own throat – it's usually men.'

'Fair enough. What do you want me to do?'

'Number one after finding next of kin, get on to the social media team. I want to know if anyone driving past here last night captured anything on their dashcam.'

'On it.'

As they descended the many flights of bare concrete steps, Kat reflected that in a few hours, or less, she'd once again be knocking on a door and ripping people's lives apart.

And it never got easier.

◆ ◆ ◆

As they went in through the staff entrance at Jubilee Place copshop, Tom stopped and looked up, something catching his attention. He pointed.

'I've been meaning to ask you ever since I arrived. What are all those dead plants poking out from that flat roof below the main one?'

Kat followed his pointing finger and smiled. A little local knowledge she could pass on.

'HR had an environmental bee in their collective bonnet three years ago. They got a grant from the council and put in a green roof. Couple of tons of special lightweight compost and about a thousand quid's worth of special drought-tolerant plants.'

'What happened?'

'This is England, right? Wet winters. Dry springs. Heatwaves followed by biblical rain. They drowned, then they dehydrated, then they drowned again. Now they're just a sort of massive brown futon.'

'Shame there wasn't one on that car park. Rosie might have lived.'

She sighed and pushed through the door, Tom behind her.

'Come on, Tomski. You can make a start on the paperwork. I'll go and brief Carve-up.' She turned to urge him in before the automatic closer swung the door shut on him. He was taking a swig from a silver hip flask. Anger, despair and concern flashed through her. 'Tomski! What the hell?'

He hastily screwed the cap back on and pocketed the flask. 'Sorry, boss. Just a stiffener after seeing Rosie like that.'

'Christ, mate, it's not even nine o'clock.'

'I said I'm sorry!' he snapped. 'Can we just leave it, please? You said we've got work to do. So let's go and get started.'

Unwilling to have a full-blown confrontation in a public place, she led him inside. She needed to find a way to reach her bagman very soon and confront him about his changed behaviour. Before he achieved the impossible and booted himself off the force.

Chapter Four

As always when she had to notify her DI of a new investigation, Kat's stomach was knotted.

It wasn't fear, or even anxiety; Kat wasn't the kind of woman to find bullies scary. But Carve-up was corrupt, and she held him in contempt – a bent officer who spent as little time as possible on any actual policework, preferring to devote himself to his beloved 'metrics', sucking up to anyone he perceived as higher up the food chain, and, presumably, doing the bidding of his various paymasters.

Chief among these was her father. He and Carve-up played golf together once a week. And there were too many times when Carve-up had known things or done things that would benefit Colin Morton for Kat to pass them off as coincidence.

She supposed it was – just – possible Carve-up *wasn't* in her dad's pocket.

It was also possible the Jubilee Place canteen served a decent vegetarian meal.

As she entered MCU's open-plan office, Kat pulled her shoulders back. Her days of letting Carve-up dictate her actions lay in the past. She had a job to do – and, in the DCI Crime, Linda Ockenden, a mostly sympathetic boss. Then Kat bit her lip, remembering the events that had seen PC Abby Greene shot and killed by a murder suspect who'd been allowed to flee the country with Linda's connivance. MI6 had been involved, but it had still dented Kat's trust in Linda.

She looked around, hoping to see one or both of her other DCs at their desks. But Leah Hooper and Faisal Mohammed were out, working a series of fatal arson attacks. Carve-up had pulled Leah and Fez out from Kat's team after Abby's murder, while Kat was answering questions from the Independent Office for Police Conduct. A naked power play designed to bolster his standing and weaken Kat's. The only mystery was why Linda hadn't backed Kat when she'd protested.

She marched through the crowded desks, nodding to various detectives she knew, and then knocked on Carve-up's office door. He'd taken to keeping the Venetian blinds closed as well. What was *wrong* with him? It was as if he'd abandoned even the pretext of being a manager, not bothering to suggest he might be watching the people on his team. Instead, he spent his days poring over spreadsheets, writing or reading reports, and presumably figuring out ways to advance his career without doing any actual work.

Sadly, it wasn't the worst strategy a second-rate detective could employ. The really good thief-takers were always the ones the brass were reluctant to promote. Bump a successful DS up to DI and you might get a senior manager who understood how things worked on the streets, but you lost a 'closer'. But take someone who never rose above average in the front-line squad and you got a twofer: a makeweight removed from the business of closing cases, and a replacement who might actually want to solve crimes.

'Come!' he barked. Kat started; she'd had enough time for her thoughts to drift.

She went in, deliberately leaving the door open behind her. His lips tightened as he glanced past her at the lack of a barrier between him and the business of catching the perpetrators of the major crimes he was responsible for solving.

'Close the door, would you, DS Ballantyne?' he said, fiddling with his mouse and avoiding eye contact.

'I won't be long, Stu,' she replied, using the nickname guaranteed to irritate him.

It was childish, she knew. And when he found the grace to call her 'Kat', like everybody else in the station, she'd repay the favour. Until then, 'DS Ballantyne' or 'Kitty-Kat' and 'Stu' it was.

'Well, spit it out, then, I've got a report to write.'

'It's a dirty job, but somebody . . . et cetera?'

He eyeballed her. And a sneer deformed his upper lip.

'I know what you think of me, DS Ballantyne.'

'I sincerely doubt that, Stu.'

'What do you call me behind my back? Pen-pusher? Metrics Monkey?'

'What makes you think we talk about you when you're not around, Stu?'

The tension between them crackled. She was glad Carve-up claimed to prefer working on-screen. Any stray papers on his desk would, she felt sure, have spontaneously combusted.

'Did you come in here to insult your line-manager? Is that it? Want me to write you up for insubordination so you can spend a few days at home with your adult colouring books or however you spend your free time?'

'I don't get any free time, Stu. Too busy on real policework. Catching murderers.'

There. That shut him up. Some half-formed insult died on his lips, which compressed into a thin white line. His cheeks paled, then flared as the blood in his face tried to decide how to represent the emotions roiling in his chest. Shame? Anger? Guilt? Confusion?

'Yes, well, me neither. A DI lives and breathes the job, so I'll thank you to get on with it and then get out of my office.'

She had to suppress a smile. The combined lie-and-boast was so transparently false she wondered how Carve-up himself wasn't winking a 'gotcha!' at her.

'A young girl was pushed to her death from the multistorey car park in the Old Town. I'm opening a murder investigation.'

He raised his head slowly and finally focused his gaze on her, full-face.

'Of course you are. I've already heard the preliminary feedback from the scene, because . . .' He held up a hand, even though Kat hadn't made any attempt to interrupt him. 'Let me finish. Yes, I do, still, have a finger on the pulse of this town. And what I'm hearing is some student, probably with mental health issues, because let's face it, they all do these days, don't they? Anyway, she's gone up to the top of the car park and taken the easy way out. But you do you, as they say. I know it's pointless trying to suggest there are other cases that deserve your time when you've made your mind up, so have at it.'

She willed her breathing to stay slow, deep. She hated needing something from him, but she had to try. Again.

'I could investigate it a lot more effectively if you'd let me have Leah and Fez back.'

His lips did something weird, then, as if he'd eaten a bad prawn. After a moment she realised he was trying to look sympathetic.

'You *know* why they're reporting to me for the moment. After that terrible business with Ali Greene – *your* mentee, remember – we agreed that having less people to manage would give you some space to heal.'

'Her name was Abby,' Kat snapped. 'And any healing I'm ever going to do is already done.'

'Whatever. Silly bitch only had herself to blame.' He clapped a hand to his mouth, then removed it to reveal a smirk. 'Whoops!

Did I just call a dead police officer a "silly bitch"? Linda would have me on the naughty step for weeks. Lucky there were no witnesses, eh, Kitty-Kat? Now, was there anything else? Only, this report won't write itself.'

Kat's fists were clenched. Like a lot of people, she did the lottery. And in the billion-to-one event she won, her first act would be to drag Carve-up through MCU by his ears and kick him down the stairs. Twice. Yes, there'd be a charge of assault. But with her winnings she'd be able to afford the best legal team in Middlehampton. And she had a strong suspicion Carve-up's lawyer would find it hard to find a single witness to back their man.

'Try ChatGPT, Stu,' she grated out, then she spun on her heel and left, budging the door wider with her hip.

Chapter Five

The drive to the village where Rosie Duggan's parents ran a pub would take two hours. Plenty of time for what Kat had planned.

'We'll take my car,' she said to Tom.

They chatted aimlessly, as cops often do, while she navigated the morning traffic in Middlehampton. Who was shagging who. Which canteen breakfast was best. Whether Carve-up would make DCI – his stated aim – and free them from his glowering presence.

Whereas talking to Carve-up had provoked no anxiety at all, broaching the subject she wanted to with Tom had her stomach squirming. She tried out various openings in her head, and in each case imagined the short, sharp retort she'd earn. Nothing sounded right. Finally, she just opened her mouth and let her lips decide what she was going to say.

'I'm worried about you, Tomski, and I don't like it. The drinking on duty? The bad-tempered outbursts? The attitude? If this carries on you won't just be off the fast-track, you'll be off the force altogether. And you're too good a detective for that to happen. Plus, if you get shit-canned that only leaves me, and I can't be a DS with no team, everybody will laugh and point.' She gulped in a breath. Too late to change course now. 'So we're going to find a way to get you sorted and I'm going to be your friend as well as your boss . . . and please *please* don't be cross.'

She tightened her grip on the steering wheel. The traffic on the northbound carriageway of the M1 wasn't too bad this morning, but she didn't want to swerve under the verbal onslaught her bagman was about to unleash.

'I'm worried, too, boss.'

Shocked, Kat risked a sideways glance. Tom was turned away from her, staring fixedly out the side window.

'Are you, Tomski? What about?'

'What you said. The drinking. Picking fights. Generally being an unpredictable, moody arsehole. Will that do for starters?'

Kat relaxed. What was to come would be hard, but she no longer thought it would be unpleasant.

'Can I tell you what I'm seeing, Tomski? What I feel is happening?'

'I'm all ears,' he said.

He sounded defeated. Tired. But also relieved. As if the burden of putting on a brave face had suddenly become too much to shoulder, and he was relieved someone had told him it was OK to put it down.

Kat inhaled. People management was right at the top of the 'skills to be mastered' section of her internal staff appraisal form. Or possibly second, behind 'stop fantasising about committing violent assaults on DI Carver'. But if she could approach Tom as one human being to another, she thought she could make it work.

'Those things you just mentioned. I've noticed. How could I not? Everyone else has, too. But they're not the problem, Tomski. They're just the, I don't know, the symptoms. The outward signs.' It wasn't a bad start, but Kat felt she was groping in the dark as she tried to find a way to the heart of the matter. 'Remember your first day in MCU, Tomski?'

'Of course. You all looked at me like I'd arrived fresh from Planet Uni with a laminated degree certificate in my back pocket.

Trying not to get my new suit dirty before I flew off to the next stop on my fast-track. Someone even put a plastic Bambi on my desk.'

Kat laughed briefly. It was funny. And it was true. Or it was funny *because* it was true.

'Craig supplied the Bambi,' she said, referring to Craig Elders, the other DS who worked under Carve-up. 'And Leah put it there.'

'Yeah, I figured it out when she kept saying "Bird, bird, bird!" loudly whenever I walked by.'

'She loves you, Tomski, you know that.'

'I'm not sure she does anymore.'

'Don't be an idiot! Of course she does. It's like in a family. Your little brother acts up and you rub his toothbrush on the soap but you don't stop loving him.' A lump formed in her throat and she swallowed. 'Oh, God, this isn't going well, I'm getting all teary, mate.'

He huffed out a breath.

'Don't expect me to help you out, boss. You started it.'

'Fair enough. Anyway, on your first day, you were so eager to please. To show you weren't that annoying fast-track kid. And you've proved yourself, Tomski. You're a good detective. You've helped put some really evil bastards away. When we went after Will Paxton, you didn't stop to consider whether taking him on without backup was a wise move. You were right there with me, shoulder to shoulder. And because of that, you were injured in the line of duty and you went into that . . . that *fucking* coma.'

'Would it have made any difference if I'd tried to stop you going in, Kat? I mean, you're not exactly known around the station for your reticent, safety-first approach, you know.'

'Ha! More like "The villain's holed up in that china shop, find me a bull to ride"?'

'You said it, not me.'

'I spoke to your neurologist, Tomski. I know they regard comas as brain injuries.'

'I did, too. She said it ought to get better on its own but there's always a few per cent of cases where it never does.' He swallowed audibly. 'That's what I'm afraid of, Kat. I mean, what if I never get better?'

Oh, shit, was he crying? Kat's heart clenched. She risked another quick sideways look. Tom still had his face turned away but his hand was just going into his pocket. For a tissue? Actually, was that bad? Here, where it was just the two of them, it would be all right if he let out some emotion. She'd only seen him cry once before, when his girlfriend dumped him.

'Let's not worry about the future,' she said. 'It's out of our control. But here's what we *can* do. Number one, I want you with me 24/7 – not literally, but we're a team, yes?'

'Yes.'

'You're my bagman, I'm your DS. Then let's work cases as a team. Properly close. You shadow me and learn as much as you can. Then when your inevitable promotion comes through and you fly the nest for the glories of counter-terror or intelligence or HQ or wherever you fast-track kids go next after the streets, you'll be ready to step up. And I'll be there if you have a wobble. Someone you can talk to off the record without going to HR or occie health or anywhere they'll record your concerns. That's what's bothering you, isn't it, Tomski? That you could derail your own career by admitting you need help?'

In truth, Kat wasn't sure this was right, but she'd spent enough time thinking about all of this to be reasonably certain. Usually in the middle of the night when she was lying awake with too many thoughts revolving in her head for sleep to come.

Tom didn't say anything for a mile. Kat nudged the Golf up to eighty miles per hour for a while, just until she cleared a slow-moving clump of traffic.

He spoke as she pulled into the middle lane again.

'It is,' he said.

'Sorry, Tomski, what?'

'I mean . . . You're right. That *is* it. Part of it, anyway. I don't know how much you know about how the fast-track works but there's a certain expectation that you continue to make progress. It doesn't necessarily mean you solve loads of crimes. More that you're active on high-profile cases. You volunteer for any inter-force operations going. You go on all the courses, cultivate contacts with other departments. All that.'

Kat nodded. She'd suspected as much. That the fast-track included a module almost certainly not called 'Greasy-Pole Climbing for Beginners'. But it was nice to have it confirmed by somebody actually in the VIP lane.

'Oi'm jes' glad to 'ave a job where oi gets to whack villains wi' me truncheon,' she said, going for the most over-the-top bumpkin accent she could manage.

Tom laughed. 'That's literally the worst deep-country Hertfordshire accent I've ever heard.'

'Thank you kindly. Please look out for my Bafta nomination.'

'I got so anxious after I woke up from it, Kat. I thought the brass would chalk me down as a failure. I mean, it's not as if there aren't plenty of other ambitious young DCs they can pick from, is it?'

'Is that why you started drinking again, Tomski?' she asked quietly.

'Mm-hmm. And then because I knew everybody'd noticed I got defensive. I was angry with myself for falling off the wagon and I started lashing out. I'm so sorry, Kat. It was unforgivable.'

'Are you kidding, Tomski? Of *course* it's forgivable. That's the one thing it truly is. If this was America and you'd been shot in the line of duty' – she swallowed as her critical internal voice spoke up, *like Abby, who you were going to shit-can with a negative evaluation after her rotation in MCU finished* – 'you'd be a hero. Nobody would be surprised if it affected you.'

'Sometimes I think it would have been better if Paxton had shot me instead of just pushing me through a coffee table.'

'You don't mean that, Tomski. Now, listen to your Auntie Kat. When you say "falling off the wagon" it makes you sound like an alcoholic. But correct me if I'm wrong – your decision to stop drinking was because of what happened at uni. The bar fight with the biker. Not being in control. It was a voluntary thing.'

'It was. I felt so bad when he died, I just didn't feel like drinking anymore.'

'So – and it's not that I'm judging anyone who does have a drink problem, but – that's not you, OK? So let's start by renaming the drinking. You were in a life-threatening confrontation with an armed murder suspect and you got really seriously injured. You came out of it suffering from anxiety and you tried to self-medicate with alcohol. Can we agree that's actually what happened?'

'I guess.'

'Pardon, DC Gray?' Kat put some steel into her voice but smiled at the same time, hoping Tom got the intention behind her words.

'Yes, boss, that's what happened.'

Kat relaxed. *Baby steps, Kat, baby steps.*

'Good. So let's decide our first step is for you to . . . not *stop* drinking, like it's a moral failing if you have a pint with the team after a long day. But stop drinking at *work*, OK? Ditch the hip flask. Is it on you now?'

'Yep,' he said quietly.

'Why don't you let me take it? And then, the next time you feel anxious, or you just reach for it out of habit, it won't be there so you *can't* drink, and you tell me what's going on instead and I'll listen until you feel better. Would that work?'

She heard a rustle of clothing. Then a subtle pressure in her lap. She glanced down. A silver flask lay across her legs. She put it in the door pocket. Smiled. It was going to be all right.

Unlike the next conversation on their schedule. That one was assuredly not going to go well.

Chapter Six

The Goat's Head represented an idyllic kind of Englishness Kat imagined foreign tourists cooing over as they faced away from its black-and-white beamed exterior and took smiling selfies.

What lucky people, the publicans, to live in and run such a pretty watering hole. One with *Beer Garden, Skittles, Children's Play Area* chalked colourfully on an A-board outside. Kat wondered whether Rosie might have been the creative talent behind the flowers and smiling stick-kids in the corners.

As she led Tom inside, passing beneath the neatly painted sign advising patrons that Andy and Madeleine Duggan were licensed to sell intoxicating liquor for sale on these premises, she wondered whether Rosie Duggan's parents would be better off if she just doused the place in petrol and tossed a match like the arsonist Leah and Fez were hunting.

It would cause damage, yes, but of the kind insurance companies could put right. What Kat and Tom were about to do would scar the couple whose names were above the door for the rest of their lives, and no amount of bleach, new carpets or specialist wood-restoration chemicals would ever heal them.

She turned to Tom. 'Ready?'

He nodded. Grim-faced. 'Let me do it.'

'Come on, then. Let's get it over with.'

They went in, Kat grateful that only a few punters were inside. Presumably most were enjoying the beer garden. They approached the bar. A girl roughly the same age as Rosie Duggan smiled brightly, revealing braces on her teeth.

'Hi, guys. Welcome to The Goat's Head. What can I get you?'

'Are Mr and Mrs Duggan available?' Tom asked.

The barmaid frowned. 'Are you from the brewery?'

'No. We're police officers.'

Her eyes widened as Kat and Tom produced their warrant cards.

'We've not had any trouble. Is everything all right?'

'Could we speak to Mr and Mrs Duggan, please,' Tom said, his voice level.

'Of course. Sure. They're upstairs. Can you hold on a few minutes? I'll call Madeleine.' She offered an apologetic smile at Tom as she took her phone out. 'I know it looks silly but I'm on my own and I can't leave the bar.'

He smiled back. 'It's fine. I understand.'

Kat glanced at Tom while the barmaid made the call. Raised her eyebrows.

You OK? she mouthed.

He nodded.

'They're coming down,' the barmaid said. 'Are you sure I can't get you anything? We've got a new zero-alcohol lager in this week. I know you guys aren't allowed to drink on duty. Or can you? Is it only on the telly where the cops say that?'

'We're fine, thank you. And you're right,' Tom said, then glanced at Kat, 'we're not allowed to drink while we're working.'

A door opened to their left and a couple, both in their early forties, walked into the room. To Kat they looked more like the kind of people she imagined worked in advertising agencies than publicans. Tanned, in great physical shape, and dressed in expensive-looking but casual clothes.

Madeleine Duggan had a pencil poked through her messy bun and wore her pink-striped shirt in a French tuck, the loose fabric sitting just so on her right hip. Her husband, sporting what Kat thought of as a golfer's tan, overtook her and shook hands, first with Kat, then with Tom. His deep-set grey eyes were clear but there was something around the mouth, a tightness, that betrayed the anxiety he must surely be feeling at an unannounced visit from the police.

'Is everything all right?' he asked. Then bit his lip. Laughed nervously. Overloud in the quiet bar. 'No, of course it isn't, is it? Plainclothes police don't generally make social calls, do they?'

'I am DC Tom Gray and this is DS Kat Ballantyne, from Hertfordshire Police. Is there somewhere private we could talk, please?'

'What is it?' Madeleine asked. 'Is it the summer house? Have we been burgled?'

Her husband laid a hand on her arm.

'They're *Hertfordshire* Police, darling. They're not here about the summer house.' He turned to Tom. 'Why don't you come upstairs? We live in a flat above the pub.'

Her stomach squirming in anticipation of what was to come, and hoping that Tom would be able to handle his first death-knock since coming back to work, Kat followed the Duggans up the narrow staircase and into a comfortably furnished sitting room.

Once they were all seated, Tom leaned forwards and looked first at Andy Duggan and then at Madeleine Duggan. He took a breath and spoke.

'At a quarter past seven this morning, a young girl's body was discovered in Middlehampton. That's the town where we're based.' He paused. Just for a second. 'From her student ID, we believe that she is Rosie Duggan. Your daughter. Evidence recovered from the scene suggests she was murdered. I am so sorry for your loss.'

And then, just as she'd taught him, he closed his mouth and waited.

Madeleine Duggan reacted first.

She laughed. A crackly, crazed sound in the otherwise tomb-silent room.

'No. Rosie's not dead. I only spoke to her yesterday. She's fine. You must have her mixed up with another girl.'

But as Kat looked at Andy Duggan, she could see that he was processing Tom's news differently. He was looking down at his hands, which had gathered his wife's into his own. He swallowed. Looked at Tom, then Kat, as if she might – like a better-trained or more sympathetic GP – give a second opinion.

'How?'

'We believe Rosie was pushed from the top storey of a car park,' Kat said. Then, weighing up the bitter merits of a distressing explanation versus the unbound horrors of newly bereaved parents' imaginations, she supplied a couple of details. 'Her neck was broken. I'm sure it was quick. I'm so sorry.'

Madeleine Duggan screamed so loudly a glass lampshade over their heads rang sympathetically. Andy Duggan reared back as she hammered his chest with her fists, then enfolded her in his arms and pulled her to him. She struggled and writhed in his grip, her ongoing wails muffled in his shirt.

His eyes were blank as he looked at Tom. 'Who?'

'That's what we're going to find out, Mr Duggan,' Tom said. 'I know you must be in shock at such terrible news, but I would really like to ask you some questions about Rosie. Is that all right? And can I record our conversation, please?'

'Fine. Ask whatever you want. But before you ask,' he said, then paused as Tom placed his phone on the arm of his chair and launched the voice recorder app, 'Rosie had no enemies. She was popular. Right from her first day at infant school, people just warmed to her. She was a golden child. Always ready to help others, worked hard at school without being a teacher's pet. She was sporty, too. Captained her school's football team.'

'She sounds like a really lovely person. May I call you Andy?'

He nodded.

'Thanks,' Tom said. 'Well, Andy, just now I said we believe Rosie was murdered. But it's really important we rule out other causes. I know how distressing and painful this must be for you, but do you think there's any way Rosie might have decided to take her own life?'

Madeleine Duggan tore herself free of her husband's enfolding arms and sat bolt upright, glaring at Tom like he'd just suggested her daughter had turned to sex work to augment her student loan.

'Rosie would never do that! I know those poor kids today have their mental health problems, and Lord alone knows, Covid did nothing to help that, but not our Rosie.' She accepted the little packet of tissues Tom had ready and ripped the cellophane cover off before fussily separating one from the sheaf and blowing her nose. 'She had everything to live for. Oh my God. How are we going to tell Lloyd?'

'And Lloyd is . . .?' Kat prompted.

'Her boyfriend. Lloyd Kenney. They've been together since they were fourteen. We always hoped they'd get married.'

A dead woman. An intimate partner. Homicide detecting 101. Lloyd's name shimmered into view at the top of Kat's mental list of potential suspects.

'How was her relationship with Lloyd?' she asked. 'Sometimes when one partner goes to uni and the other stays behind, it can put pressure on a relationship.'

'They were fine. I just told you!'

Kat nodded. Madeleine might be sure of what she was saying. Or she might be hiding something. Or she might even be simply unaware. Even those Instagram mums who posted photos with their daughters above hashtags like #besties and #morelikesisters didn't know everything. Kat looked at Andy, but his expression was vacant. Kat knew that look. He was somewhere else. A place where his precious, beloved daughter was alive and there weren't two grim-faced detectives sitting in his lounge asking intrusive questions about her.

Madeleine looked up at Kat. 'I know it sounds young to be getting married, but in my opinion people wait too long these days before settling down and having children. Andy and I were only seventeen when we got engaged.'

Kat nodded. 'I met my husband when I was eighteen. It happens when it happens.'

'Exactly! Why wait when you know it's perf—'

Something strange happened to Madeleine's features then. Kat knew what lay behind the tortured expressions that flickered across her face, flipping from surprise to confusion to gut-wrenching grief and then to blankness. It wasn't the first time she'd seen how shock could rob people of even the ability to know what emotion they were feeling, let alone compose their features into an appropriate expression.

'Is Lloyd at university, too?' Tom asked.

'No. He's not the academic type. But don't let that fool you,' Madeleine said, her eyes flashing with suspicion even as they glittered with tears. 'Lloyd is a smart young man. He's an apprentice tree surgeon. He'll have his own business before he's thirty, mark my words. And no student debt, either.'

Tom asked for Lloyd's contact details. He lived in Abbots Bromley, too, not a mile from the pub's front door.

Kat leaned forwards. 'You mentioned mental health just now, Madeleine. Did Rosie ever discuss her mental health with either of you?'

'Don't be ridiculous! Why would she? I told you, she had nothing to worry *about*!'

Andy Duggan laid a hand on his wife's knee. He spoke in a monotone, as if even the effort of varying his voice was suddenly too immense.

'She's only asking because they have to be sure. Aren't you, DS Ballantyne?'

'That's right. And, please, both of you, call me Kat.'

She almost added, *Because we'll be spending more time together in the next few days and weeks than any of us wanted.*

'She had no money troubles, we made sure of that,' Madeleine said. 'Not mollycoddling her, but the fees, the cost-of-living crisis, all that? We wanted Rosie to enjoy her time at uni, not be burdened with financial worries.'

'So you'd say Rosie was a happy girl?' Kat prompted.

'She had her moods. Like we all do. But they were just summer storms. We used to joke that Rosie entered the teenage tunnel for about a minute and a half when she was fifteen. She rolled her eyes and tutted, then went to lay the table.'

Tom shifted his weight. For the first time in the interview he looked nervous. Kat knew why. Her bagman was expecting a bad reaction to the next on his list of standard questions.

'To the best of your knowledge, had Rosie ever experimented with drugs of any kind? I don't mean to insinuate anything,' he added hurriedly. 'It's just a line of enquiry we have to look into.'

'Why?' Andy asked in that detached, flat tone. 'Are you saying she was murdered by a drug dealer?'

'No, nothing like that. But if, and this is only an if . . . if she'd taken something, even just a pill, and she wasn't used to the effects, she could have become disorientated, possibly believing she was invulnerable.'

Madeleine dropped the tissue she'd been shredding into soggy white curls and sniffed loudly.

'An accident! That's what you're saying, isn't it?' Then the momentary look of relief on her face vanished, replaced by a frown and a defeated sag to her eyes. 'But Rosie would *never* take drugs. I *guarantee* it. She was a good girl. She didn't even drink. She was *perfect*!'

Kat refrained from pointing out what every cop knew, and eventually every parent. What you knew – what you *thought* you knew – about your children and what they got up to in their private lives was so often at variance with the truth you'd be better off believing the opposite.

Kat looked at Tom, offered a minute shake of her head, then turned back to face the Duggans.

'We may want to ask you further questions about Rosie and the people she knew, but for now, are there any questions you want to ask us?'

'When can we see her?' Andy asked. 'Don't we have to formally identify her?'

'You do, yes. Although, because of her student ID, we're not really in any doubt. Would you like to come to Middlehampton tomorrow morning? Rosie is in the chapel of rest at Middlehampton General Hospital. It's very peaceful. Very respectful. We can do it there.'

'You'll be with us?' Madeleine asked.

'I will. Tom, too.'

'We'll come tonight. Find a hotel,' Andy said.

'We'll also appoint a family liaison officer. They'll keep you informed about the process of our investigation,' Tom said. 'We call them FLOs. I'm afraid you'll be hearing quite a lot of police jargon over the days and weeks to come. I'm sorry. But please ask me or Kat if there's anything you hear that you don't understand.'

Andy levered himself to his feet and regarded the two detectives in turn. 'Our daughter wasn't on drugs. She wasn't what you'd call a risk-taker,' he said quietly. 'Sometimes I wished she'd been a bit more adventurous, but there you are. And she wasn't suicidal. If she fell from a car park, then your suspicions are right. She was pushed. And I want you to catch the man who murdered her.' He set his jaw, which had started to quiver. 'Or we will.'

Kat stood. 'Thank you both. And once again, I . . . *we* are so sorry to have to bring you such sad news about Rosie.'

And then it was over.

They were out on the street again. The warm sun beating down on them, the scent of flowers from the hanging baskets flanking the pub door heady in their nostrils.

From inside, Madeleine began screaming.

Tom flinched.

Kat reached up and laid a hand on his shoulder.

'You were brilliant in there, Tomski. Honestly, I'm proud of you.'

It was an easy compliment to give. Speaking to the Duggans, Tom had reminded her just how good her bagman could be when he wasn't fretting about his career progression.

He shrugged. 'They reminded me of my mum and dad. It made it easy to talk to them, I suppose.'

'Don't do yourself down. That was professional, it was courteous, it was empathetic. And you got some really valuable information in the process.'

'What do you think Andy meant, "Or we will"?'

'Just the grief talking. I've had parents threatening to kidnap their kid's killers, take them into Ashridge Forest and torture them to death over months.'

'Good to know. What now? The boyfriend?'

The voice of one of Kat's early mentors floated down to her through the years.

Sure, Kat, it's always the husband. And if it's not the husband, it's the boyfriend.

Chapter Seven

They heard Lloyd Kenney, or at least his machinery, a minute or so before they arrived.

An ear-splitting howl with edges as rough as old bark shattered the silence in a rising and falling pulse that suggested to Kat some infernal instrument of torture. The sort, in fact, to which a recently bereaved parent might willingly subject their daughter's murderer.

As they crossed a vast lawn the size of the Jubilee Place sports club's football pitch, the harsh wailing was joined by a second tone, this one harsh and buzzy, higher-pitched. A hissing, crackling crash came next, adding its own discord to the two-part disharmony.

Standing beside a beaten-up white Honda pickup, a guy in his thirties was feeding fallen branches into an orange woodchipper the size of Kat's Golf. The side of the pickup bore a green tree logo and the legend *Jay Weekes, Arborist*.

The gaudy orange machine seemed to suck the lengths of timber right out of his gloved hands, spitting them out in a tight cone of bright yellow sawdust and wood fragments that rustled and pinged against the sides of a metal hopper.

Above their heads, invisible in the foliage, someone – Lloyd, presumably – was wielding a chainsaw. Leaves fluttered to the ground, green with chlorophyll.

Nose filling with the pleasant smell of fresh sawdust, Kat held up her warrant card.

The man by the chipper – Jay, presumably – nodded and thumbed the Off button. The machine whirred to a standstill with a jagged throat-clearing sound as it ejected one last mouthful into the hopper.

'Can I help you?'

'We need to speak to Lloyd,' Kat said.

Jay looked up into the trees and cupped his hands round his mouth. He waited for a pause in the screams of the chainsaw and bellowed into the canopy.

'Lloyd! Get yourself down here!' He lowered his gaze to meet Kat's eye. 'He'll be down directly. What's this all about?'

'We just need a few minutes with Lloyd,' she replied, watching the orange and blue nylon ropes ripple and curl as the apprentice arborist made his way to the ground. So Lloyd had no fear of heights. She made a mental note.

'He's not in any trouble, is he? The gear's all mine, if that's what this is about. I haven't been sending the lad out nicking off other arborists.'

He went for a smile, but it dropped like a half-sawn-through branch before falling off his face altogether.

Kat didn't think he was guilty of anything beyond the usual worry that members of the public exhibited whenever she and one of her colleagues came a-calling. Only natural, really. You were living your life, getting on with things, and then, from out of nowhere, a copper turned up and told you your best friend had been taken by a serial killer and choked to death, her hair cut off like the world's worst pixie crop. She shivered. Reminded herself Liv was alive and soon to be married. With Kat as her matron of honour. Now there was a party worth dropping everything for.

'You all right?' Tom asked.

'Goose walked over my grave.'

A young man in a complicated harness slithered down to the end of the rope and unclipped himself with a series of metallic clinks and pings. He came over. He was tall, muscular, his face ruddy from working outdoors.

'Lloyd Kenney?' Tom asked.

''S'right. What's this about?'

'I'm afraid I have some very bad news,' Tom said. 'This morning, Rosie Duggan was found dead in Middlehampton, in Hertfordshire. That's where we've come from. It looks like she was murdered. I'm really sorry, mate. Honestly. Gutted to be the one giving you this news.'

Lloyd seemed to have put down roots. He swayed backwards as if blown by a sudden wind only he could feel. But he didn't topple.

'Is he winding me up?' he asked Kat. 'I was only messaging her on Sunday. She can't be dead. She's coming home next weekend. We're going to see a band.'

'I'm afraid it's true, Lloyd,' she said, already homing in on his body language, his tone of voice, the words he chose to express his feelings.

He'd used the present tense, as if he were unable to process the information Tom had just imparted. Grief-stricken? Maybe. But he seemed calm. No tears. Or not yet. It didn't necessarily signify anything. Shock hit different people in different ways. One might scream till her voice cracked and her throat bled. Another might retreat into his shell, afraid that if he came out he might be overrun by emotions he was unable to deal with.

But his eyes were flicking between her and his boss. And when they came to rest on her, she thought that what she was seeing was calculation, not sorrow. A note appeared on her imaginary whiteboard below his name.

Lloyd Kenney – boyfriend

No obvious grief. Odd? Bad actor? Murderer?

For the moment she gave Lloyd Kenney the benefit of the doubt. Barely out of childhood and given the worst possible news anyone could expect to receive in a lifetime. If his emotions were off, well, she'd allow him quite a lot of leeway. No need to go looking for a psychopath just yet. But an angry young man? One trying to weigh up the risks of appearing unconcerned versus delivering a tearless performance of fake grief? That was an angle she wanted to explore just a little further.

'Can you think of anyone who might have wanted to harm Rosie?' Tom was asking. 'From home? Or did she tell you about anyone at uni? Someone she'd had words with, or got into an argument on X or Instagram or something?'

Lloyd frowned. About to tell Tom Rosie was a saint, just as her parents had described her.

'*X?* What are you, like, thirty or something? Nobody our age is on X. It's like this toxic dump. Only losers and incels are on it these days.'

'Sorry. Better not tell you I have a Facebook account, then.'

Lloyd smiled, the first genuine-looking expression he'd mustered since they'd arrived.

'Now I *know* you're old.'

Joking about social media platforms when you'd just been told your girlfriend had been murdered? Kat underlined Lloyd's name.

'How about enemies, though, Lloyd,' Tom persisted.

'I mean, yeah, it's possible. But Rosie? She was like this perfect girl. Not like a try-hard. She never did anything just so people would like her. She was just, I don't know how to put it . . .'

Jay, who had been listening attentively, saying nothing and not moving beyond laying a protective arm around Lloyd's shoulder, now broke in.

'You said she never needed to try because she was a natural, didn't you, mate? Like, people just gravitated towards her.'

Lloyd sniffed and rubbed his eyes. Wiped his nose on his forearm.

'I can't imagine anyone wanting to hurt my Rosie. That's the truth.'

Kat watched him carefully. His cheeks were dry. *Was* it the truth? She doubted it.

'OK, well, we'll leave it there,' Tom said. 'I'm sorry for your loss, Lloyd. Truly, I am. Here's my card. Can you have a think about whether Rosie ever mentioned anyone she thought might not have been so keen? Call me if you do, yes?'

Lloyd took the card, inspected both sides and pocketed it. He shrugged, powerful shoulders straining the material of his sweat-soaked T-shirt. She found she could picture Lloyd hefting Rosie's body over the car park railing. But why? According to the Duggans, he'd been ready to propose. Or had he already, and been knocked back?

She thought back to the time she'd been on her way out to meet Liv on the night she disappeared. Kat had cancelled at the last minute after her boyfriend dumped her by text, saying he wanted a clean break before going off to university. Had Rosie done the same thing to Lloyd?

'So you and Rosie . . . your relationship was good?' she asked, hoping that was the right phrase. 'Her mum said you were going to propose this summer.'

Lloyd wouldn't, or couldn't, meet her eyes.

'We were taking it slow for a bit,' he mumbled. 'Things changed a bit after Rosie went to uni. It was temporary, but you know, she was adjusting. It didn't mean anything.'

Kat saw her chance. 'What didn't mean anything, Lloyd?' she asked quietly.

'Like just, I don't know, not messaging every five minutes. I was focused on my work and she had her studies, obviously.'

'But you were still together?'

He nodded. But said nothing. Interesting. She doubted Lloyd would tell them if he *had* been dumped. Even if it were true.

But Rosie's friends would know, one way or another. And if Rosie had dumped him, Kat would ask them why.

Because right now, she had Lloyd pegged as a potential suspect.

Chapter Eight

Normally at the start of a murder investigation, Kat felt excitement thrumming along her nerves. But as she opened her front door that night, all she really felt was a sense of crushing sadness.

When all was said and done, Rosie Duggan had been a child. Yes, an adult in the eyes of the law, permitted to vote, drink, marry without her parents' permission. But in so many other ways just a fledgling making her first wobbling flight from the nest.

She dropped her bag to the floor and called out. 'Hey! Mummy's home. Also wife, who really needs a drink!' As soon as she said that, however, she thought about Tom and their conversation earlier that day. 'Of tea,' she added, loudly, wanting to convince herself that's what she'd meant as much as Van.

The first of her three boys came skittering down the hall to greet her, his stumpy tail wagging furiously, his pink tongue hanging out and his winky right eye, the result of a seizure in his first month alive, giving him that cheeky-chappie look everyone who met him fell for hard.

'Hey, Smokey,' she said, crouching to scratch the over-eager Cairn terrier behind the ears. 'Didja miss me, huh? Didja?' Judging from the ecstatic grunts emanating from deep in his throat, she assumed the answer was in the affirmative.

She went into the kitchen, Smokey trotting alongside.

Van was working at the kitchen table on his laptop. 'Hey, love,' he said, glancing up at her. 'All right?'

She bent to kiss him, got a cheek offered up. She turned his face up to meet hers and kissed him properly, on the lips.

'How was your day?' he asked, when she released him.

'I've had better. It started with a young girl pushed off the Five Cups Lane car park.'

Now he did look round, first clicking on whatever he was working on then closing his laptop.

'Oh, love, I'm sorry. How old was she?'

'Eighteen. Christ, Van, she had her whole life ahead of her. She was only a few years older than Riley.'

'I'll make you a tea and you can tell me all about it.'

'Thanks. A proper one, please, in the pot. I've had too many teabags squashed against the side today.'

He snorted. 'Don't want much, do you? How about some Rich Tea biscuits on a side plate?'

'Who are you, my mother?' She looked out the window, into the garden. 'Where's Riley?'

'He's at Millie's.'

Millie. Riley's first girlfriend. He was besotted. In a very Riley-ish way. Off-hand when asked directly, but unable to stop himself bringing her into every conversation. Kat's stomach clutched. She forced herself to avoid thinking how she'd tell Riley if Millie had been murdered. Would he be outwardly calm, like Lloyd Kenney? She doubted it. With Riley, emotions were never in short supply.

Kat messaged him.

hey home for tea?

His reply came so fast it was as if he'd been waiting for her to ask.

millies mums making pizza

Kat tutted. *She* could make pizza, too. But she typed out the dutiful reply a chilled-out mum would and left it at that.

coolio laters

She hesitated. Then added an *x*.

As Van fussed around looking for some leaf tea, she told him about Rosie Duggan's untimely end. About the parents' reactions, and the boyfriend's, too. But mostly, she just vented about the unfairness of a world in which a young girl could have started the day with no bigger concern than what to write about in an essay and ended up in a fridge in Jack Beale's mortuary.

'I'm sorry,' he said when she paused to accept the mug of tea he placed before her. 'I guess that's the job, though, isn't it? You always say you want to deliver justice for the victim and their family, see the killer put away. Now's your chance. Again.'

She sighed deeply, earning an inquiring look from Smokey.

'Yeah. It just feels so unfair.'

Van came and sat across from her, pulling the laptop towards him.

'Murder is always unfair, though, isn't it?'

She could only nod. Not really in the mood for Van's suddenly irritating 'eh, whaddya gonna do?' brand of pragmatism.

'What are you working on, anyway? Tell me about *your* day.'

He shrugged. 'The usual. Websites running slow. Forms not loading. Storage issues. Cloud stuff. You know.'

'Not really. Whose websites? Distract me, husband. I need it.'

'Dove & Charcoal's the main bugbear right now. Marnie's launched this new option and it's playing hell with the algorithm.'

Kat experienced a pang of jealousy. Marnie. Full name, Marnie Pryce. Actually, cancel that: full name, Marnie *If only my bum didn't look so good in these tight white jeans* Pryce. Proprietor of a figure that had the effect on men's gazes that black holes did on celestial bodies, and a website whose stated and only purpose was to facilitate hook-ups between married people.

Kat remembered with a flash of embarrassment the day Van told her about his new client. She'd naively asked why married people needed a dating website. Surely being married meant they'd succeeded in that particular endeavour.

'What's the new service?' she asked, dreading the answer.

'She calls it "Soar".'

Kat frowned. 'Sore? That doesn't sound so good.'

Van grinned. 'Soar, as in fly high. It's for people who don't want a relationship—'

Kat snorted. 'I thought that was pretty established from the outset.'

'A traditional one-to-one relationship, I meant. It covers what Marnie calls "diverse sexual dynamics". Swinging, people who want to try an open relationship, couples looking for a third person to join them, which, if you're interested—'

Kat held up a hand. 'Really not.'

'—are called unicorns. Anyway, it's for all sexualities and genders, different sexual outlooks, kinks and fetishes in a consensual, safe and playful environment. That's what Marnie's blurb says.'

'Very progressive of her,' Kat deadpanned, wishing at that moment it had been Miss *If only my tits weren't so perky in this T-shirt I accidentally bought a size too small* who'd been pushed off a tall building.

She shoved the half-drunk cup of tea aside. 'Actually, do you fancy a glass of wine? Because I do.'

He shook his head.

'Can't, love. Need to finish this. But you go ahead.'

Feeling a sudden need for her husband, she persisted. 'Come on, Van. How about a beer? And seeing as Riley's out for the evening, why don't we take them upstairs? See if you've got any kinks I can work out for you.'

Was that too obvious? It felt like she was acting in a porn film. But men loved that kind of thing. The more obvious the better, as far as she could tell. Her friend Jess Beckett had once observed, over a bottle of Pinot Grigio, that 'the day Mike doesn't go glassy-eyed if I wear my Agent Provocateur undies is the day I know he's cheating'.

Van smiled, but it came across as patient. The kind of smile a parent bestows on a child angling for an extra half hour before bedtime.

'That sounds lovely, but I can't. I'm sorry. I really do have to work.'

She stood up too fast, sending stars sparkling around her vision.

'Fine. I'll take Smokes out then. What are we having for tea because I don't fancy cooking.'

'I thought we'd get Chinese. What do you fancy, kung po prawns like usual?'

'How about sweet and sour unicorn?' She turned away, cross and frustrated that her obvious 'move' had failed her. 'Come on, Smokes. Walkies!'

With the little dog clattering along behind her, she changed into jeans and a T-shirt, grabbed his lead and was out the door five minutes later.

If Van wasn't interested in her, there was another man who might be.

Chapter Nine

When she needed to think, or when she let Smokey decide on their route, Kat usually ended up in a wide field known among the local dog walkers as The Gallops for the grassy swathe down one side.

As soon as they reached the field, which was already lush with crops, she unclipped Smokey. With a delighted yelp he raced off into the growing wheat or whatever it was, arable farming not being one of Kat's specialist subjects, zig-zagging and barking frenziedly. He flushed out a pair of brown birds she thought might have been female pheasants, which cackled and hooted as they flapped their ungainly wings and sought sanctuary in the air.

As she'd been hoping, Smokey was soon joined by a black-and-white streak. Leggy where he was, charitably, stumpy. And possessed of a long, noble snout and an air at once aristocratic and glamorous, like a supermodel born into a landed family. Lois was Smokey's best friend, and Barrie Price's lurcher. Kat met the ex-copper halfway down the long path on the south side of the field.

A gust of wind raised a tuft of his thistledown hair, which glowed like a halo as the evening sun shone through it. He smoothed it down with a liver-spotted hand.

'Evening, Skip,' he said, holding out a crumpled white paper bag. 'Liquorice Allsort?'

'Why not? I feel like treating myself.'

She selected a bright blue jelly covered in tiny bobbles and crunched it between her back teeth, releasing a powerful aniseed hit.

'Everything all right?' he asked, as he picked out a pink coconut drum with a liquorice centre for himself.

'We found a dead girl who'd been pushed off a car park this morning, my husband seems more interested in his bloody client's website than he does in his own wife, but other than that, yeah, all good, mate. You?'

'Oh, dear. Trouble in paradise, Skip?'

She debated whether to open up to Barrie. Normally she kept relationship stuff for her girlfriends. The Malbec Mafia netball team, or just one of her nights out with a friend like Jess. Or Liv, when they could arrange a get-together in Wales. But Barrie was old enough to be her dad, without any of the obvious baggage. And he was a man. And right now, she needed a male perspective.

Hoping she wouldn't embarrass him, she ploughed on. 'Barrie, if you're happily married, and your wife suggests, you know, a bit of a cuddle upstairs while the kids are out. Even hints' – she swallowed the aniseed jelly and coughed as it stuck going down – 'you know, at being a bit *playful*, you'd go for that, wouldn't you?'

His china-blue eyes twinkled. 'If I was twenty years younger, I'd take that as an invitation, Skip.'

'Come on, Barrie, spare my blushes. Would you? As a man, I mean?'

'Because we're all enslaved by our willies, you mean? The old "men think about sex every six seconds" fallacy?' A beat. 'No pun intended.'

'Barrie, please, I'm dying here.'

It was the truth. Her cheeks felt as if she'd caught the sun. Caught it, embraced it, and possibly even entered into a monogamous relationship with it.

His smile faded.

'You really mean it, don't you, Skip?'

'No, Barrie. I always like to talk about my sexual anxieties in public! I find it freeing. *Yes*, I'm serious!' She shook her head angrily. 'Sorry, mate. That was rude. But, yes, I actually am serious.'

'OK. Then here's my answer. Nine times out of ten, yes he would. Especially if she looked like you.'

She smiled. 'Flatterer. What about if you had a ton of work, though?'

'We're talking about you and Van, aren't we? Look, what if he really is up against it? Deadlines are bastards. Especially in his line of work. IT and that.'

'It's just . . .'

She stopped. How far did she want to go with this? She didn't mind talking to Barrie about it. But if she said out loud what was on her mind, that would give it a kind of life. A legitimacy. Keep her counsel and she could tell herself she was just being paranoid.

'Just what, Skip?'

She took a deep breath. 'He's got this client, OK? She's a bit older than us, but you know, she's really sexy. I mean in this totally obvious way, all tight clothes and husky voice. But that's what men love, isn't it?'

He shrugged. 'Takes all sorts. Some blokes do like that kind of thing. Others love a girl in specs who looks like she reads books all day. Horses for courses, isn't it?' He paused, whistled for Lois. 'I've got to go, but look, Skip, if you really want my advice, rather than all this speculating about what "men" want, or like or do, why don't you talk to *your* man? You're a good detective, from what I hear. Better than those fast-track Bambis who breeze in expecting the world to fall into their lap. So do what you do best. Ask questions.'

So she did. Later, lying beside Van in bed, her belly distended with kung po prawns, special fried rice, and beef with ginger and spring onion. Too full now to consider sex even if Van belatedly decided he was interested.

'Did you get your work done?'

'Most of it. Just a few bits and bobs to sort out in the morning.'

'Marnie'll be happy, I expect.'

'Should be. But there's always something else she wants.'

There. That was the opening she needed. 'Van?'

'Yes?'

'It's not you she wants, is it?'

'Pardon?'

'There's nothing, you know, going on – is there? I mean I trust you, obviously, but she's divorced and I just . . . I just wondered if she's made a play for you, that's all. I thought that was why you didn't want to come upstairs with me earlier.'

Van raised himself on one elbow and turned to look down into her eyes. She couldn't make out his expression, but she heard the concern, the shock, in his voice.

'With Marnie? No, of course there isn't! I know you were a bit worried about her before, but I swear to you, love, it's strictly business.'

He was saying the right things, and he sounded sincere. Why didn't she feel reassured?

She sighed. 'Sorry. I just had a bit of a day of it, having to tell Rosie Duggan's poor parents their daughter had been murdered. I was just upset.'

He gathered her into his arms and she laid her head on his chest.

'Who wouldn't be? You do an amazing job and people don't appreciate how much you take it to heart. But that's what makes you so good. I know you'll find who killed her – and yes, I know it won't bring her back, but they'll have some closure, won't they?'

'Yeah. And when it's her birthday every year until they die, they can invite the bloody closure to the party, can't they?'

She closed her eyes. But sleep refused to come. Instead, Marnie Pryce took up residence, the word 'Unicorn' stretched across her T-shirt-clad chest. Kat batted her away. Barrie was right. Van *did* have deadlines. Too many, in her opinion. And it wasn't as if she was exactly guilt-free, either. She'd lost count of the date nights she'd cancelled at the last minute when a case reared its ugly head.

She woke at 5.47 a.m. An hour later she was at her desk, putting everything she knew about Rosie on a whiteboard.

It wasn't much. But as the day progressed, she and Tom would add more, and somewhere in that growing body of information, she knew, they'd find Rosie's killer.

But before all of that, they had an unpleasant but necessary duty to perform.

Chapter Ten

The chapel of rest was too hot. Kat was sweating inside her black suit jacket. Claustrophobic, too, with Kat, Tom, the Duggans and Ashleigh Collinson, Jack Beale's assistant, waiting patiently until the Duggans signalled by word or gesture that they were ready to see the face of their dead daughter.

No doubt some well-meaning soul had read, or perhaps simply knew, that the smell of lavender had a calming effect. For Kat it brought up sickening images of more dead girls, these choked to death on wheat grains soaked in a homemade concoction that smelled pungently of the herb. She breathed as shallowly as she could manage through her mouth.

'Ready, darling?' Andy Duggan asked his wife.

She was dressed, as he was, in dark clothes. Not black. Perhaps they felt it was too funereal. Too final. As if by opting instead for navy and dark grey they could preserve a sliver of hope that it had all been a terrible mistake. Perhaps some other girl had borrowed their daughter's student ID and she'd call them at any minute to say she'd been off on a jaunt. Somewhere with no signal.

Madeleine Duggan nodded. Her eyes were wide, unblinking. Her cheeks were bloodless, and she clutched her husband's hand so tightly her knuckles had whitened in his grasp.

With infinite delicacy, Ashleigh pinched the edge of the pale blue sheet covering the body and drew it back in a steady, continuous movement.

Madeleine shuddered and fell sideways against Andy.

'Oh, my darling!'

Andy stared down at his dead daughter. Then, releasing a hand from his wife's grip, he reached out and stroked the backs of his fingers along Rosie's left cheek, the specialist mortuary technician's make-up doing an almost perfect job of disguising the bruises, grey beneath the peach-coloured foundation.

Breath escaped him in a long hiss, and he seemed to deflate not just physically, his chest sinking, but as a person, pulling away from the world – even from his wife – into himself.

'That's our Rosie,' he murmured. 'Is that what you need to hear?'

'Thank you for confirming it,' Kat said. She nudged Tom with her hip. The tiniest of pushes.

'Is there anything we can do for you, Mr and Mrs Duggan?' he asked. 'Would you like some time with Rosie to say goodbye?'

'Please,' Andy said.

Kat, Tom and Ashleigh withdrew in silence, leaving the two grieving parents alone with their daughter.

In the adjoining room, Ashleigh handed Kat a form to sign.

'It's for the coroner.'

Kat scribbled a signature in the box Ashleigh indicated.

'Thanks, Ash,' she said. 'How are you doing?'

Ashleigh shook her head. Poked her glasses higher up on her nose.

'I'm all right. But I prefer doing the post-mortems to this part. How can they go on?'

'Honestly? I don't know. I've met people afterwards, you know, like a year later. They're divorced, as often as not. One parent couldn't let it go, or the other simply pulled away or closed themselves off.'

'That's terrible.'

'Life's shitty. Sometimes they hang in there, though. It brings them closer in a strange sort of way.'

'Do you think the Duggans will be like that?'

Kat could only shrug.

'I hope so.'

'Where now?' Tom asked, once they'd seen the Duggans off from the hospital.

'The university. I want to talk to Rosie's friends.'

Chapter Eleven

Kat rang the bell at number 37 on Keeley Street, a long, winding residential road of Victorian terraced houses a quarter of a mile from the university. The day was warming up and both she and Tom were in shirtsleeves.

The boy who answered the door looked to be about Rosie's age, eighteen or nineteen. Wearing baggy, brushed-cotton tartan trousers and a long, scruffy but clean T-shirt. Dirty blond hair sticking out at angles. Not an early riser, then.

Kat took out her warrant card.

'Hi. We're with Hertfordshire Police. I'm DS Ballantyne and this is DC Gray. Can we come in, please?'

'What's this about?'

'It's about your housemate, Rosie Duggan. Could we come in, talk somewhere quiet?'

'Has something happened? Only, she didn't come home last night.' He scratched his stubble. 'Or Monday night, actually. Is she all right? Wait. You lot didn't arrest her, did you?'

Always control the conversation. Ask questions, make proposals. Molly Steadman's advice echoed inside Kat's head.

'What's your name? I'm Kat.'

'Harry.' He waited, but she said nothing. He sighed, 'You'd better come in, then. We're all in the kitchen. Nobody's got lectures this morning,' he added as if he needed to justify the fact he appeared to be in his pyjamas.

Kat followed him down a narrow hallway tiled in geometric patterns of turquoise, chestnut and cream.

The kitchen had been extended sideways and lengthways at some point and was dominated by a large table at which three girls sat. They looked far healthier and more glamorous than Kat remembered her peers looking during her brief sojourn at Nottingham University. On a ratty-looking sofa facing sliding doors into an unkempt garden, two more – a boy and a girl – lolled, their fingers intertwined.

They all sat straighter when Harry introduced them with a laconic 'Feds. I think Rosie got into trouble last night.'

Kat wished he'd shut up. It was only going to make things worse.

'I'm afraid we have some very bad news,' she began. 'Rosie is dead. We believe she was murdered on Monday night. I'm so sorry for your loss.'

If ever she'd questioned the point of that final six-word phrase, her doubts hit with full force now.

Three seconds passed in total silence, and then, as if commanded by an unseen director, all six burst into tears. The raw emotion was shocking as their crying filled the kitchen. As she took in the weeping boys, Kat thought back to Lloyd Kenney's dry-eyed stare.

Suspect.

Tom looked at her, panic-stricken. His eyes pleading, *What do we do?*

For once, Kat stayed her hand in the act of reaching for a packet of tissues. It felt inadequate as a gesture in the face of such grief. Nothing for it but to wait out the storm.

Slowly, the six students found their own ways to clamp down their emotions. Through tear-streaked make-up and reddened eyes they looked at her for answers.

'I know this must be such a shock to you,' Kat began. 'And I'm just so, so sorry to have to bring you this really awful news. But we do need to talk to you about Rosie. To ask you about her. Would that be OK?'

One of the girls sitting at the table, a ring through her septum, drew herself up a little straighter in her seat.

'How did it happen?'

'She was pushed off the top level of a car park in town.'

One of the other girls cried out and buried her head in the crook of the neck of the girl sitting next to her.

'What do you want to know?' the girl with the nose ring asked.

'Can I ask your name first of all, lovely?'

'It's Thalia. She was the Greek muse of comedy. Sorry, why am I telling you that? Thalia Garrick.'

'Thanks, Thalia. To begin with, can you think of anyone, anyone at all, who might have wanted to harm Rosie?' Kat asked.

Tom retreated a few paces and took out his notebook. Good man. Not wanting to put the students on their guard by placing a recording device in front of them.

Ready to hear a blanket denial that anyone could possibly wish Rosie Duggan ill, Kat was taken aback by what Thalia said next.

'Greg Fanning. Write that down,' she instructed Tom. 'F-A-N-N-I-N-G.'

'Who is Greg Fanning?' Kat asked.

'He's like this incel. A total creep. He was obsessed with Rosie. Kept taking photos of her when he thought we couldn't see,' she said, wiping her nose. 'He asked her out about a month ago.'

'How did Rosie respond?' Kat asked, thinking with a flicker of disgust of her own obsessive fan – a local celebrity true-crime podcaster. She'd known Ethan Metcalfe since school.

'She said no, of course! The guy's like this real loser. Probably spends his time on Reddit talking about school shootings or how to roofie girls or whatever.'

'It's true.' This was Harry. 'There's a bunch of them at the uni. They're all convinced women are like plotting to keep them celibate, but you only have to take one look at them. I mean, no wonder they can't get laid.'

The girl next to him spun round.

'Jesus Christ, Harry, show some respect!'

He flushed. 'God. Sorry. Inappropriate.'

Kat smiled sadly. 'You're all in shock. It affects people in all kinds of weird ways.'

'You ought to talk to Libby,' the girl on the sofa said, untangling herself from the boy's arms and coming to sit at the table. 'Her full name is Libby Spare. Mine's Tallulah. Gordon. Libby's in our year and she had a falling-out with Rosie just before Christmas.'

'About what?' Tom asked.

'Libby asked Rosie if she'd write an essay for her. Like pay her to? Because lecturers are starting to spot ChatGPT now? And Rosie said no. She wasn't like prissy about it or anything, like "Oh, that's against my moral code". But she still said no. You know, because it *is* wrong. And Libby's just lazy. She's like this privileged rich girl who spends all her time partying, so no wonder she fell behind with her work.'

'How did Libby take it?' Kat asked.

Tallulah rolled her eyes. 'Well, duh! How do you *think* she took it?'

For once, Kat abandoned Molly's 'we ask the questions, we don't answer them' strategy.

'I'm guessing not well?' she said.

'She went fucking mental. Said Rosie was just being a bitch. You know, like she didn't understand how other people didn't find everything as easy as she did.'

'And when you say she went "fucking mental", can you be more specific?'

One of the other girls giggled, then clapped a hand over her mouth, her eyes wide above it.

'She said Rosie would trip up one day. And then . . . wait!' Tallulah's eyes popped wider even than the giggling girl's. 'She said, "Pride comes before a fall."'

Kat didn't need to turn her head to check that Tom had noted down that particular little nugget verbatim.

'Did any of you ever see Libby be aggressive towards Rosie, either verbally or physically?' Kat asked.

'Isn't that enough?' Thalia asked.

'Sorry, let me be a bit more specific. Did anyone here ever see Libby threaten Rosie? Either tell her she was going to hurt her in some way, or actually make physical contact?'

The six students exchanged glances. Whispers filled the room. Eventually Thalia spoke again.

'No. Not literally threaten her. But like, telling her pride comes before a fall. That has to be relevant, doesn't it?'

'We'll be looking at everything. Is that it? Greg Fanning and Libby Spare?'

Kat made eye contact with each student in turn. Sometimes people felt unable to speak up unless directly invited.

The girl who'd cried out raised her head and looked directly at Kat. Her eyes were bloodshot, strikingly green beyond the red.

'I'm Bridie Trevithick. Me and Rosie were best friends. Have you spoken to Rosie's boyfriend yet?'

'Would that be Lloyd Kenney?' Kat asked, all her senses sharpening.

Bridie nodded. 'What did you think of him?'

That was a strange question. But Kat felt the end of a thread being dangled right in front of her and went along with the girl's Q&A routine.

'I think he was shocked, like all of you are. He said he loved Rosie.'

Bridie snorted. '*Said.* Yeah, well, words are cheap, aren't they?'

Kat snagged the end of the thread between thumb and forefinger. Didn't tug, not yet. Threads this fine were apt to snap without warning.

'Rosie broke up with Lloyd a few weeks ago,' Bridie said. 'He was getting way too clingy and she told me she'd had enough of him trying to control her. It wasn't like there was anyone else. She just wanted to enjoy being at uni, you know? Anyway, you think Libby didn't take rejection well? Lloyd's completely toxic. He threatened to put nudes she sent him online unless she got back with him.'

They had a motive for murder. A jealous, obsessed ex-boyfriend who'd made threats of that kind was already breaking the law. Kat had seen men commit murder for slenderer motives than that. Add in the fact Lloyd had lied to her face about the state of his relationship with Rosie, as well as his lack of obvious grief, and the name on her whiteboard gained a double underline in red. As lead investigator it was her job to assign priorities.

OK – well, she'd just assigned one.

'Do you know if he carried out his threat?' she asked.

'There's this search engine? It's called Am I In Porn? We put in a selfie, just of Rosie's face I mean, and it came up with a hit.' Tears leaked from her eyes again and she dashed them away with a fist. 'I want to kill him!'

'Bridie!' Tallulah said, glancing worriedly at Kat. 'Shh!'

'I do! I don't *care* if she hears me.' Bridie glared at Kat. 'I wish Lloyd was dead instead of Rosie. There! Happy now?'

'Can you tell me if Rosie drank at all?' Kat asked, ignoring Bridie's outburst.

Bridie frowned. 'Why are you asking that? I thought you said someone killed her?'

'I did and that *is* what I think happened. But we need to build up a complete picture of her life. Did she?'

'Not really. I mean, like half a glass of wine if we were having dinner together. But she just didn't. Lots of our generation don't.'

'How about drugs? Weed? Ket? Benzos? Molly?'

Another surprised look rippled across the six tear-streaked faces. A cop who swore *and* used the right names for 'their' drugs? Whatever next?

'Rosie didn't touch anything,' Bridie said. 'She was really into wellness. She went to the gym. She was vegan. She did yoga, played hockey and football. I know that makes her sound unbearable, but she was just . . . nice, you know?'

'She sounds lovely. I'm sad I didn't get to meet her,' Kat said, unleashing another bout of crying.

She wasn't sorry. Thought it was probably for the best if they got a good bit of crying done now so they could learn to accept the grief and how it made them feel. Because what was the alternative? Squashing their feelings down, getting off their faces on drugs and alcohol, then begging tranquillisers and sleeping pills off the university medical centre before having a full-blown nervous breakdown and fleeing to Thailand, where they met and married a boy after a month together? *But enough about me,* her internal stand-up comic deadpanned. *Let's talk about you. What do* you *think about me and my troubles with my supposedly dead best friend?*

'Would it be all right if we had a look in Rosie's room?' Tom asked, dragging Kat back to the present.

'Don't you need a search warrant or something?' Harry asked.

'Not really. I mean, technically, yes, if you objected, we'd have to get one. But as Rosie was the victim of a crime, normally people are happy to let us go ahead.'

Harry coloured. 'Sorry. Been watching too much true crime on YouTube.'

'That's a yes?'

'Knock yourselves out,' Harry said, slumping back in his chair.

Kat and Tom snapped on gloves and let Bridie show them to Rosie's room.

Kat had been expecting a tidy, well-ordered space, make-up ranged neatly on a dressing table, a few tastefully framed prints on the walls, folders and textbooks stacked on IKEA Billy bookcases.

But when Bridie opened the door it was to reveal a real rat's nest of a space. Clothes strewn everywhere, crockery and cutlery stacked haphazardly on the carpet and desk. An ashtray overflowing with cigarette butts on the windowsill.

'I know, right?' Bridie said wryly from just behind Kat. 'But Rosie once told me she was so fed up with everyone assuming she was like this golden child. It was her little act of rebellion, you know? Like being a slob just in this one place. Not succeeding, not winning, just *being*.'

'I wasn't judging,' Kat said with a smile. 'You should have seen my room at uni. It made this place look like the British Museum.'

Bridie smiled briefly. 'Let me know if you need anything.' She turned and pulled the door to behind her.

Wordlessly, Kat and Tom donned gloves, then got to their knees and started a methodical search among the dead girl's things. Tom turned up her laptop, a battered MacBook covered in stickers.

'Digital Forensics will have kittens,' he said. 'They hate Apple stuff. By the way, did she have her phone on her?'

'Nope.'

'Unless it's here, it probably means her killer took it.'

'That's a reasonable assumption, but I'll check with Jan.'

Jan Cable was an experienced police search advisor, or POLSA. Kat had set the parameters and now Jan and her team were scouring the area around the car park and the florist's shop on Five Cups Lane. If she'd found Rosie's phone then they could assume it had come out of her pocket or hand as she fell.

Kat rummaged around under the bed, then her fingers closed on something hard yet wielding. A book of some kind. She pulled it out.

It was bound in soft, burnt-orange suede and secured with a simple brass lock. No key in sight. A journal? Another reasonable assumption. She bagged it. She could probably pick it with a hair grip back at the station. Failing that, a pair of pliers and a screwdriver would have to do.

After half an hour more, Kat called it a day. They'd found no evidence of drugs beyond a packet of contraceptive pills and some paracetamol in a blister pack missing the box.

But as they were leaving, Bridie came out on to the front doorstep with them.

'You know what Harry said about watching true crime on YouTube? Well, that made me remember something. There's this guy who does guest lectures on our course. We both do media studies. He's this like famous true-crime podcaster. Anyway, a couple of weeks ago, Rosie had this massive row with him literally in front of everyone. She called him a vulture. He wasn't helping anyone, he was only doing it to sell advertising. He went really quiet but you could see he was like mega pissed-off. I can show you a video. It's on TikTok.'

Kat and Tom stood shoulder to shoulder as Bridie loaded the video. But she really didn't need to watch it. Because she already knew the guest lecturer's identity.

How could she not, when he was her former stalker?

Bridie turned the phone towards Kat and Tom, and there, on its small but high-definition screen, Rosie Duggan was tearing Ethan Metcalfe a new arsehole.

'Be honest, your show isn't about helping bring closure for victims' families or helping the police, is it? You just turn up at crime scenes like a vulture at a kill. You poke your nose in and get what you can, but really you're just feeding on people's grief so you can sell advertising. It's disgusting.'

Ethan's face, now transformed by contact lenses, cosmetic dentistry and a mild tan, displayed an unmistakable emotion.

Hatred.

Kat kept her face neutral. But inside, she experienced a dislocating sense of confusion. Ethan was a total sad-sack. Yes, he'd stalked her, but after being arrested and warned, he'd backed off completely. He'd transformed his looks and even managed to snag himself an attractive girlfriend. Stalkers could very easily go on to murder the object of their obsession, but that would be Kat, not Rosie.

Could she see Ethan murdering Rosie Duggan? Over a shouting match? She wrinkled her nose. It wasn't impossible. But it was a stretch. The boyfriend, Lloyd, still looked a far likelier suspect. They'd TIE Ethan – trace, interview, eliminate – but with the emphasis on *eliminate*.

After thanking Bridie, she got back into the car. Tom drove back to Jubilee Place, where they separated – Tom to do more digging into Rosie's past, and Kat to look at her journal.

Kat took the journal out of its evidence bag and grabbed a paperclip from a plastic desk-tidy. Straightened it, then bent the top over against the edge of an old penknife. She inserted it into the simple lock holding Rosie Duggan's secrets.

Would one of them point to her killer's identity?

She started at the final entry. The one closest to Rosie's murder. Helpfully, Rosie had dated it. As Kat started to read, she looked for evidence that would help her bring Rosie's murderer to justice. And she found it immediately.

Chapter Twelve

ROSIE DUGGAN'S JOURNAL

3 April 2026

Well that went well.

Not!

I finally got up the courage to tell Lloyd I was breaking up with him.

He went mental. Accused me of being a slag. He said I was sleeping around. I tried to tell him that wasn't it, that I just had this growing feeling we weren't right for each other in the long run, but he wouldn't listen. Then he totally changed tack. He said he could forgive me anything. He'd prove he was the one for me.

Oh, God, I am literally crying right now. I have to stop for a minute.

◆ ◆ ◆

I'm back.

Why couldn't he see it? I said we'd been together since we were fifteen, and surely he could see that people change fundamentally every year at this age, let alone if we were twenty-five or even older? But he just used that against me. He said that was the whole point. We'd got together at fourteen and we should get married because I was 'the one'.

He actually used that phrase. But I told him there's like eight billion people on the Earth so statistically the odds of there only being one person on the whole planet who you can be with is just ridiculous.

That may not have been the wisest way to put it but I was cross with him. He was acting really entitled.

Then he threatened me. He said if I dumped him he'd post nudes of me online. Revenge porn? Really? He wouldn't do that. He was upset but Lloyd's a good person underneath. He's not one of those guys who follow T___ B___ (I'm not going to write his name down because he's so f***ing toxic, but you know who I mean).

I told Bridie and she said I should report him to the police, but what can they do? The average ten-year-old probably knows more about online safety than the police. You can't stop someone who wants to do it. I just have to hope Lloyd was only saying it to upset me.

Well, it worked.

Chapter Thirteen

Someone swore. Kat raised her head from the journal.

A new DC was carrying a coffee mug and had just spilled hot liquid over his hand. Then she saw the design on the side of the mug. A jokey font reading *Hands off, you tea leaf! This is Abby's Mug.*

Kat jumped to her feet and approached him, heart thumping. Why was it still in the kitchen?

'Hey! You can't use that!'

He turned, aggrieved.

'What? Who are you, anyway?'

'I'm DS Ballantyne and that mug's off limits. Give it to me.'

He backed up a step. 'No! Get your own.'

'It belonged to a friend. A cop. She was shot last year.'

Shrugging, he held it out. 'Sorry.'

She snatched it away from him, spilling more hot coffee on to her wrist, not even feeling the burn until it was too late. She turned her back and marched back to her desk, where with a trembling hand she placed the mug beside the phone.

She knuckled tears from her eyes.

Tom appeared by her side, and placed a tea in a plain white mug on her desk.

'Hey, boss. Got this for you,' he said quietly.

'Thanks, mate,' Kat said, clearing her throat and twisting Abby's mug round so the text faced away from her.

'You all right?'

'Yeah. Probably owe that new guy an apology.'

Tom wrinkled his nose. 'Don't worry. I'll have a quiet word.' He pulled up a chair. 'Was I OK back there? At the university, I mean?'

'You were great. How you dropped into student-speak to build rapport with Harry was really good.'

'It's called code-switching. Using somebody's own way of speaking to gain trust.'

Kat raised her eyebrows. 'Is it, now? Well, we live and learn. Must've taken you back, being on campus?'

'That feels like a lifetime ago.' He sighed. 'And, as you know, it didn't end well, so . . . happy to have moved on.'

'You were good with the Duggans too, mate. It's a side of the job I don't think they teach in criminology courses. I'm not even sure they *can* teach it. But you've got it. Not the common, touch, because I've seen you with people from all walks of life. But that ability to put people at their ease.'

He smiled. 'Really?'

'Yes, really! Don't sound *too* surprised. When I tell you you're a good detective, I don't just mean you memorised *Blackstone's Crime* or PACE. I mean you get *people*.'

'Speaking of which, we got quite the haul of people of interest, didn't we?'

Kat nodded, rose from her chair and grabbed a purple whiteboard marker. She crossed to the board and starting jotting down names in messy but still legible capitals.

'In order of discovery, Lloyd Kenney, the disgruntled and clearly very unpleasant ex. Then Greg Fanning, identified by Rosie's flatmates as an incel. Rejected for a date. Next, Libby Spare. An entitled rich girl who had her nose put out of joint when Rosie wouldn't help her cheat. Finally, your friend and mine, Middlehampton's own new media sensation, Ethan Metcalfe. Publicly humiliated by Rosie and caught on video.' She turned back to Tom. 'Now, how about we put them in order of suspicion-slash-probability of being the killer?'

Tom straightened in his chair and leaned forward, eyes scanning along the list of names. It made Kat smile, seeing him display the attentive eager-to-please body language he'd evidenced on his first day riding shotgun with her.

'Can I start from the other end? I put Libby last.'

'Because?'

'She's female.'

'Women can be murderers.'

'I know, but statistically – as I think you know' – he offered a teacherly look from under his eyebrows – 'women are less likely to be murderers of adults. More likely, babies or young children. Rarer, abusive spouses. Incredibly rare, to the point of being rounding error, murders of non-intimate partners or strangers.'

'Go on, Tomski. I'm enjoying this.'

'Second-to-last place is Ethan. The guy's a weapons-grade pain in the arse, but he has a lot to lose. And could easily turn his little contretemps with Rosie into more content. As long as he's monetising it, he's probably happy.'

Privately, Kat agreed with Tom, but she wanted to push him, all the same – get him thinking rationally, analysing evidence rather than reacting emotionally. *What? Like you do?* her inner voice piped up. She ignored it.

'But as I think *you* know, he also has form as a stalker,' she said. 'Namely of yours truly. So he's not above making women feel unsafe. And I've known him since school. There's always been something a bit off about him.'

'OK, but for now can I leave him in third place?'

'Carry on. It's your show.'

'So, in second place, I put Greg Fanning. If we believe the flatmates, then he's an incel. Spends all his time in chatrooms or on Reddit venting about how women are engaged in an anti-male conspiracy to prevent them having sex. Rosie turned him down for a date so he has direct evidence to support his bonkers world view.'

'Which leaves Lloyd as *el primo* person of interest and probable suspect?'

'A former intimate partner. One who posted revenge porn after she dumped him, which he lied about to us. He also seems to have convinced Rosie's parents that the sun shines out of his arse, so we can add *practised* liar to the list. How am I doing?'

Kat went and sat beside him, then looked up at the board. 'I agree. And, for the record, I think there's a big distance between Greg and Ethan, with Libby a very distant fourth. So, first things first, we invite Lloyd to come in for an interview under caution.'

'Should we check out the revenge porn first?'

Kat sighed. 'We probably should. I just need to steel myself for more evidence of the messed-up state of the world.'

'What was that search engine called again?'

Kat checked her notes. 'Am I In Porn?'

'Should we look?'

Kat raised an eyebrow. 'Not squeamish, are we?'

'No! Of course not,' Tom said. 'But it's just, you know, Rosie's dead. Murdered, and we're going to be looking at her naked or whatever.'

'I admire your sensitivity, Tomski, but we're detectives, are we not? So we detect. A witness claims Lloyd shared nudes of Rosie online. We need to know if she was telling the truth.'

She opened her laptop and typed in the name of the search engine. The site had the URL *amiinporn.io*. And it wanted an image of the user's face. Kat opened a social media site and within seconds had dozens of selfies of Rosie to choose from. Wondering, not for the first time, whether it was safe to have so many images of yourself online, she picked one in which Rosie was smiling, the background relatively plain – looked like a beach somewhere – and downloaded it.

She switched back to the porn discovery site and uploaded it.

A dark pink button pulsed. Kat's heartbeat pulsed with it.

SEARCHING . . .

Three grey dots faded in and out in turn. Her stomach shifted queasily as she imagined some sort of robot sifting through billions of sexual images looking for Rosie Duggan.

Kat turned to Tom. 'This could take a while, I guess. Tell me what our next steps are.'

Tom sat straighter. Kat suppressed a smile.

'I'm assuming that if Lloyd did post sexual images of Rosie, he didn't use his own name,' Tom said, 'so it could take Digital Forensics a while to connect him to the images. But we might get him to admit it under caution.'

'I agree. Now, he's over eighteen, so we don't need to worry about an appropriate adult, but he's still basically a kid, so no heavy-handed tactics.'

Tom frowned. 'But revenge porn, Kat. . . That's serious.'

'I know. And if we find out he posted any, we'll take the next step. But if and when we charge him, I don't want any blowback from his lawyer saying we coerced him or used any other tactics that a jury wouldn't like.'

Tom's eyes flicked to the laptop's screen, and lit up. 'Kat! We got a hit!'

The screen displayed a textual report.

Am I In Porn? has discovered one website that appears (97% level of confidence) to show a sexual image of you, Rosie Duggan.

Links: www.paythebitchback.biz/users/758993/rosieisaslut

We're sorry to give you this news. As part of our Digital Dignity project, we have created several tools to help you remove it and advice on legal actions you can take in different countries.

There followed links to what appeared to be blog posts and downloads. For now Kat ignored these. She clicked the link.

The page that opened wasn't as bad as she had feared. No explicit video. But what was there was bad enough. Half a dozen images, clearly taken on a phone, of Rosie posing in a bra and knickers or topless. Kat studied her face. She looked, not uncomfortable, not exactly. But there was something guarded in the look she bestowed on the camera. Her hands were crossed in front of her pants.

Tom tapped a circular avatar icon and a username at the top of the screen. The icon was hard to make sense of. An orange, black and white . . . thing.

'That must be Lloyd,' Tom said. 'What is that? Part of a motorbike? A cosplay helmet or something?'

Kat pointed to the username. 'StihlCrazy. He's a tree surgeon, right.'

'Apprentice.'

'And his chainsaw was a Stihl. That's what the icon is, look. The engine of the chainsaw and the handle.'

'Sorry, boss. Should have seen that.'

'Well, there's always the chance it's a deranged Paul Simon fan, so we should keep our options open.'

'Funny.'

'I try.'

'What now?'

'I'm going to call Lloyd. Get him in here as soon as possible. While I'm doing that, can you go and talk to Digital Forensics? See if they can pin the username to Lloyd Kenney. And put wheels in motion to get the images removed. Urgently.'

'On it.'

While Tom went to talk to the legal and technical specialists in DF, Kat called Lloyd.

'Hello? Who is this? Is it you, Moxie? Did you get a burner, you wanker?' He laughed.

'Lloyd,' Kat said, interrupting him and his clearly grief-stricken good humour, 'it's DS Ballantyne. We met yesterday.'

'Oh, yeah. Right. Sorry about that. Moxie's. . . I mean Cam Moxbury . . . he's a mate. Always pranking people.'

'I'd like to invite you to come into Middlehampton police station to talk to us. It's what we call a voluntary interview under caution. That means—'

'I know what it means. I watch a load of videos on YouTube about the cops. Why?'

Kat breathed in and out. Giving herself time to refocus. One thing she was still struggling to rise above was men, even eighteen-year-old men, talking over her.

'You would be entitled to legal representation and you'd be free to leave at any time. Can you get here today, Lloyd?'

'No. I'm fifty metres up a beech tree. I can't just leave halfway through a job, can I?'

'How about tomorrow?'

'I'll be working on the same job, won't I?'

Kat tightened her tone a touch. 'I could come and see you at home, if you'd prefer? You still live with your mum and dad, is that right?'

Was it 'heavy-handed'? The tactic she'd warned Tom about. On balance, she thought not. If anything, she was trying to be accommodating in the face of a witness's reluctance to interrupt his workday.

'Yeah. But look, what's this about?'

'I just wanted to ask you a couple of questions. Routine stuff. You were Rosie's boyfriend, after all.'

A cautious note entered his voice. In the background, Kat could hear the woodchipper going full-tilt.

'Questions about what?'

'Home or the police station, Lloyd? Which is it going to be?' She turned the screw. Just a little. 'I can't compel you to attend the station, which you probably know, what with all the YouTube videos you've been watching. But I am completely within my rights as the lead investigator in Rosie's murder to visit you at home.'

'Can you come here? Tonight? I really can't take time off during the day.'

'Of course. What time do you get home from work?'

'Six. Then I need a shower. I'm covered in sawdust.'

'I'll see you at seven.'

'That's when we have tea.'

'Ask your mum to put yours in the oven for you. I'll see you later.'

She ended the call.

It was interesting. He'd been pugnacious. Borderline hostile. Clearly he didn't know they'd found his revenge porn posting. Or he didn't think he could be traced from an anonymous account. These days, everyone thought they were a bloody CSI. Watch a YouTube video and listen to a podcast and you were a qualified homicide investigator. But there was more than one way to get to the truth. Sometimes simply asking uncomfortable questions and then sitting back silently yielded more than a hundred DNA tests.

As Lloyd Kenney would shortly be finding out.

With time to spare, she went to see Jan Cable, the POLSA. Rosie's phone hadn't turned up in their search.

'The killer could have taken it, Kat,' Jan said. 'But he could just as easily have chucked it in the river or down a drain.'

'Can you widen the search?'

'Can you give me more budget?'

Kat puffed her cheeks out. That would be a hard no without even asking Ma-Linda. Rosie's phone would have to stay lost for now. It'd be locked anyway, and that would mean weeks of waiting. Which wouldn't matter if Kat could think of another way to find her killer.

Chapter Fourteen

Kat frowned as she took another look at the revenge porn site.

Why did they do it? In her day, you got dumped, you went out and got drunk with a mate while you called him every name under the sun. Cried about it if you really liked the boy. Sat around moping for a few days. Then got over him. She'd always supposed it was the same for boys.

But now, apparently their first thought was, *The bitch dumped me. Right, let's stick a video of us having sex online so a bunch of perverts can wank over her.*

Not for the first time, her thoughts turned to Riley, her son. He'd never do that, would he? To Millie? If she broke up with him?

Kat and Van had raised their son to be respectful of women. Well, of other people in general. But she'd interviewed enough sex offenders to know that the old-fashioned but still surprisingly common conception of rapists, flashers and nonces as slavering weirdos in dirty macs and greasy hair hanging over their eyes was just a fantasy parents told themselves to obscure the truth. The man who'd raped their child, or coerced them into performing sexual acts, was just as likely to be a clean-cut teacher, popular sports coach or, of course, the old favourite, a priest. Or, and at this her stomach heaved properly, because it was the most common scenario of all, a member of their own family.

She shook her head. No. They'd talked before about porn. Ever since Van had found Riley looking at some pictures on a school WhatsApp group of one of the boys' older sisters in her undies. Riley had been tearful, ashamed. And now he had Millie, he seemed more settled somehow. Less prone to outbursts. Neither of them was sixteen yet and she prayed their physical relationship was still at the experimental stage—

Oh, God, not another talk!

She flicked back to the start of the journal. Rosie documented her life, and her inner world, at Middlehampton University, and the media studies course. Nothing very useful in terms of identifying a suspect, but lots that revealed the thinking of a girl from a tiny village finding her feet in a bigger world.

Kat wondered how she herself would have fared if she'd lasted longer than two weeks at university. A sense of sadness crept over her. Regret mingled with a sort of grief for a life she'd now never know. It wasn't as if her own life had turned out too badly. A husband, a son, a career that, even without a fast-track turbocharger strapped to it, seemed to be going in the right direction. But there it was, nonetheless. A sense of a future unglimpsed. Where she might have moved away from her home town, as Rosie had done, and reinvented herself.

Kat texted Van to let him know she'd be late home. Got one of his trademark brief replies – *kk* – then went to see Linda.

Linda's PA, Annie, looked up from her computer and smiled at Kat.

'All right, Kat?'

'Is she in?'

Annie's eyes slid towards her boss's office door, which was open.

'What she's mainly in is a bad mood. But her next appointment's not for another fifteen minutes, so if you're up for a challenge . . .'

'Thanks,' Kat whispered.

She knocked softly and entered.

Chapter Fifteen

DCI Linda Ockenden looked up, and when she saw who her visitor was, ran a hand through her hair then gestured to the visitor chair.

'Just the woman. Park your arse and tell me about Rosie Duggan.'

So the big boss had heard about the case.

'Young girl, student at the university, found dead by a member of the public at 7.15 a.m. yesterday. It looks like she was pushed off the top of Five Cups Lane car park.'

Linda eyed Kat like a secretary bird eying a snake. *One false move and I'll kick you to death.*

'"Looks like"?'

'One of her nails was ripped out. We found it on the top storey by the railing. No suicide note at the house she shared. No history of mental ill-health. Everyone said she was happy, well adjusted, popular. Literally the least likely candidate for suicide you could imagine.' She swallowed. 'I think she was murdered, Ma-Linda.'

Kat deliberately used her nickname for the DCI Crime to try to lighten the mood. It had come about when, as a new transfer into MCU, she'd become flustered and dithered between 'Ma'am' and 'Linda'. It had stuck.

Linda's baleful stare intensified.

Kat swallowed nervously. What was wrong? She ran a lightning-fast audit of her actions so far, flicking back through her mental policy book. Had she missed some obvious aspect of protocol? Failed to order a search? Trampled through the crime scene without a noddy suit? Linda solved the mystery for her.

'Yes, well, you're going to have to work a bloody miracle on this one, Kat. This quarter's budget's down to the sticky stuff at the bottom of the jar.'

'I've got several promising leads already.'

'Which is great, my love, and don't think I have any doubts about your abilities. But I just had her father on the phone bending my ear and chewing it off at the same time.'

Ah. Here was the source of Ma-Linda's bad mood – and her knowledge of the case.

Linda continued: 'Rosie was a perfect child. No enemies, which' – she held up a hand, palm outwards – 'before you say anything I know almost conclusively means she did, but anyway, as Andy Duggan was at pains to point out, Rosie didn't deserve to die. As if some murder victims do, but anyway. Then he gave me an ultimatum, Kat. A bloody ultimatum! Said I had a week to solve it before he went to the media direct and accused us of dragging our heels or some such rubbish. I mean, Lord, Kat, I sympathise with any victim's relatives, you know I do.'

Kat nodded. Then, feeling Linda was looking for more, said, 'Absolutely.'

'Exactly! But he was basically threatening me.'

'I think there's a good chance we can actually wrap this up in a week,' Kat said. 'Wait, did he mean till the end of this week or seven days?'

Ma-Linda's eyes widened, revealing the fine red capillaries at the margins. It gave her a slightly unhinged look.

'You know what, Kat, I didn't get down to the finer points of his deadline!' She sighed and puffed out her cheeks in evident frustration. 'Sorry, sorry. You didn't deserve that. But there's more. He said regardless of what we did, he wasn't going to, and I quote, "sit on my arse while the police go through the motions" before telling the world his daughter took her own life.'

Kat could only imagine what would have happened if one of *them* had spoken to Ma-Linda that way. Images of detectives sailing groundward out of a third-floor window crowded into her vision. If only one of them could be Carve-up.

'I'm going to see the ex-boyfriend this evening,' she said. 'He posted revenge porn pics online. And he lied to me and Tom about the fact Rosie had dumped him.'

'That sounds hopeful. What else?'

'Got a male student, a so-called incel, who asked Rosie out and got turned down.'

Linda wrinkled her nose.

'Anyone else?'

'A female student who wanted Rosie to write an essay for her and lost it when she refused.'

'Sounds a bit thin. Don't they all use ChatGPT these days?'

'Apparently the uni authorities can spot it now.'

'That's it? The ex-boyfriend – my pick, by the way – and two disgruntled students?'

Was it worth mentioning Ethan? Linda still had a predatory look in her eye. Expecting more. Kat gave it to her, despite her own doubts.

'Then there's Ethan Metcalfe. Rosie publicly humiliated him in a lecture. I've seen a video. If looks could kill, et cetera.'

'Seriously? Middlehampton's very own true-crime-podcast celebrity a murderer? Sure you're not indulging in wishful thinking?'

Kat acknowledged Linda's doubts with an inclined head.

'He's there because a witness mentioned him, that's all. I don't like him for it. And if he has an alibi then he's not guilty of anything.'

'Apart from being a massive bell-end.'

Kat laughed, surprised once again by Linda's talent for the well-judged descent into gutter talk. 'Apart from that, yes.'

'Do your best, OK? And if you can avoid racking up a massive bill for DNA testing that would be lovely. Think you can manage that, DS Ballantyne?'

'I'll do my best, Ma-Linda.' She saw her opportunity to put her team back together and score a point over Carve-up in the process. 'If you could just let me have Fez and Leah, I could clear this one so much faster.'

Linda regarded her through narrowed eyes. 'What did Stuart say?'

'He said no.'

Linda shrugged. 'I'm not going to override your DI, Kat. This is a straight operational matter, and you know why he did it. I agree with Stuart – Abby's murder took it out of you. You're not ready.'

Kat forced herself to take a breath. 'Look, Ma-Linda, I admit it. I *was* traumatised when Abby got shot. But I've had my sessions with the psychologist just like you ordered. And now I'm ready. She agrees.'

Linda's lips tightened to a thin line. An impending storm. In that moment, Kat knew she'd blown her chances. Her DCI's eyes sparked as she leaned across the desk, all traces of her lightened mood gone. 'Consider yourself lucky you've got friends in high places or that whole thing could have blown up in your face. Losing Fez and Leah for a while was the least worst thing that could have happened.'

'But it's just one of Stuart's stupid power-plays!' Kat protested. 'Why can't you see that? He doesn't care about me, or Abby. In fact, you know what? He just called her a—'

Linda smacked a palm down on to the desk. Kat jumped. 'Stop! Do not finish that sentence! I know you don't have a lot of respect for DI Carver, but please don't question *my* management decisions.' Linda aimed a scarlet fingernail at Kat like a gun. 'Work this case with Tom. It sounds straightforward enough. That's it.' Linda bent to her paperwork. Kat stayed sitting for a few seconds longer, but Linda clearly had no interest in prolonging the conversation.

She stood, feeling more than ever like a sullen teenager dismissed from the headmistress's presence.

'Yes, Ma'am.'

Wondering who her 'friends in high places' were, and what lay behind Linda's lightning-fast mood swing, she went to find Tom. He was the one whose aunt was the Police and Crime Commissioner. Had he pulled strings for her?

'Did you get your auntie to put in a good word for me, Tomski?' she asked in the kitchen, where Tom was making himself a coffee. 'After Abby was murdered?'

'No, why?'

'Nothing. Just something Linda said.'

'Aunt Elaine says she's not going to stand for re-election next time. Nobody takes her seriously.'

Kat nodded, feeling at that moment a certain level of kinship with the PCC.

'She's not wrong.'

She left Tom to his coffee and paperwork and was on the road towards Abbots Bromley ten minutes later. Maybe she could wrap it up inside forty-eight hours. Now that really would put the smile back on Ma-Linda's face.

Kat called the MCU media liaison officer from the car. Freddie Tippett looked like a choirboy, but told the filthiest jokes in Jubilee Place.

She pictured his pink, just-shaved cheeks and that innocent 'who me?' expression he'd assume after turning the air blue. Smiled.

'Hey, Freddie. Can you organise a press conference for me? It's the girl who fell from Five Cups Lane car park.'

'I can,' he said, drawing out the final word. 'But we're kind of stacked out with requests at the moment. The arson case Leah and Fez are working is generating such a lot of interest from the nationals. They're on daily updates.'

'So I guess tomorrow's out of the question?'

He laughed abruptly. 'That's a joke, right? I can fit you in late-ish Friday morning. It's the best I can do.'

'Then it'll have to do. Thanks, Freddie.'

Brilliant. The Duggans would no doubt seize on the delay as yet more evidence of police 'foot-dragging'. Could she keep them onside if she spent some time filling them in personally on the progress of the investigation?

She decided to call in on them after speaking to Lloyd Kenney.

Chapter Sixteen

The Kenneys lived in a bungalow on the outskirts of a village a mile from Abbots Bromley. Kat parked on the street, walked up the path and rang the bell. While she waited, a man mowing his front lawn called out to her.

'Police, are you?'

Kat smiled. Said nothing. The guy had that look about him. Eyes glinting like a magpie after a shiny thing. Probably ran the local Neighbourhood Watch.

She looked at the front door. *Come on, come on.* The man had white hair like Barrie's, but dark, resentful eyes where Barrie's looked like he'd just been crowned King of the Faeries.

'If it's about that lad's motorbike, I don't know why it's taken you so long. I've made several noise complaints.'

Noise complaints were council business usually. Surely he knew that?

'And don't tell me to contact Environmental Health. He's out all hours. That's a public order offence. I know my law.'

It wasn't. He didn't. She smiled.

A shadow appeared behind the swirly pressed glass of the front door.

A woman opened it. On the young side to have a teenage son was Kat's first thought. But then, people probably said that about her, too.

'Mrs Kenney?'

'Yes?'

Kat held up her warrant card, trying to keep it hidden from the inquisitive neighbour who had advanced to within eavesdropping distance.

'Police. Could I come in, please? I arranged to talk to Lloyd.'

The woman glanced over Kat's right shoulder. Tutted.

'Go home, Les. Don't you need to update your spreadsheet?' She stepped back and beckoned Kat inside. 'Nosey old git,' she continued, as she led Kat into a kitchen bright with late evening sunshine and redolent of cooking smells. Sausages was Kat's guess. And onion gravy too. 'Runs the local Neighbourhood Watch. He spends every waking moment spying on us all. Says he's doing it out of public-spiritedness. His wife walked out last year after fifty years of marriage. Said he was driving her round the twist. I don't blame her.'

'He could be lonely,' Kat said.

'Whatever. Wait here.'

Kat waited. The kitchen was neat. *Spick and span*, her own mother would say.

She heard footsteps on the stairs. She turned in her chair as Lloyd's mum entered the kitchen together with her son. And a man in a jacket and open-necked shirt. Lloyd's father?

'This is Jeremy. He's a solicitor,' Mrs Kenney said.

The family were going to play it carefully. That was fine. In fact, Kat thought it might work in her favour.

The man was urbane, in his late forties. Good-looking in an M&S-underpants-poster way. Dark hair, good cheekbones. Nice teeth. He offered his hand, which she took. Warm and dry. A grip a man could be proud of.

'Jeremy Reith. How do you do?'

'DS Kathryn Ballantyne. Hertfordshire Police. This isn't an interview under caution,' Kat said.

'I'm just here as a friend of the family,' he said smoothly. He opened a pad and took a fountain pen out of his jacket pocket. Saw her watching and smiled. 'Just an informal record of the conversation.'

Kat smiled thinly. She turned to Lloyd. His hair was wet and he'd masked the delicious cooking smells with Lynx Africa. Kat would recognise its pungent aroma anywhere. Riley was equally fond of it. The stubby black canisters might say 'body spray' but the boys who bought it seemed to think that was secret code for 'room freshener'. Or, possibly, 'industrial fumigator'.

'How are you coping, Lloyd?' she began.

He scrunched up his features. 'It's hard.'

'Of course it is. I understand. You loved Rosie very much.'

'Yeah.'

'He was going to ask her to marry him this summer, weren't you, love?' his mum said, laying a protective arm across his broad shoulders.

He nodded, head down. After viewing the revenge porn, Kat was sure Lloyd was putting on an act. Time to ratchet things up a notch.

'It must have come as quite a shock when Rosie broke up with you, Lloyd,' Kat said. 'I can't quite see how she would have agreed to marry you after that.'

Kat watched all three of them as she delivered the line. Mrs Kenney reared back in her chair, staring at Kat with wide eyes. The solicitor turned to Lloyd then, frowning, made a note on his pad. He didn't bother to use any kind of code and Kat's practised eye had no trouble reading the inverted words. *Break-up? Motive?*

But it was Lloyd she focused on. His head jerked up and he glared at her. His cheeks flared.

'That's not true!'

'I spoke to one of Rosie's housemates who said it was.'

'She's a liar. They all are!'

'Who are, Lloyd?' Kat asked.

He glanced at his mum and clamped his lips together.

'Lloyd's right,' Mrs Kenney said. 'They were in love. Rosie was like a daughter to us. She'd have told me. You must be mistaken. This, this *housemate*, whoever she is, must have got the wrong end of the stick. It's what do you call it . . . hearsay. Or something,' she added, as if needing to convince herself.

Kat shook her head. 'Rosie wrote it in her journal. I read it myself.' She focused on Lloyd until he looked up at her. 'Rosie said, "He went mental. Accused me of being a slag. He said I was sleeping around." Did you say those things to her, Lloyd?'

'No! I didn't!'

'Well, can you explain to me why Rosie, who you say you loved and who your mum says loved you back, would write that in a journal she kept locked, out of sight under her bed?'

He was blushing furiously now, darting glances at the two adults flanking him. Finally he shrugged again.

'No idea. She could've had mental health issues. Like, exam stress or whatever.'

'I don't think she did. I've spoken to her housemates and her parents. Nobody said anything about Rosie suffering from mental illness. In fact, she seems to have been extremely well adjusted and really enjoying university life.'

'DS Ballantyne, forgive me, but do you have a question for my client?'

That hadn't taken long. Kat looked at the solicitor with the good teeth and the firm dry handshake. Waited him out. He wouldn't bite. Fine.

'Your "client"? I thought you were here as a friend of the family?'

'I am. But if, as seems likely, you are going to treat Lloyd as a person of interest in a murder investigation, I think we might drop the pretence, don't you?'

'Fine by me. Presumably then, you won't mind if I record the rest of the conversation?' She placed her phone on the table and launched the voice memo app. 'To recap, then, Lloyd, you say Rosie hadn't dumped you, everything was fine between you and you never called her a slag? Despite Rosie writing that she had, and you did, in her journal. Have I got that right?'

He glanced at the solicitor, then his mum, then back at her. He seemed to have gained in confidence now his lawyer had shown his true colours.

'I'm not saying she didn't write it. I'm saying it's not true.'

'I see. And despite the fact you think she might have been suffering from a mental health condition that caused her to accuse you of saying those things, you were still willing to propose?'

He looked confused. She almost felt sorry for him.

'I could have helped her,' he said.

'"Helped her".' Kat let the phrase hang in the air between them. 'Well, let me move on because I'm sure Mr Keith wants me to. I only have one more question for Lloyd.'

'Good, because his tea's in the oven and it won't be as nice if he doesn't eat it soon,' Mrs Kenney interjected.

Kat smiled at her. Just a little, to be polite, before she turned back to Lloyd.

'I'll come to the point, then, before your tea gets cold. Lloyd, did you post sexual images of Rosie Duggan on a revenge porn website called paythebitchback.biz under the username StihlCrazy?'

The room temperature plummeted. Mrs Kenney gasped and spun round in her chair to look at her son. He couldn't meet her gaze and was staring down at his fingers, which were locked tightly together so the knuckles whitened. The lawyer made another note, then his pen nib stilled over the page and he frowned.

'Pay the bitch back. Dot biz,' Kat said slowly, looking at him. 'All lower case, which I don't think matters. No hyphens. Well, Lloyd?'

'No comment.'

'We're not in an interview room, Lloyd. You're not under police caution. Let me ask you again. Did you post revenge porn pictures of your ex-girlfriend, Rosie Duggan, on that website?'

'No! OK? I did not post pictures like that. I would never.'

'We've given the details of the pictures and the user account to our Digital Forensics team, Lloyd. There's so much metadata in digital images these days, and most people either don't know about it or forget it's there. You'd be surprised at how many criminals get caught that way. So, I'll ask you again, did you post those images? I can understand it. You were hurt that she dumped you. Angry, even. You had the photos on your phone. Why not?'

She used the word 'dumped' rather than 'broke up with'. Heavy-handed? No. Designed to elicit an emotional reaction? Absolutely. She got one.

'Even if I did, it's not a crime, is it?'

Before the solicitor could intervene, Kat set him straight.

'Actually, it *is* a crime, Lloyd. It's an offence under the Online Safety Act 2023. Are you now telling me you did post those images?'

'I don't want to talk about this anymore,' he said sullenly, folding his arms.

'DS Ballantyne, you said you had one more question,' the solicitor said. 'That was it, I believe.'

'I changed my mind. Lloyd, can you tell me where you were on Monday night between 6.00 p.m. and 7.00 a.m. the following morning?'

'What? You mean, like, an alibi? Jesus! Do you think I killed her? I loved her, man. You're insane!'

'Please answer the question, Lloyd. It would be really helpful.'

'Well, I was at home, OK? You can like, check my phone, can't you? Ping it or whatever?'

'That's right.'

It *was* right. But all it would prove was the *phone*'s whereabouts. And although when it came to people under the age of thirty – *hell,* she thought, *under sixty* – ninety-nine per cent of the time where the phone was, so was the owner, evidentially it meant very little. You could have a suspect's phone at a murder scene, but if there were credible eyewitnesses or CCTV that placed them a hundred miles away, that was the phone evidence in the bin. Now, DNA. That was a different story.

'So that's that, then. That's my alibi.'

Kat turned to Mrs Kenney. 'When was the last time you saw Lloyd that night?'

Mrs Kenney was white-faced now, no doubt still trying to process the information Kat had shared, and starting to question what she knew about her son.

'Eight? A little after? I think he came down to get a snack from the kitchen while we were watching telly.'

'So, and I'm not holding you to this, but say, no later than 8.15 p.m.?'

'I suppose that's right, yes. But Lloyd wouldn't . . . he couldn't . . . He's a good boy.'

Kat looked at Lloyd but said nothing for a moment. She tried to see beyond the gaze, which was equal parts defiance, confusion and shame.

'You own a motorbike, is that right?'

The lurch in topic had him frowning, screwing up his features as he tried to figure out what she was getting at.

'Yeah.'

'What kind?'

'A Honda.'

'What model?'

'Rebel 500, why?'

'Any good on fast roads? Motorways?'

'I guess. I mostly just use it for work. Why?'

'Wait!' Mrs Kenney was staring at Kat. 'I remember! I got up in the night. I needed the loo. I met Lloyd in the hallway.'

'What time was this?'

'It was 3.30 a.m.,' Mrs Kenney said triumphantly. 'I remember because I always wake up at that time and I checked the time on my phone.'

Kat said nothing. She was working out timings. Lloyd could have checked in with his parents at 8.30 p.m., then rode fast to Middlehampton. Arrived at 11.00 p.m. or thereabouts, murdered Rosie and been back home in plenty of time to meet his mum on the upstairs landing at 3.30 a.m. without any trouble. Apart from the most obvious and dreadful kind, of course. His alibi was worthless.

Kat switched off the voice recorder. Put the phone back in her pocket. She stood and looked down at Lloyd Kenney.

'If it was you who posted those images, Lloyd – I mean if you *are* StihlCrazy – I'd strongly suggest you take them down and delete the account. But just so you and I suppose Mr Reith here are aware, I'll be referring the evidence we collected to our Digital Forensics team, and they *will* be investigating.'

Mrs Kenney stared at her, eyes red-rimmed. 'You can't! He's only eighteen. You'll ruin his life!'

Kat had heard this line, and variations, many times since becoming a cop. It hadn't washed when she was in uniform. It didn't now. People chose to take the actions they took. If they didn't like the consequences, well, they shouldn't have taken them in the first place.

'He's denied posting them, Mrs Kenney, so he has nothing to worry about. But I must remind you that, at this point, the only person whose life has been ruined is your son's ex-girlfriend, Rosie Duggan. Rosie was also eighteen, and she had *her* whole life ahead of her. But she won't see nineteen because somebody pushed her off a car park roof and killed her. My job, my *only* job, is to find out who murdered her.' She held up a hand, Linda-style, breathing deeply. 'Please don't get up. I'll see myself out.'

On the Kenneys' front path she took a moment to compose herself.

From a potential suspect to the bereaved parents.

Time for a complete change of approach.

Chapter Seventeen

The pub was closed.

The chalkboard under the front porch bore a sombre message. No more flowers and stick-kids.

Closed due to family bereavement.

Kat went round to the back of the building and found a door with a bell push. She rang it and waited – glad, not for the first time, that her preferred outfit of black suit and white shirt would match the mood.

After what felt like hours, the door swung inwards. Madeleine Duggan stood there, lank-haired, wearing no make-up and a look of profound sadness. If the eyes really were the window to the soul, Madeleine was in the depths of hell.

'Hello, Madeleine, can I come in?'

Madeleine nodded wordlessly, turned and shuffled along the flagstone passageway and into the deserted back bar. Once there, she subsided into an upholstered side chair and rested her elbows on the tabletop.

'Andy's out,' she said tonelessly. 'He just walks all day.'

'Has your FLO been in contact?'

'Mick's nice enough. He makes tea. Asks about Rosie. But that just makes it worse. Andy's not coping. He cries all the time.'

'How about you? How are you coping?'

For the first time, Madeleine's eyes showed something beyond despair. They flashed.

'How do you *think* I'm coping?'

'Sorry. I know this must be the worst possible time. I can't imagine what it must feel like.'

'You got kids?'

'A son. Riley. He's fourteen.'

'Then I pray you never lose him. Because it *guts* you.'

'Madeleine, is there anything I can do to help you and Andy. Anything at all?'

'When's the press conference? Mick said that's standard.'

Kat swallowed. 'Friday, 11.45 a.m. Do you think you and Andy would be able to come down to Middlehampton and take part?'

Madeleine nodded. 'It's important, isn't it? The grieving parents read out a statement, then look right into the camera and plead for anyone who knows anything to come forward?'

She'd nailed the rationale in a single, bitter-edged sentence. Because why else would anyone subject themselves to an ordeal like that? And it was true. Murderers, rapists and arsonists might have the moral sense of a black widow spider. But one of their friends or family might possess a conscience.

'If you could manage it, we can make sure you have all the support you need. We have a dedicated media specialist and a family support team – plus Mick, of course. He'd be with you right the way through. He can drive you to Middlehampton and back, too. You wouldn't have to worry about a thing.'

'Except the man who took our daughter from us, you mean?'

'We're making progress with our investigation. I hope we can give you some news soon.'

Madeleine straightened in her chair. Turned her body so she was facing Kat.

'You've got a suspect?'

'Not a suspect. That means someone we have evidence on that supports our belief they committed the crime. But we have several persons of interest.'

'Who? Who? You have to tell me!'

Mindful of what Ma-Linda had told her about Andy Duggan issuing barely disguised threats to take matters into his own hands, Kat tried to walk the line between supporting a grieving mother and protecting her own investigation.

'As I said, these are people who appear to have had a grudge against Rosie, nothing more. At this stage we have no concrete evidence against any of them.'

Madeleine's eyes widened, revealing sclera pink from crying.

'"Any of them"? How many are there, for Christ's sake?'

'We've identified four individuals.'

'Well, men, women, what?'

'Three men, one woman.'

Madeleine frowned. She drew her lower lip between her teeth and commenced chewing. It made Kat squirm, fearful she'd draw blood.

'And one of them killed our Rosie? Is that what you're saying?'

'Madeleine, you know I can't say anything that might compromise the investigation.'

'Just tell me!'

Just then, the back door banged and a heavy stride on the flagstones announced the presence of a man.

'It's me.'

Kat recognised Andy Duggan's voice. He strode into the bar and froze when he saw Kat. Then he folded muscular arms across his chest.

'You arrested someone yet?'

'No. Not yet. Do you want to take a seat, Andy? I was just updating Madeleine on our progress.'

'Nice of you to offer me a seat in my own pub,' he said, but he pulled a chair out with a squawk of its legs on the stone floor and sat heavily before refolding his arms. 'Go on, then. Update me.'

This was a different Andy Duggan to the hollow-eyed man at the chapel of rest. He seemed more focused. Grieving, obviously, but engaged with her investigation.

'We've identified four people who we want to look at in more detail. As of right now, there's no evidence that directly points to any one of them, but I'm confident we'll find Rosie's killer. If not among these four, then somewhere else in Middlehampton, possibly on campus.'

'Have you looked at the Kenney boy?'

That was interesting. Not 'Lloyd' or 'her boyfriend'. Sounded like Andy Duggan didn't much care for his daughter's choice of boyfriend.

'Why do you ask?'

'She split up with him, didn't she? I'd say that was a pretty strong motive.'

Beside him Madeleine Duggan's eyes widened. She twisted round in her chair to face him.

'She what? Why didn't you tell me? Why didn't Rosie tell me?'

Andy glared at his wife. 'Because you think the sun shines out of that boy's arse, that's why. Rosie knew you'd be upset. Try to change her mind. She asked me not to tell you. Said she wanted to wait until she was back in the summer.'

Tears sprang to Madeleine's eyes and dropped on to the front of her sweatshirt, its pale blue cotton darkening in irregular splotches. 'But we were best friends! She told me everything.'

'You're her *mum*, Mads, for God's sake! Her mum! *Bridie's* her best friend.'

'I know, but we were always messaging. And I do *not* think the sun shines out of Lloyd's arse! I just think he's got his head screwed on right. He's not academic, but that's hardly a crime, is it? I mean, look at us. One A level between us but we've got our own business. We're doing all right for ourselves.'

'Leave it, all right? They're investigating and I have a feeling they'll want to look at him a bit more closely.' He turned back to face Kat, glowering. 'That's right, isn't it? When a woman or a girl's killed, you look at the partner. The husband or boyfriend . . . or the ex-boyfriend. Do you think Lloyd murdered Rosie?'

'It's too early to say. But . . .' Kat hesitated, unsure whether she should continue.

Should she reveal what she'd learned about the revenge porn pictures? It was almost certainly Lloyd who'd posted them. But, again, without firm evidence linking him to the StihlCrazy account, she could be creating a world of trouble for an innocent, if troubled, boy, and certainly for herself. The public mood towards sex offenders was unforgiving to say the least. She would not want to be behind a witch hunt, whether or not its quarry was guilty.

'But what?'

'There are a couple of things I need to look into more closely. That's all I can say, Andy, I'm sorry. I wish I could tell you more.'

She left after promising to put them in touch with Freddie Tippett, having secured their agreement to take part in the press conference. She just hoped they'd make it through without Andy threatening to string up his daughter's murderer live on air.

Twenty minutes into the drive back to Middlehampton, she realised with a sigh that she should have texted Van before leaving the Duggans. Shaking her head, she pushed on, thinking of the potential treasure trove that was Rosie's journal.

It would be almost 11.00 p.m. by the time they got back to Jubilee Place. Updating her policy book and the rest of her paperwork would take another hour. Still, Kat resolved to read another of Rosie's soul-baring entries before she left for home.

Chapter Eighteen

ROSIE DUGGAN'S JOURNAL

19 January 2026

It's the start of the new term and I ought to be feeling so optimistic. Christmas with Mum and Dad was lovely, and it was great hanging out with the old gang from school.

So why am I feeling trapped and anxious? Easy! One word.

Libby.

I thought we'd sorted it out last term. She wanted me to write her essay for her – so, basically, help her cheat. She made it worse by offering me money. I said no, she lost her temper, called me a few names and that was that. We both went home for the Christmas holiday and I thought it was over.

But I got back to find a long letter literally handwritten and pushed under my door from Libby. She's got it into her head that I don't like her. That somehow I'm holding a grudge against her and trying to, her words, 'turn the faculty against me'. She said I ought to get down off my high horse or somebody might push me off it.

There's something not right about her. I see it now. Some sort of disorder. It could be why she's here and not at some posh uni like Oxford or Cambridge, which she pretty much told me was her right.

Anyway, like I said, it made me really anxious and I'm not normally like that. I don't really even get exam stress. Not properly, like some people. Just a few butterflies in my tummy.

So [takes deep breath] I went to see one of the lecturers in the psychology department about her. Just to see if I needed to be worried.

Dr Capstick was really cool about it. Obviously I didn't give Libby's name, and Dr C said she couldn't offer anything like a diagnosis about a specific individual. But . . .

I said there was this 'person' who'd left me this sort of weirdly obsessive letter and what did she think about it? I took it with me so she could see for herself, just in case the handwriting revealed something. I didn't have to worry about the name because Libby hadn't signed it. She just put 'Your ex-friend'.

Dr C said it looked to her like someone just really angry and venting on paper. She said it was pretty old-school for someone of our generation to be writing an actual letter but that didn't mean anything in itself. She said not to worry. 'Letter writers aren't generally violent,' is what she actually said. 'It's why they reach for a keyboard, or a pen in this case, and not a weapon.'

So, basically, Libby's like this clicktivist. Only, the cause of the injustice she's furious about is me!

I wish she'd just grow up. Or leave.

Yes. Leaving would be good, too.

Chapter Nineteen

Van had been so deeply asleep when Kat finally crawled into bed at 1.15 a.m., he hadn't even stirred. She'd apologised for her lack of communication by way of a mug of tea in bed at 7.00 a.m. and a quickie before leaving for work, promising Smokey that 'Daddy'll walk you this morning, Smokes.'

That was an hour ago. She was now completing even more paperwork, trying to get ahead of it before returning to proper policework: getting out there and talking to people. Tom tapped Kat on the shoulder. She looked up.

'Digital Forensics are working on tracking Lloyd's phone,' he said. 'Could be a few days though, they're snowed under.'

Kat huffed.

'What's new? Anything else?'

'I've been looking at our other three people of interest. Libby Spare, Ethan Metcalfe and Greg Fanning.'

'Go on, then, impress me.'

'Right, first of all, none of them has a criminal record. Libby Spare's from a wealthy family in London. But apparently money can't buy you smarts. She seems to have taken an offer from Middlehampton as something of a last resort. She could have been struggling with her studies and needed Rosie's help with the essay to avoid being booted off her course. But honestly, Kat, the way universities are funded these days, that nine grand a year means a student has to have done something egregious before they're kicked out.'

'Like murder?'

'That would do it.' A beat. 'Probably. But at the point we're looking at, she hadn't done anything, had she?'

'Fair enough. Although I just read one of Rosie's journal entries. She was worried about Libby's behaviour after the Christmas holiday. Even consulted one of the psychology lecturers about her.'

'What did she say?'

'That it was probably nothing. Letter writers aren't murderers, was the general gist. What about Greg Fanning, our incel Romeo?'

Tom shrugged. 'I've looked at his socials. If she did turn him down for a date, I can see him venting on Reddit or Telegram, but murder? It looks like a stretch.'

'It often does, though, Tomski, until it doesn't. Did he post anything about Rosie specifically?'

'Nope. He seems a bit pathetic, actually. Just posting these self-pitying screeds about how women won't give men like him a chance.'

Kat's mind went to the page in Rosie's journal and her barely coded reference to a notoriously misogynistic online influencer named Tony Butcher.

'Any signs he was being groomed in any way? Radicalised?'

'Nope. To be honest, I think he barely qualifies for the term "incel". It looks like he had a girlfriend at sixth-form college.'

'Have you checked that?'

'I have. Her name is Poppy Whitfield. Lives in Middlehampton. I called her while you were with the Kenneys. She confirmed she went out with Greg Fanning for three months in 2024.'

'Were they having sex?'

'She said they were intimate and I didn't want to push her on that.'

'He sounds less like an incel and more like some kid Rosie's friends just didn't take a shine to. Perhaps he was a bit too Dungeons & Dragons for them.' She frowned. 'Is that still a thing?'

'I think so. But you may be showing a wee bit of prejudice there, boss.' Tom grinned. 'I believe even D&D guys get laid from time to time.'

She punched him lightly in the shoulder.

'Fine!' she said. 'So he liked going drag racing or visiting the opera. Anyway, I see you've saved the best till last.'

'Yes. Now you're drunk on the box wine of Libby and Greg, may I present the fine vintage that is Ethan Metcalfe.'

'Please don't.'

'You know the background.'

'I *am* the background!'

'I watched the video where Rosie tears him a new one about ten times.' Tom tilted his head to one side. 'I think I've changed my mind, Kat. He looked properly pissed off. I mean, really, really unhappy. And it's not just his face, either. Can I show you?'

'Be my guest,' Kat said, wheeling her chair closer to Tom's and turning to look at his monitor.

He launched the video player with its now-familiar thumbnail image clipped from a point roughly halfway through Rosie's tirade against Ethan.

And pressed play.

Chapter Twenty

AUDIO STRIPPED FROM INSTAGRAM VIDEO UPLOADED BY USER MEDIAMONKEYSHINES, 17 APRIL 2026

Speaker 1: identified as Rosie Duggan (RD): Yes, Dr Monk, I have a question for Ethan. Ethan, you say you're interested in delivering justice for murder victims and their families, but isn't it more accurate to say you're interested in monetising people's grief?

Speaker 2: identified as Ethan Metcalfe (EM): Not at all. Rosie, isn't it? It's a sad fact that in today's economy, where governments of all stripes have to make budgetary decisions about every aspect of society, from defence to social care, building motorways to law and order, that sometimes our police services, hardworking though they are, simply don't have the resources to investigate every crime thoroughly—

RD: But that's not really true of murder, is it?

EM: Rosie, I did you the courtesy of listening to your question, so please listen to my answer without interrupting. As I was saying, this is why true crime podcasts like mine play an increasingly vital role in delivering justice. As to monetising people's grief – well, it's true, I have my mortgage to pay like everyone else, but if you think podcasting is the way to get rich, you've obviously never tried it.

RD: But you don't have a mortgage, do you, Ethan? I looked it up. You inherited your house from your mother.

EM (raising voice): Leave my mum out of it! It doesn't matter. I have bills to pay, that's what I meant.

RD: But that's just it, isn't it? You have bills to pay and so you need to maximise your income. What did you call it last time you spoke to us? You have to prime the pump in order to maintain a steady revenue stream from your platform. Be honest, your show isn't about helping bring closure for victims' families or helping the police, is it? You just turn up at crime scenes like a vulture at a kill. You poke your nose in and get what you can, but really you're just feeding on people's grief so you can sell advertising. It's disgusting.'

[Many speakers. Laughter. Catcalls. Whistles.]

Chapter Twenty-One

Tom paused the video with a quick stab of his mouse.

'There. Ethan clenches his fists.'

Kat turned in her chair, gazing at Tom with frank admiration.

'Nice spot, Tomski.'

'And look at his expression.'

Kat turned back to the screen. With his (newly fixed) teeth bared, the bridge of his nose crinkled and his eyes – now clearly visible thanks to his laser surgery – narrowed, Ethan looked seriously pissed off.

She reckoned if she showed that image to a dozen random uniformed cops and, without giving them any context, asked them what happened next, they'd all answer the same way.

He attacks someone.

Kat knew from personal experience that Ethan had a thin skin. She'd met onions that were better protected. Had Ethan attacked Rosie Duggan?

Had Ethan *murdered* Rosie Duggan?

Then her instincts came crowding back in, like bystanders at a crime scene breaching the blue-and-white tape.

Yes, Ethan was, in Ma-Linda's memorable phrase, 'a massive bell-end'. But Kat simply couldn't imagine him murdering Rosie Duggan over a spat in a lecture hall. She inhaled.

'Let's leave Ethan near the bottom of the list for now.'

Tom frowned. 'Really? After what I just showed you?'

'Look, Tomski, Ethan's an inadequate loser. And before you say anything, I know that description fits of lot of male perpetrators of violence against women. But that's not Ethan. He'd do something sneaky, online probably, if he wanted to take revenge.'

Tom jabbed a finger at the frozen on-screen image. 'Look at him, though!'

'I am! I still think he's not our man. And I'm not sure getting owned by Rosie in a lecture hall is sufficient motivation for murder.'

Tom's eyes widened. 'This is your former stalker we're talking about, Kat. How much more motivation does a guy like that need? Why can't you see it?'

Kat looked at Ethan's contorted features. *Was* she avoiding seeing what was right in front of her? Was she unwilling to give credence to Tom's theory because it would mean that she'd been in more danger from Ethan than she was willing to admit?

She took a moment. No. There were priorities to assign, decisions to take. Both were her responsibility. For now, Lloyd Kenney was a far more credible suspect than Ethan.

'Leave him for now, Tomski. Lloyd's our focus.'

Tom's lips twisted. Kat braced herself. He looked like he was about to lose his temper. But then something strange happened.

He closed his eyes and took a deep breath. Let it out with a sigh and rolled his shoulders. Opened his eyes.

'Sorry, boss. You're right. What do you want me to do?'

Tom had obviously been practising mindfulness, or meditation. Either way, she was impressed. Now if only a certain fourteen-year-old could learn some of that, she'd be home free.

'It's just you and me and about three pound fifty's worth of budget,' she said. 'Keep looking at Lloyd. I need to go and talk to Darcy about forensics.'

Kat went down to Forensics. Surely Darcy Clements, the forensics coordinator, would have something for her by now?

Darcy did.

As soon as Kat pushed through the double doors, she hurried over. 'Kat! You saved me a call. Guess what I recovered from Rosie Duggan's clothing?'

'Hopefully the murderer's DNA, along with a signed confession tucked into her jeans pocket.'

'You're half-right.'

'You're joking. You got DNA?'

Darcy's pale blue eyes grew serious. 'Semen on her jacket. Looks like the bloke murdered her then masturbated over her body. Bastard. I've sent it off to NDNAD but it's going to be slow, Kat.'

'That's OK, Darce, Linda's already told me to watch my budget. It's brilliant you got it. I've got my own leads and something tells me we'll have a match to at least one of our persons of interest.'

'That's not all, though. We took samples from under Rosie's fingernails and collected some from the guardrail on the top floor of the car park. They're off with a lab. Should get the results in the next day or two.'

'You're a star.'

Darcy grinned. 'I bet you say that to all the girls.'

'Yeah, but when it's you, Darce, I mean it.'

'Tart!'

Kat left Forensics practically skipping. Three male POI. Ethan's DNA was already on file: an easy way to eliminate him for their enquiries. They just needed voluntary DNA samples from Greg Fanning and Lloyd Kenney.

Tom rose from his chair as soon as Kat arrived back in MCU.

‘Greg Fanning’s at home. He’s agreed to talk to us.’

‘Let’s go then. And I bring news from Forensics: the bastard left semen on Rosie’s body, so we’ve got his DNA.’

Tom wrinkled his nose. ‘What the hell’s wrong with them, Kat? I mean, seriously, what makes these men go so evil?’

‘I have literally no idea, Tomski. Not a scooby. But if I can catch another one and stick his perverted arse behind a nice strong set of bars, I’ll take that.’

After grabbing a couple of DNA swab kits, and asking Tom to drive, Kat grabbed Rosie’s journal and took it with her, intending to read another entry or two on the way to the university.

The first time Tom had sat behind the wheel on a job in Middlehampton, he’d reached for the satnav before Kat forbade it, suggesting any detective worth their salt knew their own patch without recourse to technology. Now he chose shortcuts like a native.

Kat smiled to herself.

Then she opened Rosie’s journal.

Chapter Twenty-Two

ROSIE DUGGAN'S JOURNAL

5 February 2026

I just need to say something about one of my lecturers.

Dr Monk is amazing! She is so perceptive. The way she talks about the changing media landscape and the tectonic shifts in power between producers and consumers is so insightful. I wish she'd spend a little more time on her appearance, though! I know it's playing the patriarchy's game to talk about another woman – correction, a successful woman – in terms of her looks, but she's got such good skin and she's got a lovely smile.

Sometimes I imagine she comes to me and asks for advice on a new image. We talk about how she could style her hair, like get it cut really short. Buy some new clothes, try a few different looks. I say she could be a goth, and she laughs and says could I imagine her with black panda eyes and fishnets? Actually, I could. I may have the tiniest bit of a girl-crush on her. I don't think it means anything. Not really. I still like boys. There's one in my class, Flynn, who is so hot. Half the girls and at least a quarter of the boys want to go to bed with him. (I exaggerate. Haha.) But, you know, I would, if she asked me.

The only thing I really don't like about her – well, not her but her choices – is she's got this new boyfriend: Ethan Metcalfe. Who, by the way, is so punching. I mean she is totally out of his league!! God knows what she sees in him.

She calls him 'Eeth' – which looks weird written down, but I don't know how else to spell it. Eath? Ethe? Eith? He's got this podcast. Really morbid. One of the true crime ones only it's all serial killers and murderers. He dresses nicely, and he looks all buff and he's clearly got veneers but I found a picture of him online. Jesus, he has had one hell of a makeover. He used to look like a proper nonce. Or a serial killer. Greasy hair, old-fashioned gold-rimmed glasses, saggy Black Sabbath T-shirt covering his man-tits.

He comes in and does these guest lectures where he patronises everyone and drones on about monetising content. If I had the courage, I'd call him out on his stupid bloody podcast. Maybe next term I will. See how bright his smile is then.

gulp

Chapter Twenty-Three

Kat made a note. If Dr Monk was so insightful, she might be able to help Kat understand more about the dead girl and the people who might have wished her harm.

'The forensic evidence lets Libby off the hook, then,' Tom said, as he took the exit off a roundabout signposted to the university.

Kat tended to agree with Clare Capstick, who she'd consulted herself on her first case after joining MCU. Villains who wrote threats tended not to carry them out. Although plenty of serial killers wrote to the papers boasting of what they were doing and how the police would never catch them. She made a mental note to consult Clare to talk about Libby. Not a priority. Just some investigative housekeeping.

'Yep. Although Rosie wrote about her in her journal. Looks like Libby got really angry about the essay. Anyway, if we're going to the university, I wouldn't mind having a quick word if we can find her. Just for completeness. But in all probability, it's going to be that depressingly familiar figure: a man who kills a woman. Lloyd Kenney most likely, or Greg Fanning.'

'Or Ethan Metcalfe.'

'Who I've said I doubt did it.'

'Sure, yeah. I was just trying to keep an open mind.'

'Which is admirable in an ambitious young detective eager to get his career back on track.'

'Are you taking the piss, boss?'

She grinned. 'Does it *sound* like I'm taking the piss?'

He pointed at a sign for a car park. 'Oh, look. We've arrived.'

'Guess we'll never know, then, will we, rookie?'

Tom climbed out. She followed. He locked the doors. Regarded her across the roof of the car.

'Rookie? Now I know you're taking the piss.'

Kat's grin widened. She felt optimistic.

'If the cap fits.' A beat. 'Rookie.'

Tom rolled his eyes. Which Kat took as a good sign. He was getting some give back in his elastic, which had felt stretched to breaking point for months now.

Greg Fanning had a room in a shared flat in Halliwell House, a student residential block at least twenty storeys high.

Kat stepped out of the lift, grateful it had been working, unlike half the lifts in the town's less salubrious estates.

She knocked on the door. Turned to Tom.

'Want to lead?'

He nodded.

The door opened.

'Greg?' Tom asked the tall, strongly built if paunchy youth filling the doorway.

'Yeah. Are you Tom?'

'That's right. This is my boss, DS Ballantyne. She likes people to call her Kat.'

Greg looked down at Kat. At well over six feet, he made her feel like a child. She smiled up at him.

'Thanks for agreeing to see us at such short notice, Greg. I hope you're not missing anything important.'

'Not really. Do you want to come in?'

He led them into a long, narrow kitchen at the far end of the flat. The windows gave on to a lake bordered by a grassy slope dotted with gaggles of students sitting chatting, smoking – weed, Kat assumed – and even, in one case surely a candidate for 'Ironic Throwback of the Year', strumming an acoustic guitar.

'Do you want coffee? Or I've got fruit juice, or there's plain water.'

'Coffee would be great, Greg, thanks,' Tom said with an easy smile as he sat down at a long grey-topped table. 'I'll have mine with milk, and my guv'nor takes hers black.'

Interesting approach, Kat thought, the way Tom was speaking for her. Clever, too. Showing Greg that it was essentially a chat between two men. She, nothing more than an appendage, despite her rank.

Coffees made, Greg sat opposite them with his back to the window.

Also an interesting choice. The light was behind him, giving him a slight advantage. Was he less innocent in the ways of police procedure than he was suggesting?

While Tom warmed up his interviewee with a few general questions, Kat used the time to study him.

He had a look she associated with a certain breed of young man. She'd seen them at Riley's school at parent-teacher evenings. Put kindly, socially awkward and favouring the kind of shapeless beards that crept from chin to collar and which seemed to be the result of simply ceasing to shave.

His hair needed a wash, and as for his clothes, black was the dominant colour, punctuated by a lurid airbrushed design on his T-shirt of a naked woman astride an enormous snake. She dimly remembered the band from school. Whitesnake had been very popular among the metalheads.

She found that she could imagine, with precisely zero effort, Greg Fanning lifting Rosie Duggan bodily over the railing and overcoming her desperate efforts to hold on. But immediately she had another thought. If Rosie had turned down Greg's offer of a date, how on earth had he persuaded her to meet him on top of Five Cups Lane car park in the middle of the night?

Tom was getting down to the gnarly questions. She tuned back in.

'Can you tell me about Rosie Duggan, Greg?'

'Like what? I mean we do – did – the same course. Media studies. But we didn't exactly hang out in the same group, if you know what I mean?' He sketched a gesture with his right hand towards his T-shirt. 'Rosie was one of the Populars. I'm more into classic metal and gaming.'

'Yeah, no, I can see that.' Tom's voice shifted into a 'duh, how could I have missed that!' tone. More code switching? 'Only, you must have seen something in her to ask her out. What was it?'

Greg's reaction was fascinating. His face blanked for a second, like a device going into standby mode. Not a muscle twitch for at least three seconds. It was as if he'd had a full-face Botox treatment. Then life flickered back. He frowned.

'I didn't ask her out.'

'No? Oh. I must be mistaken. Only we spoke to Rosie's housemates yesterday and one of them told us you asked Rosie out and she said no. In fact, she also said you'd been taking surreptitious photos of Rosie. Did it slip your mind, Greg? What with the pressure of uni work and everything? Do you think you could have another try for me? Did you ask Rosie Duggan out on a date?'

Greg flushed and looked down at his hands. Pudgy. Large. Kat envisioned them clamped around Rosie's upper arms, pushing her backwards until her back banged into the guard rail.

'It was just a casual thing. That's why I forgot just now.'

'Of course, I get it. No probs,' Tom said with a smile, as if to say, *Hey we're both players, we ask lots of girls out, it's hard to remember every attempt.* 'And how did it feel when she rejected you?'

'I wouldn't exactly say she like *rejected* me. I asked her, she said no thanks, end of story.'

'Fair play. How about the photos, Greg? What's the story there?'

Greg shook his head. 'Didn't happen. I don't know which one of Rosie's mates told you that, but there's a couple of the girls who were like this protection detail.' His eyes slid away, towards the ceiling, and his lips twisted into an ugly grimace. 'They sort of stopped anyone getting to know her. It's like if they disapproved of you, they wouldn't let you even speak to her.'

'No, of course, I get it. Girls can be quite cliquey, can't they? So, for example, if we were to take a look at your phone, we wouldn't find any candids of Rosie? No up-skirts or down-blouses? Nothing like that?'

Greg's eyes flash-bulbed, but whether it was from guilt or shock, Kat couldn't tell.

'No! Of course not!'

'Can we then? Take a look?'

'What?' Greg's hand went to his trouser pocket. Then his eyes narrowed a fraction. This was a look Kat had no trouble whatsoever interpreting. He was starting to think like a suspect. Or was it just the suspicion of a typical teenager?

'No, you can't. Not without a warrant.'

Tom smiled, even rubbed his chin. Doing his *junior detective confronted with a tricky puzzle* act.

'A warrant? Just to look at your phone, mate? I mean, you just said you didn't have any pics of Rosie on there.'

Greg folded his arms across his chest, obscuring the naked woman but leaving the legend below her in full view. *Lovehunter.*

'I'm not an idiot, you know. I haven't done anything wrong, and I don't have to show you my phone. Unless you've got a warrant, which you won't get on account of there's no evidence because, as I think I just said,' he enunciated pedantically, 'I haven't done anything wrong.'

Kat leaned forwards, a signal most cops used and which Tom reacted to with perfect timing, leaning back and raising his coffee to his lips, the better to fade from Greg's attention.

'Greg, could I just ask, where were you between 6.00 p.m. on Monday just gone and 7.00 a.m. the following morning?' Kat asked.

Greg looked up again. Closed his eyes. 'I did some work here, then I went out for a bit, walked into town, did some shopping at the Aldi on Market Street. Then I came back. Put my shopping away, made something to eat, then I watched some videos on YouTube, went out for a couple of drinks, got back here about ten-thirty, played a bit more, went to bed. Got up at ten.'

'Can you email Tom with the details? Especially what route you took into town and back, anyone you spoke to or interacted with. And anyone you talked to either here in the flat or in the bar. Was that on campus?'

'Yeah, the student union. There were loads of people there though, I can't remember them all.'

'Of course not. Do the best you can.' Kat reached down for her bag and took out one of the DNA testing kits in its crackly plastic wallet. 'Before we go, Greg, I wonder whether you'd mind letting me take a DNA sample? It's from the inside of your cheek and it doesn't hurt or even feel uncomfortable.'

He looked at it. Then at her.

'I'm going to say no.'

◆ ◆ ◆

Out in the sunshine again, Kat suggested they walk around the lake to get to Libby Spare's flat.

'Thoughts on Greg?' she asked as they skirted a large group of students who all suddenly had reason to cup their smokes behind their hands.

Kat had to smile. The smell of weed was so strong she felt a mild buzz just from passive smoking. She looked down at a girl who was just now peering up at Kat from under a mop of frizzy ginger hair.

'Relax. We're Major Crimes. Your secret's safe with us.'

The girl grinned guiltily and uncurled her palm. She held out a smouldering joint less than an inch long.

'Want some?'

'Cheeky!'

They made their way down to the water's edge, where ducks waddled into and out of the lake.

'He's a big, strong lad,' Tom said. 'He lied about asking Rosie out. And I bet if we did get a warrant for his phone, we'd find plenty of photos of Rosie on it, taken without her permission or knowledge.'

'Agreed. How about his alibi?'

'Lots of detail. But lots of people to track down and interview. Could be a smart move.'

'Or a frightened boy doing his best to prove his innocence.'

Tom shrugged. 'Time will tell. I'll get on to it as soon as we get back to the station. What about not giving a DNA sample?'

'Can't really hold that against him. Lots of members of the public are losing faith in the police – for obvious reasons. Make that person a student and that loss of faith turns into downright distrust.'

According to Tom's research, Libby lived in an almost identical block to Greg's, this one called Skinner House.

Kat rang the doorbell and a young woman answered. She seemed taken aback by the presence of two strangers and blinked rapidly six or seven times.

'Can I help you?'

Kat and Tom produced their warrant cards.

'Hi, lovely, yes. We're looking for Libby Spare. Is she in?'

The girl shook her head. 'She's in a lecture.' She checked her phone. 'It should be over in five minutes.'

'Whereabouts?' Kat asked.

'The media studies department. You go across the main square and turn left by the sculpture of the horses. There's a massive sign with like a montage of screens on it. You can't miss it.'

Without waiting to be asked, she closed the door in their faces.

They hurried back the way they'd come, and after making the correct turns, found themselves waiting for Libby on a patch of grass centred on a flowering cherry tree opposite the media studies department.

'It would be funny if Ethan was giving the lecture,' Tom said, leaning against the tree trunk. 'We could kill two birds with one stone.' He coloured. 'Sorry, boss. That came out wrong.'

Kat shook her head. 'Curse of the job, Tomski. Your mind gets infected with murder and then pulls out these awful puns at the worst moment. You know Molly?'

'Your mentor, right?'

'Yes. So, back when I was her bagwoman, we had to visit the coroner in his office. Old guy, really, really senior and extremely formal. He used to wear a three-piece suit whatever the weather, and a gold watch across the front of his waistcoat like it was the 1930s. Anyway, Molly had to report to him on a murder investigation and she said, "I'm sorry, sir" – because you always called Old Man Wilkie "sir" unless you wanted a bollocking – anyway, poor old Mols says, "We've been burning the midnight oil but it's still early days."'

Tom frowned. 'What's wrong with that?'

'Well, it was an arson case. A nightwatchman was burned alive at an oil refinery. Poor old Molly shrank to three inches tall.'

Tom grinned. 'Speaking of arson, how're Leah and Fez doing?'

'You haven't spoken to them?' Kat asked, feeling a pang as she pictured her other two DCs having to report in to Carve-up.

'Yeah, a bit, but they're always deep into it. They're really pulling all the stops out.'

'Let's round everyone up for a drink. Soon, OK? We could all do with a catch-up.'

Tom pointed at a young woman striding confidently across the tarmac towards them. She was on the phone, and even from here Kat caught the posh-sounding drawl half the kids at Middlehampton College, Riley's school, affected.

'That's her,' he said.

Kat took a path that would intercept Libby just at the edge of the patch of grass. She called out to her, stopping her dead.

'Libby? Can we have a quick word?'

Chapter Twenty-Four

Libby pulled up sharply in front of Kat.

She was extremely skinny, with downy blonde hairs on her jawline. Her eyes were bright, perhaps overbright, darting from her face to Tom's and back again. Her dirty blonde hair was scraped back from her face in a high ponytail. Kat wondered whether she had an eating disorder.

'What do you want? Wait. You're police, aren't you? You have to be.'

Kat produced her warrant card.

'Why "have to be", Libby?'

The girl rolled her eyes. 'Come on,' she said. 'Did either of you look in the mirror when you got dressed this morning? My dad says back in the eighties when he used to go to festivals you could always spot the drug squad because they all had shiny shoes poking out of their jeans. It's like that. You might as well wear badges.'

Kat took in the young woman standing in front of her, seeing the person inside that rail-thin body. What amazing self-confidence. Accosted by two detectives on campus, and her first instinct was to make fun of the way they were dressed.

Kat smiled. 'Nice one. Could we talk about Rosie?'

Libby's face changed. The mocking grin melted like candlewax too close to a flame. The corners of her mouth drooped and her eyes filled with tears that overspilled the smudgy black lids.

'Oh, no, please don't. Not my Rosie.'

The tears seemed genuine. Nobody could turn on the waterworks that quickly. And 'my Rosie'? That didn't sound like somebody who might have murdered a girl for not agreeing to write an essay.

'I'm sorry. Were you two close?' Kat asked, drawing Libby under the shade of the cherry tree.

Libby nodded. She wiped her nose on the back of her hand. It was a curiously childlike gesture and stripped away her earlier swaggering attitude. Kat offered her a packet of tissues. Libby blew her nose and then drew another tissue from the packet and blotted her eyes, smearing the kohl.

'She was this radiant personality. I can't believe someone would want to wipe her away like a note on a lecture-hall whiteboard.'

Kat nodded sympathetically, but her mind was whirring. That was an odd sort of simile for a grieving friend to use. It seemed contrived. As if she'd played around with some ideas ahead of time.

'That's why we need to talk to all of Rosie's friends,' Kat said. 'Am I right in thinking you and she had a falling-out over Christmas? Or just before? Over an essay you wanted her to write for you?'

Libby jerked her head up. Her eyes flashed. It should have been comical, given the state of her make-up, but it gave her a dangerous look instead. A warrior from an all-female tribe who took no prisoners.

'Who told you that?'

'Is it true?'

Libby shrugged and looked away to her right, as if spotting something far more interesting than a murder detective standing right in front of her.

'Libby?' Kat prompted, injecting a little heat into her tone.

'It was nothing, OK? I was short of time. Rosie never seemed to have any stress about work. I thought she might like to make some easy money. She said no. End of story.'

'So you didn't bear a grudge?'

'No. It was only a stupid essay, it wasn't like she shagged my boyfriend.'

'You didn't say "pride comes before a fall"?'

Libby smiled. 'Er, no, I didn't. Because I don't come from the nineteenth century.'

'Or that Rosie ought to get off her high horse or somebody might push her off it?'

Libby sighed theatrically. Drew out her answer. 'No-o-o, I did not use some line from one of my mum's dopey Agatha Christies. Is this really why you stopped me? To ask if I threatened my friend. My actual *friend*? I mean, can you even *hear* yourself? What? Do you think I killed her?'

Kat flashed a quick look at Tom. He nodded. She wondered whether he'd remember what he'd said about Libby on the drive over. Decided to keep her counsel for now. See where he took it.

'Did you?' he asked.

Libby started. She'd been so focused on dissing Kat she'd clearly forgotten he was there.

'Of course I didn't! What a toxic thing to suggest! Jesus, you're such a pig.'

Tom kept his voice level. 'Where were you, Libby,' he said, 'from 6.00 p.m. on Monday to 7.00 a.m. on Tuesday?'

She wrapped her arms around herself. Turned to face him. Scowling.

'That's none of your business.'

He shook his head. 'I'm afraid it literally *is* our business, Libby. Can you tell me where you were, please?'

She shook her head. Then turned to Kat.

'You're his boss, right? Do I have to answer that?'

'It would be a good idea if you did, Libby,' Kat said carefully.

Libby smiled slyly. 'Which is a "no", isn't it? Well, in that case, I'm going now. My dad's a barrister, and he told me never to talk to the police without a lawyer present. If you want to arrest me or whatever, fine, but I'll ask for a lawyer straight away – and believe me, my dad knows some really good ones.'

She stalked away, her skin turning white-gold as she merged into the sun from the shade of the cherry tree's blossom-laden branches.

Tom turned to Kat. 'Wow!' he said, when Libby was out of earshot. 'Quite the act.'

'I feel like we just met three people. The grief-stricken bestie. The self-confident girl-boss. And the spoilt little princess.'

'What did you think?'

Kat thought for a minute. You could read Libby's reactions in at least two different ways:

One: an innocent person so overwhelmed by her bereavement that her emotions were all over the place. No need to provide an alibi because she hadn't done it.

Or two: a guilty party, so confident she'd concealed her hand that she could afford to play the sarky, entitled rich girl who wouldn't alibi herself on principle.

Except for the small matter of the male DNA on Rosie's corpse.

'I think students really, really irritate me,' she said finally.

Tom laughed loudly. 'Oh God, boss, I'm sorry. Do you want me to handle any more interviews on campus?'

She grinned at him, happy to see him becoming more relaxed, despite the occasional near-miss.

'No, I'm good, Tomski. And in answer to your question, do I think she could have done it? It's a stretch. But it's possible. Rosie would probably trust her if she asked for a meeting at night at the top of the car park. Libby could have just said something like,

"Oh, Rosie, I'm so sorry for being such a bitch to you. I'll explain everything, but not on campus, blah, blah, blah."'

Tom's brow furrowed. 'And that would work? Despite the letter and the remarks her flatmate told us about?'

Tom had forgotten something, but she was happy to answer his questions for now until he remembered. It would be good practice – for both of them.

'Tomski, let me tell you something about Planet Woman. Unlike men, we are complicated. If another woman hates us, we want to know why. We want to fix it.'

He nodded. 'Eleanor once said to me that if two blokes turn up at a party in the same clothes they do a fist-bump and go, "Nice! We're dressed like twins." Two women do it and one either leaves in tears or spends the evening spreading gossip about the other one.'

Kat waggled her head. 'Like I said. Complicated.'

'So, Libby tricks Rosie into meeting her at the car park and then pushes her off. They struggle, Rosie gets the wood under her nails, losing one in the process, and falls to her death.'

'Could be.'

'Then why not offer an alibi?'

'Because she doesn't have one.'

'But surely if she's as "complicated" as you say she is, she'd have thought of that?'

'She might have done. But here's the thing, Tomski. A person can't be in two places at once. So if they're at Point A, committing murder, they can't also be at Point B, listening to a band in a club, or studying in a library full of students. It's why murderers' alibis always fall apart in the end.'

'So, why not just say she was in her room all night?'

'I don't know. Her dad's a barrister, so she presumably knows that kind of alibi isn't worth anything. She'll know it's better to clam up and let us try to find some evidence.'

'Which she knows we won't.' Tom slapped his forehead. 'Wait a minute! It *can't* have been her, can it? Darcy found semen on the body. What are we doing even *talking* about it?'

Kat smiled. He'd remembered. This was a good sign. If she was going to set him back on the fast-track, he'd need to use his brain, not his emotions.

'I was wondering when we'd get back to that. You were doing such a good job with Libby I wanted to let it run its course. Thoughts?'

Tom looked up into the candyfloss blossom clusters above their heads. 'What if she had an accomplice? She did bear a grudge. She was complicated. And we know she's rich, or at least has access to money. What if she paid someone to kill Rosie? She could even have said to leave DNA to complicate things.'

'It's an interesting idea. But the male killer would have to be monumentally stupid to leave his DNA.'

'Or he knew because he didn't have a criminal record, it wouldn't matter. And because he had no connection to Rosie, he'd never be in the frame for her murder. He might not even be at the university. He might not even be from Middlehampton. He could come from Leicester. That's Libby's home town. Or she could have found him online.'

'Wow, Tomski, slow down! I think we're getting a little too deep into the weeds, here. A Leicester-based contract killer Libby found on the Dark Web?'

He grinned. 'OK, when you put it like that it does sound a little bit Jason Bourne. What's your theory?'

'Simple. It wasn't Libby. We find semen at a crime scene, we look for a male perpetrator. It fits the forensics, it fits the statistics and it fits the psychology.'

Tom blew out his cheeks. 'Here endeth the lesson?'

'Something like that. Come on, let's see if we can track down our third male person of interest. Even if I don't think he's guilty, I'm going to enjoy his reaction.'

Was it unprofessional of her to look forward to discomfiting Ethan? Very probably. But then, she'd had to reorganise her life and take safety precautions just because he'd developed a weird obsession, and thought it entitled him to waylay her in public.

Now it was her turn to have him on the defensive.

Chapter Twenty-Five

Ethan lived in a semi-detached house in Fawcett's Field, a quiet neighbourhood on the south side of Middlehampton with the air of a 1950s suburb. Box hedges, lace curtains and sparklingly clean Mercedes, BMWs and Jaguars were everywhere.

Kat turned to Tom as they stood ready on Ethan's cleanly swept doorstep.

'Ready?'

He nodded. 'You going to lead?'

She flashed on her various unpleasant interactions with Ethan over the years.

'Oh, yes. I'll lead.'

She faced front and rang the bell.

They waited.

And waited.

Nothing.

Frowning, she pushed the bell again, left her finger there for ten seconds, then delivered a loud triple-knock on the door, making the stained-glass panels in the upper half rattle. Ethan needed to get those fixed or one could fall out.

'Yes, yes, yes! For God's sake, wait a fucking minute!'

Ethan's voice didn't so much float out as barge its way right through those loose panes of glass. The door swung inwards to reveal the master of the house dressed in a grey roll-neck sweater and jeans.

His eyes widened when he saw who was standing waiting, her warrant card out. Then they narrowed. A smile stole across his face, like a second-rate actor waiting in the wings.

'Oh, Kat. Hi.'

'Hello, Ethan. Can we come in?'

'Why?'

'We'd like to ask you about Rosie Duggan.'

He bit his lip. 'It's not a good time, I'm in the middle of an edit.'

'Can it wait?'

He looked up and down the street, then stepped back into the shadows.

'Not really. No.'

'Where were you on Monday night, Ethan?' Kat asked hurriedly as he started closing the door.

'What?'

'On Monday night? Between 6.00 p.m. and 7.00 a.m. Where were you?'

He shook his head. 'No. We're not doing this now. I have to go. Sorry.'

He slammed the door in her face.

'Definitely nothing to hide,' Tom deadpanned.

Her stomach twinged. She put it down to hunger, and not the first stirrings of a gut-feel about Ethan.

'Hungry?'

He smiled. 'I could eat.'

'Good, because I'm starving.'

◆ ◆ ◆

Hatî, the Kurdish-owned cafe on North Street, had become Kat's favourite spot for a sandwich and an Americano. Or, if her jeans weren't too tight around her middle that week, a cannoli filled with vibrant green pistachio paste and covered in crushed roasted hazelnuts.

Tom had bagged a table by the window and accepted his latte and mozzarella, tomato and basil panini gratefully.

Kat pulled out her chair and sat, sipping the perfect Americano – rich, dark and without a hint of bitterness – before trying her lamb and spinach pastry.

'You're doing well, Tomski,' she said after swallowing the first, delicious bite. 'How are you coping without the hip flask?'

He regarded her over the rim of his coffee mug before placing it on the table. The look he gave her melted her heart, so full was it of regret and boyish guilt, like Riley when he knew he'd let her down in some way.

'It's fine, Kat. Really. I think I was partly doing it because it was, you know, a role. Like the shell-shocked soldier returning from war. I'm surprised I didn't take up smoking, too.'

She stretched out a hand and covered his on the tabletop.

'Hey, Tomski, don't make a joke out of what Paxton did to you. If you had started smoking or, I don't know, doing a hundred down a country lane at 3.00 a.m. with your lights off, I would have understood.'

'Not sure Traffic would have. But anyway, thanks, boss, I'll take that.' He sighed. 'The thing is, I just felt my life was finally going well. I'd put the business at uni behind me, I was on the fast-track. I was going out with Eleanor. Then Paxton put me into a coma and everything went into reverse. I really wanted to be a detective. Everything from the moment I got my offer to study criminology went towards that. I'd built my whole self-image on it.'

Kat listened with an ache behind her breastbone. Tom's words struck a deep chord with her: after she'd thought Liv had been murdered, becoming a cop, becoming a *murder* cop, had seemed like the only way she could come to terms with it.

'But, Tomski,' she said finally, 'you *are* still a cop. A homicide detective with a very promising future ahead of him. Just keep doing what you've been doing this week and the sky's the limit.'

He frowned. But it was a sorrowful expression rather than the many varieties of scowl she'd witnessed over the previous year or so.

'Yeah, but that's just it, isn't it? The sky used to be the limit, but now other people are already flying higher than me.'

Kat smiled. He reminded her again of Riley, in one of his down-in-the-dumps moods, usually related to his not being picked to run out with the first team.

'You know, rookie,' she said slyly, hoping Tom would catch the gleam in her eye, 'there are more tracks than the fast-track. I believe even grubby little homicide detectives can get reasonably high in the pecking order. Our very own Ma-Linda being a case in point.'

'You say the nicest things, boss. Where now?'

'I'm not finished with the campus yet. I want to talk to a psychology lecturer about Libby.'

'I thought she wasn't a suspect anymore.'

'Just dotting i's and crossing t's.'

Chapter Twenty-Six

Clare Capstick was working in her office and readily agreed to talk to Kat and Tom.

Kat thought that a quick conversation with Clare would confirm her own feelings about Libby – that while she might be a troubled young woman, she wasn't a murderer.

Since Kat had last met her, Clare had grown her hair out, wearing it today in a high ponytail. And it was a fiery red. It set off her green eyes perfectly.

They shook hands. Then Clare sat down again and clasped her hands loosely in front of her on the desk.

'So,' she said, looking at Tom with her head tilted to one side, a smile on her face, then at Kat, 'what can I do for you? Not another serial killer, I hope?'

'We're investigating the murder of Rosie Duggan. She was a student here, on the media studies course.'

Clare frowned. 'Murder? I thought it was suicide.'

'Did you think that was likely, given what you knew about her?' Tom asked.

'Well, I didn't really know her at all. She came to see me about a letter another student had sent her.' She ran a hand over her ponytail. 'She seemed a little put out, but I wouldn't say suicidal.'

'What was your take on the letter writer?' Tom asked. 'Just that, or would somebody like that have it in them to turn their epistolary animus into real-world violence.'

Clare opened her mouth in apparent delight, her green eyes flashing. 'My goodness! "Epistolary animus"! Now there's a fifty-dollar phrase for poison-pen letters if ever I heard one. Did you swallow a dictionary, DC Gray?'

Tom smiled, shifting in his chair to face Clare more fully. 'It must be the surroundings. Takes me back to my own uni days.'

Her smile widened. 'Aha! One of those legendary fast-track detectives we all love to read about.'

Kat started feeling like a third wheel.

'I don't know about that,' Tom said. 'I'm a regular homicide detective at the moment.'

'Oh, I doubt there's anything very "regular" about you, Detective Constable Gray.'

'Please, call me Tom.'

'Well . . . Tom . . . it sounds like you know something of what I said to Rosie. But perhaps I can elaborate. I told Rosie—' She bit her lip. 'Poor girl, so much ahead of her.' Shook her head. 'Anyway, I told her she had nothing to worry about. That letter writers rarely if ever take their grudges into the real world. It's why they write letters in the first place. They're usually quite inadequate people, preferring to conduct their mischief from the shadows.'

'But?'

'But that was because I wanted to reassure her, not add to her anxieties. In truth, I can imagine plenty of scenarios in which an individual begins by writing letters – which, by the way, I thought was really old-school for a student – but then, perhaps if they feel they aren't getting what they want, escalate to a face-to-face confrontation. Even a violent one.'

'The student who wrote the letter talked about pride coming before a fall. She also told Rosie that she ought to get off her high horse before somebody pushed her off it. Given Rosie was pushed off a tall building, do you think that points to guilt?'

Clare sat back, laced her hands behind her head. The action pushed her chest out. Kat wondered if Tom noticed that Clare was acting like a chimpanzee on heat for his benefit. If so, he was maintaining an excellent poker face.

'That's a little outside my field of expertise, Tom. You'd probably tell me that the only thing that points to a person's guilt is evidence.' Clare dropped her hands to the desk again. 'Does a person's choice of metaphor indicate their preference for a particular MO? I've no idea. Sorry.'

'But it's possible.'

'Well, it's *possible*. But they could have written Rosie would be, I don't know, hoist with her own petard. But I wouldn't necessarily expect a murderer to blow her up with a cannon.'

Kat leaned forwards, feeling an unreasonable need to remind them this was a three-way conversation. 'The letter writer was female. To come back to *your* field, Clare, what about the idea she might have become obsessed with Rosie in some way? How does that play out?'

Clare pursed her lips. 'OK, yes. So, you probably don't need me to tell you this, Kat. . . but you might, Tom. In close female friendships, especially where there's what we might call a dominant and a submissive personality, that friendship can spill into obsession.' As she got into her stride, Clare sat straighter then leaned across the desk towards Tom. 'Generally speaking, we'd expect the submissive one to become overawed by the dominant one. The dominant might not realise it but she's exerting a very powerful form of control over the submissive. She might suggest risky activities, or a new look for her friend, and the submissive feels powerless to resist.'

'Are you saying Rosie was the dominant one in this particular relationship?' Tom asked.

'Not necessarily. Psychological dominance takes many forms. It may not have anything to do with outward signs, like popularity, or attractiveness. If you've ever seen a group of dogs in a public park, they like to establish a pecking order straight away. But it isn't always the biggest dog who ends up as the alpha.'

Kat smiled. 'That's right on the money. My dog's a cairn terrier but he thinks he's a Dobermann.'

'Let's assume, for now,' Tom said, looking directly at Clare, 'that the letter writer was the dominant personality. Is it possible she could have found a lever to pull that would persuade Rosie to meet her at night on the top floor of a car park?'

Clare smiled. 'Entirely. You wouldn't even have to be a dominant personality. Some people will happily meet up somewhere risky if the payoff is inviting enough.'

As Clare and Tom had been talking, Kat had been thinking about her and Liv. Were they in that kind of relationship? And if so, who was the dominant personality? Well, no contest – Liv, of course. She had a kind of electric energy that had the young Kat following her into all kinds of escapades, from shoplifting lippy from a department store in the next town over, to the blood oath carved into the skin of their thumbs at school with Liv's rule-busting penknife.

She refocused. Clare was talking about her job. The teaching schedule. Her research into abnormal psychology. Tom was leaning forwards, eyes locked on to Clare.

Kat got to her feet. 'You've been really helpful, Clare, but we've got more people to talk to. Thanks again.'

'No problem. Happy to help.'

Tom handed Clare his card, then headed for the door and Kat followed him. But as she placed her hand on the door handle, already thinking about Ethan's curt refusal to let them in, Clare interrupted her thoughts.

'Kat, quick word?'

'I'll see you outside, Tom,' she said, then turned and re-entered Clare's office.

'Yes?'

Clare looked out of the window, smiled briefly, then turned to face Kat again.

'Your bagman. That *is* what you call them, isn't it?'

'That's right. What about him?'

Clare grinned. 'Is he single?'

Kat smiled back. 'As a matter of fact, he is.'

Clare turned Tom's card over and over in her hand.

'OK, thanks.'

Kat left Clare in her office, and a transparently obvious glow of excitement, and went outside to find Tom sitting on a low wall, his face turned up towards the sun.

'All right, Tomski?'

'Yep. Just catching some sun.'

'I wonder if Clare likes a man with a tan.'

He frowned. 'Pardon?'

'Oh, come on, Tomski, you fancy her, don't you?'

'Do I?'

'OK, so my female intuition was off back there. Maybe you always have hearts coming out of your eyes when you interview people. But *she* fancies you.'

He looked at her intently. 'Do you think so?'

'I *know* so. Did you not clock her body language? Listen, when a woman puts her hands behind her head like she just did, it's like sending in the advance battalions. Please tell me you noticed?'

He grinned. 'I may have detected a certain spark.'

Kat smiled. She felt absurdly happy for her bagman. 'Well, whatever message she sends you, I'm thinking it won't be any "epistolary animus".' A beat. 'Tosser.'

That cracked him up. He laughed loudly, causing two passing students to turn his way and smile.

She held her hand out and dragged Tom to his feet. They had another lecturer to see. And this time Kat would take the lead.

◆ ◆ ◆

Ada Monk's office was minimalist, where Clare's had been cluttered. And this time, Kat detected not so much of a flicker of interest in Tom from the woman she'd come to talk to.

'We were just wondering whether Rosie had ever confided in you about anyone she was worried about, Dr Monk,' Kat said, unable to bring herself to call Ethan's girlfriend by her first name.

Ada nodded thoughtfully. 'I know there'd been some friction between her and one of my other students. Libby Spare, do you know her?'

'We've spoken to Libby, yes.'

'So, there was that, although I believe it was all resolved amicably in the end.'

'Did she mention anyone else?'

Ada shook her head. 'I honestly don't think Rosie had an enemy in the world. I just can't understand how or why anyone would want to kill her. I mean, she was perfect.' She smiled sadly. 'Well, not perfect. Nobody is, right? But she was popular without being mean. Sporty without being a jock, or whatever the female equivalent is. It's baffling.'

'She seems to have admired you a lot,' Kat said. 'I'd go so far as to say she had a bit of a crush on you.'

Ada smiled self-consciously. Rubbed her arm. Shrugged. 'I know. It was a bit embarrassing, to be honest. Not just because I have a boyfriend.' She coloured. 'As you know. But someone like Rosie, as almost-perfect as she was, didn't need to worship anyone. If anything, she was the object of desire. I know of at least one student who wanted to go out with her.'

'Oh, who would that be?'

'He's another of mine. Greg Fanning.'

'Anyone else?'

Ada shrugged. 'Search me. I mean, there could well be. She just had this glow about her, you know? Like, why *wouldn't* you want to go out with her?'

'If I can ask,' Tom said, 'how did you know she had a crush on you?'

'Eeth told me. He overheard Rosie telling one of the other girls during a break in one of his guest lectures. Sweet boy, he thought I might be at risk from the university authorities.'

At the mention of Ethan, Kat scowled involuntarily.

'Everything all right, Kat?' Ada asked.

'Oh, yes. Onions in my lunchtime sandwich, that's all.'

Finally, after feeling that if she spent another minute on campus she'd start joining a student society, Kat called it a day.

At home, after walking Smokey round the block, she sat at the kitchen table as Van served up his 'signature' spaghetti Bolognese. Normally a reliable if unexciting dish involving minced beef, a tin of tomatoes and plenty of garlic, this time he seemed to have skimped on the seasoning. It tasted bland and Kat had to add a few grinds of black pepper.

'How's your case going, Mum?' Riley asked, sucking a sauce-coated strand of spaghetti into his mouth and flicking a few vermillion droplets on to his cheek.

'It's going quite well, actually. We have a number of promising leads.'

'Yeah? I hope you catch him. Bastard,' he added. Maybe he felt the closeness in age between him and Rosie, as Kat did. She reached over and squeezed his hand quickly. 'So, what's next, Mum?'

'Press conference in the morning.'

'You all right about that?'

Kat realised she was fine about it. No butterflies and she'd cleaned her plate, despite the under-seasoned sauce. She smiled at Riley.

'I can't wait.'

On the night before a press conference, Kat would usually toss and turn, before waking at 3.00 a.m. in a flop sweat, pulse hammering, a sense of doom making her want to hide beneath the covers. But when she rolled over beside her husband – who was snoring lightly but annoyingly, every five seconds, not that she was timing it – the display of her phone read 6.37 a.m.

She smiled. She'd slept through. With not even a dream of standing in front of an audience of journalists in her underwear to sully an unbroken seven hours of sleep.

Leaving Van to his own, noisy slumbers, she gathered the clothes she'd left out the night before and took them into the bathroom.

Showered and dressed, she went downstairs and made herself breakfast. She felt ready to face the beasts, as Carve-up never failed to call the media.

She smiled to herself for the second time that morning, early as it was. Carve-up. She'd hardly thought of him all week. After telling him about Rosie, she'd been so busy at the university campus and in Abbots Bromley, she'd barely set foot in MCU. And when she had, he'd either been absent or hunkered down in his office behind that perpetually closed door.

She bent to scratch Smokey behind the ears, eliciting a little grunt of pleasure from the dog. Then she grabbed her keys and was out the door.

Kat had the press conference at 11.45 a.m. But first, there was Rosie Duggan's post-mortem.

Chapter Twenty-Seven

Never watch someone cut a dead body open on an empty stomach.

Of all the pieces of advice Molly Steadman had given her peachy-keen bagwoman, DC Ballantyne, this had earned its place on the podium over and over again.

It seemed counter-intuitive, and Kat had seen more than one rookie run for the sick-bucket after ignoring her when she shared Molly's wisdom. But it worked. With two slices of Marmite toast inside her, she waited while Jack completed his external examination of Rosie Duggan's body. Beside her, Tom stood silently.

She was calm. Expectant. Whatever his flaws, Jack was a brilliant forensic pathologist and she'd yet to feel she could have solved a murder faster without him.

'Cause of death was massive blunt-force trauma, caused by the impact when Rosie hit the metal canopy,' Jack was saying. 'Specifically, her neck was broken. I'll give the precise site in my written report.'

He noted the torn-out fingernail. Then he moved on to a set of bruises on Rosie's upper arms. Kat was certain she knew what had caused them, but held her tongue. Jack would confirm it one way or another.

'Contusions to the upper arms. One oval on the anterior surface of each bicep.' He lifted Rosie's left arm and peered underneath. Nodded, as if satisfied. 'Four roughly circular impressions on the posterior surface. Thoughts, Ashleigh?'

Ashleigh held her arms out with her elbows slightly bent, hands in claws. 'Her assailant took her by the upper arms and squeezed hard as they pushed or walked her back to the railing.'

'You may be veering into Kat's territory there, but yes, in essence, I think that's what happened. For my report I'll simply say that the bruising on the victim's arms is consistent with the standard evidential pattern indicating a strong, crushing, two-handed grip from an assailant facing the victim. Can you help me turn her over, Ashleigh?'

On Rosie's back, buttocks, thighs and the curves of her calves, the tell-tale deep red patches of livor mortis revealed the exact pattern of the square corrugations of the steel awning.

'As we can see,' Jack said, 'blood settling indicates that she lay there for at least five hours.'

'Any thoughts on why she fell to the ground after so long, Jack?' Kat asked.

He looked at her from the narrow gap between his green scrub-cap and his surgical mask.

'Could be a number of factors, including the two you mentioned at the scene. My best guess? As the blood settled in her body, and the outside temperature increased, the internal weight distribution shifted by a small fraction.' He moved his hands in the air, rocking them back and forth. 'If she was already balanced precariously, it might have been enough to shift her centre of gravity over the edge of the canopy, leading to the final fall to the pavement.'

She nodded. It sounded plausible. The Duggans hadn't asked yet. They might never ask. But she'd be ready with an explanation if they did.

Jack peered at Rosie's back. He pointed to a spot over the right kidney.

'Tell me what you see there, Ash?'

She leaned closer, then fetched an illuminated magnifier and shone its bright circle of LEDs on to the purplish-red skin.

'There's a darker patch beneath the livor. It looks like a contusion. It may have been caused when the assailant pushed Rosie backwards into the railing.'

They concluded the external examination. Jack and Ashleigh settled the transparent plastic visors over their masks and then she handed him the large-bladed PM40 scalpel so he could create the Y-incision that started every internal examination.

During the next two hours, Jack confirmed that Rosie was neither a virgin, nor pregnant. But also that she had not had sexual intercourse, consensual or coerced, in the twenty-four hours before her death. Nor were there any external signs of sexual assault, from bruising or bite marks to semen on her skin. At least Kat could comfort the Duggans with that shred of information. She would hardly call it good news, but parents always wanted to know.

What they almost certainly wouldn't want to know was that their daughter had, in addition to the fatal neck injury, suffered catastrophic internal injuries to her spleen, left kidney, lungs, liver and her upper intestine. And had suffered the insult of a post-mortem sexual assault over her clothes.

Kat checked the time. She and Tom had a press conference to prepare for and two devastated parents to coach.

'We're going to have to leave, Jack. Press conference.'

He looked up and nodded. 'You'll have my report this afternoon.'

Back at Jubilee Place, Darcy confirmed that the wood and paint beneath Rosie's nails had come from the guardrail, placing her on the top floor of Five Cups Lane car park.

And now, without any doubt, Kat knew her instincts – and her strict adherence to protocol – had been correct. Rosie Duggan had been murdered. Her killer had enticed, coerced, persuaded or tricked her into meeting him on the top floor of the car park. Then grabbed her tightly by the arms and propelled her backwards, ramming her into the guardrail and lifting or tipping her over the top, where she'd frantically scrabbled for grip, tearing out a nail, before falling to her death.

Kat was positive she'd already spoken to Rosie's killer. Of the people they'd interviewed, Lloyd was still her pick. The crime stats said it was most likely to be him. He had means, motive and opportunity. And he'd lied to them more than once already.

But if it wasn't Lloyd – the evidence they had on him was circumstantial, after all – then who had murdered Rosie? Greg Fanning, a rejected suitor? Libby, a pissed-off cheat? Or Ethan, a podcaster with a problem with assertive women?

As much as she might wish it were Ethan, what she wanted now was solid evidence. The imminent press conference was her chance to shake the tree.

Chapter Twenty-Eight

Kat ducked into the ladies on the ground floor of Jubilee Place. Bared her teeth at her reflection. No wayward piece of this morning's breakfast lodged between two incisors. She put on some Chanel Pirate, the vibrant carmine lippy that always made her feel strong and powerful, and misted her wrists with Elie Saab Girl of Now.

From the ladies, she strode, head high, to the media centre on the far side of the large, open-plan reception area, shooting Polly, her favourite front-desk employee, a quick smile.

The conference room was packed, and loud with the excited chatter of about fifty journalists. Far better than the usual ten- or twelve-strong cadre of locals who attended when there'd been what everybody in MCU called, with contorted cop humour, a 'BDSM' – a basic domestic stupid murder. Barely any need for Forensics to zip themselves into their noddy suits. The husband, because of course it was always the husband in a BDSM, confessed in person or called 999 from his blood-spattered bedroom and, sobbing, asked for the police.

Kat attributed the boost in attendance to a single depressing factor. The victim. Rosie Duggan was the sort of attractive, fresh-faced girl who, in happier times, might have been plastered on the front page of the *Daily Mail* in mid-August, shrieking delightedly with two or three other pretty girls after getting their A-level results.

Such a cliché. As was the one her shell-shocked parents, flanking Kat at the top table, would soon be reading in their own newspaper or on their phones.

> *Tragic Murder Victim Rosie Had Everything to Live For*

Kat, Madeleine and Andy Duggan didn't have the table, which was draped in French-blue Hertfordshire Police cloth, to themselves. They'd been joined by the Duggans' thirty-something solicitor – a woman by the name of Emma Kingsmill. She had a black leather folio in front of her, its polished brass corners winking in the downlighters.

To one side of the media pack, Kat could see Freddie leaning against the wall. He always wore a suit for press events, though it only served to give the impression of a schoolboy wearing his dad's work clothes. He raised enquiring eyebrows. To Kat the meaning was clear. *Shall I call them to order?*

And, normally, her heart running like a marked car in full pursuit tune, palms slick with sweat, Kat would have nodded back with an anxious half-smile plastered on her face.

She smiled at him and shook her head.

Then she leaned forwards and amazed herself with the calm, level and, yes, authoritative words that emerged from between her Piratical lips.

'Good morning, ladies and gentlemen, my name is DS Kathryn Ballantyne.' The room stilled as if Freddie had hit a mute switch. She caught his eye during a careful, three-second pause. He nodded, and smiled. 'I am the lead investigator on the tragic and senseless murder of Rosie Duggan. Joining me today are Rosie's bereaved parents, who have very courageously agreed to read a prepared statement. But before that, let me update you on the progress of the investigation.'

Something strange, but not entirely unpleasant, happened to Kat as she sketched out the circumstances of Rosie's murder, and the steps she and Tom had taken so far. She became aware that she was listening to her voice as if from behind a one-way mirror in an observation room. She sounded confident, yes. But there was something else, too. Because confidence could always be faked, if you knew the postures to hold, the words to utter, the hand gestures to demonstrate. What was it?

When it came to her, she felt a thrill of delight course through her.

The female DS holding fifty or so journalists in the palm of her hand *actually knew what she was doing*.

With a snap she felt somewhere just forward of the nape of her neck, she re-entered her body, and the strange doubled sensation disappeared.

'I'll now ask Madeleine Duggan to read a prepared statement.' She turned to Madeleine, whose hands were white-knuckled as they clutched a sheet of paper. Offered a quick smile of encouragement and murmured, well away from the mic, 'You OK?'

Madeleine nodded briefly, though her bloodless lips and taut facial muscles told their own eloquent story. No, of course she wasn't all right. She was about as far from all right as it was possible to get and still be breathing. But the woman had guts. And a dead daughter's murderer to see rot in prison.

She looked out into the sea of faces, blinking rapidly as the snappers all unleashed their digital flashes in one go with a sound like a swarm of locusts, and started reading.

'Rosie was an extraordinary girl. Whoever murdered her didn't know who they were taking out of the world. If they had, they wouldn't have committed their crime. My daughter was a very special person. She was bright, already doing well at university here in Middlehampton, the first in her family to go. She was sporty, too, and captained her school football and tennis teams. Rosie achieved so much in her short life, including the Gold Duke of Edinburgh's Award and being head girl at her school.'

Madeleine paused, lifted a glass of water with trembling fingers and took a nervous sip, spilling a few drops on the blue cloth as she replaced it on the table. Andy Duggan took her free hand in his briefly, and squeezed. He looked barely capable of motion, let alone speech. His eyes betrayed nothing, as if someone had scooped out the real ones and replaced them with painted marbles. Madeleine cleared her throat. The room was utterly silent.

'But, despite all the certificates, all the trophies, all the Guiding badges' – she smiled brokenly, and then wiped a tear away, causing another flutter of locusts to pierce the silence – 'that wasn't what made Rosie special. What made my daughter such a wonderful girl was the way she put herself out for others. She volunteered at a care home once a week, singing old songs to dementia sufferers, and was, at the time of her death, helping local children with learning difficulties right here in Middlehampton, not even her home town.'

She swallowed. Now for the crunch. Beneath the tablecloth, out of sight of the cameras and iPhones, Kat pushed her right leg against Madeleine's left, hoping she'd understand the gesture. *I'm right here with you.*

Madeleine Duggan put her paper down on the table and looked into the dark eye of one of the TV cameras.

'If you know anything about how my daughter was murdered, and by whom, please contact DS Ballantyne. A friend or a relative of yours might have been acting out of character since Tuesday morning. You may have noticed bloodstained, torn or dirty clothes in a rubbish bag, or put in for a wash. Someone you know might have let slip that someone *they* know is behaving oddly. *Please* do not dismiss these suspicions. Come forward.

'If you have your own reasons for not wanting to speak to the police, I understand. It's not a problem. Call Crimestoppers instead. Just, please, I am begging you' – she turned to Andy and took his hand in hers, occasioning yet another burst of insectile digital shutters to explode in the room – 'help us find our daughter's killer. Help us end this torture we're enduring.'

There followed five seconds of silence so complete Kat heard the buzz of a phone on vibrate.

Then the room erupted with questions and demands, the flashes of cameras and a certain amount of ill-tempered jostling as journalists left their seats to thrust microphones towards the Duggans.

Madeleine physically recoiled. Kat pulled her wand mic towards her.

'Ladies and gentlemen, please! That's enough!' The cacophony diminished to a murmur, then petered out altogether. Those on their feet, or knees, retook their seats. 'The Duggans do not feel able to answer your questions, but their lawyer, Ms Emma Kingsmill, will respond on their behalf.'

A hand shot up with the velocity of a bottle-rocket. Its owner didn't wait to be called.

'Ethan Metcalfe, *Home Counties Homicide*. Have you considered the possibility that Rosie was murdered, not by someone she knew, as you outlined in your excellent summary of the case, DS Ballantyne, but by a stranger?'

Kat maintained a neutral expression. Though inside, she was seething. Where was a throwing knife when you wanted one? Why would they consider Rosie's death a stranger-murder. Based on what?

'As most *serious* crime reporters know,' she began, catching the eye of Dawn Jacobson, the *Echo*'s vastly experienced editor, and a personal friend, and getting an approving nod in reply, 'when a woman is murdered, in the vast majority of cases the killer is known to the victim. And in fact, is often a current or former partner. At this point, we have no evidence that points to this being a stranger-murder.'

Ethan wasn't finished. 'Ah, but that's just it, isn't it? It's impossible to prove a negative.'

Kat frowned. Was it? It sounded like something Ethan had read off the back of a cereal box.

'And if it *was* a stranger,' Ethan continued, 'then have you considered the *further* possibility that what you're dealing with is another serial killer operating in Middlehampton?'

The buzz in the room intensified. Kat used it to gain a few precious seconds of thinking time. Ethan almost sounded as if he wished it *was* a serial. And then she saw why. His bloody podcast. Riley had gloatingly informed her recently that Ethan's numbers were slipping. An active serial killer would give Ethan traction with the mainstream media all over again, win him new subscribers and boost his revenues. Or was there an even more troubling explanation for Ethan's obvious enjoyment in derailing her press conference? Was he performing a textbook action and inserting himself into the investigation? Goading the investigating officer to catch him out?

No.

She still couldn't see Ethan as a murderer, much less a psychopath. For now what mattered was closing him down. She fell back on officialese. As boring as she could make it.

'While following several promising lines of enquiry, involving several persons of interest, my colleagues and I are keeping an open mind as to the motives of the person who murdered this lovely young woman. However, at this point, we feel the most likely explanation for Rosie Duggan's murder, as tragic and senseless as it was, is that . . .' She blanked. What the hell could she say?

Certainly not 'it was a BDSM', which had been on the tip of her tongue. Talk about sending your career down the shitter. She'd have gone viral in three seconds flat. Her pulse jacked up and she felt heat rising from the front of her shirt.

She took a breath and rallied. '. . . is that it was the result of personal enmity felt by her killer. Unlike our local true-crime expert, my team and I are professional homicide detectives, and what we do is follow the evidence we *do* have, not the evidence we *wish* was there to support a far-flung theory.'

Freddie intervened before Ethan could respond to the slap-down, selecting another journalist, and then another, making sure Ethan never got another chance to air his views.

Once Emma had signalled she didn't want any more questions, Kat addressed the room for the final time.

'Before we close, I have one last request, and it's an important one. I would like to ask anyone who was driving down Five Cups Lane between the hours of six on Monday evening and seven on Tuesday morning, and who has a dashcam, to contact me at Jubilee Place police station. Your footage might have caught the murderer.'

Kat brought the press conference to an end.

With the room empty apart from the top table, Freddie Tippett and Tom, who had left his post at the back of the room and joined them, Kat turned to Madeleine Duggan.

'You were brilliant. Thank you so much. I know how hard that was for you. You too, Andy. I don't think Madeleine could have managed it without your support.'

'Will it work?' he asked.

'I think so. The tip line always lights up after a press conference. And in this case, well, you said it yourself, Madeleine, Rosie was a star. I'm sure the public will want to see her murderer caught as much as we all do.'

With a promise to keep them updated, Kat let Emma escort her clients away. Tom waited until the door had closed behind them.

'Did you mean that? About the tip line?'

'Every word of it. The trouble is, Tomski, wanting and doing aren't the same thing. Not the same thing at all. Plus we'll also have to sift through all the serial confessors, the UFO-spotters who think every homicide is an alien abduction, the conspiracy theorists, the psychics offering help from the grave, the vicious little shits trying to settle scores by dobbing in an enemy. Shall I go on?'

He smiled. 'I get the picture.'

'Come on,' she said, 'let's grab a coffee and get back to it.'

She thanked Freddie and preceded Tom out of the door of the media centre, where she bumped into Dawn Jacobson, who was on her phone. She frowned, then smiled when she saw it was Kat.

'Tomski, get the coffees in, mate. I'll see you back in MCU.'

Dawn put her phone away. 'Hi, Kat.' She looked over Kat's shoulder. 'Hi, Tom!'

He lifted a hand in a wave. 'Dawn.'

'It's so sad, isn't it? Another student dead.'

'Another?'

'You probably don't remember, seeing how it wasn't murder, but a year ago there was another beautiful young girl who died from a fall. Rebecca Poole. Ring any bells?'

'Sorry, Dawn, no.'

'She was eighteen, just like Rosie Duggan. Studying at the university, too. Wonderful girl, really had it all going for her, just like Rosie. But unlike Rosie, she wasn't pushed. She fell from a bridge over the old railway line. Lots of alcohol in her system. The coroner recorded it as suicide. These poor kids, Kat. The mental health epidemic is frightening.'

Kat nodded, thinking of Tom's remark at the crime scene. He must have been talking about Rebecca Poole.

And, from a quiet little place in her cop brain, a voice whispered to her.

Two girls, a year apart? Both died after falling from a height. Are you sure *Ethan was reaching?*

And then it sidled closer and whispered something else.

Does he know something you don't?

Several strands of reasoning twined together in her brain like badly wound string. Ethan had always been a bit off around women. Even as a schoolboy. His animus – to use Tom's fancy word – could have metastasised into violence. But he was Kat's age: mid-thirties was a late start for a serial killer. Could he really be a serial? Or was she the one who was reaching? Boosting his podcast was a simpler explanation for his cocky remarks in the press conference just now. But then, he'd refused to give them an alibi yesterday.

She shook her head. *Follow the evidence, Kat.* Everyone from Molly to Ma-Linda had told her that. So that's what she would do.

But she might spend a little bit of energy looking for it in Ethan's vicinity.

Chapter Twenty-Nine

While Tom stared into a monitor on which CCTV and dash-cam footage played relentlessly, Kat reviewed the transcripts of their interviews so far. Nobody leapt out – except, by his absence, Ethan.

At 4.40 p.m. her email app pinged with a new message from Jack. The subject line – *RD PM report* – had her opening it in a hurry. She scanned his findings, which Jack always helpfully summarised. She'd save the main report for that night's reading.

Cause of death:

a) spinal cord severed between C4 and C5 (cervical) vertebrae, caused by:

b) fall from car park on to steel shop canopy

Manner of death: homicide

Time of death: 11.00 p.m., 5/5/26 - 2.00 a.m. 6/5/26

Observations:

Blood alcohol concentration (BAC) measured at 0.16%. This is twice the legal limit for driving. Allowing for the natural production of ethanol during decomposition, we can still say with confidence that Rosie Duggan's judgement would have been significantly impaired. However . . .

I also detected the presence of benzodiazepines in her bloodstream. In combination with the alcohol, this would not just have disorientated Rosie, but rendered her extremely liable to suggestion.

Bruising to both arms indicates an assailant grabbed Rosie shortly before her fall.

Kat sat back, the events of Rosie's last hours becoming clearer in her mind. The murderer had drugged her with benzodiazepines, the active ingredient in many prescribed anti-anxiety medications, then plied her with alcohol – which as a light drinker, Rosie would normally have refused. Then, having disabled most or all of Rosie's natural reflexes for self-preservation, he'd found a way to get her to the top of the car park and forcibly pushed her off.

She frowned. When had he deposited his semen on her body? It could have been before she went over, but afterwards seemed more likely. He'd assumed she'd land on the street, so when she fell on to the canopy he'd had to climb up. And he could have been caught by a passing motorist's dashcam. She hoped her appeal at the press conference wouldn't only bring the crazies out.

Another question presented itself. How had the benzodiazepines found their way into Rosie's bloodstream? Kat had assumed the murderer had administered them, but they could have been Rosie's own medication.

She called Madeleine.

'Do you know if Rosie was taking any prescription medication for anxiety?'

'I don't think so. Rosie and I talked about everything. I'm sure she would have told me if she was struggling with her mental health. The last time we spoke she was her usual happy self. I mean, she never had any of the troubles a lot of them have, even during A levels.'

But kids were adept at hiding things. Kat had met plenty whose misdeeds had completely blindsided their parents, who'd only discovered the truth when a uniform had brought their offspring home in a marked car, or on receiving a call from the duty officer.

Then there was the fact that Rosie could easily have gone to the doctor on her own for anti-anxiety medication.

'Do you know which GP practice Rosie was registered at?'

'Well, ours, I assume. In Abbots Bromley. It's called Park Street Medical Practice. Do you need me to get you the number?'

'It's OK, I can find it.'

'What's this about, Kat? Was Rosie on drugs? Is that what you're saying?'

'The pathologist found benzodiazepines in her system. I'm just checking on possible reasons why they were there.'

Kat thanked Madeleine for her time and immediately looked up and then called the GP. After a little bit of back-and-forth about patient confidentiality and GDPR, the practice manager confirmed that Rosie had registered with the university medical practice.

Five minutes after speaking to Madeleine, Kat found herself speaking to one of the university GPs.

'As Rosie's dead – which we're really shocked about, by the way – I can tell you we'd not prescribed any anti-anxiety medication,' the GP said. 'No antidepressants or sleeping pills, either, if that's relevant. Her last visit was to get a prescription for oral contraception.'

If Rosie hadn't taken prescription medication, that only left street drugs. Whether she'd bought them herself for recreational purposes or her killer had bought them, there was one person who might be able to steer Kat in the right direction.

Chapter Thirty

'Hello, Isaac.'

The skinny young man in a grey Adidas tracksuit jumped. He whirled round, then smiled, revealing brownish teeth.

'Oh, hi, Kat. Didn't hear you. Been practising your ninja skills, have you?'

'Night and day. How's business?'

'Oh, you know.' He scratched his patchy ginger beard. 'Up and down.'

'How are *you* doing?'

She meant since his mum had died. She'd been touched that Isaac had invited her to the funeral. It wasn't every drug dealer who'd willingly welcome a cop to a family affair.

Isaac wiped his nose on his sleeve. Shrugged bony shoulders.

'I still miss her, but, you know, I try to remember the good times, like you said to. Birthdays, Christmas, holidays, when we had them.'

'I'm glad, really, Isaac, I am. You're doing great.'

He looked up and down the street. Back at her. 'I guess you're buying?'

'You still work the uni campus?'

He grinned self-consciously. 'I mightn't have been clever enough to go, but I know a market when I see one.'

She caught a sense-memory of the sweet smell of weed smoke by the lake. 'What's popular with students these days?'

'The usual. Weed, of course.'

'Of course. What else?'

'Molly, ket. A bit of coke if the rich kids are partying.'

'Ever sell any benzos?'

He wrinkled his nose. 'That stuff's addictive. Worse than heroin. Which, as you know, I don't touch.'

'Don't worry, I'm not looking to pinch you.'

'Is this about Rosie Duggan?'

'Why, what have you heard?'

'Nothing! Only, obviously she's been murdered and here's you, Middlehampton's answer to Clarice Starling, asking me, a local chemicals entrepreneur, about benzos. Doesn't take a genius to see the connection.'

'Just as well,' Kat said with a grin, then grimaced guiltily. 'Sorry, mate. Couldn't resist it. No offence.'

'None taken,' he said flashing her another unwelcome sight of his gruesome dentition. 'I already said I wasn't the uni type.'

'So, have you?'

'Sorry, Kat, have I what?'

She groaned inwardly. Having a snitch like Isaac had its upsides, but his inability to concentrate for longer than a few seconds was something of a trial. 'Have you sold any benzos to students recently?'

'Some? A few? They're not as popular as they were a couple of years ago. Trends happen in the recreational pharmaceuticals market like everywhere else.'

'Boys, girls?'

'Girls. The lads all want ket these days.'

'How recently?'

'Sunday, I think. I was up there – the campus, I mean – after lunch.'

Kat showed him a photo of Rosie on her phone. 'To her?'

He scrutinised the photo, scratching his chin. 'Could have. She's pretty. Who is she?'

She sighed. 'That's Rosie, Isaac. The murder victim. Remember?'

'Oh, yeah. Course. Sorry.'

She swiped until she found a selfie Libby Spare had taken for her Instagram. 'How about this girl?'

'Can I?'

She handed him her phone.

He stared at the photo, pinched and zoomed. Screwed up his face. 'There's this look, isn't there? Pretty, but like a bit Insta-ready. Sometimes it's hard to be sure. She was definitely blonde. It could have been her. Or the first one.'

'Does anyone else work the campus? One of your competitors, I mean?'

He shook his head. 'Frank makes sure people know that's my patch.'

He was talking about Frank Strutt. A local gangster with whom Kat shared an uneasy if occasionally mutually beneficial relationship.

Kat took her phone back. Slipped Isaac a tenner.

She returned to Jubilee Place. With nobody else to help her, and Tom already red-eyed from staring at CCTV footage all afternoon, she joined him in the viewing suite and loaded the first clip.

It was going to be a long evening. But somewhere in the hours of footage, she felt sure there'd be something that would show them who Rosie had been meeting at Five Cups Lane in the middle of the night.

Chapter Thirty-One

Without Leah and Fez, and with Linda keeping a tight grip on the budget, Kat felt under pressure like never before. Saturday-working was normal on a murder case, but it didn't make it any more fun. After walking Smokey at 6.00 a.m., she was pushing through the doors into MCU at 6.59 a.m.

To find Tom at his desk.

'Bloody hell, Tomski!' she said, clocking his dark grey jeans and rumpled blue shirt. 'Please tell me you didn't pull an all-nighter.'

He turned his head. The movement suggested a machine that had once been pampered and was now several months off its maintenance check. She fancied she could hear the shriek of unlubricated joints grinding.

'I went for a sleep in the quiet room at about three. Been up since five.'

'Jesus, Tomski. Right, stop what you're doing' – which she now saw was reviewing dashcam footage. 'Lean back, close your eyes, because they look like someone poured lemon juice into them, and let me fetch you some coffee. Actually, breakfast too. What do you want?'

'A bacon sandwich with tomato sauce, please.'

'You know, normally I'd have to write you up for your continuing selection of the wrong sauce for a bacon butty, but given how hard you're working, I'm going to let it slide this time.'

He managed a weary-looking half-smile.

'You're a star.'

'But I'd caution you to remember it's brown sauce on a bacon sandwich, tomato sauce on chips.'

'Noted.'

He leant his head on his hands and closed his eyes.

Kat hurried downstairs to the sandwich van in the car park. Further than the canteen but the new guy's coffee was the real thing, unlike the weirdly sweet, frothy concoction the stainless-steel machine behind the canteen counter dispensed.

She returned to find her bagman sound asleep, snoring, a slender rivulet of saliva dribbling from the corner of his mouth. Smiling, she set the coffee and paper bag down and plucked a tissue from the pack in her pocket. As gently as she could, she wiped the drool off his chin.

While Tom slumbered, she sat beside him and took over mouse duties, reviewing the latest emailed dashcam footage to arrive from the night Rosie was murdered.

Tom had been keeping track in a spiral-bound notebook by the left side of the keyboard. There was a huge gap between 9.12 p.m. and 10.51 p.m., then sporadic coverage until 11.10 p.m. He'd cued up two clips that provided another slice of the night. The clip she'd interrupted began at 11.11 p.m. The driver had been coming into town from the west, slowly making their way through the Old Town. Sipping her Americano, Kat peered at the screen.

The driver turned into Albion Street at 11.27 p.m., travelled halfway along, then made a right into Five Cups Lane, coming towards the florist's shop from the southern end of the road. No pedestrians were visible. Certainly nobody keeping their head down, or ducking away from potential council CCTV cameras using a hoodie or hat to hide their face.

Kat hit pause as the car passed in front of the shop. The canopy above the front door looked fine. No dent. She let the video run then wound it back and played it again, watching the canopy. The frame cut off the top of the steel sheeting but it would be clear enough if a body hit it at speed. Nothing. The driver drove the length of Five Cups Lane then turned right into Chalk Street.

She closed the file and opened the next one Tom had already lined up. She watched for five minutes as the driver headed towards Five Cups Lane. Two figures came into view. Briefly, Kat's interest spiked, but then, as they revealed themselves to be a couple of old men weaving drunkenly away from the Queen's Head, she shook her head with a wry smile and dismissed them. Neither looked capable of hoisting a full pint glass to their lips, let alone a young woman over a railing.

At 11.50 p.m., the driver passed the florist's. Kat's pulse picked up. Was something different about the canopy? It was dark, but it looked deformed. She ran the video back and played it again, pausing it just as the car approached Blooming Miracles. No mistake. Whereas, on the last clip she'd watched, the canopy was straight and true, now its lower surface was clearly bowing down. The angle of the camera meant the top of the canopy was out of shot, just as it had been on the previous video. But the deformation was unmistakable. At some point between 11.27 p.m. and 11.50 p.m., Rosie Duggan's body had hit the canopy over the shop. She'd just narrowed time of death down to a twenty-three-minute window.

Beside her, Tom snorted, then sat bolt upright. 'What did I miss?'

'Relax, Tomski, you were sleeping like a baby. I didn't have the heart to wake you.' She gestured to the grease-soaked paper bag.

'Bacon sarnie's in there. With the devil's sauce. Latte, too. May need thirty seconds in the microwave.'

'Thanks, Kat,' he said, sliding the sandwich out and taking a huge bite. Then he slugged half the coffee. 'Tepid, but delicious. What did you find?'

Kat showed him the two clips. He hunched forwards as the second clip played. 'Is that Rosie?'

'Has to be.'

'Poor girl. Everything to live for and then wiped out.'

'We'll catch whoever did it, mate.'

'Should we keep watching? What if the murderer came down to check on his handiwork?'

She nodded. 'Good idea. Wouldn't that be sweet if they were caught by another dashcam?'

They reviewed another fifteen clips. Each with the same evidential value: zero.

'Every time I close my eyes all I see is grainy dashcam footage.' His email program bleeped. Tom sighed. 'Incoming. Please, God, let it not be another clip.'

But it was.

He ran it at quadruple speed from 11.50 p.m.

Suddenly he jabbed a finger at the screen. 'You are shitting me!'

Kat paused the footage and stared at the rectangular viewing window. 'That's him,' she said. 'It has to be.'

Frozen in the act of climbing on to a wheeled council rubbish bin at the side of the shop was a figure dressed in dark clothes. A hoodie – of course – obscuring his features. The figure was looking up at the canopy where, despite the top being cut off by the edge of the screen, Kat now knew Rosie's body lay.

She rewound and played again.

The passing car had caught Rosie's murderer on its dashcam. The trouble was, being a moving source and not a static council CCTV camera, it gave them just that brief clip.

But what they could see was damning. The figure climbed on to the lid of the bin and then hauled himself up on to the canopy, where he moved out of shot.

'What's he doing up there?' Tom asked as Kat froze the video again.

'Given Darcy found semen on Rosie's clothing, I'd say he went up there and masturbated over her body,' Kat said. 'Pervert.'

Tom peered at the still image, which was rendered grainy by the lack of light. 'Think we'll be able to get anything usable in the way of a physical description?'

Kat studied the image. The hoodie meant they'd not get a single square centimetre of facial features. Beyond that, what did they have? A figure of, what, average height, average build? Even that was hardly provable, given the baggy clothes he was wearing. Reasonably fit, if he could haul himself up on to a steel canopy from a rubbish bin.

Great. Half the population of Middlehampton. And at least one member of the population of a little village a mile outside Rosie's home town of Abbots Bromley.

A young man who resented Rosie for dumping him. A young man easily capable of climbing on to a shop canopy given his job as an arborist. A young man who'd supplied a partial alibi at best.

Rosie Duggan's ex-boyfriend. Lloyd Kenney.

Chapter Thirty-Two

'Lloyd's Stihl-crazy.'

Kat and Tom shared a look as Lloyd's grinning boss pointed up into the boughs of a sycamore tree in a park just outside Burton upon Trent.

'Sorry Jay, what did you just say?' Kat asked.

'My little joke. He loves Stihl chainsaws. First thing he asked me when I took him on was, "When do I get to use an MS 881?" I told him,' Jay narrowed his eyes and dropped his voice into a dusty growl, '"Son, the Stihl MS 881 is the most powerful series-produced chainsaw in the world. It can take a tree's branch off in one and a half seconds. So do you feel lucky, punk?"'

Kat regarded him with bafflement. What the hell was he on about? Jay caught her look.

'*Dirty Harry*?' His eyes pleaded with her to understand. 'Clint Eastwood? This is a .44 Magnum, et cetera? Come on, you must have seen it?'

'Nope. More of a *Mamma Mia* girl, myself.'

Clearly, they weren't going to bond over a shared love of Clint Eastwood films. He sighed, and yelled up into the foliage for Lloyd to come down. As before, Lloyd rappelled to the ground, landing with balletic poise before unclipping himself from his ropes.

His face fell. 'Now what?'

Kat turned to Jay. 'Could you give us some privacy, please?'

Jay hesitated, but she eyeballed him until he moved away, climbing into the cab of his truck. Kat turned back to Lloyd. 'Do you still claim you were at home when Rosie was being murdered, Lloyd?'

'I told you, didn't I? In the presence of my solicitor.'

'That's quite a legalistic phrase to use, mate,' Tom said. 'Did Mr Reith tell you to use that?'

'It doesn't matter what he told me. I didn't kill Rosie, all right?'

'The trouble is, Lloyd,' Kat said, 'after your mum saw you in the kitchen at around 8.15 p.m. on Monday night, nobody can put you in your house until the small hours of the following morning. We now know Rosie was murdered between 11.27 and 11.50 p.m.'

Tom cleared his throat, dragging Lloyd's attention away from Kat. 'Lloyd, the only two fixed points we've got are when you met your mum in the kitchen at around 8.15 p.m. and again on the landing at 3.30 a.m. You could have ridden to Middlehampton and back between those times, do you see what I mean? So, regardless of where your phone says you were, I need you to help me put you at home in person.'

Kat thought that was a nice touch. Tom asking for Lloyd's alibi as a way of helping Tom prove his innocence rather than establish his guilt.

Lloyd looked from Tom to Kat and back again. There was something there, behind his eyes. He was weighing up two different stories. The truth, which would get him into trouble of one sort or another, and the lie, which was crumbling under the basic pressure of a few mileage and speed calculations from his home to Middlehampton.

His lips tightened, a subconscious effort to keep from blurting out something incriminating. He was going to refuse to cooperate. A smart move, really, given he already had legal representation, and the absence of an alibi was a long way from evidence of guilt.

Then they softened. Parted. He no longer looked defiant. He looked embarrassed. Bit weird for a boy about to confess to murder.

'I was with someone. You know, having sex.'

Kat tipped her head to one side. 'Someone?'

'A woman! I was with a woman. An *older* woman.'

For a second Kat envisaged Lloyd in bed with a woman of Linda's age. But then corrected herself. He wasn't out of his teens yet. 'And when you say "older", Lloyd . . .?'

'She's twenty-six. But you can't go see her. She'll kill me. Or her husband will. He's a soldier.'

Kat tried not to smile. Either this was the world's most creative false alibi or Lloyd had really got himself caught between a rock and a very hard place indeed.

She looked at Tom, passing him the invisible ball. He'd had some success with Lloyd already. If he could just find the right tone to ask him about his married girlfriend.

'Lloyd, mate, just for now, OK, we can keep this between us. Just you and me. Don't worry about who she is for now. What I can't get my head round is why you didn't tell us this before?'

Lloyd pulled a *duh!* face, his jaw slack and eyes rolling. 'Are you literally having a laugh? In front of my mum you think I'm going to come out and say I'm shagging a married woman?'

'Fair play. But you could have called me afterwards. I gave you my card the first time we met, didn't I?'

'I was trying to protect her,' Lloyd said, trying and failing to meet Tom's eye.

It could have been to shield a lie, but he was blushing from his throat to his cheeks, and Kat had a feeling he was telling the truth.

'A minute ago you sounded more like you were trying to protect yourself,' Tom said. 'Is her old man really a soldier?'

'Yes! I told you! I forget the regiment, but he's totally ripped. You can't tell anyone.'

He looked straight at Tom, and then Kat, too. 'My mum knows them. Manda used to babysit me. It's how I know her.'

And in his eyes she saw the truth. He was desperate to keep his activities with his former babysitter a secret – not just from her husband, but from a much more frightening figure in his life. His mum.

She softened her voice and imagined she was talking to Riley. There was only a few years between the two boys after all.

'Lloyd, I'm going to ask you a question, and I want you to answer me straight away and completely honestly, OK? And I'll know if you're lying. It's what I do. Yes?'

He nodded. Mumbled, 'OK.'

'Look me in the eyes.' He complied. 'Did you kill Rosie?'

'No! I swear to you.'

And in that moment, seeing him as she might her own son, she believed him. He fell off her list of potential suspects altogether. Which meant the remaining three individuals all moved a place higher. Including Ethan.

'Right, then. In that case, you need to do what Tom said and help us to help you. If you really were with this lady – Manda, was it?' He nodded. 'Then we need to talk to her to confirm your story. If she does, then you're in the clear.'

'But do you have to tell my mum?'

'I don't see why. You're an adult. What you do in your private life is no concern of mine – or hers.'

'Oh, thank God! OK, then, her name's Manda . . . I mean, Amanda Bell. She lives at 27 The Vale, Hademore Barracks. I can get the postcode if you want, or do you guys use Google Maps?'

She smiled at his eagerness to help. She felt she could, now she no longer liked him for Rosie's murder.

'It's fine. We'll manage.' She was about to go when she turned back. 'Look, Lloyd, I said what you get up to is nobody's business but yours, but if you're involved with a married woman, you need to think very carefully about that. Manda might be unhappy in her marriage, but it's not a good idea to get between a husband and a wife, even if he's not a soldier. It's messy. A good-looking lad like you could get a single girlfriend, I'm sure. Even an older one.'

She thought she'd just earned herself a sarcastic, and probably justified, retort. *Thanks, I thought it was only Iran that had the morality police.*

Instead he merely nodded and said, 'I know. It was just, after Rosie dumped me, I was really low. I met Manda in the pub and, you know . . .'

'One thing led to another?'

'Yep.'

'Look, Lloyd, we do need to go and talk to her, but we'll be ever so discreet. And I promise, we won't tell your mum.'

Before they left, Tom took a swab from inside Lloyd's cheek. Kat thought they wouldn't need it, but it was best to be sure.

They left Lloyd with his treasured Stihl, ascending into the canopy of the sycamores. She shook her head. How could there be such conflicting instincts warring in such a young man's breast? On the one hand, so angry that he posted revenge porn. One the other, embarrassed that his mum would discover he'd been sleeping with the married ex-babysitter?

'Above my paygrade,' she muttered.

'What's that, boss?'

'Nothing, Tomski. Come on, we've got to visit the lovely Manda.'

Chapter Thirty-Three

The Bells lived 'outside the wire', meaning Kat didn't need to show any police ID to a gate guard as she approached The Vale.

She pulled up outside number 27, a neatly kept red-brick terrace with a front lawn mown to a military buzz cut, dotted here and there with daisies and dandelions.

With Tom beside her she walked up the path and rang the doorbell.

There was no answer.

'You looking for Manda?'

A young woman's voice.

Kat turned. A woman of perhaps twenty-one or -two was watching from the opposite side of the road, a baby on her hip.

'That's right. She not in, then?'

'Took Charlie up the shops.'

'Would that be the ones we passed on the drive in?' Tom asked. 'On Cordingley Road?'

'That's right. The Co-op. I think she needed nappies.'

'Thanks.'

They climbed back into the car and waited.

'How're you doing after your dashcam all-nighter, Tomski?'

He rubbed his chin. In the confines of the Golf's cabin she could hear the bristles beneath his palm.

'I won't lie, I've felt better.'

'Nothing some caffeine won't fix. I'll buy you a coffee after this. I bet the Co-op has a little machine.'

'Actually, it's my turn.'

'You know what, Tomski? It *is* your turn.' She grinned. 'Which is great because I also saw a very nice-looking cafe in the village. I bet they do a lovely Americano. Probably a panini, too.'

'Oh, so now it's me paying, she wants lunch, too. God, talk about overbearing bosses.'

'Tell you what. You buy me lunch and I'll repay the favour by inviting you for dinner. How about Sunday?'

'Tomorrow, you mean?'

'Unless you've got a date?' she said mischievously. 'With a clever, attractive psychology lecturer, for example.'

He grinned. 'I haven't. And dinner would be lovely. What time shall I come round?'

'Seven?'

'Cool. Thanks, Kat.'

'So, come on, Tomski, how *are* you doing? Not about the CCTV. I mean in general?'

He rubbed his chin again. Turned to her and smiled. 'Honestly? I feel pretty good. It's good to be back in the car with you, Kat. I know I was always angling to be given my own investigations, but this feels good. I'm starting to feel I'm getting the hang of talking to witnesses, too.'

'Oh, mate, you really are. What with the code-switching and the compassion, I might have to start brushing up my own skills.'

'I thought when you made sergeant you just went around giving orders. Leaving all the soft stuff to the rookie.'

'That must be some other sergeant, then, because I love this part of the job. It's how you find stuff out. I mean, don't get me wrong, we need the physical evidence – DNA, blood, digital forensics, all that. But you don't know *where* to look, or *who* to look at, until you've put in the groundwork. That's my theory, anyway.'

'Judging from your clearance rate, it appears to work.'

'Carve-up doesn't seem to think so.'

'Carve-up's an arsehole.'

She opened her mouth, then closed it again. She'd never shared her suspicions about Carve-up's role in their violent and – for Tom – near-fatal confrontation with Will Paxton before, thinking it might send him into a full-blown depression.

But now was the time.

'I think Carve-up might be worse than an arsehole, Tomski,' she said. 'I think he pulled our firearms support when we went to arrest Paxton.'

He twisted round in his seat, a half-smile playing on his lips. 'What? You're not serious? I mean, we all know he's a twat, but that would be taking his animosity towards you to a whole new level.'

'After I got back to the station that day, once you were with the paramedics, I went to see Tony Kaminski. He was in charge of the firearms team that day. I tore him a new one for abandoning us and he said Carve-up stood them down. Said the op was cancelled.'

Tom looked stricken. All the colour had leached out of his face. 'Kat, please tell me you're not serious?'

'I confronted him and he denied it. But then he said it was my word against his. I took it to Linda and she said something about the fog of war. I can't remember her exact words, but that was that. I felt worse because she wouldn't back me up than I did about Carve-up, to be honest. She's always been there for me.'

Although not when you asked for Leah and Fez back, her mischievous inner voice piped up.

'Jesus Christ, Kat, if that's true—'

'It bloody is true, Tomski! I swear to you on Riley's life.'

'Do you think he told Paxton we were coming? Warned him so he could get a weapon sorted?'

'I don't know. I don't think so. It was a golf club after all. Half the male cops have a set in their house. You do too, if memory serves.'

Tom lapsed into silence. Kat felt terrible. Hoping desperately she hadn't undone the progress Tom had made. She stretched out a hand and laid it over his, briefly. Squeezed.

'That bastard,' he grated out. 'We have to get him.'

'Look, Tomski, don't do anything rash. He's a DI. That brings a lot of power. And he's connected, as well,' she said, thinking not just of the police brass, but wealthy and powerful individuals in Middlehampton, her father among them. 'Mostly thanks to that bloody golf club. I mean MGC, not the one Paxton was swinging around. I want him, too, but we have to go carefully. Don't do anything to damage your career. He's not worth it.'

'But I've built my whole view of my career on emulating people like him. Not him, specifically, but, you know, DIs in general. On the fast-track, you head for that because that's the first real target rank.' He coloured. 'No offence.'

'None taken.'

'And now it turns out my own DI tried to have us killed in the line of duty.' As if the thought had only just occurred to him, he thumped the dash. 'Hang on a minute. Why would he do that? It's a bit much even for a contender for douchebag of the year.'

'I'm not sure, mate. I'm pretty sure he's in my dad's pocket. He had something to do with me getting investigated for taking bribes, which turned out to be my dad's money. And now I'm starting to wonder what else he's been up to for my father.'

Tom shook his head – then, perhaps feeling that wasn't enough, blew his cheeks out too. 'Perhaps I should just stay as your bag-man, boss?'

'I'd love that, Tomski, but I think you've got bigger and better places to go than that. Anyway' – she pointed through the windscreen – 'here comes our witness.'

'You're sure?'

'Young woman in her mid-twenties, really pretty – which she'd have to be for Lloyd to think it was worth the risk – baby in a buggy, big bag of Pampers. Come on.'

They left the car. Kat called out, keeping her voice light and her tone friendly. 'Hi, lovely, are you Manda Bell?'

The woman stopped. Regarded Kat and Tom with a look of suspicion.

'Yes. What's this about?'

'We're police. Could we come in, please? We need to ask you a couple of questions.'

'Can I see some ID, please?'

They produced their warrant cards, which Manda scrutinised for a few seconds each.

'Fine. But can you carry the nappies? I need a hand for my keys.'

'Here, let me,' Tom said with a smile, taking the oversized Co-op carrier bag from her. He bent to look at the baby in the buggy, who appeared to be about one or one and a half. 'Hello. I'm Tom, but you can call me Tomski.'

The baby looked up and smiled, revealing two white pearls just breaking the gumline.

'How old?' he asked Manda.

'Seventeen months.' She smiled tightly. 'He likes you. Got any of your own?'

'Not yet.'

Once inside, and the nappies put away, Manda gestured for them to sit at the table in her small but immaculate kitchen. 'Tea?'

'Please,' Kat said.

Once the tea was made, Manda sat facing Kat. She'd put the little boy in a playpen, where he was now stacking coloured plastic cups and laughing delightedly each time the tower toppled.

'It's not about Johnny, is it?'

'Is he your husband?'

'Yeah. He's in Kenya at the moment. Training their lot.'

'It's about Lloyd Kenney.'

Kat watched Manda's expression carefully. Obviously Manda would know him, having been his babysitter. But how she reacted to hearing his name in this situation would go a long way to forming Kat's impression of her as a witness.

Manda took a sip of her tea. Buying time. Masking the lower half of her face behind her mug with a printed message in bright, primary colours. *My Daddy's protecting his country.*

'What about him?'

'You used to be his babysitter, is that right?'

'Oh, yeah.' Manda smiled. Relieved to be on safe ground. 'Right little handful he was.'

'What's the nature of your relationship with him now, Manda, if I can ask?'

'I haven't got a "relationship" with him. I mean, he's a bit old for babysitting now, isn't he?'

She went for an amused look but her cheeks were pinkening.

'At the moment, we're investigating the murder of a young woman in Middlehampton,' Kat said. 'That's where we've come up from today. And until quite recently, Lloyd was this young woman's boyfriend. When we asked him for his whereabouts the night of her murder, he said, eventually, that he was with you. Rosie Duggan was killed between 11.27 and 11.50 p.m. on Monday night. The one just gone. Was Lloyd with you at that time?'

Mandy shook her head and answered at once. 'No.' Her blush deepened.

'No? Lloyd seemed like he was telling the truth to me, Manda. If he *was* with you, you need to tell us the truth. If you don't, you could be landing Lloyd in a lot of trouble.'

Manda swallowed the last of her tea, put her mug down and stared out of the window. She sighed.

'Does my husband have to know? Could this come out in court, or whatever?'

'I don't think so. If Lloyd is telling the truth, and you confirm it, then his whereabouts at the time the murder was committed won't be relevant to any eventual court case. As to your husband, that's between you and him.'

'Because, and I'm not joking, Johnny would literally tear him in half. He's like, incredibly insecure and jealous. He once decked this bloke in the pub for looking at me. Only he wasn't even looking at me, it was my mate.'

'He won't find out from us, Manda.'

'Look. I'm not proud of what I done. But Lloyd's a nice boy. Handsome, too. It just happened.'

'Where did you meet the first time?'

'In the pub. Then we came back here.'

'And did it happen again? On Monday night?' Kat waited. 'Manda?'

'Yes, OK? Yes! Lloyd came round here at about nine-thirty. He stayed until about two and then I told him to go home.'

Kat had what she wanted. But something inside was telling her to push just a little bit harder. She hadn't seen a video doorbell, but then, she hadn't been looking.

'Manda, have you got a doorbell cam?'

'Here? Are you joking? The Army doesn't even pay for decent loft insulation. They're hardly going to lay out for a Ring or whatever.'

Thinking about Lloyd's predilection for pictures of his sexual partners, Kat had a brainwave. One that would cause her and Manda a certain amount of embarrassment.

'Manda, forgive me for asking this, but while you two were intimate, did either of you take any pictures or video?'

Manda's eyes widened. 'You're seriously asking me that? What, so you can take them back to the police station and share them on some WhatsApp group? No thank you!'

'Does that mean you did? Only, they'll have timestamps that will prove beyond all question Lloyd is innocent.'

Manda folded her arms across her chest.

'Well, we didn't, OK? You've got what you wanted, haven't you? I'd like you to go, please. Benji needs his lunch and then a change and then a nap.'

Outside, Tom turned to Kat and asked, 'Do you believe her?'

'I do.'

'She could have conspired with him to murder Rosie. Supplied a false alibi.'

'Why would she do that? What's in it for her? If he'd murdered her husband and then they were covering it up together, that I could understand. But there's no upside for Manda. And without video evidence neither of them can prove he was there.'

'On which subject, we should check CCTV, ANPR. He probably rode through Lichfield both ways. As soon as we get back, see if you can find his bike.'

They drove the next half hour in silence.

As she navigated the route back to Middlehampton, Kat found she was growing unaccountably angry with both Lloyd and Manda. Why was she feeling such hostility? Lloyd could hardly be blamed. He wasn't married and, at his age, was at the mercy of his hormones and poorly developed ability to assess risk.

Manda, then? But why? Kat had met plenty of married people who'd had affairs before. Sometimes it led them to commit murder. She hadn't felt this overpowering sense of personal emotion then.

Was it her father's affair with Tasha Starling? If he'd kept his dick in his trousers, her half-sister would never have been born, and Kat would not now have a murder board in her spare bedroom.

It sounded plausible. But the trouble was, identifying it didn't make the feelings go away, as she would have expected them to if that was really the cause of her anger.

She drove on for another mile or two. And then it came to her.

It was Van. Or, to be more accurate, it was Marnie Pryce and her loathsome website that actually provided a platform for married people to betray their spouses. A website *her* husband maintained.

But why should that bother her? It wasn't as if Van was having an affair. They'd already cleared the air about that. The person who'd been obsessed with Marnie Pryce's perfect little arse had been Kat herself.

Sighing, she signalled for the motorway. What mattered was that, in all likelihood, they had eliminated Lloyd Kenney as a person of interest in Rosie Duggan's murder. Kat didn't like Libby Spare for it, although they'd still have to formally eliminate her. That meant focusing on Greg next, and finally – Ethan.

She cursed Ethan inwardly. Every time she thought about him, she felt conflicted. A stalker with, at best, dubious attitudes to women. Yet one she simply couldn't see as a killer. She shoved her doubts down. *Focus on policework, Kat. Leave the psychology to Clare Capstick.*

She nodded to herself. She could do that.

Chapter Thirty-Four

One of Greg's flatmates answered the front door to the flat.

'We're looking for Greg. Is he in?' Kat asked with a smile.

The young man pointed to a door halfway down the hall. 'That's his room. Haven't seen him come out this morning.'

He turned and walked away.

Kat knocked on Greg's bedroom door. They heard the sound of stumbling. A muffled 'Hold on.'

He appeared in the doorway, rubbing his cheeks, clad in pyjamas.

'Hello, Greg, can we come in?'

He rubbed his cheeks. 'Bit cramped in here. Kitchen's better.'

Kat turned to Tom. Smiled brightly. 'Fine by us, isn't it, Tomski?'

Greg pulled the door to behind him but the latch didn't engage. He looked down. 'Sorry about the . . .'

Kat followed his gaze. The door had caught on a discarded sock.

'Heavy night?' Tom asked with a sympathetic smile as they followed him into the kitchen.

'Something like that. What's this about?'

'Well, we're still looking at the possibility that Rosie Duggan was murdered by someone close to her, Greg,' Kat said, taking a chair, seeing as he wasn't about to offer one.

He huffed impatiently as he slumped into a chair.

'Not me, then.'

'No? Meaning what, exactly?'

He turned and looked straight into her eyes. She found the experience disturbing. There was a darkness there. Or was it just a hangover? She cautioned herself to follow the evidence, not her gut. Although it was often her gut that pointed her at the evidence she ought to be following.

'As I think I told you,' Greg said carefully, 'she wouldn't even go on a single date with me.'

'And that bothered you?'

'Yes it *bothered* me! Girls like that think they have the right to just treat everyone like shit, just because they won the genetic lottery.'

Kat wrinkled her nose. What a lot to unpack in such a short little outburst.

'Sorry, Greg, "girls like that"? What do you mean?'

'Oh, come on. You know exactly what I mean. They get the looks, which they didn't work for. They're naturally clever – again, no work required. Sporty, ditto. Popular, double-ditto. So, they have all the cards, and if you don't have such a good hand as them they despise you.'

It sounded to Kat like Greg might have been spending too much time online watching YouTube videos aimed at vulnerable young men, blaming women for their problems.

'But apart from not going on a date with you, what evidence do you have that Rosie treated you, or anyone else, like shit. That she despised you?'

He sneered. 'I've got the evidence of my own eyes, haven't I? She looked at me like I was nothing.'

'That must have really hurt, mate,' Tom said. 'Being rejected like that. Especially by a girl who'd never had to try like you have.'

'Of course it hurt! You don't know what it's like, I can tell by looking at you. You've got predator eyes, the works.'

Kat glanced at Tom, baffled by Greg's reference. He ignored her. Fine, he was winning Greg over, she could see that. She'd ask him later.

'Listen, mate, it's not the eyes that matter,' Tom said. 'It's what's behind them. Force of personality, OK?'

'Yeah, that's what Tony Butcher says in his videos. But it's easy for him. He's got it all, hasn't he? The money, the cars, the bitches.'

Kat recoiled mentally, but kept her body still, wanting to see how deep Greg would dig the hole he was sinking into.

'I might look like I'm a hunter,' Tom said, 'but believe me, mate, it's hard for me, too. My girlfriend dumped me. Do you want to know why?'

Greg leaned towards Tom, eyes greedy for an apparent alpha-male's secrets. 'Why?'

'I got wounded in the line of duty. I fought back and brought the guy down. She said violence was a sign of toxic masculinity.'

Kat really felt for Tom. Using his own personal heartbreak – even if he was twisting the facts to suit his story – to wheedle secrets out of Greg was going way beyond what was necessary. But Greg was lapping it up. 'That's what I keep saying in the group.'

'What is it, Telegram? Reddit?'

'Signal.'

'You must have talked about Rosie. What with her being murdered?'

Greg seemed to have forgotten Kat even existed, so wrapped up was he in what he imagined was his and Tom's shared ill-treatment at the hands of women.

'Look, Tom . . . Can I call you that? I mean, it's OK not to say DC Gray?'

Tom smiled easily. 'Course it is. All my mates call me Tom.'

Greg smiled. 'Yeah, so, look, this isn't me speaking ill of the dead or anything, because nobody deserves to die, OK?'

Kat's pulse quickened. Was Greg about to incriminate himself?

'Sure, of course, mate,' Tom said, leaning forwards, mirroring Greg's posture, drawing him closer into a private, two-person conversation.

'But Rosie getting killed like that? Well, it was sort of poetic justice, wasn't it? She put herself above other people. Like, way above. And then someone pushed her off her pedestal. Like a real-world metaphor for her personality flaw.'

Kat got to her feet slowly, quietly. Not wanting to break the flow of the conversation Tom was weaving.

'Just need the loo,' she whispered with a smile she hoped would come off as simpering. Even though she wanted dearly to slap Greg Fanning round the chops and tell him to stop being such a self-pitying, whiny little baby.

He barely acknowledged her. Just waved his hand. 'End of the hall.'

She reached Greg's room before the loo. Pushed the door open and toed the discarded sock to one side. She was hoping they'd disturbed Greg mid-rant on social media, his laptop screen bearing the evidence of his crime. Or at least something for which they could arrest him. But the lid was down and, as she feared, when she lifted it, the password screen was all that came up.

Sighing, she turned away from the desk.

Taped in a neat row were girls' faces. Clearly cropped and blown up from images taken on a phone. Five in total, all blonde, all attractive. Rosie Duggan on the left, her face partially obscured by a scrawled cross in red marker. Along the bottom of the photo, a legend: *Target 1*. And, in blue biro, so presumably written later: *Reap what you sow, bitch*.

Kat unpeeled them from the wall and took the sheaf of paper back to the kitchen. Her heart was hammering in her chest. Were they sharing a student kitchen with a serial killer?

Tom looked up as she re-entered the kitchen. Greg swung round in his chair. His eyes fell upon the papers in Kat's hand.

'Where did you get those? Wait! Did you go in my room? You can't do that without a warrant! Give them to me!'

Kat held her hands wide, flapping the incriminating photos by her side. Yes, they were inadmissible as evidence, but she didn't want them for court. She wanted them to start a very difficult conversation for the doughy young man sitting facing her with hostility towards women.

'Honest mistake, Greg,' she said. 'I took a wrong turn. But, sure, you can have your pictures back.' Standing across the table from him, beside Tom, she began spreading them out on the table. She looked down at Tom. 'I found these taped up on Greg's bedroom wall.'

When she'd arranged the pictures in a line, she put her hands flat on the table and stared at Greg. He looked terrified. Face pale, eyes darting from the pictures to Tom, then Kat, then over his shoulder.

'You were targeting Rosie Duggan,' Kat said, her voice hard. All pretence that this was a friendly chat erased by her discovery. 'And, presumably, these other girls. Did you murder Rosie, Greg? Did you drug her with benzos, entice her to the top of the car park and push her off because she wouldn't go out with you?'

His eyes were wild. But he made no attempt to jump to his feet. Just as well, as he would have found himself in full-body contact with the kitchen floor seconds later.

'No! I didn't! You can't possibly believe I killed her!'

'Can't I? Why not? I've just had the unpleasant experience of listening while you described Rosie and young women like her as bitches. You made admiring remarks about Tony Butcher, a so-called influencer currently awaiting trial on charges of rape and human trafficking in Thailand. And, in your bedroom, you have a picture of Rosie Duggan on which you wrote "Target number one", then crossed out her face and added, presumably after you murdered her, "Reap what you sow, bitch".'

He held his hands out. 'You've got it all wrong. She wasn't my target. I mean, she was, but it's like, sexual. She was the one I had to try first. It's what Tony says. You have to prepare a target list and work through it. It's not about killing them.'

Kat's stomach turned at the way he was describing his female contemporaries. But she wasn't here to engage in student politics or a debate about ethics or toxic masculinity. She was here to find out who'd murdered Rosie Duggan.

She took a steadying breath.

'Greg, I want you to come in to Jubilee Place police station for a voluntary interview under caution. That means you would be entitled to legal representation, and you would be free to leave at any time. Given the seriousness of the situation, that really would be in your best interests. Don't you think, Tom?'

Tom got to his feet. Stood shoulder to shoulder with Kat. 'Honestly, mate, it's probably for the best. You could say no, but we'll just get an arrest warrant and come back for you.'

Greg appeared to be on the verge of tears. His eyes were red and glistening. 'When?'

'No time like the present,' Tom said.

Chapter Thirty-Five

Kat stared at Greg Fanning, eyebrows lowered to hood the tops of her eyes. A basic take on Tom's explanation of 'predator eyes'. Basically mimicking the glare of big cats, and yet another piece of pop-psychological bullshit employed by the online influencers Greg seemed so enamoured of.

She tried to see beyond the mix of bewilderment and anxiety. Was it an act? If it was, it was a good one. Wide-open 'prey' eyes and all.

'Gregory Fanning, you are attending a voluntary interview at Jubilee Place police station. You do not have to say anything, but it may harm your defence if you do not mention when questioned something which you later rely on in court. Anything you do say may be given in evidence. Do you understand?'

'No! I *don't* understand. I thought this was just voluntary. Now you're saying I'll be going to court.'

'It's the legal wording. And the keyword is "if". Basically, it's a strong suggestion to tell the truth, OK?'

He nodded. 'OK.'

'So do you understand?'

'Yes.'

'Greg, did you murder Rosie Duggan?'

'No, I didn't.'

'But you agree that you had a picture of her on your bedroom wall marked "Target Number One"?'

'Yes,' he said in a voice dripping with regret. 'But it didn't mean murder.'

'And you crossed Rosie's face out and wrote, "Reap what you sow, bitch" on it?'

'Yes. But I didn't kill her.'

'Where were you between 11.27 and 11.50 p.m. on Monday night?'

'I already told you.'

Tom leaned forwards. 'You did, and I checked the details you emailed me. I can put you with other people until about 9.40 p.m., then it all gets a bit hazy. People were drinking, or smoking weed: their memories weren't so sharp. By your own admission you were in your room between 10.00 p.m. and 9.00 the next morning.'

'Greg, you refused to supply a DNA sample last time we spoke,' Kat said, pulling a testing kit from her pocket. 'I'd like to ask you again if you would be willing to provide one? Again, I can't compel you, but I really do think it would be in your best interests.'

He looked at the kit in its crackling plastic bag. At Kat. Back at the kit again. She kept her breathing nice and even. If he refused a second time, she'd arrest him and then he'd have no say in the matter.

'Fine. But does it stay on file if I'm innocent?'

'No. It gets deleted.'

He tilted his head back and opened his mouth.

Kat broke the seal on the kit and removed the swab. Keeping her fingers well away from his teeth, she inserted the tip into his mouth and rubbed it firmly against the inside of his right cheek. And the left. Just to be sure. Brought the swab out and capped it in the collection tube.

'Thank you. While we're waiting for the test results to come back, I'd ask you not to leave Middlehampton without informing me first. Can you do that?'

'Yes. But how long will it take?'

'Shouldn't be longer than a week.'

◆ ◆ ◆

Tom returned to MCU after escorting Greg out of the station.

'Well?' he asked, pulling his chair over.

Kat tugged on her left earlobe. Time to share the troubling thoughts that had started revolving in her brain the moment Greg agreed to give her a DNA sample. It was the one thing Rosie's murderer wouldn't willingly do.

'So far we've been following homicide detection 101, right? Murdered women are almost always killed by an intimate partner,' she said. 'Which gives us Lloyd Kenney. Failing that, someone who has a grudge against them for a different reason.'

'Greg Fanning, Ethan Metcalfe, Libby Spare. And given the semen at the crime scene, it makes the two men the more likely suspects. And we have both their DNA.'

'But what if it's *not* someone Rosie knew? Then it's a stranger, just like Ethan said in the press conference.'

'Someone like Stefan Pulford, you mean? A serial?'

'That's exactly what I'm thinking, Tomski, and it terrifies me. What if the man we're hunting isn't going to show up in the victimology because he picked Rosie for some perverse sexually sadistic motive only he understands?'

Well, he didn't laugh, so that was a bonus. Instead, her bagman frowned and looked up to the ceiling. She said nothing, valuing the way he let his thoughts come together before answering.

He lowered his head and made eye contact.

'You always say follow the evidence. Which we're doing. And we now have DNA samples from Lloyd and Greg to go with Ethan's, which is already on file. The probability is that one of them did it. We should eliminate them before we go on to other theories. Although,' he paused, and resumed his inspection of the grubby suspended ceiling tiles, though she could still see the smile on his face, 'I suppose Ethan *could* be a psychopath. I mean, think of the impact on his ratings. A true crime podcast produced by an actual serial killer. He'd go global.'

Kat frowned. At the press conference she'd wondered about Ethan and his own motives. He'd appeared to enjoy baiting her with the idea of Rosie having been murdered by a serial killer. She'd squashed the idea down at the time. But then he'd flat out refused to supply an alibi or even let them into his house.

Once again, her doubts demanded to be heard. The school loner Liv had christened 'Mutt-calf', was a creep and a stalker, but a killer? Surely she'd have seen his darker side if it existed. Or had she been wrong about him her whole life?

'Work it through for me, Tomski. What do we know about Ethan?'

Tom straightened in his seat. 'He stalked you before. You had him arrested. He gets a makeover, and a girlfriend. But he's still around, popping up at the press conference. He can't let go of his obsession with you. And he figures, "Well, if she won't accept me as a friend, or even a colleague, I'll have to get her attention by becoming her opponent." Or am I the one reaching now?'

'I don't know. He did bring up the idea of a serial killer in the press conference, after all.'

'Yeah, and I thought at the time he was pushing it. But what if that's his way of taunting us? Talk about inserting yourself into the investigation. I mean, that's serial killing for dummies, isn't it?'

'But we've got his DNA. And Greg's. Hardly the smart move.'

Tom shook his head 'Psychopaths aren't criminal masterminds, Kat. That's what this visiting DCI told us on our course. He said, in the real world, away from books and TV shows, they're just twisted little losers who get off on causing pain.'

'But it's still a massive risk, isn't it?'

'Love of risk-taking's a known marker for psychopathy. Anyway, it might not have been his semen on the body. He could have stolen some.'

Kat pulled a face. 'I don't even want to ask how.'

Tom grinned. 'I can think of at least three ways without even trying.'

'Now I really don't want to ask.'

'From a friend's bathroom. From a sperm bank. From a used condom on the towpath . . . shall I go on?'

'I'd prefer you not to. But that's a good point.' Then a troubling thought knocked at the door of her brain. 'If Ethan's a serial killer, then Ada could be in danger.'

'She's blonde like Rosie.'

'Yes. Not as pretty, but for these guys it can just be one thing. Hair's really common.'

'I don't see there's much we can do. Not without evidence linking Ethan to the murder.' Tom spread his hands wide. 'If we get it, fine, we can arrest him and then you can talk to Ada. Although I guess at that point she'd probably dump him anyway. It'd be a double-win for you, though, boss.'

She turned to him. 'What do you mean?'

'Well, you catch a killer and you put the twerp who's been making your life a misery behind bars.'

It was a tempting thought. Kat squashed it down.

'Look, Tom, I don't like Ethan.' Tom raised an eyebrow. She frowned. 'OK, I *hate* Ethan. But I don't want to see him in prison for a crime he didn't commit, just to make my own life simpler, OK? What I want is justice for Rosie. That means arresting her killer, not settling a score with Ethan-bloody-Metcalfe.'

Tom shrugged. 'Follow the evidence?'

'Follow the evidence.'

Chapter Thirty-Six

Until the DNA results came back, Kat could only fill her time with more research into her potential suspects.

She stayed late, digging into Ethan's past, listening to as many of his podcasts as she could stomach. She found that switching to double-speed meant she could still pick up the gist without his smug, self-congratulatory tone.

Should she talk to Ada about him? What would be the point? Ada would probably run straight to Ethan and tell him, especially if he was controlling her in some way.

Then an even more worrying thought entered her mind. Ethan was obsessed with serial killers and gruesome murders. Now she came to think about it, he'd always been going on about them at school. In fact, hadn't someone in sixth form said he'd be just the kind of kid to do a school shooting? She must have blotted out the memory once he started appearing in her adult life.

Was Ethan more than just an observer of serial killers? If Ethan *had* killed Rosie, was she his first victim or had he started long before the podcast was even the glimmer of an idea? Instead of shaking off the idea like Smokey trying to dislodge a flea, she gave it some space in her brain.

Serial killers had patterns. Rituals. What was Ethan's?

She chided herself. *Who says it's him?*

We're just brainstorming here, the suspicious part of her brain shot back.

Then she remembered what Tom had said to her at the crime scene. *That would be the second suicide since I arrived in Middlehampton. Last year, a girl threw herself off a bridge.* Dawn Jacobson had also mentioned it.

Kat ran a search and had the results she wanted a few seconds later.

An eighteen-year-old student at Middlehampton University named Rebecca Poole had been found dead beneath a railway bridge to the north of Middlehampton. Cause of death: head trauma. The coroner had recorded her death as suicide, despite the absence of a note or any history of mental illness.

Kat pulled up a picture. Rebecca was conventionally pretty with a less pronounced version of the tan, teeth and eyebrows look favoured for Instagram. But whereas Rosie Duggan was slim and blonde, Rebecca was curvy and dark-haired. Nobody could say they were a 'type'. Except, possibly a psychopathic killer who'd selected them both for reasons that only made sense to him.

She returned to the coroner's report, and when she saw the date the student had apparently taken her own life, she stopped, eyes wide, and checked she wasn't imagining it.

Rebecca Poole had fallen to her death from the Brearley Woods railway bridge on 6 May 2025. The same day of the year as Rosie.

It could be a coincidence.

Could be.

Before calling it a day, Kat put in a query to the National Crime Agency's Serious Crime Analysis Section – a so-called SCAZ request. She wanted to know if the Violent Crime Linkage Analysis

System had any records matching her perp's MO. Female victims aged 17–21. Pushed from a height. No trophies taken from scene. Signs of sexual assault. Date of crime 4–8 May.

And a second to the National Heads of Crime Network. The same parameters as for ViCLAS.

Chapter Thirty-Seven

Telly detectives never slept. They were also burnt-out cases with alcohol problems, a framed set of divorce papers, an amazingly reliable classic car and a love of that squealy, wince-inducing jazz that Kat, personally, would rather have needles in her eyes than listen to.

She, on the other hand, had a life. Or she tried to, at least.

Which was why, this Sunday morning, she resisted the urge to get up early and do some work on Rosie Duggan's murder. Instead, she tiptoed out of bed and gently pushed the bedroom door closed until it clicked firmly shut.

With anticipation fizzing low in her belly, she slid back beneath the covers and slithered her hand down over Van's stomach.

He grunted, and turned towards her.

The sex, though, was perfunctory and – for her anyway – unsatisfying. Afterwards, lying with Van's arm slung over her chest, she lay awake while he drifted back into a doze. He'd seemed enthusiastic enough, but there was something missing from their lovemaking. Like she had the body, but not the man.

He was tired, though. As was she. Working for a living could be a grind, especially when you had to ferry a teenage boy around to football games all over the country, which Van had done the previous evening. She left too much of the parenting duties to him, she knew that. It was just, the Job was so important. Nobody died if an IT consultant was late doing a backup or recovering a hard disk.

Leaving him to sleep, she got out of bed and went for a shower. Even this didn't wake him so she dressed and went downstairs to have breakfast and take Smokey out.

While he indulged in his ongoing big game hunt with the pheasants who liked to potter about the wheat field, she rang Liv.

'Thelma!' Liv said. 'How's it going?'

Their shared love of *Thelma & Louise* as kids had given them private nicknames as well as a series of catchphrases.

'All right, Louise. Got time to talk? You're not mucking out the llamas or whatever you Welsh hill farmers do?'

Liv's accent, which had shifted over the years from Middlehampton seasoned with a bit of London-street to a soft Welsh lilt, thickened like over-cornfloured gravy.

'Oh my God, Thel, what are you sayin'? Tha's the North where they 'ave the sheep an' that! We're the Valleys down yer.'

That cracked Kat up and she laughed with the sheer unalloyed joy of hearing her best friend's comedic indignation down the line.

'Soz, mate. How are the wedding plans?'

Kat completed a full circuit of The Gallops, waving a greeting to Barrie as they crossed paths, while Liv enthusiastically relayed the strategically important aspects of her upcoming marriage to Dafydd Jones.

'. . . course it's a right pain in the arse counting out exactly seven sugared almonds each into a hundred fiddly little lilac net bags but, I'm no' gonna lie to you, Thel, i's gotta be done, 'asn' i'?'

By now her accent was that of a lowlander who'd never strayed much beyond the precincts of her patch of heaven and regarded a trip into Swansea as venturing to the mouth of Babylon. Then she flipped back into her normal voice.

'Oh God, Thel, I've been banging on about my wedding and I haven't even asked you about the case.'

'Which you know about because of our favourite podcast?'

'Natch. God, that man's a right pain, isn't he?'

'Like a boil on the bum.'

'Or a bad case of cystitis.'

Kat grinned. 'Period pain.'

'Having an IUD put in.'

'Or taken out.'

Liv cackled.

But the smile died on Kat's lips as she framed the question she wanted to ask her best friend. The question perhaps only Liv was qualified to answer. Given she knew Ethan and had fled Middlehampton to escape the attentions of a serial killer.

'Liv, have you been following Ethan's latest podcast?'

'About Rosie Duggan? Of course! Someone's got to keep you in the loop about Mutt-calf's sweaty little outpourings, haven't they?'

Kat swallowed, then spoke quickly before she could change her mind. 'I think there's a chance Ethan might be the killer and I wanted to know whether you think I'm way off beam here, or could he be a murderer?' The line went quiet. 'Liv? Hello? Are you still there?'

'I'm here,' Liv said, her voice flat. 'You're serious, Kat? You think Mutt-calf could have done it?'

Kat screwed up her face. *Did* she think that? How sure was she?

'Honestly, I don't know. He's a world-class slime-ball.'

'Obvs.'

'And he got his arse handed to him by Rosie on video. But against that, I just don't see him as a serial killer.'

'A serial killer?' Liv's voice shot up at least an octave. 'You mean he's done others?'

'I don't know! There's another girl, died the same way, exactly a year before Rosie.'

'Look, Kat. You want my opinion? Yes, it could be him. I mean, you wouldn't even be asking me if you didn't have your suspicions. I met Stefan Pulford, remember, back when he first started killing those girls. He was good-looking, charming, bit of a rogue, but all the girls love a bad boy, don't they? None of them look like serial killers until they do.'

'So you're saying I should keep investigating Ethan?'

'Exactly! Wait! He got arrested, didn't he? For stalking you. So his DNA's on file. Was there DNA at the crime scene?'

'I can't say, Liv, sorry.'

'Doesn't matter. You're the detective, not me. But if there was, you just need to run a comparison or whatever you do. If it matches Ethan, it's him. If it doesn't, it's not. Right?'

Kat remembered Tom's delight in coming up with scenarios for procuring semen without being the originator. They were all feasible, but could she imagine a jury giving any of them weight? She could not. DNA was considered gospel among cops, and not far off in the CPS. Juries loved it.

She inhaled deeply, forced a smile back on to her face. Ethan would be the subject of further scrutiny in the days ahead. But she wanted to keep at least some of her weekend for personal stuff.

Kat reached her front door with Smokey tugging at his lead to be let inside.

'Lou, I've got to go. We've just done a whole walk and I'm bursting for a wee. I'll talk to you soon, yes?'

'I love you, mate.'

'I love you, too. Now let me go before I wet myself.'

With Smokey let into the back garden and her own needs met, Kat made herself a coffee and took it upstairs. She poked her head round the bedroom door. Van was still asleep. Bloody hell, there was tired and there was wiped. She made a mental note to tell him to take some time off next week. All work and no play made Van a dead-to-the-world boy.

She didn't even bother checking on Riley. Since turning fourteen, his sleep patterns had practically inverted themselves.

When he did, finally, put in an appearance, she gave him the good news. Well, she hoped he'd take it that way.

'We've got a guest for dinner tonight,' Kat said brightly, as Riley hacked at a loaf of bread, separating a thick wedge that he then squashed down into the toaster.

'Who?'

'Tom.'

Riley smiled. She loved it when he had that uncomplicated look of pleasure on his face. Such moments didn't come round very often at the moment – he was a teenager, after all – but when they did, it lifted her spirits like nothing else.

'Cool. Tom's nice.'

'He is, isn't he? You can help me cook if you want.'

'Yeah, OK. What are we doing?'

'No idea. I guess we better get a couple of cookbooks out.'

Chapter Thirty-Eight

Tom placed two bottles – one red, one white – on the table.

'I wasn't sure what we'd be having so I brought one of each.'

Van nodded appreciatively as he picked up the white and put it in the fridge. 'Nice.'

Tom grinned.

Kat winked at Tom. 'You ought to taste it first, Van. It could be horrible.'

'Not the wine, nitwit! The quote,' Van said.

She frowned. 'What quote?'

'From *Jaws*? Richard Dreyfuss, remember? He goes to the police chief's house and that's his line.'

'Oh, right. Sorry. I didn't realise boy-time had started so soon.'

'Which do you want, Tom, red or white?' Van asked.

Tom brought out a four-pack of no-alcohol cider from the carrier bag dangling from his left hand. 'One of these, please.' He caught Kat's eye. Just for a second. But a great deal of information passed between them.

Drinks poured, Tom and Van fell into an easy banter. Kat felt unaccountably irritated with Van. He loved his classic movies and sometimes derided her preference for what he always called 'chick flicks'. But he usually managed to conceal his exasperation with her lack of interest a little more subtly.

Riley arrived in the kitchen. He'd shaved, and the room filled with his signature scent. Half a can of Lynx Africa.

'Hi, Tom,' he said.

'Hey. How's it going, Riley?'

Riley picked up a wooden spoon and stirred the pasta sauce. He'd opted to make rigatoni Amatriciana, and the bacon, onions and tomatoes were blending nicely.

'Football today. We got trashed, five–one.'

'Mate, what happened? Were you playing with your boots on the wrong feet?'

Riley laughed.

As the three males bantered, Kat sipped her Pinot Grigio. Tom seemed to be mending faster than she'd ever thought possible. Was it just because she'd started keeping him under her wing, or was it the potential romance with Clare Capstick? Or just the simple passage of time?

Whatever it was, she started to relax. Her bagman was back. Not exactly the way he was before – an experience like the one he'd had would change a person, possibly for ever – but he was showing up. Doing the job. And not drinking.

Riley served up, and when Van offered him wine, he looked shyly at Tom and said, 'Can I have one of those, Tom, please?'

'It's only pretend, I'm afraid.'

'I don't care.'

Kat's heart swelled. Only a few months back, Riley had been loudly insisting on trying wine with dinner, and even though his first experience had been, to put it charitably, suboptimal, he'd persisted. But here he was, being offered alcohol and instead opting to follow Tom's example.

Conversation flowed, Tom entertaining them with stories of growing up in pubs. During a lull, Riley piped up.

'So, like, have you got a girlfriend?'

Kat smiled. 'Riley! Personal, much?'

He coloured. 'Oh. Sorry, I was just, you know, trying to make conversation.'

Tom shook his head. 'It's fine. I did. But it ended. Although' – he glanced at Kat – 'there might be someone on the horizon. How about you?'

Kat thought Riley might blush and get tongue-tied, or clam up, like he did whenever she tried to ask him about Millie.

'Yeah. She's called Millie.'

'Cool.'

What happened next puzzled Kat. If it had been her and one of her friends, the next logical question would be 'What's she like?' Or, perhaps, 'Where did you two meet?' 'Have you been together long?' Or one of about two thousand other questions.

But they just started talking about Tom's work.

She swallowed her wine. 'Sorry, can I just ask, what just happened?'

'What do you mean?' Tom asked.

'You just asked Riley if he had a girlfriend and he said yes and now – what? – you're talking about being a detective?'

Tom and Riley looked at each other. Some sort of male-only message passed between them like an exchange of electrons concealed in a cloud of Lynx Africa molecules.

'I asked a question,' Tom said.

'And I answered it,' Riley finished.

She groaned. 'Ohh, right. Because you're men, and that's what men do, right?'

Now Van chipped in, slurring his words a little. 'That's right, darling. Like, when you say, "have you loaded the dishwasher" and I say "no".'

'Let me guess,' Tom said, grinning. 'Then she gets cross because you didn't realise that meant "I want you to load the dishwasher"?'

Kat rolled her eyes in her best imitation of her son, who was looking pleased with himself.

'Right, well, for the avoidance of doubt, put your hand up if you want pudding. It's apple pie and ice cream.'

Three hands shot up, and for a disconcerting moment, she felt like she used to on the rare occasions she had time to help out at Riley's primary school.

'Cool,' she said, looking pointedly at Tom, though she couldn't prevent the grin that slid on to her face. 'But you guys will load the dishwasher while I get pudding.'

Riley dug into his bowl of pie and ice cream as if he'd not just consumed a huge bowlful of pasta. He paused after a few mouthfuls though, and turned to Tom.

'How's the case going? That student, the one who got pushed off the car park?'

Tom looked at Kat. Seeking permission. She nodded. He knew better than to share confidential information.

'Well, we have some promising leads. In fact, I was at work today and I think we might have a new witness.'

'Why didn't you call me, Tomski?' Kat asked, feeling like he'd deliberately kept her in the dark.

'I tried, but it wouldn't connect. I left a message. Have you checked voicemail?'

Crap! She hadn't. She'd been so wrapped up in thinking about Ethan, and then preparing for tonight's meal.

'Who is she? Or he?'

'It's a he. Says he was drinking in the Five Cups Inn until closing time on Monday night. Apparently, he saw two girls walking along Palmer Street. He thinks one of them might have been Rosie Duggan.'

'Have you been to see him?'

'He's in Manchester with relatives, back tomorrow. We arranged for me to talk to him in the morning. Do you want to come?'

'Er, yes! What time?'

'Ten.'

◆ ◆ ◆

Yiannis Demetriou had a flat on Palmer Street in a block at the other end from the junction with Five Cups Lane, where the Five Cups Inn stood. Had stood, in fact, since 1531.

He offered, 'Greek coffee. Best in the world.' And sweet, crisp triangles of pistachio-filled baklava leaking so much honey it formed little pools on the King Charles III coronation side plates.

He stroked his bushy black moustache – a triumph of testosterone and styling wax. 'I must apologise for not coming forward sooner. I had had a lot to drink. I thought it wasn't important. But my wife, Athena, she said I must say something. I saw your press conference.' He looked directly at Kat. 'You are very persuasive.'

She smiled, then took a sip of the coffee, wary of its potency given the tiny cup Yiannis had served it in. It was like drinking adrenaline dissolved in silt. Her heart stuttered.

'Wow!'

Yiannis laughed, a big, booming sound in the daintily decorated sitting room.

'Like I said! I hope you weren't planning on sleeping before midnight, Detective Sergeant Ballantyne.'

She grinned ruefully, and took a bite of the baklava to try to take the edge of the caffeine hit currently elevating her pulse to the red zone.

'Perhaps you could tell us what you saw on Monday night, Yiannis?'

'Of course. I come out of the pub. It is 11.15 p.m. A little later, perhaps. And I, you know, wobble a little in the fresh air. I steady myself on the wall and turn for home. As I do this, I bump into two young girls. I say "sorry, my dears", something like that, and I walk down Palmer Street to my home – here, where we are sitting.'

'And Tom says you think one of the girls was Rosie Duggan.'

'Yes! I recognised her from the photograph they showed on the TV.'

Kat's thoughts whirled. She'd been so sure it was Ethan, but now an eyewitness put Rosie in the company of a female within minutes of her death. The only girl they'd so far identified with a motive to want Rosie dead was Libby Spare.

'How about the other girl? Do you think you might recognise her if we showed you a photo?'

He shrugged bulky shoulders. 'It was dark and I am in the pub since seven. But, sure, show me, please.'

Kat found a photo of Libby and held her phone up to Yiannis.

He frowned, and stroked his moustache. 'It could be. She was nice-looking like her. Not beautiful or anything, but, you know, nice. Attractive. Right hair colour, too. Sort of dark blonde, or, what do they call it? Athena would know.'

'Dirty blonde?' Kat hazarded.

His eyes lit up. 'Exactly! Dirty blonde.'

'Did either Rosie or this other girl say anything?'

'Oh, yes. Rosie, she just smiles at me and says something kind, like "steady there" or, I don't know, "careful, my dear". You know, considerate. But this other one, she gave me a look would freeze your b—' He blushed. 'Forgive me. I mean freeze your heart. She said, "Keep your hands off her you toxic pig!"' He held his hands up. 'I swear on Saint Photini the Samaritan Woman, I didn't touch her.'

'It's fine, Yiannis, I'm sure this young woman was just lashing out. And thank you for coming forward, this has been really helpful.'

Outside on the street again, Kat turned to Tom. 'Did you hear what he said?'

He nodded. 'She called our friend Yiannis a toxic pig. Libby pretty much did the same to me when we talked to her on campus.'

'Problems with our wit?' she prompted, seeing another teaching opportunity.

'One, he was pissed when he bumped into them. Two, "toxic" and "pig" hardly count as notable language these days. Half the female population of Middlehampton – let alone those at uni – probably use them.'

'Agreed. Having said that, at the very least we have to take another look at Libby. And your theory about stolen condoms, too.'

Tom nodded. 'Ah, the joys of policework.'

Kat offered him a wry smile.

Chapter Thirty-Nine

Kat asked Tom to invite Libby in for a voluntary interview under caution, then went to visit their other prime candidate for murder suspect.

She took a breath and rang the doorbell. She was still struggling to believe he could be a serial killer. She'd known him since they were both awkward, nervous eleven-year-olds on their first day in secondary school.

It was hard to define the feeling she was getting, or rather not getting. And it had zero connection to the concept of evidence. But every seasoned murder detective would privately admit that you just knew when you were in the presence of 'a wrong'un'. And Kat wasn't getting it.

Ethan opened the door and took a step back when he registered that it was Kat calling on him first thing on a Monday morning.

Then he did something she always associated with guilty individuals. Or at least those with something to hide. He looked past her, up and down the street.

'I'm alone, Ethan,' she said.

He smiled but it didn't reach his eyes. More of the sort of ingratiating toothy grin one saw chimpanzees offer dominant individuals on a wildlife documentary.

'Is that wise, Kat. What with, you know . . . our history?'

'You mean when you used to stalk me, Ethan?'

'Ada said—'

'Yeah, I'm not really interested in what Ada said. Can I come in, please?'

'What's this about?'

'Rosie Duggan. What else?'

Now the smile became genuine, lifting the corners of his mouth one millimetre at a time before reaching, and crinkling, the outer corners of his eyes.

'I don't believe this! You want to work together? After all these years, all the cases, Kat, you've come round. Oh my God, this is so cool!' He literally swelled with pride. 'First, I get a girlfriend, who as you've probably noticed is clever, beautiful and totally into me, then I get asked to consult on a live murder investigation. Yes, of course, of course! Come in, come in!'

He held the door wide and stepped aside. Whatever had prevented him from inviting her and Tom in before, he'd clearly had a change of heart.

The house smelled of cleaning products. Lavender, which ignited a flicker of nausea. Bleach. Air freshener. For a second, she envisaged a blood-spattered bathroom, then banished the thought. Rosie Duggan's killer favoured a bloodless MO.

'You should let me give you the tour,' he said excitedly. 'The studio's downstairs. The basement. It's better for audio purity. Come on!'

He hurried down the hallway and into the kitchen, which was clean to the point of obsessiveness, and furnished in a style that had been outdated when Kat was growing up.

Ethan unlocked a door and switched on a light. Carpeted stairs led downwards.

'Follow me,' he said. 'No need to watch your step, it's solid as a rock and there's a handrail.'

Heart trotting along, hand straying to the Taser clipped to her belt beneath the flap of her jacket, she followed him down into a well-lit, low-ceilinged space.

She looked around. So this was where he did his work.

Blue-and-white crime-scene tape criss-crossed the walls. A blond-wood desk was clear of everything except for a tablet, a paper notebook and a pen. A foam-shielded microphone with a circular mesh pop-filter hung above it on a multi-angled black stem.

A tower PC bore a foot-tall Wonder Woman figurine. A web-cam sat atop the monitor. Another, superior-looking camcorder was mounted to a bookshelf on a clamp. A large, professionally designed and printed signboard fixed to the wall declared in a stencil-style type-face, *Home Counties Homicide – where true crime comes alive!*

She turned round. Another desk held a second computer and a stack of rectangular black boxes that resembled hi-fi components. Other boxes with knobs, buttons and VU meters on, at whose purpose she could only guess.

He swung round, eyes shining, and held out a hand to encompass the presumably expensive studio set-up. 'What do you think? Impressive or what? Bet you never thought old Mutt-calf would make a success of himself. Well, you got that wrong, didn't you?' He shot her a sly look. 'Oh, yes, Kat. I know what you and Liv Arnold used to call me. But it's fine! *We're* fine, aren't we?'

Trapped below ground with him, whether or not she detected the presence of 'a wrong'un', she felt a squirm of anxiety in the pit of her stomach. She swallowed, nodded.

'Yep.'

'This is where the magic happens,' he said, sweeping an arm in a semicircle. 'My old set-up was rubbish. So amateurish. But when Mum died and left me the house and the money, I could totally kit it out. This is state-of-the-art, Kat. You're looking at fifty grand's worth of professional audio and video equipment here.'

'How did she die?' She stared hard at him. *Did you drug her with tranquillisers and push her down the stairs?*

Ethan looked at her as if he'd heard her inner question. 'It was a heart attack. We were eating tea. Fish fingers and chips. A salted caramel Viennetta for afters. One minute she was there, and then she just frowned at me and died.'

'I'm sorry.'

'I'm not. She used to bully me, Kat. Just like you did at school. But anyway, every cloud – she's dead and I'm rich. Well, not rich, but I'm secure. Even if *HCH* wasn't the mega-successful show it is, I'd never have to work again. She was pensioned up to the eyeballs.'

Under the pretext of inspecting the hi-tech equipment on the second desk, Kat stepped back from him. He was playing nice but every few sentences he'd slip in a little barb, like that one he just made about the bullying.

'Ethan, do you know anything about what happened to Rosie Duggan?'

'Well, I've been digging, obviously, as I'm sure you have. She was popular, well liked, sporty, academically quite brilliant apparently. All the things I wasn't. Nobody had a bad word to say about her. So my conclusion, as I think I may have mentioned at the press conference, is that we're looking for a serial murderer. Perhaps one just starting out on his journey.' He paused – somewhat theatrically, Kat thought – and scratched the back of his head. 'On which subject . . . press conferences, I mean. When you hold another one, just give me a bit of notice and I'll speak to the media for you. As a consultant, obviously. I could probably save you wasting money on a profiler, too. I know at least as much as any of those frauds.'

Kat stared at him. How could he exhibit such a spectacular blend of grandiosity, narcissism and sheer wrong-headedness?

You know perfectly well why, her inner voice whispered. *Because despite your famous 'copper's gut', there is something deeply off about him.*

'Last time we spoke,' she said carefully, 'I asked you if you remembered your whereabouts on the night Rosie was murdered. You were busy with editing, so you didn't answer. But I'd like you to have a think now, Ethan. Just so I can eliminate you from our enquiries.'

He frowned. Shifted his weight from foot to foot. Looked down at the Wonder Woman model. Was it heavy, Kat wondered? Plastic? Or painted metal.

'I don't understand. Why am I even *in* your enquiries? I thought you were here to ask for my help.'

'I am here to ask for your help, Ethan. I'm here because, as you might remember, you had a rather public falling-out with Rosie in a lecture. She humiliated you in front of, what, thirty other students? Someone posted the video. I've checked. It's had over three hundred thousand views.'

He smiled crookedly. 'I wouldn't say she *humiliated* me, Kat. She was just venting. It's what they do. Students I mean. As for the video, bring it on! It's all publicity for my podcast.'

Just as Tom had suggested, Ethan was a fully paid-up member of the 'there's no such thing as bad publicity' school of thought.

'Either way, Ethan, it puts you on our radar. And the quickest way to get you off it again would be to tell me where you were on Monday night.' A beat. 'Please.'

He'd started chewing his lip. Now he wouldn't meet her gaze. 'You know, I thought now we'd cleared the air, me apologising and everything, we could be friends.' He shrugged. 'Not bosom buddies, but at least you might have extended me some professional courtesy as one investigator to another. But now I see that nothing's changed. I'm still Mutt-calf to you, aren't I, Kat?'

'No, you're not, Ethan. And I'm sorry we gave you that horrible nickname.'

She meant it, but that did nothing to stop the trembling that had begun in her left knee, before spreading to her right, and then to her entire body, right the way down to the finger-tips, now hovering a few inches from the Taser in the back of her waistband.

'Are you, Kat? I hope so. But anyway' – he checked his watch, a flashy gold number that bore a resemblance to the Rolex she suspected her father had given to Carve-up – 'I'm live-streaming my next episode in ninety minutes and I need to get ready. You'll have to go.'

'Ethan—'

He held up a hand sharply, making her flinch.

'No! I've done nothing wrong, unless you count having ambition and a desire to escape the past. I didn't kill anyone and I don't need to prove it, either.'

He pointed to the stairs.

'I'll show you out.'

She preceded him up the stairs, feeling a prickling low in her back beneath the Taser. She practically ran up the last few steps, down the hall and out of the front door.

Chapter Forty

Kat locked the Golf's doors and then let out a long, slow breath. Shook her hands about, to release the tingling sensation that had been building during the previous few minutes in Ethan's basement.

Ethan had refused to supply an alibi for the night of the murder twice now. *Could* he be hiding something? Had his podcast made him curious about what it felt like to kill? He wouldn't be the first to wonder.

Tom was more suspicious of Ethan than Kat was. Should she give him some credit? After all, she was always telling him what a promising detective he was. The thought already lodged in her brain surfaced once more. *Have I been downgrading Ethan because otherwise I'd have to admit I was in more danger from him than I want to admit?*

She started the car, fighting down a sudden wave of nausea.

If forced right now to choose between Greg Fanning and Ethan Metcalfe as Rosie Duggan's killer, she knew who she'd pick.

She arrived back at MCU twenty minutes later. Tom was waiting for her, along with an email from the NCA informing DS Ballantyne her ViCLAS request had come back negative. Meaning there was no official trail of murders of young women disguised as falls from heights.

'How did it go with Ethan?' he asked.

Kat shuddered involuntarily.

'Refused to give me an alibi again. And he made me feel really uncomfortable, Tomski.'

'You think it could be him?'

No delay in her answer this time.

'Yes, mate. Yes, I do.'

'Well, this is just snipping off a loose end, then, but I've got Libby Spare in the friendly interview room. You ready?'

'Let's go. You lead, Tomski.'

'You're sure?'

She smiled. 'Come on. The way you've been handling yourself on this case, you should be lead investigator, not me.'

He smiled back. 'I don't think you mean that, but I'll take it anyway.'

Libby was engrossed in her phone when Kat followed Tom into the interview room and took a seat beside him on the sofa. At once, the look of boredom on Libby's angular face was replaced with one of outright hostility.

'I'm only here because your boyfriend here threatened to arrest me if I didn't come in voluntarily,' she said, glaring at Tom.

'I'm sure Tom would have done no such thing, Libby,' Kat said. 'And I do need to reiterate that you're here of your own free will. *Would* you like to leave?'

'Let's just get it over with.'

Once the official business was out of the way, Kat sat back and watched Libby as Tom began with a gentle question.

'How would you characterise your relationship with Rosie Duggan?'

'We were friends, I already told you that.'

'What kind of friends? "Saying hi in the street" friends? "Sharing a joint" friends? Was she your bae?'

She rolled her eyes, the whites contrasting sharply with the thick lining of kohl.

'"Bae"? What is this, 2015? We were friends, OK? Just the regular kind.'

'Fair enough. And you've already told us that the falling-out you two had before Christmas was, what, a . . .' He wrinkled his nose. 'Sorry, I don't want to get the terminology wrong, but a "beef"?'

'Oh, Jesus! Listen to him. It's like in *Animal Farm*, if you've read it? Pigs trying to act like humans.'

Tom smiled. 'I *have* read it. As a critique of Stalin's regime, it's a bit too obvious. "On the nose", you'd probably say. I prefer *1984*, although that novel has its detractors, too.' He paused. 'One of the things I liked about it, though, was how Orwell focused so much on language. Newspeak. You remember? His term for the way Big Brother wanted to end dissent by erasing the words people used to express it. Like how you use the word "pig" for police officer. It's a bit old-school, isn't it? Pig. Like you're at Kent State or Berkeley in the 1970s, and not Middlehampton in the 2020s.'

Kat knew exactly where Tom was headed, but Libby was clearly bamboozled by his digression into literary criticism and the history of student protest.

'I'm sorry, but where are you going with this?' Libby checked the time on her phone. 'I've got a lecture at 11.00 a.m.'

'We won't take long, Libby. I'll make sure you don't miss your class. You've called me a pig twice now.'

She pouted. 'Sorry if I hurt your feelings.'

He smiled and shook his head. 'You didn't. But the funny thing is, we spoke to an eyewitness yesterday who bumped into Rosie and a female friend on the night she was murdered. And this friend, you know, the regular kind, called our witness a pig.'

Libby shrugged her bony shoulders. 'Am I supposed to care?'

'He said she looked like you.'

'Let me guess. Blonde. Skinny. Pretty. That's like the standard toxic-male bullshit description for any girl who isn't a curvy redhead or a woman of colour.'

'She also called him toxic. Just like you just did.'

'Again, so what?' She pulled herself straighter in her chair and folded her arms across her chest. Eyeballed Tom. 'In case you've forgotten, my dad's a barrister. We used to play a game called "police interview" when I was little. Dad played the *pig*' – a little extra emphasis on that word – 'and I was the suspect. Let's just say you wouldn't have won a single round.'

'Fair enough. But let me recap, as we're playing it for real. On the night Rosie Duggan was murdered, by being pushed from a height, she was seen not two minutes from the scene in the company of a young woman who bears a resemblance to you. This young woman used language you use. And, while we're on the subject of language, we have Rosie's written testimony that you talked about knocking her off her high horse and pride coming before a fall. Finally, you and she had a major falling-out – a "beef", if you prefer – when she refused to help you cheat with your academic work, giving you motive. You can keep refusing to give us an alibi, which is your right, but why not tell us where you were and we can clear this whole thing up?'

While he'd been talking, Kat had been watching Libby minutely, looking for a little flicker of the eye muscles, a tightening of the lips, a sudden inability to meet Tom's gaze, a heightening of her colour, or a draining of blood from her cheeks. Anything that might indicate the moment when Tom hit on the truth. But all she could see was a stroppy, hostile witness entirely sure of her ground. Which appeared to be formed from several metres of granite.

'You've got literally no evidence I killed my friend. And suspicions are cheap. I've got mine about you. You want to hear them?'

'I'll pass,' Tom said.

'I bet.'

'Do you ever take benzos recreationally, Libby?' Kat asked.

The effect was startling. Libby whirled round, eyes blazing. 'What the actual fuck?'

'It's a simple question. Do you take benzodiazepines for fun?'

'No, I do not. They're highly addictive, which I assume you know. Anyway, I'm on prescription medication for depression and anxiety. Mixing them would be a really bad idea.'

'Can I ask which ones?'

'You can *ask*.'

'Have you got the NHS app on your phone?'

'Yes. Why?'

'Could you show us your medical records?'

'Could you get a warrant? Otherwise, no, I couldn't show you my medical records. In fact, you know what? I'm done.'

She stood up, shot Kat a look so filthy it made her feel unclean, as if she'd been caught viewing child pornography, and left, slamming the door behind her.

Tom sighed. 'That went well.'

'Don't worry, Tomski,' she said with a wry smile. 'And top marks for keeping your cool. Can you have a chat with the university medical practice? See if they'll cooperate?'

'I can try. But you know what they'll say.'

'I know, but try anyway.'

They left the interview room and walked back to MCU. Kat's bottom had barely touched her chair when her phone rang.

It was Darcy. She sounded excited. And after hearing what she had to say, Kat turned to Tom, a sick feeling making her whisper. 'Forget about the uni doctors. It's not Libby.'

And with that, she led him down to Forensics.

Chapter Forty-One

Wondering how she could have been so blind, Kat arrived in Forensics, Tom on her heels.

Darcy was grinning as she held out a single sheet of paper. Kat plucked it from her fingers and glanced at the paragraph in bold a third of the way down the page.

The paper shook in her trembling fingers. She should have been feeling triumphant. Instead, her nausea increased. They had their perpetrator.

Shock and guilt mingled queasily in her gut. She still found it hard to believe, but there was no doubting the evidence. Half-cut eye-witnesses, grainy council CCTV, smudgy fingerprints: all could be discredited by a skilful defence barrister. But that double helix of inter-twined molecules was the silver bullet that could slay the werewolf.

She held the sheet out so Tom could read it.

'It's him, Tomski.'

Standing shoulder to shoulder with her bagman, she checked again just to be sure. There was no mistake.

Sample type: SEMEN

Crime scene: (1) VICTIM [ROSIE DUGGAN]'s BODY

Location: FIVE CUPS LANE, MIDDLEHAMPTON, MH1 7AV

NDNAD match (%): 100

NDNAD record: Ethan Metcalfe

Chapter Forty-Two

'Stuart, I need an arrest warrant for Ethan Metcalfe. He murdered Rosie Duggan.'

From behind his desk, Carve-up looked up at Kat. For once his expression was neither irritable nor contemptuous.

'Say again?'

'We have a hundred per cent DNA match. The semen deposited on Rosie Duggan's body is Ethan Metcalfe's. Please can I have an arrest warrant?'

He smiled up at her humourlessly. 'Well, well. You've actually done it. A genuine twofer. Closed a case and put that sorry little excuse for a man in prison greys. Carry on like this and we might have to reinstate your team.'

He created a warrant, typed in a few details, then printed it out and signed it.

She gathered a full-strength team including a method-of-entry officer, skilled with the steel ram everyone called the Big Red Key. Then, with Tom riding shotgun, she followed the marked van and two patrol cars as they tore through the traffic, blues and twos screaming joyfully.

'It's actually him,' Tom was saying, as Kat blew through a red traffic light behind a chequerboard Volvo in full pursuit tune. 'I can't believe it. He *must* be a psychopath. To murder her and then keep bloody podcasting about it.'

Kat didn't answer. Her own thoughts were too loud between her ears. She'd known Ethan since they were kids and at worst had pegged him for a pathetic individual who'd turned to stalking as a last resort to get her attention. How could she claim to be a good murder investigator when she'd failed to spot he was a murderous psychopath? If she had, Rosie might still be alive. And then there was the earlier death. Rebecca Poole. Had Ethan murdered her, too?

Kat swung the Golf round a roundabout, tyres screeching. She speared through a traffic-calming chicane, barely moving the wheel, letting the car's weight help it shimmy between the posts that flew by, inches from the wing mirrors.

Five minutes later, heart pounding, she hauled the car to a stop outside Ethan's modest suburban semi at 98 Oxford Road in Fawcett's Field. The marked cars had closed the street at both ends, and in front of her the transit's rear doors opened, releasing four uniformed officers. Behind it, a prisoner transport van, which everyone still called a Black Maria, even though they hadn't been painted black for decades.

Kat strode over to face them. Forced her self-doubts down. For now. The team needed her to stand tall. Her only priority was to get Ethan into the Black Maria without anyone getting hurt.

Better late than never, her inner critic mocked.

'I knock, then stand back with DC Gray. Suspect comes to the door. I arrest him. Then you cuff him and it's into the back of the Black Maria with him. Suspect is to be considered extremely dangerous and unpredictable. Any signs of violence, you use reasonable force, up to and including strikes, to render him passive. Understood?'

Nods all around.

'Everyone got their body-worn cameras on?'

More nods.

'Right, let's do it.'

They approached the front door. Kat turned to see Ethan's neighbours peering from around their lace curtains. One had her phone pressed up against the glass.

Her heart was beating hard, and fast. But this was a different kind of energy from the anxious thrum she'd felt on her earlier visit that morning. Now she had her quarry in her sights, and enough reinforcements to subdue an elephant.

Kat marched up to the front door. Rang the doorbell. A good, long push. Then she hammered with the side of her fist on the central wood panel between the stained glass. *Good and loud*, as Molly had once told her. *He might be asleep*.

Or recording his last podcast for a while.

She tried again, adding a loud shout. 'Police! Ethan Metcalfe, it's DS Ballantyne. Open up!'

Nothing.

'He's definitely in?' Tom asked.

'He should be. He said he'd be live-streaming an episode in ninety minutes before he shoved me out the door.'

She turned and hammered again. Hard enough this time to rattle the delicate glass panels with their beautifully painted scene of sheep grazing beneath an Art Deco sunrise.

'Police!' she yelled. 'Open up or we will force entry.'

She waited for five seconds. Could just imagine the problem. Of course Ethan was in. But he'd be down in his bloody basement, headphones on, riding his hobby horse: that the police in general and Kat in particular were incompetent, blinkered, failing to spot the obvious. Yeah? Well, they'd spotted it now, hadn't they? His filthy DNA all over a murder victim.

She turned and beckoned the method-of-entry officer and his red battering ram. MOE guys were generally selected for a certain amount of physical bulk as well as an affinity for manipulating cumbersome and weighty bits of steel. He was a fine example of the breed. She suspected he might wrestle bears in his spare time. And win.

'Break it down.'

He nodded, dropped his visor and took up position. With very little preparation, he swung the ram backwards and then smashed it into the door just below the lock.

With a loud crack and several flying splinters, the door gave way and swung inwards, bouncing off the hall wall and shattering the left-hand panel of stained glass.

Kat sent two uniforms ahead of her.

'Kitchen, turn right. Door to the basement.'

She turned. 'Come on, Tomski.'

They kept their distance from the uniforms, both mindful that the last time they'd worked an arrest together, it had ended with Tom almost bleeding out.

They skittered down the stairs into the basement, where the tableau presenting itself would have made a nice Victorian morality painting. One entitled, perhaps, *Finally, Justice*.

Facing two burly uniformed officers, Tasers at the ready and bellowing at him to keep still, Ethan sat open-mouthed, eyes popping, fingers clawed into the armrests of his chair. A pair of over-ear headphones lay on the desk.

She planted herself in front of him.

'Ethan Metcalfe, I am arresting you on suspicion of the murder of Rosie Duggan. We have evidence' – *oh, how we have evidence* – 'connecting you to the crime. You do not have to say anything, but it may harm your defence if you do not mention when questioned something which you later rely on in court. Anything you do say may be given in evidence. Do you understand?'

His opening and closing mouth made him look like a koi carp gopping at the surface of a pond. But this one was definitely out of water.

'What?'

'Do you understand your rights as I have explained them to you?'

'Yes, but I didn't kill her. Kat, it's me, Ethan.' His lips quivered, and for a moment she thought he was about to cry. Then they curved upwards into a sickly, ingratiating smile. It turned her stomach. 'It's me, sad little Mutt-calf! I'm not a murderer, you know that. You've made a mistake.'

Kat stood back and nodded to one of the uniforms. He stepped forwards.

'Stand up, please,' the officer said.

Ethan gripped the arms of his chair tighter.

'No! This is all wrong. You can't. I'm literally live-streaming my podcast where I talk about—'

The officer looked at Kat. She nodded.

Together with his partner, he hauled Ethan to his feet and spun him round.

'Hands behind your back!'

Ethan was a little too slow, and yelped as his hands were yanked behind his back and secured with cuffs.

Kat called Jan Cable, the POLSA. Gave her the address.

'Seize everything. Devices, notebooks, the works.'

Then she led Tom back up to the light. They drove back to Jubilee Place behind the Black Maria. She waved to Darcy, who was driving a forensics van towards her.

From nowhere, she barked out a savage laugh, then clapped a hand over her mouth.

'Relieved?'

She glanced across at Tom.

'Tomski, you have no idea.'

Ethan's trajectory was pathetic. From lonely, bullied outcast, to stalker, to celebrity true-crime podcaster, to murderer. If only it hadn't ended in a young girl's death. Once again, Kat's doubts insinuated themselves into her mind.

She might still be alive if you'd taken Ethan more seriously.

I thought you were supposed to be good at sniffing out wrong'uns?'

And then Carve-up's sneering tones added to the unpleasant jumble between her ears.

Not as good as you think you are, eh? . . . Kitty Kat?

With a huge effort, she silenced them all.

Perhaps she should have seen past Ethan's sad-sack exterior sooner.

But they'd got him.

She pushed her foot down on the accelerator.

She didn't want to miss the fun.

Chapter Forty-Three

Julia Myles had the long-suffering demeanour of the seen-everything breed of custody sergeant. All of them, in other words.

Yet when Kat marched the handcuffed Ethan Metcalfe up to her desk, she raised her eyebrows.

'Well, well. A celebrity in our midst.' That was as far as she permitted herself to deviate from her script. 'And who do we have here, then?'

'Suspect is Ethan Anthony Metcalfe.'

Julia tapped the name into her computer. 'Charge?' she asked, fixing an errant braid behind her ear.

'Murder. Rosie Duggan.'

More keystrokes, then Julia stared at Ethan. 'You have a number of legal rights, which I shall now explain to you. Please don't interrupt. If you have any questions, not opinions, I'll be happy to answer them when I've finished. OK?'

'OK,' he mumbled.

'Good. You have the right to legal representation. If you can't afford a lawyer, one will be provided for you.'

As Julia ran through the prisoner's rights, Kat tuned out and examined her own thoughts and feelings.

She felt not just the tension of the last week leaving her, but what felt like years of it flushing from her system like dirty water from a blocked bathroom drain. So what if she had been wrong about Ethan all that time? She'd arrested him now.

'I'll use my own lawyer,' Ethan was saying. 'He's very good. But you'll have to wait. He's a busy man.'

And then that was it. A custody officer took him away and seconds later a heavy steel-faced door was clanging shut. The host of *Home Counties Homicide* had assumed a starring role in one of his own shows.

Kat thanked Julia then made her way back to MCU, and applause. Once the hubbub had died down and she'd taken a sip from a plastic cup of warm Prosecco someone handed her, she sat at her desk with Tom.

'He's getting lawyered up,' she said.

'Would you expect him not to?'

'I suppose not. I guess I was hoping he might just break down and confess there and then.'

Two hours later, the arrest paperwork still only half-completed, a guy from Digital Forensics called her. 'I've just finished trawling his search history. I've emailed you the report. Guy might as well have confessed to you when you nicked him.'

Kat checked her emails. Opened the report. The details were exactly as the DF officer had stated: Ethan's search history made for fascinating reading.

On and on it went. Search after search after search. Ethan might as well have typed in *If I murder Rosie Duggan will I get caught?* She could answer that one for him.

Yes, mate. Yes you will.

At home that night, Kat had barely got through the door before Riley came barrelling down the hall and enveloped her in a hug comprising equal parts fierce love, newly acquired muscle and, as always, the heady aroma of Lynx Africa.

'You got that creep, Mum!'

Not to be left out, Smokey kept jumping up, his front paws pattering against Kat's knees as he frantically tried to get between the young master and his mistress.

Van was in the kitchen, hunched over his laptop.

He looked up with a weary smile as she came in, propelled by Riley, who was gripping her by the shoulders, with Smokey yelping frenziedly behind them.

'Well done, love,' he said, snaking a hand around her waist as she bent to bestow a kiss.

'She's a legend!' Riley crowed.

When she could catch her breath, Kat turned to Riley.

'This is all very lovely, my darling boy, but I do have one question. How did you know?'

He stood back, giving her one of his signature looks. Wrinkled forehead, lips pulled to one side in a quirky half-smile.

'Er, he was live-streaming? It's gone viral. Literally everybody at school's seen it. My mates think you're badass.'

She smiled. 'Hear that, Van? They think I'm "badass".'

Van went to the fridge. 'As does your husband. I put some champagne in to chill. Come on, let's celebrate.'

The hit of alcohol, aided by the excitement of the arrest and Riley's continuing gloating at the live-stream, went straight to her head. She even managed to ignore the complications of an arrest happening in real-time on the suspect's own podcast. By the time the takeaway Chinese food arrived, which Van had insisted on, she was halfway to being drunk.

There had been times, she admitted to herself as she cuddled up against Van in front of the TV after they'd finished eating, when an arrest had left her curiously deflated. The expected high dissipated before it had arrived, shoved aside by a negative emotion. Disgust. Disappointment. Or just desolation at the evil human beings continued to mete out to each other. But tonight, and despite her self-doubt over Ethan, she felt a sense of achievement.

She and Tom had worked hard, assiduously following every lead, gathering evidence, just as Ma-Linda wanted. It was a textbook piece of detective work. Culminating in an arrest that, while not without incident, was also a model of escalation protocol.

She sighed.

'All right?' Van murmured.

'Yeah. Just tired, that's all.'

'God, me, too.'

'You work too hard, Van.'

'Well, I work as hard as my clients need me too. Bloody Marnie's got me on my knees over this new service. I close my eyes and all I see is the backend. All these plug-ins just dancing around refusing to talk to each other, like squabbling kids at a nursery.'

Kat snickered. It was such a comic image, and unusually vivid for Van, who normally preferred to deal in realities rather than metaphors.

'Just tell her you have a life.' She reached down and gave his groin a little squeeze. Felt the first stirrings of desire. 'Tell her you have a *wife*!'

He shifted his weight. It had the effect of bringing her closer into his embrace but also twisted her arm so she had to remove her hand.

'I know,' she murmured into the crook of his neck, her voice thickening. 'Why don't we leave all this, put Smokey to bed and go upstairs. I could wear the lingerie you bought me for my birthday.'

'Darling, I know you're excited, and I am too, for you. But would you mind if we didn't? I'm shattered and I need to get up early and get to work.'

Kat sat up and faced him. Took his hands in hers.

'Are you all right? I'm not being funny, but normally if I even mention sexy undies you get all hot and bothered.'

'It's fine, love. Just been a long day, that's all. But I'd love a cuddle in bed.'

Which they did, Van falling asleep in minutes, leaving Kat staring at the ceiling, wondering whether if she made DI they'd be able to afford for Van to cut back on his work.

After listening to Van snoring for another twenty minutes, Kat slid from beneath the covers and went downstairs. She made a cup of peppermint tea and opened Rosie's journal. This time, she started with the very first entry.

Chapter Forty-Four

ROSIE DUGGAN'S JOURNAL

29 September 2025

I'm here! I'm actually here!! It's not Birmingham, or Liverpool or Manchester, let alone London, but Middlehampton is properly big. I told someone I met today where I came from and she just looked at me like I'd said Outer Mongolia. For a second I felt defensive about Abbots Bromley. Then I just laughed it off. Anyway, it turned out she comes from some little village in the depths of Cornwall, so we have a lot in common. Her name's Bridie Trevithick. Bridie. Such a cool name!

Anyway, the whole point of being here is I don't have to be *that* girl anymore. Mum and Dad were so proud, but if I have to hear 'She's the first one in the family to go to university' one more time, I think I'll scream!

Obvs my teachers were all thrilled, but it was always, 'Oh, well, we always knew you'd make it, Rosie.' As if everything just falls into my lap. Nobody seems to know or care how much work I put in. When everybody was going out, I was in my bedroom studying.

It's the same with the sports stuff. Girls at school were really mean, like I was rubbing it in people's faces how I could do all these different things really well without trying. It's not my fault! I can't help it if I'm a fast runner, or good at football. That's just me! How I was made. It's like blaming a kangaroo for being good at jumping. God, that's a bit of weird comparison. I should tell people to call me Roosie. Haha.

So 'Uni-me' isn't the bloody 'Golden Child' Mum's always going on about. I mean that's literally the person nobody wants to be friends with. You're like this try-hard goody-goody always volunteering to be editor of the student newspaper or working for some student politician's election campaign. I just want to have a good time, get my degree and get into the world. Find out how my life's going to turn out.

I spoke to Lloyd last night for ages. He actually cried at one point. Said I'd forget him. Meet some posh boy from a private school and dump him by text. But I love him. I do! I mean he is a *bit* needy, but I think that's just because he's not gone to uni. He feels I might be pulling away from him. But he's going into his dream career so I don't really understand why he's so anxious.

It'll sort itself out. One way or another.

Signing off. There's a freshers' party in half an hour and a few of us are doing pre's. Time to try out my new identity. 'Hi I'm Roosie!'

Boingg!!

Chapter Forty-Five

Ethan's solicitor arrived at 8.30 a.m. At 9.00 a.m. everything was ready for the interview to begin.

Outside the interview room, Kat paused with her hand outstretched towards the door handle.

'You lead, Tomski. You've earned it.'

But he shook his head. 'You do it. I'll sit back. I'll get more out of it by watching you.'

She nodded. 'Follow my lead.'

She opened the door.

When Ethan had loudly proclaimed his intention to bring in his own lawyer, Kat had wondered whether that would turn out to be her frequent sparring partner, Beth Sharpe. Thought by both cops and robbers to be Middlehampton's finest criminal defence solicitor, she and Kat had gone toe to toe many times.

But the lawyer sitting beside Ethan was a man in his forties, with greying hair cut in a fashionable style that reminded her of the lead actors in old movies. Ruler-straight parting, and close-cut at the side and nape of the neck. He'd given her his card on arriving in MCU. In elegant embossed black type that felt like tiny beads of coagulated blood, it informed the bearer that Edgar Wade was a partner with offices in London, Paris, Berlin, Washington and Tokyo.

All in all, quite the statement.

And with an hourly rate to match, she assumed.

Ethan had to be worried to hire someone with that kind of pedigree.

Once the pleasantries were out of the way, and Wade had opened a leather-bound folio, uncapped a fountain pen that looked as though it cost a beat cop's monthly wage, and regarded her with an expectant stare, Kat began.

'Why did you do it, Ethan?' she asked softly.

'I didn't,' he said.

He was making a great effort to maintain a calm facade, but the cracks were already starting to show. Beads of perspiration had broken out along his hairline and his lower lip kept twitching.

'You're denying that you murdered Rosie Duggan?'

'Of course I'm denying it! It isn't true!'

'You didn't entice or coerce her to the top of Five Cups Lane car park and then push or throw her off?'

'No!'

'You work out these days. I can see that. You're a lot stronger than you used to be.'

'Do you have a question for my client, DS Ballantyne?' Wade asked, in an emollient tone, as if concerned she might have forgotten how interviews were supposed to work.

'How much can you lift on one of those machines at the gym, Ethan?'

He frowned. 'I don't know, it varies by machine.'

'Give me an example.'

'Is this relevant?' the lawyer interrupted.

Kat ignored him. 'Ethan?'

'On a chest press, forty kilos on a good day.'

'You give the bars or whatever, the handles, a good hard shove and send forty kilos up and down, what, ten times.'

He shook his head. 'I do two sets of twelve. And a chest press is in and out, not up and down.'

'Wow. Impressive. So, twenty-four times forty is . . .' She turned to Tom. 'What's that add up to, DC Gray?'

'Nine hundred and sixty kilos.'

Kat widened her eyes. 'Nearly a tonne is really impressive. You'd have no problem pushing a girl weighing just fifty-five kilos off a car park roof, then?'

The nod had already started before he fully processed what she'd just said.

'No! I mean, that's not how it works. Anyway, I just told you I didn't kill her.'

'But you wanted to.'

'No.'

'She humiliated you, Ethan. I've watched the video. According to the latest figures, so have six hundred and eighty-seven thousand people worldwide. The caption says "Incel 'vulture journalist' owned by savage girl".'

'I already told you, it meant nothing but extra subscribers for my podcast. I was actually grateful to her.' He smirked. 'And "incel"? Hardly. I told you, I'm having plenty of sex with my girlfriend.'

Trying extremely hard not to let her mind paint a picture of *that* particular scenario, Kat picked another sheet up from the sheaf in front of her. Regarded it for a moment or two. Returned her gaze to Ethan.

'How's your mental health, Ethan?'

He pulled his head back. 'My . . .?'

'Your mental health. How is it? It's OK not to be OK, you know?'

'It's fine,' he said, shortly.

'Are you on any prescription medication, Ethan?'

'What is that,' he said angrily, pointing at the sheet of paper she was holding. 'Are those my medical records? You have no right to have them!'

'Yes they are, and yes I do. Are you on any prescription medication, Ethan?'

He crossed muscular arms over his chest. 'Obviously, you know I am.'

'What kind?'

'Anti-anxiety medication. And statins.'

'Bit young for statins, aren't you?'

'It's precautionary, after Mum's heart attack, I thought . . . wait! Why are you even asking me about statins? That's completely irrelevant.'

'Sorry, Ethan, you're absolutely right. Statins *are* irrelevant to the murder of Rosie Duggan. Which anti-anxiety medication?'

'Xanax. As you obviously already know.'

'Xanax. What dosage?'

'I take nought-point-two milligrams three times a day.'

'What's the active ingredient in Xanax, Ethan, do you know?'

'Benzodiazepine, why?'

'Do you take your tablets religiously? Ever miss a dose?'

He shrugged. 'Sometimes you miss one. Sometimes if I'm feeling better than usual I might choose not to.'

'I see. So you might end up with a few left over at the end of the month?'

'Yes, but you just keep taking them. That's the idea.'

'Rosie Duggan had a high concentration of benzodiazepines in her bloodstream, Ethan. Did you give her some of your Xanax tablets before you walked her up to the car park roof?'

He opened his mouth, then clopped it closed again. He might be on the back foot but he'd still spotted her trap, a variant on the old 'have you stopped beating your wife?' gambit.

'No comment.'

'I see. So just to confirm, your story is, you didn't want to kill Rosie, you weren't with her the night she was murdered, you didn't drug her with your prescription Xanax, you didn't walk her up to the top of Five Cups Lane car park and you didn't push her off. Is that about it?'

'That's completely it – and, by the way? It's not my "story", it's the truth.'

Kat looked sideways at Tom. Their usual signal. He leaned forwards, she leaned back.

'I've been looking through your search history, Ethan,' Tom said conversationally, tapping a sheet of paper in the folder he'd just opened. Ethan's eyes flicked down to the printout and back up to meet Tom's frank stare. 'Interesting stuff. Can you explain what you were doing when you typed in the following phrases? "Height to guarantee death from falling on to concrete. Is pushing off tall building always murder? Is rigor mortis affected by high-speed impact? Date-rape drugs not Rohypnol. Defences against murder charges ranked by number of acquittals. Fast-acting hypnosis techniques. Is phone-cam footage admissible in court if no consent given at time of filming?"'

Ethan smiled. Which was odd. Kat would have expected something akin to guilt or shame. That's how a normal person would react, surely?

'You're barking up the wrong tree, Tom. That's just research for a book I'm writing. Not true crime, by the way. It's a novel. I've already had expressions of interest from several publishers.'

'A novel. What's it about?'

'Well, it's about—' Ethan began eagerly, then a sly look stole over his face. 'Trying to get me to reveal the plot so you can steal it? Not going to happen.'

'I'm really not, Ethan. Let me guess. It's about a true crime podcaster who bumps up his falling ratings by committing murder and then investigating it himself.'

Ethan shook his head. Smiled again. 'Nice try.'

Kat's pulse was comfortable, but a flicker of excitement still ignited in her as she prepared to land the killer blow. She closed her folder, looked first at the solicitor, then Ethan, and smiled.

'That's just about it, then.' She turned to Tom. 'Do you have any more questions for the suspect, DC Gray?'

'Nothing from me, Skip.'

Kat nodded. Turned to face Ethan again across the scarred and scratched table.

'Well, then. We're done. Oh, apart from one last question. Ethan, can you explain to us how your DNA, your semen, to be specific, ended up on Rosie Duggan's dead body?'

The air inside interview room 1 thickened. Silence descended like a heavy blanket. Kat became aware of everyone's breathing, including her own.

Ethan's eyes performed a funny little dance, jittering in their sockets, the lids narrowing as if he was about to fall asleep, then widening until the whites were visible above as well as below the irises. His mouth opened slowly. That koi carp again. Then it closed. The droplets of sweat on his forehead coalesced into a larger bead. As she watched, it trickled with agonising slowness into his right eyebrow, in which she saw a few flakes of dry skin trapped among the coarse dark-brown hairs.

He swallowed, noisily. 'You can't have my DNA. It's impossible. Kat, you have to believe me. You *know* me!' He looked to his left. Towards his solicitor. His panic was clear.

'I think I'd like a few moments in private with my client,' Wade said levelly.

'I'm sure you would,' Kat said. 'Interview suspended.'

Chapter Forty-Six

Tom reopened the interview ten minutes later.

'Ethan, before we broke so you could talk to your lawyer, DS Ballantyne asked you how your semen got on to the body of the murder victim, Rosie Duggan. Could you answer now, please?'

Ethan glanced at Wade, then addressed Tom. He frowned as he spoke, as if an amateur actor had been given a complicated script and insufficient rehearsal time. In truth, the script was a simple one.

'I am unable to explain the presence of my DNA on Rosie Duggan.'

'I think you're going to have to do better than that, Ethan,' Tom said calmly. 'Juries love DNA. I would have thought you of all people would know that.'

'I am unable to explain the presence of my DNA on Rosie Duggan.'

Kat stayed quiet, leaning back in her chair. So that was how they were going to play it. Wade would have advised Ethan that with DNA evidence on their side, there was nothing Ethan could say that would persuade them to release him under investigation, let alone without charge. His best bet was to leave it there and put the onus on the police to prove his guilt.

Tom shrugged. 'Have it your way, Ethan. But we can place you not just near the crime scene at the time of the murder, but literally right in it. We've even got dashcam video showing you climbing up on to the canopy to masturbate over that poor girl's broken body.'

'I am unable . . .' Ethan frowned. Then he shook his head violently. 'No. No! This is bullshit! It wasn't me, OK? It *can't* have been me because I wasn't there.'

'Where were you, then?' Tom asked. 'Did you send your semen to the crime scene on a drone?'

'I was with my girlfriend, OK? She came round to mine and we were in bed. Having sex,' he added, shooting Kat a triumphant grin as if to say, *There! I told you she was into me. Even if you never were. I got a better girlfriend.*

Beside him, Wade did a decent job of keeping his features impassive. But his lips tightened, just a fraction. Enough for Kat to notice. He wasn't pleased with his client. In fact it looked very much as though he'd just been blindsided.

'Why have you only told us this now, Ethan? You've had ample opportunities to provide an alibi before today. Even before we suspended the interview.'

'Given I was innocent, I saw no need to drag her into this. Plus, I've been in shock since your stormtroopers invaded my house and violently arrested me.'

'Body-worn camera footage will clearly show that, despite repeated attempts to get you to come to the door, you made no effort to answer. All force used was reasonable and proportionate to the circumstances,' Kat said. She faced Wade. 'I'd be very happy to share copies of all footage taken, unedited and untreated.'

He nodded. 'Thank you. We'd like to see that.'

A stock response. She could tell he knew it would be a waste of his time and his client's money.

Back to Ethan.

'You were in shock?'

'Yes.'

'But your shock lifted when I presented you with incontrovertible evidence that you murdered Rosie Duggan, is that it?'

There! She saw it. The defiant spark in his eyes flickered and went out.

In a flat voice, shorn of the previous emotion, he muttered, 'On the advice of my legal representative I decline to answer that question.'

Kat didn't bother cajoling him. She'd had enough. She'd had *more* than enough.

Ethan would remain in custody until trial.

It was over.

Chapter Forty-Seven

With Ethan back in a cell, Kat set Tom to work compiling the reports and paperwork the Crown Prosecution Service would require to proceed with charges.

'I'm going to see Ada. The alibi's bullshit, but I still need to confirm it with her.'

He nodded. 'That reminds me. I found Lloyd Kenney on CCTV on the night of the murder. A council camera picked him up in Lichfield at 9.15 p.m. heading towards the barracks and again at 2.17 a.m. heading away. Another loose end snipped off.'

As she drove towards the university, Kat felt the tension of the last week leaving her. She'd be able to debunk Ethan's alibi and then, with the last piece of the puzzle in place, let Carve-up, and then Ma-Linda, know that she'd closed the case.

She found Ada in her office. She looked up when Kat knocked and entered.

'Oh. Hello, Kat. Actually, can I call you that or are you here on official business?' She looked stricken. 'Of *course* you're here on official business. It's about poor Rosie, isn't it?'

Kat sat down and leaned forwards across the desk. She pinned Ada with a frank gaze.

'Ada, I'm afraid I have some news you may find shocking and upsetting. Ethan was arrested this morning for the murder of Rosie Duggan.'

Eyes wide, Ada slumped back in her chair. Kat steeled herself for an outburst. It wouldn't be the first time she'd suffered an onslaught of invective by a woman convinced of her murderous boyfriend's innocence. Wouldn't be the last, either. But when Ada spoke, she shook Kat's faith in her own predictive powers.

'Oh, thank God!'

Kat frowned. Why *thank God*? Not wanting to deviate from her planned exchange, she ploughed on.

'He has denied the charge and alleges he was with you at the time of her murder. Now, we have DNA evidence that places Ethan at the scene, but as a formality, I need to ask you, where were you on the night of Monday last?'

'I had some essays to mark so I worked here in my office until about 9.30 p.m., then I went back to my place and went to bed.'

'Alone?'

'Yes. I didn't see Ethan the whole night.'

Hearing the final tumbler lock into place on Ethan's murder conviction, Kat doubled down, just to be sure.

'So, to be entirely clear, at no point in the evening or night were you with Ethan Metcalfe, having sex at his place?'

Ada's head twitched to the left and she emitted a strangulated groan. Her arms wrapped around her chest seemingly of their own volition.

'Ada, are you all right?' Kat asked.

'I'm . . . I'm fine. But I have to tell you, our relationship is celibate. I had childhood trauma. I was an only child, and my stepfather . . .' She bit her lip and turned away before speaking again, in a low voice just above a whisper. 'Because of what he did to me, I can't bear to be touched intimately. So, to answer your question, no, we weren't having sex. On Monday night or any other time.'

Kat looked down at her notebook. Time to satisfy her curiosity.

'Ada, just now, when I told you we'd arrested Ethan, you said, "Oh, thank God." Can you tell me why?'

Ada looked out of the window, apparently unable to meet Kat's gaze even as she began speaking.

'At first, it was lovely. He was kind, considerate. He bought me flowers for no reason. He was respectful of my, you know, condition. Never pushed me to go to physical places I wasn't comfortable with. But lately, he's become really controlling. Telling me what to wear, what to say. Even how to run my lectures. And then' – she drew in a shuddering breath – 'I got a job offer from a US university. It's on the tenure track. That means I get job security after five years, guaranteed. But Ethan didn't want me to go.' She laughed brokenly. 'Ha! That's a joke. He *forbade* me to go.'

Ada had stopped calling Ethan 'Eeth', painting him as a man exerting coercive control.

Part of Kat wanted to believe what she was hearing. After all, she'd arrested Ethan herself just that morning, so clearly he was someone with a dark side. But part of her – possibly the same part that had never once smelled psychopath on Ethan's person – doubted Ada's sincerity. Kat thought any woman who Ethan tried to control would probably just slap him and leave. Was Ada trying to put distance between her and Ethan? Presumably being the girlfriend of a murderer would hamper one's chances of getting tenure at a US university, to say nothing of a green card.

But what was even more interesting, and relevant to her case, was that Ada had flat out denied that Ethan had been with her on the night of Rosie's murder.

Carve-up's smug, cocky phrase echoed between her ears. And for once she didn't find it repulsive. *Slam dunk.*

'I'm sorry to hear that,' Kat said. 'But Ethan's in custody, and with the evidence we have on him, I can promise you he won't be coming out this side of a trial. And I doubt he will after, either.'

Five minutes later, convinced that even the most liberal jury would bring back a guilty verdict after the shortest spell they felt was respectable, Kat was blipping the fob on her car when her phone rang. It was Clare Capstick.

'The students are holding a candlelit vigil for Rosie tonight,' Clare said. 'I thought you might want to come?'

'Thanks, Clare. I would. What time's the vigil?'

'It's at 10.00 p.m. Down by the lake. It was Rosie's favourite spot on campus apparently.'

'Will you be there?'

'I wasn't planning to attend. I didn't have Rosie for any classes. But if you're going . . .?'

'I think I will. Just to pay my respects. I'll bring Tom, too.'

'Oh.' Kat could hear Clare's mental cogs whirring. It wasn't difficult. They were as loud as factory machinery. 'Well, I might see you there.'

Kat paused before answering. Should she try to help things along a bit? It couldn't hurt.

'Clare, I hope I'm not speaking out of turn. But, if you're wondering about Tom, I'm pretty sure he likes you.'

'Do you think?' Clare sounded eager, but anxious, too.

'I've worked with him for nearly three years, I know his tells.'

'OK,' Clare said with a smile in her voice. Again. 'OK.'

Chapter Forty-Eight

The full moon cast a melancholy silver-white light over the campus. A light breeze had sprung up, ruffling the surface of the lake, so the water shivered the moon into silver splinters.

Kat met the Duggans, who were accompanied by their FLO and a female PCSO – a police community support officer – but made sure their meeting was brief, feeling that three cops to two bereaved parents was the wrong balance.

Several hundred students had gathered down by the shore, holding tealights in bowls, glass jars, cut-down drinks cans, whatever they could find. Many held candles pushed through cardboard circles. Some were singing, others weeping. Girls in particular were taking it hard, clustered in small groups, hugging, crying, or staring out at the water, where more tealights floated on little wooden rafts.

Kat found Tom standing with Clare Capstick. While Clare asked Tom about his work, careful not to stray into details on the case they'd just closed, Kat looked around at the young people who'd come out to pay their respects or show solidarity. Despite all the depressing news stories about toxic masculinity, there were plenty of boys here, too. Maybe there was hope.

Then her eye snagged on one boy in particular. Greg Fanning. He was standing with a group of young men, all dressed in black. Together like this, they resembled some sort of paramilitary outfit, or even a cult. She told herself off. Greg wasn't guilty, and lots of male students favoured the all-black look. It meant nothing.

Another male joined the group. At first she didn't recognise him because he wore a hoodie. But when he turned, Kat started. Lloyd Kenney had made the trip down to Middlehampton. Was that really so surprising, though? After all, Rosie had been his girlfriend. Yes, he'd posted revenge porn, and she couldn't simply forget that, but grief did strange things to people and it would take a better psychologist than her to interpret his behaviour.

She decided to ask Clare about it. But when she turned, Clare and Tom weren't there. A lit-up food truck was doing brisk business a few hundred yards away, on a patch of tarmac. Maybe they'd decided to test the water with a casual coffee date. She smiled. Good for them.

She moved through the crowd, no destination in mind, just her copper's instincts kicking in, wanting to know who had come out to say their goodbyes to Rosie Duggan.

A group of eight or nine young women were huddled together around an improvised shrine. Framed photos of Rosie, flowers, candles in jars. Their crying was audible from several yards away. Among them, Libby was standing transfixed by the shrine, a glass of red wine in her hand. Her face was streaked with tears, lit like snail trails by the moon. One of the others turned to comfort her. It was Ada.

Kat went over to say hello.

Ada smiled sadly. 'Even though it's over, I feel so empty. Losing Rosie and now freed of Ethan. It's like my emotions don't know what to do.'

'This is probably a good idea, then,' Kat said, moving a hand around in a semicircle to encompass the still-growing crowd. 'Let it out. Don't worry about how you're supposed to feel.'

Ada smiled. 'Thanks, Kat. That's actually quite helpful.'

Kat left her with Libby and walked around the fringes of the crowd. Not looking for anything in particular, but unable to stop. Why, though? She headed for a quiet spot at the top of the slope. Why did she feel so restless? They had Ethan in custody, his alibi shot to pieces, DNA placing him at the scene. He had means, motive and opportunity. Then it came to her.

It was his reaction in the interview when they'd told him about the DNA.

His agonised plea floated back to her. *Kat, you have to believe me. You* know *me!*

In his eyes and the agonised expression on his face, she'd seen shock, confusion, disbelief. And damn him, it had seemed genuine.

Could he be innocent? Were her instincts right about him after all? Despite the confidence-shaking evidence from the DNA report, and his lack of an alibi? Although why *would* a true-crime podcaster leave his DNA at the scene? Surely he'd know better? She shook her head. If he was a psychopath then he'd see himself as invincible. He'd just assume he could get away with it because he *wanted* to.

She drew a two-column table in her head. Labelled them *Guilty* and *Innocent*. As she filled it in, some of the anxiety she was experiencing left her. Thinking of it this way – cold, hard, factual – the picture of who Ethan was became clear.

Guilty	Innocent
DNA at crime scene	Shocked facial expression
Motive	Plea to be believed
No alibi	My (admittedly) wonky instincts
Known stalker	Remote possibility someone 'acquired' some of his semen.
Access to benzodiazepines	
Physically strong enough	

The list vanished. Molly Steadman had always been insistent. *When you've a choice between hard evidence and your gut, always trust the evidence, Kat. It's not sexy. It's not the stuff movies are made of. But it is what gets convictions.* Ma-Linda was much the same. *Follow the evidence.* Even Jack Beale's predecessor Dr Feldman had liked to say, in his speech to rookie detectives attending a post-mortem, *This is a scientific space. When you enter, you leave your hunches, gut feelings and 'copper's intuition' at the door.*

Kat yielded to the collective wisdom of her mentor, boss and the former pathologist. Unless someone provided incontrovertible proof that Ethan couldn't have killed Rosie Duggan, she'd see him charged for her murder and, on the DNA evidence alone, almost certainly sent down for life.

Sighing, she glanced down the slope. The group of black-clad male students had thinned a little. Greg Fanning had left them. She looked around, trying to spot Lloyd, but he'd gone, too.

She set off to track down Tom and Clare. She wanted to ask Clare to help her develop an interview strategy to get a confession out of Ethan. It would save money, but more importantly, it would offer some shred of comfort to the Duggan family not to have to go through the hell of a murder trial at which the accused pleaded not guilty.

A scream shattered the atmosphere of quiet grieving.

It came from behind her.

The screaming redoubled in volume. It was joined by others.

Kat whirled and started to run towards the sound. It had come from the direction of a student accommodation block.

Chapter Forty-Nine

Kat sprinted up the hill, mind whirling. What the hell had happened? A sexual assault? With many vulnerable young women present, and plenty of dark corners despite the full moon, it had to be a consideration.

A small crowd had already formed at the foot of the block. Kat recognised it. Halliwell House, where she and Tom had interviewed Greg Fanning the previous week.

'Police! Let me through,' she shouted.

At the centre of the crowd, which had formed into a ring as if watching a fight, lay a body. Male, she saw that at once. Lying face up, arms and legs horribly twisted: clearly broken.

She turned and yelled angrily. 'Put your phones away!'

Tom arrived, breathless, at her side. Beside him, Clare Capstick, who looked horrified as she stared down at the face of the dead boy.

'Oh my God! That's George Seaton-Clark. He's on my psychology course.'

'Thanks, Clare, but I'm going to need you to step back now, please.'

Kat placed two fingers on the pulse point beneath the dead boy's jaw. Not expecting a pulse. Or finding one. He was dead. A thin stream of blood issued from his nose.

A second dead student – apparently dead from a fall – in a week? No way would anyone convince her this was a coincidence.

'Tomski, get Forensics up here. Unis, too. And the pathologist and coroner's officer.'

The PCSO who'd been with the Duggans ran up. She glanced at the body, then at Kat.

'How can I help, Ma'am?'

'What's your name?'

'Sofia, Ma'am. Belfelice.'

'Right, Sofia. One, get the students back ten paces, please. Two, keep an eye out for anyone acting strangely, like unemotional or watchful or even smiling. Three, I haven't seen you before. You're new, right?'

'Qualified last week, Ma'am.'

'Well done. And thanks for being here so quickly. Anyway, as we'll be working together in the future: three, please don't call me "Ma'am". Makes me feel old. It's Kat or Skip.'

'Yes, Skip.' Sofia nodded briskly and turned away, hands out in front of her as she approached the crowding students. 'Listen up, please! I need everybody to take ten big paces backwards. Count with me, please, and step back. One, two, three . . .'

Collective shock had kicked in, and as a single organism, the students began stepping outwards from the crime scene before Sofia's steady advance.

Two men in black uniforms with white 'SECURITY' patches on their chests and shoulders emerged from the innermost ring of students. They looked at the body and one, younger than the other, turned away. The older man came over to Kat.

'University security. What do you need us to do?'

'Thanks. Can you help my colleague there keep everybody back, and if possible not taking bloody photos or videos. I don't want this on social media before we've had a chance to inform next of kin.'

'We'll do our best, won't we, Aziz?' he called to the younger guy who was standing a few yards away looking lost. He wasn't that much older than the students.

Kat approached a group of girls closest to where the body lay. 'Did anyone see what happened?'

A girl with blonde hair in two plaits pointed up to the roof of the building. 'He came from there. I saw him fall. I was taking a picture of the moon and I just saw him.'

'OK, thanks, lovely.'

Kat went back to Tom. 'Stay here, wait for the cavalry. And keep an eye on the crowd. I want to know if you get a negative vibe off anyone.'

'On it.'

Kat nodded and ran for the entrance, praying the lifts were working. And wondering, again, whether she'd arrested the right man for Rosie Duggan's murder. The drumbeat of DNA was still loud in her eardrums, but it was overlaid by a shrill chorus from her inner voice: *what if . . . what if . . . what if . . .*

It was windy up on the roof.

Long, thin clouds like fingers slid in front of the moon as if caressing it. The light level dipped each time. She switched her phone torch on and walked towards the edge where the boy – what had Clare called him, George? – where George had fallen to his death. Except he hadn't fallen, had he? Someone had pushed George Seaton-Clark. Murdered him. Just like Rosie Duggan.

She crouched down. Shone her torch on to the gritty bitumen. The greyish surface was immaculate elsewhere, but riven with black scuffs pointing in all directions for a good four or five feet out from the edge. Unlike Five Cups Lane car park, there was nothing here to slow the victim's progress. Unless Kat counted the six-inch lip at the very edge. She did not.

She stepped back, not enjoying the tingling sensation behind her knees. The CSIs would need to get up here and take photos, but it was clear to her what had happened. The murderer had found a way, probably, if her hunch was correct, using a combination of alcohol and benzodiazepines, to get George up to the roof. There they'd led him to the edge, where, after a brief violent struggle, they'd pushed him off.

Had they framed it as a dare? A place to get a great video of the vigil for social media? For sex? She wouldn't know until she had them in custody. And right now, it didn't matter.

She returned to the warmth of the inside of the building. She thumbed the lift's call button. The doors slid apart with a hiss. Kat stepped inside. Two murders a week apart with the same MO. The same basic victim type, if you called them young students at Middlehampton University. Now what did that sound like? The lift juddered, making her stomach flip. It shook loose a thought. Was it two? Or was it three?

After Ethan had raised the idea of a serial killer at the press conference, Kat had looked up the details of Rebecca Poole's death, which had occurred exactly one year before Rosie Duggan's murder. The coroner had recorded the Middlehampton student's death as suicide. But what if he was wrong? If Rebecca *had* been murdered, then they had a pattern and three victims conforming to it. Rebecca Poole, Rosie Duggan and George Seaton-Clark. Two females and a male. It didn't necessarily rule out a serial killer. Especially not given the similarities in the other factors of their deaths.

But there was one glaring hole in this embryonic theory. And she was still pondering it when the lift doors opened on the ground floor of Halliwell House.

They had Rosie Duggan's murderer in custody.

Even if Ethan had also murdered Rebecca Poole, there was no way he could have murdered George Seaton-Clark. Not by himself, at least. Could he have he teamed up with an accomplice? Or had he been framed? If so, then by whom and why?

Whoever it was, they must have a grievance against Ethan to want to frame him, specifically. Mind you, that could be a long list, and it included her.

Tom came up to her. 'I've got next of kin.'

Chapter Fifty

Kat drove up the rutted track to the farmhouse where the Seaton-Clarks lived. It was just outside Gerrards Cross, a chi-chi Buckinghamshire town filled with independent restaurants, upscale boutiques, and houses that seemed to have other houses built in their driveways. Even the cars lived well here.

As she and Tom climbed out of the car, the smell of manure hit her. A loud moo from a nearby barn completed the picture for her. Cattle farmers.

The moon was unobscured by clouds, and in the silvery light the puddles of slime and liquid cow shit looked like molten metal. She walked up to the front door with a heavy heart.

'Let me take this one, Tomski,' she said, ringing the doorbell.

Kat inhaled and let it out again in a slow breath designed to calm her nerves. It didn't work. It never worked.

She readied her warrant card. Saw Tom doing the same. No sound came from the other side of the door. But they were farmers. Probably went to bed early. Should she ring again?

She stretched out a finger, then pulled it back. Frowned. Her stomach churned. She pushed the button again just as a light came on inside and a voice called out, 'Yes, yes! I'm coming.'

The door swung inwards. This must be George's father. Kat confirmed his identity with a quick question.

'John Seaton-Clark?'

'That's me. Who are you? What's this about? Bit late for Defra, isn't it?'

Department for Environment, Food and Rural Affairs. A reasonable conclusion for a farmer to draw. Just wrong in this case. He went for a quizzical smile, but she could see it already, hiding just out of sight behind his dark, tired eyes. Anxiety. Every parent had felt it, to a greater or lesser degree. It was your first thought. *Something's happened to the children.*

'I'm Detective Sergeant Kathryn Ballantyne. This is Detective Constable Tom Gray,' she said, holding up her warrant card. 'May we come in?'

He led them into a kitchen. A black and white border collie, just like Duffel at Liv's farm, raised itself from its basket and came over, sniffing first Kat, then Tom, before retreating to its bed with a soft whine at a command from its master.

'I'll ask you again. What's this all about? Is George in trouble?'

'Mr Seaton-Clark, I'm afraid we have some bad news. Is your wife here, too?'

'What bad news?'

Kat turned. A woman had come in and rounded her chair to stand behind her husband, her hand resting lightly on his shoulder. She wore a man's dressing gown. The old-fashioned kind made of soft checked fabric, held closed by a twisted silky rope.

'It's about George, Jenny,' John Seaton-Clark said quietly.

'Perhaps you'd both better sit down,' Kat said.

They sat, two parents who were bereaved without knowing it.

Kat took in a wealth of little domestic details as she readied herself. The brown ceramic teapot, big enough to serve at least eight people. The scores and dents in the much-waxed wooden tabletop. A family photo on the wall: the two older Seaton-Clarks with their arms around George and a girl of roughly the same age. A sister? A girlfriend?

And then she uttered the words she had said too many times before. She used the same basic formula as always. Not to lessen her sadness, or the tsunami of emotion that was about to engulf her and Tom, but simply to get it out.

'At 11.03 p.m. tonight, a young man died after falling from a building at Middlehampton University. We believe he was your son, George Seaton-Clark. And we suspect he was murdered. I am so very sorry for your loss.'

Ten seconds ticked by, which Kat measured out on the large station clock mounted above a huge fireplace at the far end of the kitchen. The dog scrabbled to its feet and whined piteously. She didn't blame it. The aura of onrushing grief was palpable.

Mrs Seaton-Clark stood suddenly, tipping over her chair, which clattered on the flagstone floor. She reached forwards and grabbed the teapot, raised it above her head and hurled it to the ground where it shattered with a loud crash. The dog emitted a piercing bark and ran towards the mess of pottery shards strewn across the floor.

'Stay, Gem!' John Seaton-Clark shouted.

Jenny Seaton-Clark looked wildly at Kat. 'No! You can't say that. I won't . . . You're lying, you bitch! Lying! Why would you say that? Why would you invade our home in the middle of the night with such a filthy lie? George isn't dead. He's alive. Of course he is! He's at university. He hasn't been murdered. Oh, you—'

She spun round and slapped her husband across the left cheek. The flat smack of skin against skin was shocking in its violence. He looked stunned as he raised a hand to cup his face.

'Tell her, John. Tell her to leave!'

John Seaton-Clark looked stunned. His left cheek bore a cherry-red imprint of his wife's hand, but aside from that his face was waxy.

'Is it true?' he asked as Jenny subsided into a chair, moaning low in her chest.

'I'm afraid it is. And I know you are in shock right now, but I do need to ask you some questions about George.'

'Yes, yes, of course. Whatever you need.'

'Are you aware of anybody who might have wanted to harm George?'

'No. Nobody. George loved university. He was a popular lad. Always has been.'

'Georgie is a perfect child. Why would anyone want to hurt him?' Jenny Seaton-Clark interjected in a flat voice, her eyes reddened from crying. 'He's just been elected president of the student union. That's how popular he is. George doesn't have *enemies*. Everybody loves him, from his teammates to the people on his course.'

Jenny called George a perfect child, albeit in the present tense. Madeleine Duggan had used the exact same phrase to describe Rosie, hadn't she? Kat had recorded the conversation so it would be easy enough to check.

'What sport does he play?' she asked.

'He's captain of the university rugby team, but you name it, George is good at it,' John said. 'Football, cricket, swimming, tennis. He's just a natural all-rounder.'

'How about his course?'

'Spanish and Psychology. Double-honours. He got a first in his year-end exams last summer.'

Kat made a note. Despite the difference in gender, there was an awful lot linking the two victims. Both popular, academically gifted, sporty. Classic alpha types. Their parents might not be able to see it, but she was starting to discern a new kind of motive. One borne out of resentment at those apparently blessed from birth with an easy path through life. She made another note to have Tom check Rebecca Poole's background.

Kat turned to her bagman. Tom looked about as uncomfortable as it was possible to be. He'd not experienced this kind of reaction yet.

'Come on, Tom,' she said. 'Let's go.'

She got to her feet. 'We'll come back to see you. In the meantime I'll make arrangements for a family liaison officer to be appointed for you. We will also need you to come to Middlehampton to formally identify George. But that can all wait until the morning. Once again, we are both very sorry for your loss.'

Leaving the Seaton-Clarks locked in the desperate embrace of shipwreck survivors, Kat led Tom outside and back to the car.

'I feel sick, Kat,' he said.

'Open your door and just breathe, Tomski. It'll pass.'

And the awful truth was, it would. Quickly. By the time they got back to Jubilee Place, he'd be feeling fine. Treating the murder of George Seaton-Clark as the third in a series of 'multiple linked homicides', as the College of Policing's guidelines had it.

As she drove back down the farm track, Kat glanced in the rear-view mirror, at the lighted kitchen window of the farmhouse.

Where the horror of George Seaton-Clark's murder would never pass.

Chapter Fifty-One

The next morning, Kat asked Tom to work up a profile on Rebecca Poole. When he came back to her, she skimmed his findings, which he'd helpfully summarised on the first page of his report.

As she read, she felt certainty growing steadily in her mind.

This was the pattern, she was sure of it.

Rebecca Poole had been eighteen when she died. A model student. One of her lecturers had even gone so far as to opine in a report that she was destined for a first, unless 'you wilfully decide to avoid one'. She had many friends and, according to them, no enemies. Not one. Her school career had been equally starry, including a year as highest goal-scorer for the girls' football team, and as captain of the debating team. Her father had described her as: *One of a kind. Nothing came hard to Becky, but she never boasted about it. She was as modest as she was talented.*

And, as Kat had already ascertained, Rebecca had not been suffering from – had, in fact, *never* suffered from – any kind of mental illness or distress. What on earth had the police and the coroner been doing at the time, recording her death as suicide? She flicked through the rest of Tom's report, looking for the name of the lead investigator on the case. That had been a DC Jane Roberts. But on a separate line, Tom had recorded the name of the SIO: *DI S. Carver.*

Of *course* it would be Carve-up. Anger boiled up behind her sternum like the worst-ever case of reflux. She looked over at his office door, which was closed as usual. Imagined how satisfying it would be to push Carver off a tall building.

She forced herself back to Tom's report. And an inescapable conclusion.

Someone – not Ethan, who annoyingly had an iron-clad alibi for this latest death – had murdered two other Middlehampton University students by pushing them off tall structures. Respectively, Brearley Woods railway bridge, and Halliwell House at the university itself.

The victims all embodied a particular sort of personality. Outgoing, popular, bright, high-achieving in everything they tried, from sport to student politics.

Rosie had had enemies. No doubt Rebecca Poole had, too. Kat had no doubt that, as they looked into George Seaton-Clark, they'd discover he wasn't universally liked and admired, either.

But the thought underlying all of this analysis was chilling.

She was hunting for the second serial killer of her career. And back it came, roaring into her conscious mind: the one inescapable factor that complicated matters even further.

Ethan was guilty of murder number two, but one hundred per cent guaranteed, slam-dunk-innocent of murder number three.

Tom tapped her on the shoulder. 'Kat, you're going to want to see this.'

She turned to see Tom handing her a coffee. 'Thanks, Tomski. But I've seen a mug of station coffee before.'

He pulled up a chair and sat beside her, holding out a sheet of paper. 'Look at this. It's the results of the election for student union president.'

She read the brief report, taken, apparently, from the website of the student newspaper, *Sargasso*.

After a single count (because why would more than one be needed?) George Seaton-Clark was elected President of the Student Union last night. 'Landslide' would just about cover the margin of victory . . . if you were ready to accept 'quite good predator' as an adequate description of a great white shark. Or a lion. Or possibly a great white shark crossed with a lion. And a Komodo dragon.

Those election results in full.

George Seaton-Clark: 13,891

Greg Fanning: 178 (who knew Greg had that many friends?)

Kat looked at Tom, wondering whether Greg and Ethan could have been working together. She'd considered earlier whether Ethan had an accomplice, but dismissed that idea in favour of his being framed. Had she been right to think there might be someone else involved?

'Because his pride's wounded, Greg murders George? Does that sound feasible?'

'Eminently.'

'I need to update Linda. She's going to have kittens when I tell her we're looking at multiple linked homicides.'

'You're sure it's a serial?'

'Three dead students, pushed' – she held up a hand – 'OK, *fallen* from a height. All so-called perfect kids. Two on the same date, a year apart.'

Tom pulled his lips to one side. 'The third on a different date. While the second's murderer was locked in a cell. I'm not trying to contradict you, but are you sure? I know there are similarities, but the dates could be a coincidence.'

Kat shook her head. 'I don't believe in coincidences, Tomski.'

When Kat outlined her theory to Linda – that Ethan and Greg Fanning were possibly working together as serial killers of high-achieving students – she discovered she was in a minority.

'Is Rebecca Poole's case open?'

'No. But—'

'Do we have any evidence to suggest she was murdered?'

'No. But Ma-Linda—'

Linda was in no mood to yield. 'What was the coroner's verdict?'

'Suicide.'

'Not open.'

'No.'

'You've got that toe-rag Ethan Metcalfe in custody for Rosie Duggan's murder?'

'Yes.'

Kat could feel her will draining away in the face of Linda's relentless questioning.

'With his spunk all over her corpse?'

'Yes.'

'So he did it?'

Kat hesitated. This was the sticking point. DNA was the gold-standard. She'd used it as a stick to beat Ethan with in the interview. So why didn't she *feel it*, deep down where her copper's instincts lay? Why didn't she *feel* he was guilty?

'That's what the evidence says.'

Linda regarded Kat quizzically.

'Never known you to be mealy-mouthed before, Kat. Especially where Ethan Metcalfe's concerned. I would have thought you'd *want* to see him convicted of murder.'

Kat twisted her mouth up. Unwilling to open it in case her words betrayed her. But under Linda's gaze, she felt powerless.

'I want Rosie's *murderer* convicted. If it was Ethan, then fair enough. But now it looks like George Seaton-Clark and Rebecca Poole were murdered by the same person, in the same way and for the same reason. And Ethan can't have murdered George.'

'I agree. But what am I missing here, Kat? If there *is* a serial killer at work in Middlehampton, which you haven't proved, it's clearly not Metcalfe.'

'So he's an apprentice. Doing the bidding of a more experienced killer.'

'Or a sad little man who couldn't take being insulted by a clever young girl and murdered her in revenge. Was he even in town on May sixth last year?'

Kat cursed herself for not having checked. Talk about a rookie error.

'I don't know.'

'Any trophies taken from any of the three victims? Any signs of rituals surrounding the crime scene?'

'Not obvious ones, no. But the killer might have taken pictures. That's a kind of trophy.'

Even to Kat's own ears, her suggestion was tissue-thin.

Linda puffed out her cheeks and dragged her fingers through her hair.

'Look, Kat, I can see you've spent a lot of time looking at these three deaths. And I'm not trying to force you to accept my conclusion. But from where I'm sitting, what we have is a girl who committed suicide by jumping from a bridge, a girl murdered by being pushed off a car park a year later, and a boy dead after falling from a tower block a week after that. When's the post-mortem?'

'Jack Beale's doing it today.'

'Then we might end up with a suicide, a murder and an accident in a two-year period. No pattern, no linked homicides, just a tragic set of three deaths of young kids in our town. That's a possibility, isn't it?'

'Yes, Ma-Linda,' Kat said dejectedly, feeling like she'd brought a school project home only for her mum to fail to praise it.

Linda smiled. 'Look, Kat. You're a good homicide investigator. No, scratch that. You're a *really* good one. And you're getting better. You're on the SIO track. But if you hear hoofbeats, you look for horses, not zebras. Go to the post-mortem. If Jack thinks it's homicide, then maybe, just maybe, there's a link between these two latest deaths. But I want you to run down all other possibilities before you come back here saying we're looking for a serial, yes?'

Kat nodded and left Linda's private office. As she smiled to Annie Brewster, Linda's PA, on her way out, she resolved to obey Linda to the letter *and* to prove her wrong. This was a series of linked murders. She could *feel* it.

And if they *were* linked, then Ethan Metcalfe, guilty of Rosie's murder or not, was right at the heart of it. That she *was* sure of. In her bones.

She went downstairs and grabbed Tom. Led him to a conference room and wiped down the whiteboard, trying to avoid inhaling too much of the heady smell of the cleaning fluid.

'Let's assume all three victims are a serial killer's,' Kat said, standing position by the board. 'Problem?'

Tom sat straighter in his chair. 'The serial killer can't be Ethan because he was in custody when George was killed.'

'Is it possible Ethan didn't kill Rosie, meaning the real killer was out when George was killed?'

Tom shook his head. 'DNA evidence puts Ethan at the Rosie Duggan crime scene. Literally, with her body. There's no doubt in my mind. He did it.'

'Which means . . .?'

'Ethan killed Rosie and an accomplice killed George.'

'Is it possible Ethan is telling the truth? That he didn't kill Rosie.'

'Only if we assume he was framed by the real killer, which seems like a huge stretch. But either way, George's killer is still at large.'

'So we have three possibilities.'

Kat began writing fast on the whiteboard, trying to keep it all legible as her thoughts ran on ahead of her hand's ability to keep up. When she'd finished there were three numbered theories.

> *1 Ethan = serial killer with 'disciple'. Problem: Why kill George so quickly, not one year later according to ritual?*
>
> *2 Ethan = disciple. Problem: Why would killer 'delegate' a kill in the middle of a sequence?*
>
> *3 Ethan = patsy. Serial killer framed Ethan with his DNA at RD crime scene. Problem: as 2, plus murdering GS-C while Ethan in custody invalidates frame (and why Ethan?)*

Kat stared at the board, trying to decide which theory she preferred. She flung a marker pen across the room in disgust. This was a waste of time after all. Linda, damn her, was right. This was no time for forcing facts to fit theories that might not even be true.

She grabbed the eraser, obliterated her three so-called theories then slapped it down on the desk with a loud crack.

'I'm wrong, Tomski. Completely wrong! This isn't some university philosophy problem; this is real-world policing. I'll tell you what we're going to do. We're going to follow the evidence. We have Ethan's DNA plastered over the bloodied corpse of a murder victim. His girlfriend didn't back up his alibi. But we also have a second killing to investigate. So we investigate, and when we identify George's murderer we'll understand what's going on. And, one way or another, we'll have both students' murderers behind bars. If they're master and disciple, or Bonnie and Clyde or Tom and bloody Jerry, it won't matter, because unlike Ethan Metcalfe, we're not interested in storytelling. We're here to deliver justice.'

Her phone rang. The front desk. She answered fast.

'Yes?'

'Kat it's Polly. I've got a young man here wants to talk to a detective about George Seaton-Clark.'

Surely it wasn't going to be that easy. Kat sent Tom down to collect the young man from reception and went to wait for them in the friendly interview room.

The man who preceded Tom into the room looked to be somewhere between his late teens and very early twenties. He was sweating and kept touching the side of his face.

'This is Dorian Evans,' Tom said.

Kat offered her hand. His was hot, damp with perspiration, and his grip was weak despite him possessing a muscular physique. 'Hello, Dorian, I'm DS Ballantyne. Call me Kat. Would you like a tea, or a coffee?'

'I'm . . . I'm . . . No, thank you.'

'Let's all sit down then, and you can tell us why you're here.'

He rubbed his palms on the tops of his thighs.

'Look, I know how this is going to sound, right, but I'm a mate of George's. The thing is, I had, like, this massive row with him yesterday evening. He injured me in a rugby match last weekend and kept saying it was my fault. I saw him in the student union bar last night and went to have it out with him. Then things sort of got a bit heated and then . . .'

He stared out of the window and rubbed at his eyes. He was crying.

'And then what, Dorian?' Kat prompted.

'I punched him in the face. He retaliated and it turned into this massive ruck, like I said. He basically destroyed me, but what's going to happen because it always does, doesn't it, is that someone's going to share a video from social media and you guys'll see it and arrest me and I didn't do anything wrong, I swear.'

Kat spoke slowly and calmly, lowering her voice in the hope she could encourage the young lad opposite her to do the same.

'What would we see if someone did share the video, Dorian?'

'Me on the ground screaming at him, "I'll kill you!" But that's just, you know, what you say like on the pitch. We're always sledging like that. It puts the other team off their game. It doesn't mean you're literally going to murder someone, does it?'

Kat shook her head, happy to concede that specific point. If it were true, every sports pitch from Middlehampton to Manchester would be littered with corpses every Saturday.

'*Did* you kill him?' she asked.

Not because she expected a confession, although, bizarrely, it sometimes happened, but because how people reacted to the question always revealed something about them.

'No! Of course I didn't! I just told you. But I bet you find my DNA on him and you're going to jump to conclusions, only that's why it's there, not because I killed him.'

She tried to get a sense of the frightened young man in front of her. He'd come in voluntarily, which counted for something. But then, as he'd admitted, it was only to pre-empt someone putting him on her radar. And however you looked at it, making threats to kill always led to police scrutiny.

'We know that George died at 11.03 p.m. last night, Dorian. Where were you then?'

'What?'

Interesting. She'd spoken perfectly clearly. And he'd heard all her previous questions. It was a classic delaying tactic while a perpetrator figured out the least incriminating way they could answer.

'Where were you last night at 11.03 p.m.?'

'At the vigil.'

'Did anybody see you there?'

'Loads.'

'But at 11.03 p.m. specifically. In fact, let's widen it out a little and say between 10.45 and 11.15?'

'I don't know. I had a few beers and lost track of time. I heard people screaming when he, you know, fell, and I went over there to see what the trouble was but there were all these police holding everyone back behind the tape and everything, so I just went back to my flat.'

Kat nodded, made a note.

'How well did you know Rosie Duggan?'

He blinked. 'Rosie?'

'She was murdered last week.'

'I know that,' he snapped. 'You just surprised me. Why are you asking?'

'Were you two friendly?'

'I didn't know her.'

'You're sure? No lectures together?'

'None. Look, what's this all about? You've got the guy in custody. I saw it online.'

'Would you consent to my taking a DNA sample from you, Dorian? If, as you say, we do find your DNA on George's body, this will help corroborate your story.'

'Sure.'

She unwrapped a testing kit, swabbed the inside of his cheek then inserted it into the tube, which she bagged and labelled. 'Tom will see you out.'

Kat waited until they'd left, then hurried back to her desk. Wondering: had Tom spotted the same flaw in Dorian's evidence that she had seen?

Chapter Fifty-Two

'Well?' Kat asked Tom when he returned from showing Dorian out.

'Well what, boss?'

'What did you make of Dorian's account?'

'Seemed plausible enough.'

'How about how he came to be at the crime scene?'

Tom looked up for a second. Back at Kat.

'Again, nothing out of the ordinary.'

'He said he heard the screams and went over, but he turned back when he got to the police manning the cordon.'

'Yeah, and—' Tom frowned. Then he half smiled. 'There *was* no cordon. Just the two university security guys.'

'I don't think he was there at all. I think he just described a scene he's seen on telly without thinking through the timings.'

'So where was he then?'

'I don't know, Tomski. But I'd like you to find out. See if the university has any CCTV covering Halliwell House. The moon was pretty bright. Also social media. I know it's a pain, but someone might have uploaded a clip with Dorian in it. You can probably search "Rosie Duggan vigil".'

'There's an Instagram hashtag, RememberRosie. I'll start with that.'

'Good man. Oh, and check on his account of the fight with George. I bet there's plenty of video online of that, too. Plus, check his academic schedule and any clubs he belongs to. I want to know if he ever crossed paths with Rosie Duggan.'

'On it. What are you going to do?'

'The groves of academe beckon me once more, Tomski.'

He nodded. 'Very poetic.'

◆ ◆ ◆

Despite her speech to Tom about ignoring theories in favour of evidence, Kat couldn't let go of the idea that she was hunting a serial killer. And Clare Capstick was going to help her catch him.

Kat parked and made her way to Clare's office, where the psychology lecturer poured fresh coffee from a cafetière and offered biscuits. Kat accepted the coffee gratefully but refused the biscuits.

'Feeling a bit fat at the moment.'

Clare grunted in acknowledgement.

'Tell me about it. I just bought some new jeans that I know are too small for me. Guess what I said?'

'I'll lose weight to fit into them,' Kat finished for her, smiling.

Preliminaries out of the way, although in other circumstances, Kat would happily have chatted over coffee with Clare until the end of the day, she raised the issue of a profile for the first time.

'I need some help building a profile of a possible serial killer, Clare. But I have a problem, and it's not fair on you to get you interested before I raise it.'

Clare raised an eyebrow. 'Now I'm intrigued. What's the problem?'

'My boss won't authorise any money for outside help. It's just me and Tom on the case at the moment and she doesn't want to entertain my' – air quotes – '*wilder theories.*'

'You know what, Kat. Last time you paid me such a lot more than I was expecting, I felt guilty for weeks. I can work with you on this one and it'll make me feel like I've balanced the scales.'

'Really? Because I know you have a busy schedule.'

'Really.'

'Then, thank you. But the next time we need help, I'm going to come to you with a Hertfordshire Police credit card in my hand. Deal?'

Clare smiled. 'Deal. So, talk to me.'

'Normally I'm all about following the evidence. In fact I just lectured Tom about it.'

'But?'

'But something about these deaths just . . .'

'Calls to you?'

'Yes! Call it hunch or copper's intuition, but it's there, Clare, and I can't ignore it however hard I try.'

'Perhaps you shouldn't then. There's been a lot of research, a lot of articles and books written about intuition and the role it plays in decision-making. It has its fans and its detractors, but as we're not at a psychology conference I think we can just go with it. What do you know about your killer so far?'

Kat wrinkled her nose. 'Actually, that might be a second problem. I'm not sure we even have a single killer.'

'Go on.'

Kat outlined her thinking about how there needed to be two killers working together.

'And you have one of them in custody,' Clare said. 'I saw you arresting Ethan Metcalfe on YouTube.'

Kat fought down the urge to unburden herself to Clare about her doubts regarding Ethan despite the DNA evidence.

As she spoke, Clare wrote notes on a whiteboard, much like the one in Kat's incident room, or the one in her spare bedroom.

Three victims (minimum): meets criterion for serial killer.

Two female, one male.

All three 18 or 19 when they died.

Both female victims killed on May 6.

Female victims attractive but physically different. Male obviously completely different.

All well liked, straight-A students. No criminal records.

All died after falls from tall structures/buildings.

No obvious trophies taken from victims, e.g. hair, body parts, single missing earring, item of clothing (although hard to prove what isn't there).

Evidence of post-mortem sexual assault on Rosie Duggan's body.

Clare sat back down and steepled her fingers under her chin as she stared at the board.

'Serial killers' victims usually represent a figure from their past. There may be a sexual trigger, and this trigger may have arisen as the result of sexual abuse in childhood. The presence of semen on Rosie Duggan's body certainly points in that direction.'

'We've got a male victim, too, though. Although I suppose the second killer could be homosexual.'

'You may be looking at the sexual component too literally, Kat. Serial killers almost always find the act of killing itself sexually arousing. But the obvious lack of physical similarity across all three potential victims means I think we have to discount sexual sadism as the motive here. It feels to me like there's something deeper going on. A more psychological motivation for killing.'

Kat nodded. 'Rosie's and George's mothers both referred to their children as either perfect or in some way too popular to be murdered. Could that be relevant do you think? Are we looking at someone who hates that kind of person?'

Clare flashed Kat a quick smile of acknowledgement.

'Looks like you've got there without me. I feel better about working for no fee. Our three victims are all examples of the classic all-rounder. The killer probably feels inadequate when measured against them. Now, given that serial killers are often, essentially, killing the same person over and over again, we have to ask, who do these victims represent to him? Any thoughts?'

Noticing herself sitting up straighter in her chair and staring at Clare's whiteboard, Kat thought she knew how Tom felt when she asked him a question.

'A sibling?'

Kat's conclusion made her pause. Ethan, she knew, was an only child. But if he was an accomplice then he might have been doing his partner's bidding, 'borrowing' their motivation. She continued.

'Given that the first two victims—'

'—that we know of—'

'Exactly. Given they're female, I'll say it's probably a sister.' Kat thought of her own older sister, Diana, always the favourite in their mother's eyes, however hard she might deny it. 'An older sister. So this older sister was perfect. Always got high marks at school, good at games, lots of friends, probably helped round the house without being asked.'

Clare laughed. It felt all right despite the subject under discussion. 'Sounds like a confession there, DS Ballantyne!'

Kat smiled. 'I'm saying nothing.'

'Our killer may have believed that his sister enjoyed unearned favour from their parents, thus depriving him of his rightful share of parental attention, affection and love.'

'What about George, though? He doesn't fit the pattern, either by sex or date of death.'

Clare drew in a breath. 'I know, and it does bother me. Now, you arrested Ethan Metcalfe for Rosie's murder. Either he communicated his need to kill George to his accomplice from his cell, or they'd already planned George's murder before Ethan was arrested. Perhaps, for some reason, after murdering Rosie they needed to kill again quickly, or at least know that another victim had been murdered. This escalation caused them to drop the sex of the victim or the totemic date of May sixth as a criterion.'

Kat made another note. Who had Ethan been in contact with since his arrest? Surely his suave London solicitor wasn't passing messages to an accomplice? Maybe he didn't need to. She'd met another London lawyer who'd been accomplice to some very dark crimes indeed. Sir Anthony Bone now resided at HMP Pentonville on remand, awaiting trial.

'If we accept your ideas, then do you think Rebecca Poole was the killer's first victim?'

'Not impossible. If they're roughly the same age then it could make sense: serials usually begin killing in their teens or early twenties. But if he's older, then I'd expect there to be other, earlier victims. In fact, you know what, Kat? I'd try and find the sister. She might well have been his first victim, and if she was, she would have been eighteen or nineteen when he murdered her. Probably on the sixth of May.'

Kat nodded as she tried to absorb everything Clare had told her. She and Tom needed to discover whether there were other dead young people who'd gone under the radar. ViCLAS had come up with nothing, though, which only left her outstanding Heads of Crime request.

'What about the MO, Clare? Is that significant?'

'Of course! It always is with these people. Now, on the surface, we've got no overtly ritualistic aspects to the murders. No baroque wound patterns. No contrived murder weapons. No staging of the body. No ante-mortem torture. No post-mortem mutilation, dismemberment or cannibalism. But what you *do* have is a consistent MO: the push from a tall building. Even though the sex of the victim and the date of their murder changed, this has remained fixed. It's hugely significant to the killer. It means something to him.'

'It's how he murdered his sister.'

Clare nodded enthusiastically. Funny how you could become so enthralled by the problem of catching a killer, you forgot you were dealing with real dead people. Kat didn't hold it against her, though, it happened, however hard you tried to remain focused on the victims.

'When you find him, he'll probably have pushed an older sister from an upper-storey window or off a bridge. If they were old enough to travel together, they might have been climbing together and he claimed to the police his sister died when a rope failed.' Clare glanced up at the whiteboard. 'How did the killer manage to persuade George to meet him at the top of the tower?'

'I think we're going to find alcohol and benzodiazepines in his system. They would have rendered him suggestible.'

Clare frowned. Put the tip of her index finger to the groove below her nose.

'They might. But calculating dosage for benzos isn't an exact science. You might end up with an unconscious victim at ground level, when what you want is a suggestible one at the top of the building. And even then, people still retain a degree of self-possession. They don't act in the same way as with Rohypnol, for example.'

'My feeling is, in each case the victim knew their killer. That definitely goes for Rosie Duggan.'

'So, George may have seen his killer as a friend? Another student?'

Kat thought of Ethan. 'Yes, but it could be someone he trusted professionally. A lecturer like yourself, for example.'

'I suppose you want a profile right now,' Clare said with a sigh.

'Just a steer, Clare. If you can help me profile this nutter then I might be able to break through Ethan's defences and get him to disclose the identity of his accomplice. Because until I do, they could kill again, and I don't want to find another young person dead at the foot of a tower block.'

'OK. Here's what I think.'

As Clare spoke, clearly and without pause for ten minutes, Kat made notes. After the meeting, she called Tom and asked him to compile a list of everyone Ethan had been in contact with since his arrest, including police officers and civilian staff.

But first she had a post-mortem to attend.

Chapter Fifty-Three

The snapped-branch smell of formalin wormed its way into Kat's nostrils as she stood looking down at George Seaton-Clark's broken body. The oil of camphor she'd smeared on her top lip wasn't working today, and the curdled odours of mint, tree-sap and early-stage bodily decay were nauseating.

She breathed shallowly through her mouth, hoping that the surgical mask covering her face was filtering out the worst of the airborne particles she imagined swirling around the room.

Jack went through the standard set of procedures on the body, but Kat was finding it hard to concentrate. She gave up trying and focused her attention inwards instead. On Clare's sketched-out profile, which she'd promised to write up with any additional details she could summon later that day.

Clare had said that the killer was adept at masking his psychopathy and presenting as a friendly, sociable individual. Half-right, in Ethan's case. He'd live in Middlehampton, probably within five miles of the centre of town. Yes. He would have a sibling, probably an older sister, who died in a fall aged around eighteen. No – so that had to be the accomplice.

He'd harbour deep-seated feelings of inadequacy that would lead him to envy and hate people he perceived as successful, especially if that success appeared to him to be unearned. Kat could easily imagine Ethan feeling that way. In later life he might have boot-strapped himself into a position outsiders would regard as successful, but in his inner world, it wouldn't fill the emotional hole left by his childhood overshadowing. Substitute 'overshadowing' with 'bullying' – including by Kat and Liv – and Clare was right on the money.

The only point where she and Clare had parted ways was when Clare described the male killer as someone an eighteen-year-old girl would trust. Rebecca Poole might have trusted Ethan . . . But Rosie? No. The video evidence laid bare her true feelings towards him. Unless . . .

Had Ethan pleaded with Rosie for a meeting to explain himself? Using a psychopath's glib charm and talent for lying, he might have managed it.

She shook her head. The real question was, how could she use what Clare had told her to get Ethan to crack and reveal the identity of his partner?

'Kat?'

'Huh?'

Jack Beale was looking at her. As were Ashleigh, his assistant, the photographer and the two CSIs. He raised his visor and then drew the surgical mask down over the lower half of his face. He was smiling. Her belly flipped.

'I asked you if you had any special requests before I close up.'

'Oh. No. Sorry, Jack, I don't what happened.'

Christ! She'd zoned out for the entire second half of the post-mortem.

Jack turned to Ashleigh. 'Must be losing my touch, Ash. Normally Kat finds my work fascinating.' He winked at Kat.

Another belly-flip. It wasn't always the work that fascinated her.

She thanked everyone and left, nodding as Jack promised her a preliminary email, 'As soon as I'm done here.'

◆ ◆ ◆

Traffic was heavy, and by the time Kat sat down at her desk, Jack's email was waiting in her inbox.

Hi Kat,

Full report to follow, but in summary, in the case of George Seaton-Clark:

Cause of death:

a) coronary haemorrhage caused by puncture of coronary artery by broken rib owing to:

b) massive blunt force trauma following fall from tower block.

Manner of death: homicide

Time of death: 11.03 p.m., 13/5/26

Observations:

George had a bruise on his left cheekbone, spreading to his eye. Looks like the result of a punch. Other bruising on torso and back, upper arms and thighs. Most attributable to fall, but others may be the result of personal violence.

Blood alcohol at time of death would have been around three times the legal limit. As with Rosie Duggan, I also found traces of benzodiazepines in his system. In the amounts present George would have been rendered pliant and confused.

She tried not to think of Jack's wink as she read on. Forced herself to concentrate on the report. The bruising was interesting. The black eye supported Dorian Evans's tale of a bar fight. And as a rugby player, apparently a forceful one, George could easily have sustained the other bruises in the match that had led to his altercation with Dorian.

So that settled it, not that there had been any doubt in her mind. George had been murdered. Probably by the person who had ordered Ethan to murder Rosie Duggan. She went over to Tom's desk.

Tom handed her a sheet of paper. It contained eleven names. All police or civilian staff, including the arrest team, the officers in the custody suite and his lawyer.

'That's it so far.'

They simply didn't have the time to interview them all. And Kat wasn't ready for the stink she'd create at Jubilee Place if she interviewed eleven cops and staff under caution, asking them if they were aiding and abetting a pair of serial killers.

She wanted to talk to Ethan again. Actually, what she wanted to do was go down to the cells and beat his head against the wall until he gave up his murderous partner.

She permitted herself a brief, dark smile. There were other ways to skin this particular cat.

As long as you're not the Kat getting skinned, her inner voice whispered.

On her way down to the cells, her phone pinged with an incoming email. It was her Heads of Crime request. Heart racing, she opened the message.

It was negative. No other lead investigator anywhere in the UK was currently investigating a series of linked homicides where the MO involved falls from high structures. That was that, then. It was just her and Tom.

And the man she was going to see.

Chapter Fifty-Four

The custody officer stood aside as Kat entered Ethan's cell. It smelled rank. Unwashed armpits and a sour odour she always thought of as *Eau de Misery*.

Ethan was sitting on the narrow bench that served as both bed and chair. He looked up as she closed the door behind her. He drew his knees up and encircled his shins with his arms, pressing himself backwards into the corner of the cell.

All trace of the vainglorious celebrity podcaster was gone. In his place was a dejected figure in stained grey sweats and off-white towelling slippers similar to the ones you got these days in hotels. Only, those tended not to have what looked suspiciously liked dried bloodstains on their upper surfaces.

He looked up at her and in his gaze she saw hope mingled with suspicion. She leaned back against the door.

'Hello, Ethan, how are you holding up in here?'

He looked around, as if seeing the cell for the first time. Back at her. 'Well, it's not The Garland, if that's what you mean.'

The Garland. A boutique hotel in the centre of town where a year earlier Kat had arrested the man who'd murdered PC Abby Greene. Had Ethan picked that location on purpose to taunt her?

'Have you had anything to eat since you've been here?'

'A lovely ham sandwich from the canteen. A plate of something that might have been lasagne. I think someone spat in it.'

'I'm sorry.'

His eyes flashed, although he stayed wrapped around himself in his corner, like a spider pushed into a defensive position by a questing finger. 'Are you, Kat? Are you really? You were the one who put me in this place, remember?'

'Ethan, you left your DNA on a murder victim. What was I supposed to do? Surely the host of *Home Counties Homicide* would applaud me for doing some proper policework for once?'

She cursed inwardly. She'd come down here to try to extract information from him. That required rapport-building, not the scoring of cheap points.

'I didn't do it,' he whined. 'How can you even believe that I did? Why would I do something as stupid as leaving my DNA at the scene?'

I'm still not entirely sure I do believe it, she wanted to say. *Your DNA says you did it, but my gut says something's wrong.*

She disregarded her doubts. And it certainly wasn't her job to answer his questions.

'There's been a development, Ethan. A very strange and unpleasant development. And it casts some doubt over the way we proceeded with your arrest.'

There. That should bring him out of his defensive shell.

It did. His arms loosened. His legs unfolded until those stained slippers touched the floor. He leaned forwards, eyes glittering.

'I knew it! I'm not saying you were personally guilty of fabricating evidence, Kat. I have too much respect for you to do that. But I think we both know there's plenty of police corruption out there, and someone could have seen an easy mark and fitted me up.'

It was quite the speech. And in other circumstances, Kat might have accepted the challenge and gone toe-to-toe with him. But today she had a different purpose.

'While you were locked up in here, another student was murdered. In exactly the same way as Rebecca Poole.'

He frowned. Had she caught him out already with a simple bit of subterfuge? Mixing up the two female victims 'by accident' and surprising him.

'You mean Rosie Duggan?'

'Sorry. Yes, of course. Rebecca Poole's something else I'm working on.'

He rocked back. Then a sly smile crept over his face.

'I told you,' he said in a flat voice. 'It wasn't me. I didn't kill the Duggan girl and this proves it. You have to let me go now, don't you? That's what you came to tell me. I'm a free man. Oh, my God, I have to call my lawyer. He is going to bankrupt Hertfordshire Police over this.' Then he frowned and held up a hand. 'But don't worry, Kat. I'll instruct him not to file suit against you personally. I know you were only following orders, as they say.'

Kat let the patronising semi-insults slide over her. For one thing, Ethan was 180 degrees off in his assumptions, and for another, she really didn't like the way he'd referred to Rosie as 'the Duggan girl'. Dehumanising her.

'You're quite the expert on murderers, aren't you, Ethan?'

His forehead crinkled as he adjusted to the unexpected turn in the conversation. But she was flattering him. It would work.

'Obviously. One-point-two-three million subscribers can't be wrong.'

'Serial killers especially.'

He nodded. Offered a smug smile. Held his hands out wide.

'What can I say? It goes with the territory.'

'Ever cover a master-disciple pairing? You know. That's where—'

'—a serial killer grooms a successor. Often from behind bars. I know what it means, Kat. What's your question?'

She'd asked him one, but in his rush to show off he'd forgotten. No matter.

'The thing is, Ethan, all this new murder proves is that there is a second killer operating in Middlehampton. We still have enough evidence to convict you for Rosie Duggan's murder. But if you were to help me catch George Seaton-Clark's, that could help with your sentence.'

Ethan looked around. At the camera in the top-left corner above the cell door.

'Is that thing on?'

'Yes, but it's video-only. No audio. And if you're concerned about your legal rights, nothing you've told me in here would be admissible in court.'

He smiled slowly. 'You failed to caution me. Of course.'

She let him have his little victory. She hadn't 'failed' to caution him. She just hadn't.

'So? Who is he, Ethan?'

'Sorry, Kat. *He?*'

'The person who murdered George Seaton-Clark using your MO and victim profile.'

He smirked. 'Hang on a minute. You've got a female murdered. Then a male. That's serial killer victim selection 101 out the window.'

Now he hadn't even referred to Rosie as 'the Duggan girl'. She'd become 'a female'. What next? *It?*

'It can't be a copycat, Ethan. Who would bother copying an MO with so many possibilities for it to go wrong? Why not just stab the victim or bludgeon them? Yet it's too specific to be a coincidence. Someone killed George Seaton-Clark like that because they were told to. Or you killed Rosie that way because someone else told *you* to.'

He folded his arms. 'I didn't kill Rosie Duggan. I didn't kill the other girl. And I didn't tell some' – he made air quotes – '*disciple* to kill this boy. George whatever his name was.'

'Why May the sixth, Ethan?'

'What do you mean?'

'Does that date have some significance for you?'

He looked up at the water-stained ceiling. Back at her.

'If memory serves, that was the day King Charles and Camilla were crowned. 2023.'

'It was also the date you killed Rosie Duggan. Rebecca Poole died exactly a year earlier.'

'I didn't kill those bitches!' he shouted suddenly.

It was loud in the hard-walled room and Kat flinched. He blushed violently, his throat and cheeks flushing.

'I'm sorry, I shouldn't have called them that. I'm really, really stressed here, Kat. But in any case, I didn't kill them. You have to believe me.'

'I have to believe the evidence, Ethan. Nothing else. I might come back later.' She paused at the door, wondering just how wrong she'd been about the man in grey prison sweats staring up at her from his chair. 'I'll tell them to stop spitting in your food. You've got enough on your plate without that.'

She left him in the cell with a fresh question needing an answer. One sparked by his outburst.

Those bitches!

Chapter Fifty-Five

'Tomski!'

He heeled his chair over to her desk. 'Boss?'

'What if Rebecca Poole wasn't the first victim in the series?'

'What do you mean?'

'I want you to go back ten years. Search for any deaths recorded as accidental, misadventure, suicide or unexplained that match our criteria. Keep it loose to start with. I'd rather get false positives than miss someone out.'

Tom nodded slowly. 'The criteria are pretty straightforward, aren't they? Victims aged between, what, eighteen and twenty?'

'Make it between seventeen and twenty-three. Bracket the key age.'

'Died on or about May sixth. Cause of death, a fall from a tall structure.'

'That's it exactly.'

'And if we get any hits, we can profile them to see if they match the victim profile you and Clare drew up. High-achievers. Popular.'

'All-rounders, yes.'

Kat felt it, then. The energy connecting her and Tom. It felt good. Like they were on the brink of something. And if they did find a trail of murders, they'd be able to bring closure to all those bereaved families. And somewhere along the way, they might strike lucky and find Ethan's accomplice. Either way, this was a lead she'd pursue full-force.

Then Tom's face fell. 'Wait. There's a problem. If they weren't recorded as murders at the time, the PNC won't be any help.'

'Then get creative, Tomski. I have faith.'

Tom returned three hours later. He was beaming, holding a sheaf of papers in his hand.

'I did it, Kat. I consulted NHS records, the coroner's office database, even local newspapers.'

She accepted the papers from him. 'What have we got?'

'I found fourteen cases that predate Rebecca Poole. All but one were female. Three of these were confirmed suicides with a history of mental illness and suicide notes left behind. That leaves eleven. Two were accidents, with witnesses: one in a climbing accident in the Alps, the other at a Go Ape experience when a harness failed. That leaves nine.' Tom leaned forwards. 'Listen to this, Kat. All but one of those died on May sixth, the outlier dying on October eleventh. So, if we're conservative and say we have nine historic victims that match the pattern, add our three Middlehampton victims and that gives us a total of twelve. Kat, this is bloody massive. He's been active for *years*.'

Kat scanned the top sheet Tom had handed her. 'Tomski, this is excellent work, mate. You're a star. And I love your summary table.'

'I thought it might make life easier for both of us if I tabulated the results.'

She stuck the table on to the murder board. Then stepped back and looked at a history of murder stretching back over the previous decade.

Chapter Fifty-Six

Topline results: deaths matching current criteria 2017–2026

Name	Age	Place	Year
Nicole Bagshaw	18	MH	2017
Poppy Arbuthnot	18	Liverpool	2018
Keira Davies	19	Liverpool	2019
Magdalena Radecki	19	Liverpool	2020
Norman Pettifer	19	Sheffield	2021
Elodie Johns	18	Sheffield	2021
Sneha Ashok	19	Glasgow	2022
Felicity Wise	18	London	2023
Dalilah Muhammad	19	London	2024
Rebecca Poole	18	MH	2025
Rosie Duggan	18	MH	2026
George Seaton-Clark	19	MH	2026

Chapter Fifty-Seven

Kat was at her desk at 7.57 a.m. the next day, eager to get to work on Tom's research.

The work ahead was mountainous, but she had the scent in her nostrils now and nothing would keep her away from the trail. Somewhere in all those files she knew she'd find Ethan's accomplice, and in the process solve George Seaton-Clark's murder.

Her phone rang. It was Tom.

'Hey, Tomski! Please tell me you're on your way in.'

He sounded down. 'No can do, Kat. Carve-up's pulled me off the case for the day. I've got to help him put together a presentation for the brass in Welwyn Garden City. At his place. Says my reward is he'll take me along.'

'Did you tell him you were on an active murder investigation?'

'Of course I did! But you know what he's like. I pushed back, Kat, and he pulled rank. Tried to sweeten the pill by saying it would be good for my career.'

She swallowed down the lump in her throat. It was composed of equal parts hatred for her line manager, despair that her own workload had just doubled, and sorrow. Because, for once, Carve-up was right. She'd not have Tom around for ever.

'He's not wrong, Tomski.'

'But you need me! I don't want to spend the day farting about with PowerPoint. I want to help you catch this killer.'

'And you will, Tomski. You already have. It's not going to be over today. My advice?' She sighed loudly. 'Do what he wants. Give it your best shot and make him look good. He likes to remember favours.'

'I don't have a choice, anyway. I'll see you later, yes?'

'Call me when you're done.'

Kat ended the call and began work on the files.

When the series started with Nicole Bagshaw in 2017, Ethan would have been the same age as Kat: twenty-seven. Easily old enough to commit murder, even if it did seem a little on the old side for a serial killer's first. But Greg Fanning, Libby Spare, Lloyd Kenney and Dorian Evans would have only been eight or nine at the time. She tried to imagine a pubescent disciple. Failed. They were all in the clear.

Apart from one, all the earlier deceased were female. All students. All either eighteen or nineteen. All had fallen from a height. Every coroner had recorded a verdict of suicide, accident, misadventure, or issued a narrative verdict of an unexplained but unsuspicious death. The locations were all over the country: starting in Middlehampton, then moving to Liverpool, Sheffield, Glasgow and London, before finishing up in Middlehampton again. To Kat, it looked like a Middlehampton native who had gone on a journey before returning to his home town.

The deaths had occurred one a year until 2021, when there were two deaths that met Tom's search criteria. Then, in the current year, when two students had been murdered. Clare had provided a convincing explanation for their proximity. But what about the two in 2021?

One of the victims that year sounded like a match to Rebecca Poole and Rosie Duggan. Elodie Johns. A pretty name. Kat pictured a young girl with baggy jeans and a crop top. Tattoos. A couple of facial piercings. Carrying a messenger bag stuffed with lecture notes and textbooks festooned with stickers.

But Norman? What kind of a name was that for a nineteen-year-old? She rummaged through the background files Tom had left stacked on his desk.

She found him. Norman Arthur Waverley Pettifer. She struggled to visualise this student or young worker. Gave him a mullet or a buzz cut. Dreadlocks or a goatee. Tribal tats. It didn't work. He sounded like an old man.

She ran a finger down the page and stopped at his occupation.

Retired.

This couldn't be right. Norman's cause of death was listed on his death certificate as a broken neck caused by a fall down stairs at his home in Sheffield. Tom had printed out every document he could find connected with each death.

Kat riffled through the papers until she found the hospital post-mortem. This was the basic medical PM, rather than the detailed forensic variety that Jack Beale conducted.

The first line of the report couldn't have been clearer, or more puzzling.

The deceased is an elderly male.

Kat had an idea and went online. She pulled up the 2021 census. On 21 March 2021, at Norman's address, 33 Lightgate Road, the sole occupant was listed as Norman Arthur Waverley Pettifer, born in 1930.

Mystery solved. Someone had fat-finger syndrome at the coroner's office. Norman was ninety-one not nineteen.

Kat turned to the first victim. Nicole Bagshaw had been eighteen at the time of her death. According to the coroner's report, Nicole had fallen at a popular beauty spot in the countryside to the north of

Middlehampton. Known locally as Lover's Leap, it was a steep chalk cliff overlooking open countryside. The verdict was accidental death.

When she read Nicole's home address, Kat's pulse jittered upwards. She lived at 102 Oxford Road. Two doors up from Ethan Metcalfe. Hurriedly, she went through the other files looking for connections to Ethan, but she came up empty-handed. It didn't matter. Here he was again, at the heart of the case. First, his DNA on one of the victims. Now, his address on the same street as another.

What she needed was to confirm her and Clare's theory about how and why the killer had selected his victims. That meant a lot of phone calls. And at least two home visits.

Eyes smarting from reading onscreen, she decided to start with the in-person work. She grabbed her keys and headed out.

Chapter Fifty-Eight

Joy Poole showed Kat into a neat sitting room dominated by a vast TV hung from the wall.

At the moment, it was displaying a slideshow of family photos in which her dead daughter figured in almost every shot, always smiling. Here she was, astride a glossy-coated chestnut horse. At the helm of a sailing boat. In a smart suit standing between smiling parents in front of what Kat recognised as the main building of Middlehampton University.

Kat accepted the offer of tea and waited until Joy had seated herself in an armchair.

'Mrs Poole, thanks for making the time to see me.'

'You said it was about Rebecca. Of course I'd make the time. And please, call me Joy.'

'Well, Joy, I am currently investigating the deaths of two students. You may have read about the first in the *Echo*. Rosie Duggan?'

Joy shook her head. 'I try not to see any news. Social media, either. It's all so nasty and depressing and I'm on tablets as it is.'

Kat nodded, thinking Joy probably hadn't heard about Ethan's arrest. 'Rosie was murdered. She was pushed from the top of Five Cups Lane car park. I think that whoever murdered Rosie may also have murdered Rebecca.'

She waited for this news to sink in.

Joy took a cautious sip of her tea, as if Kat might have slipped poison into it.

'My daughter took her own life. Gary and I have learned to accept that. We didn't . . . We don't . . . understand her decision. But we've come to terms with it.'

'I know that's what the coroner recorded, Joy. But new evidence has come to light that I believe may mean we have to reconsider the manner of Rebecca's death. I know this must be incredibly painful for you, but I wonder if you can remember whether Rebecca had told you of meeting anyone special around the time of her death. Someone new who she liked? Who she trusted? An older man? Mid-thirties? A lecturer perhaps?'

Joy was shaking her head from side to side. 'I can't remember anything about that time. We were both in bits for weeks.' She looked up at the TV, now showing a photo of her daughter in hockey kit, grinning past a bright pink gumshield as she held a cup aloft. 'Everyone loved Becky. We received so many lovely messages.'

'Do you happen to know if Becky kept a journal at all?'

'We kept her room exactly as she left it. You're welcome to come upstairs and see it. But I don't remember her ever having a journal.'

Kat followed Joy, who walked with the slow, careful steps of someone inebriated and striving to appear sober. Grief had obviously hollowed her out, leaving this walking, talking shell of a woman. Would grief ever loosen its grip on her? Kat wondered whether she'd ever recover if she lost Riley. A horrible thought. She pushed it down and, nodding to Joy as she held the door open, entered Rebecca Poole's bedroom.

Kat had seen it before. Parents unwilling or unable to change anything in their dead child's room might leave clothes exactly where they'd fallen. Or the mother, usually, would wash, dry and iron them before folding them neatly and putting them away, ready for the day their child, restored to them, would come back in through the front door.

Rebecca's room was painted a soft lilac. A vanity with mirror sat in front of the window. Make-up and hair slides littered the surface. But there was no dust. Joy must take everything off, dust the surface, then meticulously rebuild the chaos. How many times had she done that since the day Becky disappeared from her life? Fifty? A hundred?

'May I check the drawers?'

Joy sat on the bed and picked up a teddy bear with a red satin heart appliquéd to its chest. She held it to her nose and inhaled, with her eyes closed.

'Of course. But please be careful. And put everything back the way you found it.'

'I will,' Kat said.

She turned away and methodically went through every drawer in the vanity, the wardrobe and the white-painted desk in the corner. Then she got down on her hands and knees and looked under the bed.

No journal.

She stood up, clutching the end of the bed as dizziness momentarily overtook her. The white sparks squirming around the edge of her vision gradually wiped out one by one.

'Joy, do you know if Becky left any of her things at the university?'

Joy opened her eyes. Placed the teddy in her lap. 'Everything she had in her room there, they returned to us. This is all of it.'

'What happened to her phone and laptop?'

'Gary smashed them with a sledgehammer. I think he thought it might make him feel better.'

Kat paused, visualising a grief-stricken father taking out his rage on two inanimate devices. Social media had been implicated in plenty of teenage suicides. But in Rebecca Poole's case, the danger had come from the oldest source of all. An angry, violent man.

'Well, thank you for showing me Becky's room. She was clearly a lovely girl.'

Joy got to her feet. Came to stand right in front of Kat, no more than a foot away. She looked straight in her eyes and at that moment all traces of the drug-induced vagueness in her manner disappeared. She gripped Kat by both upper arms.

'Becky wasn't lovely. She was *perfect*. If you say she was murdered, then I want you to find the man who did it and I want to see him suffer.'

On the drive over to the Bagshaws' house at 102 Oxford Road, Kat fine-tuned her theory. What if Ethan had *always* been working with a partner? The partner had the murderous obsession with his older sister. Ethan was content, or even turned on, by acting as a spotter, researching targets, possibly even interacting with the girls to get to know them? Then he could lure the girls to the killing ground where the partner would take over? Had it given him the idea for his podcast?

Ten minutes later, sitting at the kitchen table with a glass of water in front of her, Kat told Oliver and Sarah Bagshaw the same story she had told Joy Poole. That she suspected their daughter had been murdered.

But she was taking a different approach to the one she had tried with Joy earlier.

'Did Nicole ever mention Ethan Metcalfe? Having bumped into him in the street, anything like that?'

At the mention of Ethan's name, both Bagshaws stiffened.

'Was it him?' Oliver Bagshaw gritted out, his jaw clenched. 'Did that weirdo murder Nic? I saw he'd been arrested for killing that other poor girl.'

'I'm just following a lead at this point,' Kat said carefully, visualising, with great ease, an angry mob of bereaved parents, their solicitors and a media pack besieging Jubilee Place.

Sarah's left hand was intertwined with Oliver's right. She laid her free hand on top of his.

'He would "appear" in the street when Nic was coming home from school. Try to engage her in conversation. Then, when she was sixteen, he asked her out.' Sarah's eyes bored into Kat's. 'He was twenty-five at the time. What the hell was he doing asking a sixteen-year-old girl out on a date? Well, I mean, we all know what he was doing. There's a word for men like him. Nonce!' She spat out this word like a mouthful of spoiled food. 'Nic always told him where to go. She was gay, anyway. Even if he'd been the right age, it wouldn't have mattered to her.'

'Did he ever become abusive? Verbally, for example? Or physically?'

'Nothing you could ever challenge him on,' Sarah said, looking at her husband, who nodded in agreement. 'He'd turn away and say something under his breath. Nic always knew it was some sort of slur, but, you know, he'd mutter it so he could always put it back on her. *Did* he kill her? Is that what you're saying?'

'As I said, I'm just following a line of enquiry.'

Oliver nodded. 'Of course you are. Well, here's another line of enquiry you should follow. One day, this would have been summer of 2016, I went round there. I'd had enough and I wanted to warn him off. He denied everything and then he told me not to worry because he'd be leaving Middlehampton soon. I remember his words clearly, because he was so full of himself. Grandiose, you know? Talking about himself in the third person. I wanted to punch him in the mouth just to wipe that supercilious smile off his face. He said, "No need to worry, Ethan is taking *Home Counties Homicide* on tour. He's going to be live from London, Liverpool, Newcastle, Edinburgh." That was his stupid podcast, by the way.'

This was no coincidence. It couldn't be. Two of the places Ethan had boasted of visiting were the sites of murders in the sequence. Poppy Arbuthnot, Keira Davies and Magdalena Radecki had all died in Liverpool. Felicity Wise and Dalilah Muhammad had died in London. Sneha Ashok had died in Glasgow – which was, what, an hour's drive from Edinburgh? And Newcastle to Sheffield, while longer, was still less than three hours.

Sarah placed both hands flat on the table and fixed Kat with a level stare.

'Nic was planning to leave Middlehampton to study – she had a place at Durham to read maths. She was so gifted. She wanted to go on to Cambridge afterwards to do a master's and then a PhD in the US. And what was that – that *loser* doing? Travelling to do that idiotic podcast. As if anyone was listening. A friend of mine overheard him once, in the Co-op. He was boasting to the cashier that he had two hundred listeners. Two hundred! So what? So bloody what?'

Kat nodded in sympathy, as Sarah dropped her head and let the tears that had been glistening in her eyes during the last few minutes finally spill over.

As she took her leave of the Bagshaws, she was more certain of her theory. There had been a monster born in Middlehampton who'd begun killing in his home town before spreading his wings. He'd been obsessed with murdering his older sister over and over again. And somewhere along the line he'd recruited Ethan to help him.

So if Ethan *was* the disciple, then who was his master?

Chapter Fifty-Nine

Back at MCU, Kat called Tom.

'How's it going?'

He spoke in a low voice. Clearly Carve-up was in earshot.

'OK. Going to be a long day, though.'

'He's close by, isn't he?'

'Mm-hmm.'

'Twat.'

'Yep.'

'Wanker.'

'Yep.'

She fancied she could detect a smile behind the monosyllables. Pushed for a laugh.

'Massive bell-end.'

'Yep.'

OK, Tomski had a proper poker face. Even over the telephone. 'We're going to get that murderous bastard, Tomski. One of these days. I promise you.'

'Good.'

'I have to go.'

'OK.'

As she ended the call, she caught Carve-up's voice, dripping with sarcasm as he asked Tom, 'Woman trouble?'

Oh, it was woman trouble, all right. But it wasn't Tom who'd one day find himself in the firing line.

She made herself a black coffee and got back to work. First, pulling all the files and checking every location of the nine earlier deaths. Apart from Norman Pettifer, the unfortunate ninety-one-year-old, all the youngsters – *victims!* shrieked Kat's inner voice – had died on or near their university campus. Bridges, flyovers, housing blocks, multistorey car parks, a clock tower: a depressing architectural list of crime scenes. For Kat was convinced that was what she was looking at.

If she could put Ethan at any of the universities, it would bolster her case. She closed the latest file and went down to the cells.

Alone once more with Ethan, she squatted down facing him, her back to the door.

'Ethan, will you talk to me?'

He lifted his head. It appeared to weigh more than his neck muscles could cope with. All trace of his previous preening figure in front of TV cameras had gone. In its place a pathetic figure slumped against the wall in the drab, stained police-issue sweats.

'About what?'

'About when you took *Home Counties Homicide* on the road?'

'How did you know about that? It was years ago.'

'I'm a detective, Ethan. Finding things out is what I do.'

He shrugged. 'What do you want to know?'

In that moment, Kat had an insight that she felt had been eluding her right until this very moment. TV shows and movies always gave the impression that serial killers were these twisted geniuses. Either playing games with the cops or outwitting them, always one step ahead. To a degree, Stefan Pulford had conformed to the stereotype.

But here was another example of the breed. And although he was clearly twisted, there was nothing of the manipulative genius about him.

'Do you want to have your lawyer present?'

'No need. I've had plenty of time to think. I'm going to be tried for murder, aren't I?'

'It certainly looks that way. I doubt the CPS will throw this one back at me. Not with the evidence we have.'

'Then no. I'll need all my funds to pay for my defence. Barristers aren't cheap. Not the good ones, anyway, and I've got a feeling I'm going to need a very good one.' He smiled crookedly. 'It's odd, isn't it, Kat?'

'What's odd, Ethan?'

'All these years I've been begging you to let me help you investigate a murder, and now, at last, you're asking me for my help to catch a killer.'

Your accomplice, she wanted to shout. But that would achieve nothing. She held her feelings in check.

'How did you support yourself when you were on tour?' she asked instead. 'Not being rude, but at the time you didn't have enough listeners to pay the bills, did you?'

A flash of his old swagger came back.

'We call them subscribers, actually, Kat. Just for your information. But no, it was early days. I got jobs.'

'What kind of jobs?'

He shrugged. 'IT support, mostly. I was always good with computers. You must remember at school, I founded the computer club?'

'Of course. So, IT support where? Freelance?'

'No, I needed a regular income. Local councils, small companies, universities. Whoever'd have me.'

'Do you happen to remember which universities?'

He looked up at the water-stained ceiling. 'Sheffield, I think. And I had a short-term contract in Glasgow.'

'Glasgow, not Edinburgh?'

'Yes,' he snapped. 'I'm a prisoner, but I'm not an idiot.' He shook his head. 'Sorry, Kat, sorry. That was rude. I apologise. I haven't been sleeping well.'

'Forget it, Ethan. And I'm sorry you're not sleeping. It's hard, I know that.'

His eyes blazed. 'Do you? Do you *really*, Kat? That's nice for you. I mean, given that you put me in here for a crime . . . *I did not commit!*'

He shouted the last four words, but Kat remained calm. She knew he couldn't hurt her. She couldn't let him get under her skin. For all she knew, that was his intention. And she desperately needed to wheedle the name of his accomplice out of him before he killed another student.

'Ethan, you said just now you're going to need a good barrister. I agree with you. But there is a way you can make their job easier. A lot easier. Tell me who killed George Seaton-Clark. You don't have to admit that they're your disciple, or you're theirs, or any of that pop-psychological bullshit. Help me catch him and any judge would definitely take that into account.'

He spread his hands wide and smiled. Odd thing to do, but everything about Ethan Metcalfe was odd.

'How should I know who murdered him?'

'Because he murdered George using the exact same methods you used to murder Rosie Duggan.'

'I did not kill Rosie Duggan. And I did not get someone else to kill George Seaton-Clark.' He jumped to his feet and towered above her, and in that moment, she realised just how big he'd become thanks to his newfound enthusiasm for working out. 'I. AM. INNOCENT!' he roared, so loud that her ears rang for a second.

Kat backed up and scrabbled to get a purchase on the steel door at her back so she could lever herself to her feet.

She hammered a fist on the door.

'Out, please!' she shouted, turning her head to one side without taking her eyes off Ethan. The door stayed shut. Locked. With her on the wrong side.

Ethan took a step towards her. Grinned. 'It would be pretty fucking ironic if I killed you in here, wouldn't it, Kat? I mean, I'm not getting out, am I? And you seem pretty sure I'm going down for murder. I should at least do a real one.'

She raised her hands in front of her, palms out, and took a step towards him.

'Stay back!' she yelled at him. 'Back away!'

Then she turned her head to the side again and screamed.

'Let me out!'

The lock scraped and the door swung inwards, bumping her painfully in the back.

Ethan sat down on his thin, blue plastic mattress. Smiled up at the custody officer who was staring at him, her eyes full of suspicion.

'Everything all right in here?' she asked.

'Just let me out,' Kat said, her chest rising and falling as if she'd just played a furious netball quarter. 'And next time, please come the first time I call.'

◆ ◆ ◆

Shaken, by her encounter with Ethan and unable to reconcile the two seemingly contradictory sides to his personality – creepy and pathetic one moment, roaring and violent the next – Kat stood facing the murder board, still breathing heavily. She calmed herself by transcribing Tom's table of victims on to the whiteboard. When she'd finished, she stood back and ran her eye down the column of dates.

George Seaton-Clark was the latest victim in 2026 and Nicole Bagshaw began the series back in 2017. Or did she? Clare Capstick had said the killer's older sister would have been his first victim: Nicole was an only child. So there must be at least one earlier victim.

What was the age gap between Ethan's accomplice and his older sister when he'd murdered her? Kat went for a reasonable assumption. Two years. So he'd have been sixteen at the time. Assuming he and Ethan were the same age, that would put the date at 2006.

She called Tom.

'Remind me how you compiled your list of unexplained deaths, Tomski.'

'I used the coroner's database, plus NHS records. Local newspapers, too.'

'I need to go back to 2005. Is that going to be easy or hard?'

She could hear him smiling. 'It's going to be easy-peasy, boss. I set up an automated search based on all the sources I used. It's actually a bit of custom code I wrote myself – well, with a bit of help from an AI. Just go to my PC. Log in with my details and launch the app called TomskiSearch.'

'This isn't a wind-up, is it, Tomski? Because I am seriously up against it here, especially without you.'

'That's just the point, Kat. You're not without me. It's not a wind-up. I really did it. It's something I've been tinkering with at home.'

'Then you're a bloody star! I love you, Tomski. I have to go.' She paused. 'I'm guessing Carve-up's not around this time?'

'Oh, Jesus, Kat! It's torture. Like being cellmates with . . . well, with Stuart Carver actually. And I'm asphyxiating on bloody Aramis. He's drenched in it.'

Kat failed to suppress a laugh. 'Oh, my poor Tomski. It's only for one day, then you'll be back where the real work gets done. Hang in there, yes?'

'I'll try. But if he leans over me while I'm showing him how animated slide transitions work one more time, I swear I'm going to vomit over his keyboard.'

Shaking her head and smiling properly for the first time in what felt like weeks, Kat ended the call and moved over to Tom's desk.

She followed his instructions and pulled up the app. The list of saved searches included one named 'EM killings 2017–2026'. She opened it and adjusted the start date back twelve years. Hit the magnifying-glass button and waited expectantly.

Tom may have been a computing wizard, but he wasn't Google. A creaky little hourglass started clicking round in ninety-degree increments.

Sighing, Kat went to the kitchen to make herself a coffee.

On returning to Tom's desk, the screen greeting her was not black, or showing the arthritic hourglass. It had thrown up a results screen.

There were two further instances of deaths meeting their search criteria.

The later death had been recorded as a suicide. Kat pulled up the coroner's report.

On 2 January 2015, aged eighteen, Valentina Pellegrini leapt to her death from the Clifton Suspension Bridge in Bristol. She left a note explaining she no longer felt that life was worth living. The poor girl had spent two separate periods in a residential psychiatric unit in Bristol, where she had made repeated attempts to take her own life.

No match.

Swallowing down the lump in her throat as she grieved for a young girl she'd never known, Kat turned to the second girl.

Who fitted the pattern like a jigsaw piece.

Like Valentina, Emily Siddle was eighteen when she died.

On 6 May 2013, Emily suffered a broken neck after falling from a treehouse at the family home in Middlehampton. The coroner's verdict was accidental death.

Emily Siddle was the fifth, and earliest, victim who'd lived in Middlehampton. And she'd died on the right date. She was unmarried, so they were looking for a killer with that surname.

She ran a check on the PNC. It came up blank.

No easy wins for you, today, Kat, she thought.

Chapter Sixty

Kat returned to the question of the identity of George Seaton-Clark's murderer.

Everything she and Clare had discussed held, still. The killer would have been someone George knew and trusted. They'd have to look at all his friends again, including Dorian Evans. But what about adults? Kat resolved to start with George's lecturers. Surely that was a shorter list. One she could work through without Tom to help her. Clare had said he'd been taking her course. Was he taking others?

She called Clare.

'Hey, Kat,' the other woman said. 'How's the case going?'

'Honestly, I'm in the weeds at the moment. I was actually wondering if you could do me a favour.'

'If I can, of course. What is it?'

'I need a list of all of George Seaton-Clark's lecturers. I know you said he was taking your course. And another. Italian, was it?'

'Spanish, I think, but I'll check.'

'In fact, could you include anyone who also taught Rosie Duggan and Rebecca Poole, please?'

'When do you need this list by? Or shouldn't I ask?'

'Any chance you could get it to me by the end of today? I know you have lectures to give and students to see, but this is really important, Clare.'

'Relax, Kat. It's not as hard as you think. Give me an hour, OK? I'll email it over.'

◆ ◆ ◆

Rather than waiting for Clare's email, and somehow doubting such a complex request could really be answered in an hour, Kat grabbed her car keys and headed out. She wanted to visit the Siddles to ask them about their daughter, Emily.

Lee and Deborah Siddle lived on a long, curving private road on the south side of Middlehampton. Even though Kat had lived in the town all her life, she'd never visited or even known about Chancery Lane West.

Halfway down, just after a dog-leg, she came to The Mill House. A grand residence in red brick and some kind of greyish stone, swathed in a red-leaved creeper.

She rang the doorbell.

Once again she went through the whole speech with the woman who answered the door and identified herself as Deborah Siddle.

Deborah was in her mid-fifties. She had lovely eyes, a pale green with a darker rim, but they were sunk in a face blotched with rosacea on both cheeks and scored with the deep creases of a long-time smoker. Her body was large and shapeless. She carried herself wearily, as if defeated in battle.

As Kat passed her to enter the square hallway, her nostrils filled with the smell of cigarette smoke. The house reeked of it.

'Let's talk in the kitchen,' Deborah said. 'I more or less live there.'

'Is your husband here or at work?' Kat asked, hoping she could talk to both Siddle parents at the same time.

'Lee and I got divorced ten years ago. Poor man couldn't cope,' Deborah said, lighting a cigarette and offering the packet to Kat.

'No, thanks.'

'Don't mind if I do, do you?' Deborah said, thumbing the wheel on a translucent orange plastic lighter.

'Please, go ahead. It's your house.'

Deborah nodded as she placed the tip of flame to the top of the cigarette between her lips. Drew deeply and blew the smoke out from the corner of her mouth.

'Filthy habit. My doctor says it'll kill me, but here I am,' she said in a voice Kat now heard was rattly with phlegm, 'still alive. Worse luck.'

'Mrs Siddle, I was hoping to talk to you about Emily. If that's all right?'

Deborah shrugged. Even this small everyday movement seeming to cost her.

'She'd have been thirty-one this year. Could have been married. A couple of kids, even. I could have been Granny Debs.'

'I read the coroner's report. It said Emily fell from a treehouse.'

Deborah sucked smoke deep into her lungs as if wanting it to lodge in the tissue there and bring on a fatal cancer. In the quiet of the kitchen, Kat could pick up the crackle as the tobacco burned.

'"Fell". Well, she certainly fell all right, so he got that right.'

Kat felt it then, a quickening of the pulse and a flicker of nervous excitement in her belly. Somehow, she knew that, whatever had led her to this kitchen table, she was meant to be here.

'What do you mean?'

Deborah answered a different question. Perhaps one she would have preferred to have been asked.

'Emily was perfect. You ever meet someone like that? Not a show-off, not like these awful kids you see on Instagram nowadays, boasting about all the shit they've blagged. But she was just meant to be in this world. I don't know how to explain it.'

'A golden child,' Kat said, recalling at least one comment made by a bereaved parent.

Deborah's eyes came alive, just for a moment.

'That's a lovely way to put it. Wait there.'

She pushed herself to her feet and – suddenly possessed of an effortless grace, despite her size – hurried over to a vast pine dresser. From a lower compartment she pulled out a photo album and sat beside Kat, opening the navy leather book at the first page.

She began flicking through the pages. Each displayed a different side of her daughter's character. Like Rosie, Rebecca, Nicole and all the others, Emily had been a multitalented child. Here she was helping a child with Down's syndrome to ride a charming, shaggy-maned pony. Here, rowing in an eight, water droplets spraying from an upraised blade, the cox leaning forward and yelling into a red loudhailer. Another gifted child apparently blessed with the ability to succeed at anything she turned her hand – or brain – to.

'She was obviously popular, too,' Kat said, pointing to Emily amidst a crowd of cheering girls holding A-level certificates aloft. 'Lots of friends.'

Deborah sighed. Stubbed her cigarette out in a battered brass ashtray and lit another.

'I think that's what her sister was most jealous of. The friends she had. We used to say Emily made friends the way other kids made messes. She couldn't help it.'

Kat's pulse quickened. 'Sister?'

Deborah's face hardened. 'She was with her that day. In the treehouse.'

'What is her name?'

Deborah looked at Kat. Drew cigarette smoke down into her lungs and spoke on the exhale, propelling the name out with a narrow jet of grey smoke.

Chapter Sixty-One

'Ada.'

Chapter Sixty-Two

Heart leaping wildly in her chest, Kat tried to keep her voice steady.

'Sorry, Deborah . . . did you say Ada?'

'That's right. She was playing with Emily in the treehouse. Then she strolled into the kitchen and said Emily had tripped and fallen.'

'How old was Ada at the time?'

'Fourteen.'

It wasn't a massively rare name. But not as common as say Chloe, Jessica or Sophie, especially for a girl born in 1999.

'Are you in contact with Ada?'

Deborah drew on her cigarette. 'Haven't seen her since she left home at sixteen. Haven't wanted to, either.'

'Do you know if she ever changed her name?'

'Nope.'

'Deborah, do you think Ada had something to do with Emily's death?'

Deborah stubbed her cigarette out, twisting the butt violently against the ash-encrusted brass.

'There was something off about Ada. Right from the day she was born. She never cried. When she went to nursery, that first day, I was all ready for tears, her doing that clingy act kids do, like you're sending them into a torture chamber. And do you know what? Ada just walked in. Didn't even look over her shoulder at me.

'She had friends, but she never brought anyone home. She liked to go out on her own for walks. We told her it wasn't safe but she ignored us. Lee once said the only stranger danger Ada would encounter was if she bumped into a mirror.

'Emily was an angel. She used to try and include Ada in games or take her to parties. She never gave up. It's why they were playing together in the treehouse. I mean, can you remember when you were eighteen? Would you have wanted to play with your weird fourteen-year-old sister?'

Kat thought back to her own childhood. She'd been the younger sister, not the older. But Deborah Siddle was on the money. Diana, at eighteen, couldn't put enough distance between her and Kat.

'Not really.'

Deborah reached for her cigarettes. Shook the packet, but it was empty. Tutted.

'No, me neither. But Emily did. They'd been out there about half an hour. Then Ada swans into the kitchen and calm as you like announces that Emily's fallen out of the treehouse. The way she said it she could have been talking about a book or a football, not her own flesh and blood. It chilled me.'

'Did you ever ask her about it?'

'Of course! She just kept repeating it. "Emily just fell." Lee lost his rag a couple of times. But even that didn't seem to bother her. She just used to smile at him like he was doing it to amuse her.'

'But you thought she'd pushed Emily?'

'I didn't think it. I *knew* it.' Deborah lit another cigarette. Sucked smoke deep into her lungs. 'Just like I knew she killed Tommy.'

Kat felt like she was a surfer who'd just caught the biggest wave of her life, being lifted bodily and then thrown towards the beach with terrifying, yet exhilarating force.

'Tommy?' she repeated.

'Our neighbours bought their son Alex a puppy for his birthday. Lovely little cocker spaniel. Honey-coloured. Alex came in one day screaming that someone had killed Tommy. His dad went out to look and found Tommy in the woods. Gutted, apparently. One of our kitchen knives was lying beside the body. I asked Ada about it and she denied it but I knew she'd done it. You could see it in her eyes.

'You're sure.'

'Totally.'

Kat nodded. She recognised stone-cold certainty when she saw it. And there was something she felt would be useful in the next phase of her investigation.

'Can I ask a favour?'

◆ ◆ ◆

Kat returned to Jubilee Place, arriving at just after 5.00 p.m. And, joy of joys, Tom was at his desk.

'Oh, thank God, Tomski. I so need you. Listen, this is either the end or I've gone down the deepest darkest rabbit hole you can imagine. But I just went to speak to a dead girl's mother. Not one of the first nine you pulled up. But I found her with your app. A new one. Oh, and by the way, you are a total legend. Anyway, I'm getting overexcited. Listen. Deborah Siddle, that's her name, the dead girl's mother, told me she suspected that her younger daughter murdered her old sister, Emily. And the younger girl's name was Ada.'

She paused for breath, sucked in oxygen the way Deborah had sucked down smoke.

'We know an Ada,' he said carefully.

'Yes, Tomski, we do. She's Ethan's girlfriend. She's the girlfriend of a murderer. What if it's her?'

'The younger sister, though . . . Her name would have been Siddle, not Monk.'

'I know! So I want you to find out if Ada Monk ever changed her name.'

'On it.'

While Tom started searching, Kat grabbed a sheet of paper and a pencil and started scribbling dates down. She wrote in such haste that the pencil point broke, scattering fine particles of graphite over the paper. She swore and found another one, tried to be more careful this time.

For each victim, starting with Emily Siddle, she mapped Ada's ages on to their dates of death. Proceeding from the as-yet-unproven assumption that at some point Ada Monk had been fourteen-year-old Ada Siddle.

Nicole Bagshaw had died in 2017, when Ada would have been the same age, eighteen. So a four-year gap. Easily explainable without stretching anyone's imagination. Perhaps it took four years for her murderous impulses to calcify into something pathological. Something she recognised as an urge.

From then, Ada could have killed one victim a year until 2026, when, for some reason, she'd enrolled Ethan in her scheme before killing George Seaton-Clark while Ethan was in custody.

Or had she? Was there another explanation for Ethan's DNA being present on Rosie's corpse after all? Had Ada put it there to frame him? But why?

An answer presented itself at once. Ada had said she was planning to move to the US. Framing Ethan might have given her the chance to make a clean break. Or even resume her killing in America.

But if Ada had killed Rosie, why had she almost immediately killed George rather than waiting until the following May?

As these questions whirled around inside her head, Kat's stomach turned over.

Oh, God – was Ethan innocent, after all?

Kat's phone bleeped, the alert for an incoming text. It was Clare.

Chapter Sixty-Three

Kat read Clare's text with mounting impatience.

> Sorry, got sidetracked. Student in distress! Will have list of victims' lecturers to you in next 10 mins :)

Kat made coffees for herself and Tom. Her phone pinged with the email as she carried them back to their desks.

Just as Tom had done with his list of victims, Clare had tabulated her results. They'd make a good pair.

Two names stood out from the rest.

Rebecca Poole and Rosie Duggan had both been taught by Ada Monk and Ethan as guest lecturer on the Media Studies BA course.

But George was the outlier here – both in terms of sex and time of his murder. He'd had neither Ada nor Ethan for any lectures.

'Hey, Tomski! If a student isn't down as having a particular lecturer for their course, does that mean there's no way they could have attended one of their lectures?'

He swung round in his chair.

'Not necessarily. Unis are pretty open places. You can attend any lecture you like. I once went to an anthropology lecture. By mistake, admittedly, but nobody asked to see any ID or anything.'

'So George could have attended one of Ada's lectures?'

'Definitely.'

'How's your search for Ada's name-change going?'

'I got as far as the *Gazette*. But the staff, like all good government bureaucrats, want seven to ten days to process the request.'

'We don't have that long. She could do it again.'

'Well, how else are we going to find out?'

'When you change your name, you don't have to do it officially, do you? I'm sure I heard that once on some course or other. What if Ada just *calls* herself Monk?'

'Then all her bank stuff, passport, all of that, would still be in her birth name of Siddle.'

'Which would be a problem for a normal person, but if she's a psychopath she might not care.'

'How does that help us, though?'

'Call the university. Ask for someone in payroll.'

A smile stole over his lips. '*Now* who's the legend?'

He picked up his phone.

Kat turned back to her screen. Could George have attended one of Ada's lectures for fun? Media studies sounded cool. It might even have been relevant to his own course, especially the psychology side of things. She loaded the video where Rosie Duggan had called Ethan out for his 'vulture journalism'.

Pressed play.

It took her three viewings, slowing down the playback, zooming in, then out. But then she found him.

George was half-obscured by another student, but the features visible were definitely his. There was the link between the three latest Middlehampton students. They'd all attended a minimum of one of Ada Monk's lectures. Had that been how she'd selected them? Befriending them, getting to know about their starry ascent? Marking them out as future victims?

Tom put his phone down and whooped with triumph.

'Oh, yeah! We've got her, boss, we've bloody got her!'

Kat looked up. Tom was on his feet, grinning.

'Guess who receives Ada Monk's salary every month?'

'Go on, Tomski. Tell me. Take the win.'

'Ada Siddle.'

Kat leapt to her feet and hugged her bagman. This was it. The beginning of the end. Relief flooded her system.

But they needed to work fast. Ada was still out there and, for all they knew, planning another murder. And whatever Ethan's involvement in her crimes, he was tucked up in a cell downstairs and could wait for now.

Whether Ada was escalating, bored or just plain mad as a hatter, it didn't matter. They had to stop her. But she was cunning, clearly. Rushing over to her house with a warrant wouldn't fly. She could just deny everything and tie them in knots for months.

Kat looked over Tom's shoulder and pulled back hurriedly. Carve-up had just entered MCU, casting glances left and right, presumably looking for his new secretarial assistant.

'There he is!' he crowed. 'Jubilee Place's resident PowerPoint wizard. I tell you, Tom,' he said as he came to stand in front of him, with his back to Kat, 'if coppering doesn't work out for you, I reckon there's a solid career for you making kickass presentations.'

He turned to face Kat. 'You should see the animated transitions he built for me, DS Ballantyne. The brass won't know what's hit them.'

She found she had no words. None that wouldn't land her in hot water so deep she'd need air tanks, anyway.

'Cat got your tongue? Never mind. Tom, I'm afraid I'm going to need you to work late on it. There's a few of the slides I changed after you left my place. Shouldn't take more than a couple of hours. They're really minimal.'

Kat found her tongue. 'It's going to have to wait, Stu. We'll be planning an arrest strategy all evening.'

Carve-up turned slowly to look at her. 'I beg your pardon, *DS* Ballantyne? That wasn't a junior officer telling her manager what could and couldn't happen, was it?'

Tom was right. Carve-up reeked of Aramis. She forced herself to breathe it in so she wouldn't look like a fish gasping for air.

'No. That was the lead investigator on multiple linked homicides telling him that her DC is going to be helping her catch a serial killer. Something I'd have thought a DI so focused on the *metrics*' – she shuddered inwardly as she used the hated word – 'would be pleased about.'

But Carve-up was Carve-up. A corrupt, greasy-pole-climbing excuse for a detective who'd attempted to have his DS and a DC murdered.

He curled his top lip. 'Yet, amazingly, here I am, absolutely not pleased. And you know why? Because you're at it again. Is this that daft cow who got shit-faced and fell off that car park last week? I mean, fuck me, DS Ballantyne, I know you're desperate to keep up with Tom here, but face it, it's a lost cause. He's fast-track. What are you? Born in Middlehampton. Tried to leave for university but couldn't hack it. Moved back to Middlehampton. Work in Middlehampton. You'll probably die here and the world won't even miss you.'

'Shut the fuck up, Stuart,' Tom said sharply. 'You're way out of line. Kat's a brilliant detective. I've learned more from her than I ever will from you.'

Carve-up's mouth dropped open. Kat was horrified. Tom had just torpedoed his own career.

But something had gone wrong with Carve-up's brain, or whatever passed for one in that thick skull of his. He was looking at Tom as if he'd transformed into an alien, or a gorilla or possibly a garden gnome. Something entirely incomprehensible anyway.

'What did you say?' he finally choked out.

'I said Kat's a legend, sir. A brilliant thief-taker.'

Tom eyeballed Carve-up and waited him out. Kat couldn't believe what was happening. It was like some weird play taking place right in front of her. Possibly called *An Inspector Falls*.

'He did, Stuart,' Kat said.

'No. He didn't. He told me to shut up.'

'*I* didn't hear that. Are you all right. You look pale. Shall I get you some water?'

'I'm fine,' he snapped. 'And I need you working on my presentation, Tom.'

'Sorry, sir, I can't. Kat's already given me a direct order.'

'We could talk to Linda, Stuart,' Kat said, maintaining the solicitous tone that he apparently found so confusing. 'I'll happily abide by her decision.'

That was it. Carve-up always backed down when bigger dogs were paraded in front of him. Usually he tried to curry favour, but if he showed his belly to Linda, Kat reckoned she'd lick her chops and tear it open.

'Forget it.'

He stalked off towards his office. His door slammed, rattling the thin sheet of glass beside it.

Kat looked at Tom. He had a pleased expression on his face.

'Thanks for that, Tomski. If you hadn't intervened just then, I'd have given him another nosebleed.'

'I guess we're quits now after I saved you the last time.'

She smiled. 'I guess we are. Come on. Let's go before he changes his mind. We can eat at mine and then figure out how we're going to take Ada down before she kills anyone else.'

Ten minutes later, they were pulling out of the Jubilee Place car park in Kat's Golf.

Chapter Sixty-Four

'So Ada's been killing students since 2013, after murdering her older sister by pushing her out of the treehouse,' Tom said.

'Looks that way.'

'Why do you think Ethan murdered Rosie?'

Kat bit her lip. Forced herself to give voice to the terrible doubt spiralling round in her brain.

'I'm not entirely sure he did, mate. I think Ada might have framed him.'

'Or told him what she was doing. He might have murdered Rosie to impress her. Or to taunt you. Plus he was using it to boost his podcast ratings. I checked his numbers. They always jump after he starts a new case. Wait! Do you think Ada *made* him do it?'

'Why? Would she do that?'

'I don't know, fun? *Folie à deux?*'

'Ada transfers her psychosis to Ethan and he kills Rosie believing he shares Ada's delusion about her older sister?'

'It's not that hard to imagine.'

A guilty thought of her own intruded as she straightened the steering wheel.

Life would be easier with Ethan behind bars. No more self-serving, loudly voiced questions at press conferences. No more aspersions cast on her and her team from the safety of his basement studio. No more flickering remnants of the anxiety she'd still feel from time to time when leaving Jubilee Place late at night, wondering, as she clutched her keys between her knuckles, whether Ethan had woken up that day and decided he no longer need worry about the caution Abby had delivered.

She frowned. She wanted justice for Rosie and all the other victims. If that meant Ethan spending his life behind bars, so be it. But justice would only be served if they could arrest Ada as well. All they needed was one piece of evidence.

The realisation hit her like a baton to the face.

'Crap.'

'What?' Tom asked, twisting in his seat.

'Follow the evidence!'

'Exactly! Don't worry about Ethan, Kat. He's going to go down for it.'

'But that's the point, Tomski! That's the whole, bloody point. Yes, he will. But what evidence do we have on Ada?'

'Well, we've got . . .'

The click of the indicator was the loudest sound in the Golf's cabin.

'Go on,' Kat said in a flat voice.

'A theory, unsupported by a single shred of evidence.' Tom's voice was filled with defeat. 'Except for the name-change?'

Kat adopted Ada's soft, inoffensive, light voice. 'I hated Siddle but I never got round to doing the official paperwork. This works for me.'

'Her sister's death?'

Again, speaking as Ada: 'Mum and Dad couldn't cope with their grief. Blaming me was their way of coping.'

'But it was the same MO?'

'My client's sister's death was a tragic accident, as the coroner confirmed,' Kat said in pompous, lawyerly tones. 'Were benzodiazepines found in her system? We don't know, since forensic post-mortems aren't called for in cases of accidental death. So, not the same at all, and not qualifying for the term "MO" at all.'

'But you were so sure, Kat.'

'I know,' she said, speaking in her own voice once more. 'And deep down I still am. But if I call Linda and ask her for an arrest warrant? She'd ask for evidence, and believe me, Tomski, my little bit of play-acting would be like light entertainment compared to what she'd say. I've already had her views on the subject once on this case.'

'So what do we do?'

'Not sure. Get creative. Dig more. Come up with a plan to get her to incriminate herself.'

She negotiated the last few turns and parked on the drive.

'Come on,' she said. 'I'm gasping for a cup of tea.'

'Hey!' she called as she walked into the hall and hung her bag on a coat hook.

'Hi, Mum!' Riley called from the kitchen.

With a high-pitched yelp, Smokey came tearing out of the kitchen, his claws losing purchase on the hall flooring so he skidded into the wall at the dog-leg.

Tom laughed as he bent to scratch Smokey behind the ears. 'Might need to work on your drifting, Smokes.'

The little dog grunted contentedly and butted his head against Tom's arm each time he tried to stop.

'You'll be there until midnight, Tomski,' Kat said with a smile as she went into the kitchen.

Riley looked up from his laptop. 'All right, mother?'

'Yeah, good. Homework?'

'Biology.' Riley looked past her. 'Hi, Tom. Did you do biology at school?'

'I did. Got an A at A level. And at uni, too.'

'Uni? Wait, you did criminology, right?'

'I did.'

'So you did, like, blood splatter? Crime scenes?'

'I did.'

Tom didn't correct Riley on 'splatter' versus 'spatter'. It was a small kindness, which Kat appreciated. And she saw something else, too. How, as an adult, you could relate to Riley without always having to make sure he was getting everything right. Tom was a natural. He'd make a great dad. Did Clare want kids?

Kat smiled. She was thinking like her mum. They hadn't even been on a date yet. Or not as far as she knew. She made a mental note to ask him later.

Tom sat beside Riley and answered his question while Kat made tea.

'Where's Dad?' she asked over her shoulder.

'He had to go out. Some sort of IT crisis at a client's.'

'Oh?' Kat tried to keep her voice light. 'Did he say which one?'

'Marnie.' Riley turned to Tom and murmured conspiratorially, 'She's hot.'

Kat flushed with heat herself as she poured boiling water into the teapot. But it was the heat of jealousy. IT crisis? Really? She'd been striving not to worry about Van and Marnie. But each time her name came up, or Van was working on her bloody site, she felt another wicked little pang, like a splinter under a nail.

'Did he say he'd be back for dinner?'

'Nope. Some problem with the backend, apparently.'

Riley sniggered and, to her dismay, Tom joined him. She kept her back to them so they wouldn't see the scowl twisting her mouth. There was rapport, and there was taking the piss.

After they'd eaten, Riley excused himself, leaving the kitchen to the adults.

'Everything all right, Kat?' Tom asked as she got out her force-issued laptop and waited for it to boot up.

'Yeah, why?'

'Nothing. You were a bit quiet over dinner.'

Damn Tomski for being so observant!

'Just thinking about the case. So, I've been wondering about the towns where the murders were committed. Hold on.'

She loaded Tom's table of unexplained deaths and their locations and tiled it with a map of the UK on which she'd plotted the towns.

'Quite the odyssey,' Tom said.

'Middlehampton. Liverpool. Sheffield. Glasgow. London. Back to Middlehampton. What does that look like to you, Tomski?'

'It looks like an academic CV. Ada's CV.'

'Can we prove it?'

He checked his watch. 'The university HR department could probably help but they'll be closed now. Unless they're working late. I'll give them a call. Or perhaps Clare can help.'

'Hold your horses! I've got a better idea, although I do want to ask you about Clare.' She opened a browser and typed in a web address. In a few seconds they were looking at LinkedIn.

'Nice,' Tom said, nodding his head.

Kat typed Ada's name into the search box. Three women shared that name on the professional networking site. Below a customer experience manager at a restaurant in Boca Raton, Florida, and a pharmacist at a medical practice in Bergen, Norway, was a media studies lecturer at Middlehampton University.

Kat clicked on Ada's profile.

Tom's chair legs squawked on the floor, making her jump, as he shuffled closer to the screen.

'She did her BA in English at Liverpool John Moores University,' he said. '2018 to 2020.'

'Worked in Sheffield for a year in 2021 as a PA in a marketing agency.'

'Did her master's in media studies in Glasgow in 2022,' Tom said, his voice filling with energy.

'Then she moved to London in 2023 to start her PhD at Imperial.' Kat tapped the screen. 'That's interesting, though, don't you think? She switched universities last year, coming to Middlehampton to complete her doctorate. I wonder if the Met were looking at her kills, too.'

'My client felt that there were more opportunities in her home town. Hardly evidence of a murderous temperament, more a completely understandable focus on her academic career,' Tom intoned, borrowing Kat's lawyer-voice.

She turned to him. 'I hate you,' she deadpanned.

'You're welcome,' Tom said with a sly smile. 'But it reads like a self-penned geographical profile, Kat, don't you think?'

'It does. But it's still a mile away from reaching the evidence threshold for an arrest. And even if we did arrest her, she's cunning, Tomski. She probably wouldn't even need a lawyer to walk out of Jubilee Place a free woman.'

'So what do we do?'

'You're going to go home and get some sleep. Tomorrow's going to be a big day.'

'What about you?'

'I want to do some research of my own.'

Once Tom had gone, Kat settled down at the kitchen table with a cup of black coffee. She started looking into Ada's background. Every job she'd had, every address she'd lived at. Every article she'd published. At 12.37 a.m., she found something significant. An address in Sheffield. Tucked it away for now.

Van came in at just before 2.00 a.m. Kat knew because she woke briefly, and checked the glowing red digits on her bedside clock.

'Where've you been,' she mumbled.

'John's. Playing *Call of Duty.*'

Had he been avoiding her because he knew she'd want to bend his ear about the case? Witter on about Ethan? It was true, she did use Van as a sounding board. But that was what all cops did. You had to or you would go mad. She fell asleep wondering if she should start keeping a journal.

Waking early, she went into work and settled down to read another of Rosie's diary entries. Now her plan to arrest Ada was in place, she felt she could afford to stop looking for clues and start understanding a little more about Rosie as a person. As a young woman.

Because however many murder cases Kat took on, she never wanted to forget that each case centred on a person. One who'd been somebody more than just a case number, a 'vic' or a 'DB', or even a body on Jack Beale's gleaming stainless-steel dissection table.

Chapter Sixty-Five

ROSIE DUGGAN'S JOURNAL

11 April 2026

OK, breathe, Rosie, breathe. This is freakin' awesome!

I. Have. Decided.

That's right, I've decided what I want to do after uni. I know, I know it's only my first year and everything could totally change, but this feels right.

Enough teasers, dear diary, I'm going to write it down in your pages and then I can't change my mind.

I want to do a master's, then my doctorate. Then I want to be a lecturer. I went to see Dr Monk yesterday, for some advice. She's such a good listener and I just needed to get everything into the open.

She is SO cool. I love her. I just wish I had the courage to ask her out. I know she's way older than me, but even if we had just one date I would have that memory.

sigh

God, listen to me! I sound like some lovelorn fifth-former in one of mum's old *School Tales for Girls* books!

Anyway, I asked her if she thought I had what it takes. I'd really love to do my PhD at a foreign university. I'm thinking the US perhaps, or even something really wild like Spain, although I'd have to learn the lingo. But if I do go there I could easily take on Spanish next year as a subsidiary. I've always been really good at languages anyway, so I'm sure I could manage.

But anyway, I'm getting ahead of myself. The point is, Ada said she thought if I really wanted it, I should go for it. She's even got a couple of contacts at American universities thanks to her own research projects and she said she'd put in a good word for me.

I literally can't believe my luck! I told Ada and she just smiled that secret smile of hers and said that we make our own luck. Her exact words were, 'If you want it, Rosie, go out there and grab it. Fly as high as you can.'

And I, being such a nerd, said, 'What about Icarus? He flew as high as he could and look what happened to him.'

She just smiled and said, 'Nobody's going to make you fall, Rosie, I promise you.'

Chapter Sixty-Six

Kat snapped the journal shut, chilled by Ada's promise to Rosie.

She called Ada, who answered on the first ring.

'Ada Monk.'

Kat smiled before speaking. It was supposed to make your voice sound friendlier.

'Hi, Ada, it's Kat Ballantyne. We've come into some new evidence implicating Ethan in a string of other murders similar to the way he killed Rosie Duggan. I was hoping, seeing as you're one of the closest people to him, that you could come to Jubilee Place this morning for a chat. I could really do with your help in understanding his psychology.' She paused, deliberately. 'I know how hard this is for you, and if you'd rather not, I would completely understand.'

Ada's voice was firm, resolute. Just the trace of a wobble.

'No, no. I understand. It's just, you know, I'm still adjusting to this new reality.' She sniffed, loudly. 'My boyfriend a serial killer? It's just so, so . . . unbelievable.'

Of course it was. Kat was sure now that Ethan was nothing of the kind. Just a dumb idiot who'd got in way over his head with the genuine article.

'When do you need me?' Ada asked.

'I was really hoping you could come in right away. Time is of the essence, what with the PACE clock ticking. Sorry, that's—'

'—the Police and Criminal Evidence Act clock. I know. We cover it in Media Representations of the Legal System. It's one of the most popular modules I teach. Now's fine. I'm still at home, actually, and I practically have to drive past Jubilee Place on my way to work. I can be there in twenty minutes.'

'Ada, you are a star. Thank you. I don't know what I'd do without you.'

'It's nothing. Just doing my civic duty.'

And, apparently, forgetting about your emotional turmoil of two minutes ago, Kat thought as she went to book an interview room.

'Sorry, Kat,' the departmental secretary said, consulting a calendar on her screen. 'Leah and Fez have hauled four people in on those arsons. They've booked all the interview rooms out for the whole day.'

'What about the friendly room?'

The secretary wrinkled her nose.

'Someone threw up in there last night. It's closed for a deep clean.'

Kat sighed. 'Thanks. Guess I'll have to get creative.'

'There's always the roof. Nice this time of year. Plenty of space. As long as you take your phone to record it, it's kosher.'

Kat smiled at the semi-serious suggestion. Then the expression fell from her face. Something Tom had said came back to her. She nodded to herself.

Twenty minutes later, Polly called her to say she had a visitor. Kat gave Tom a couple of instructions then went down to collect Ada.

Ada was waiting in a corner of reception. In her baggy jeans, loose crop-top and shoulder bag, she looked more like one of her students than a lecturer. An easy way to gain the girls' trust.

Kat went over, hand outstretched.

'Ada, thank you so much for coming in! I hope you're not missing anything important.'

Ada smiled, shook hands. The same limp fish as before. Act or not, Kat couldn't wait to let it go, but Ada's grip, though floppy, was unyielding. She looked into Kat's eyes.

'I just want to say, I am so sorry.'

Kat frowned. 'About what?'

'Poor Ethan. I worry that I should have spotted the signs. Called you sooner.'

'*Did* you see signs?' Kat said, relieved when Ada finally released her hand.

Ada sighed. 'I mean, not that the layperson would pick up. But I'm, well, I hesitate to use the word "expert", but I did my master's on media depictions of serial killers.'

'That's amazing!'

Ada beamed. 'Isn't it? I titled my thesis "Good Girls Do Kill: Female violence as an antidote to toxic masculinity – the female serial killer as feminist icon".'

'Wow. Bit of a mouthful,' Kat said, having prepared the line the night before after finding Ada's thesis tucked away on an academic CV site.

Ada's smile vanished. 'My supervisor said it was the best title she'd ever read.'

'Oh, well, what do I know? I never even went to university. Not clever enough, I suppose.'

Ada offered a sympathetic smile. 'It doesn't matter, Kat. Not everybody has what it takes. And look at you! A detective sergeant at, what, forty? Forty-two? That's quite an achievement.'

'Thirty-six, actually. Must have forgotten to put my slap on this morning. Come on, let's get the lift.'

They had the lift to themselves. Kat punched the button for the top floor.

'All our interview rooms are full, I'm afraid,' she said. 'But as it's a sunny day I thought I'd show you a sight members of the public never see. The roof. There might be a copper or two having a crafty smoke, but there are great views of Middlehampton.'

Ada looked up at the stainless-steel ceiling of the lift. The tip of her tongue, pink as a cat's, flicked out over her lower lip, just for a moment.

She dropped her gaze to Kat. 'Cool!' she said, eyes twinkling.

'Has Ethan been stalking you, Ada?' Kat asked, apparently out of nowhere.

'What? No, why?'

'Well, we've traced at least eight dead girls who fit a profile and who died in the same way as Rosie Duggan. They're all in places where you were either studying or working. I'm assuming he must have been following you around the country. Middlehampton, Liverpool, Sheffield, Glasgow, London, and then back to your home town, Middlehampton. Quite the odyssey.'

The good humour and 'I'm just happy to help' eagerness deserted Ada.

'I had no idea you'd been so thorough in researching him.'

'Oh, yes,' Kat said, warming to her theme. 'He's killed in every city you've lived in, including your home town.'

Ada turned to face Kat. 'How do you know where I grew up?'

'I know all kinds of things about you, Ada. It's called witness profiling. We do it as a matter of course when we're looking for people who can help us profile a murderer. It's standard practice. We can't afford to get caught out if it turns out a key prosecution witness turns out to be a serial killer themselves, can we?'

Kat's heart was thumping in her chest. It was taking all her mental strength not to scream at Ada to turn around and accept the bite of the cuffs she had clipped to her belt under her suit jacket.

'Joke!' Kat said. 'I mean, you hardly fit the bill of – what did you call it in your little essay – a "female serial killer as feminist icon"?'

'It wasn't a "little essay", it was my master's thesis!' Ada said, overloud in the small metal box that contained them both. 'Sorry, sorry. I suffer from claustrophobia. Lifts always make me anxious.'

'It's fine,' Kat said. 'Who doesn't have anxiety these days? Are you taking anything for it?'

'No. I just try to avoid closed-in spaces, or if I have to be in one, I do breathing exercises.'

'So, no prescription drugs for anxiety then? No tranquillisers?'

'No. As I think I just said, I manage it holistically.'

'No Xanax or Valium? Benzos can be incredibly effective, so I've heard. Ethan used them on his victims, you know.'

Ada smiled. It didn't reach her eyes. 'Really, nothing.'

The lift doors opened on to a featureless corridor, painted a pale gloss green.

'Here we are,' Kat said brightly. 'It's along here and then through the safety door, which, by the way, some naughty person disabled the alarm on.' She rolled her eyes. 'Coppers, eh? Worst lot of lawbreakers you'll ever meet!'

She led Ada along the concrete-floored corridor, their footsteps echoing off the hard surfaces. At the far end, the door to the roof barred their way. A large green and white sign declared: *This door is alarmed. No access except for authorised personnel.*

Kat hit the bar hard with the heels of both hands. Turned and grinned at Ada. 'As I said. Coppers!'

An array of satellite dishes and radio aerials were clustered in the centre of the roof, the wind blowing through them setting up sympathetic vibrations that sounded like distant moans.

Ada stopped beside a hutch containing air-conditioning units. 'So, Kat. What exactly is it you wanted to ask me about Ethan?'

'Let's leave Ethan for now, Ada. What I'd like to know is how, if you don't have a prescription, you got hold of the benzodiazepines you used to subdue your victims.'

Ada frowned. Then, she grinned. 'This is a joke, right?'

'No, I'm deadly serious. How did you do it?'

'I'm sorry, I don't know what you're talking about.'

'And why kill George Seaton-Clarke at all? I mean, Ethan had done this year's kill, and we'd arrested him, so you were in the clear. If you'd moved towns and started again next year on May sixth, or buggered off to America, nobody would have been there to spot the pattern.'

'Look, Kat, this is all very interesting, and I suppose you're just testing me in some weird way. But I really have no idea what you're talking about.'

The act wasn't bad. But Ada had missed the obvious move a genuinely innocent person would make. She hadn't stormed off, bristling with anger and indignation, threatening to call a lawyer and sue for defamation or police harassment. Instead, like the narcissist she was, she was enjoying being the centre of Kat's attention.

'You're a serial killer, Ada. You've murdered at least ten people because of your feelings of inadequacy. They were golden children and you're just a pathetic loser.'

Kat crossed the last few feet of grey bitumen to stand looking down at the town she loved so much. The town whose population she cared about enough to put herself in danger rather than run away from it. Like now. Turning her back on a serial killer. She shook her head and slapped her right temple for good measure. Adjusted her stance a little. Felt the comforting pressure of the cuffs in their leather pouch.

'I mean, Ada, talk about a waste of space!'

A gust of wind rattled the radio aerials. The noise almost masked the gritty scuffs of Ada's feet as she ran towards Kat.

The shove between her shoulder blades was hard enough to drive the breath from her lungs, but Kat had no time to worry about that as she hurtled off the roof, arms windmilling in the air.

The last thing she heard was Ada's hoarse cry.

'I hate you, Em!'

Chapter Sixty-Seven

Kat's scream as she fell was entirely genuine.

It was hard not to feel frightened, sailing off a roof with the hard, unforgiving pavement waiting to greet her eight storeys down.

Heart pounding, panic clouding her mind, she still managed to rotate in mid-air. She landed seven feet lower down – a human starfish – on HR's green roof. It was dried out, but as springy and yielding as moorland heather. Winded, she got to her feet and rushed over to the steel inspection ladder bolted to the wall.

By the time Kat had reached the roof, Ada lay at Tom's feet, struggling against her cuffs. Tom was finishing the arrest script.

'. . . given in evidence. Do you understand?'

But Ada was silent. Mouth open, she could only stare at Kat. Kat found she could quite easily imagine Ada's state of mind. A tumult of basic emotions, in which rage and confusion currently reigned, but which, very quickly, calm calculation would replace.

'Do you understand your rights as I have explained them to you?' Tom said again.

Ada turned her face away from Kat. It appeared to cost her a great deal of effort. She looked up into Tom's face and smiled as she said, 'Of course I do, Tom. I'm not an idiot.'

◆ ◆ ◆

Arrested in the commission of a crime, no warrant needed, Ada allowed herself to be led back to the lift. While Tom took Ada to the custody suite, Kat went to see Linda.

'We just arrested Ada Monk.'

Linda put her pen down. 'Charge?'

'Attempted murder.'

Linda frowned. 'Attempted? From what you've told me all her victims died. Horribly, I might add.'

'She attempted to murder *me*, Ma-Linda,' Kat said, preparing for a grilling.

Linda removed her black-framed reading glasses and regarded Kat for a few seconds. Kat's pulse had slowed down after her encounter with Ada on the roof. Now it ticked up again and she felt that familiar squirrely feeling of anxiety in the pit of her belly. She'd not crossed the line. But she thought she'd probably been pretty bold in walking along it. Like a kid doing a highwire act on a tall brick wall. Or a roof parapet.

'Attempted how? Exactly.'

'I was interviewing her. On the roof. I turned my back. She pushed me off.'

Linda's eyes widened, then narrowed.

'Few questions?'

'Please.'

'The roof?'

'All the interview rooms were booked.'

'And you thought, well, I could wait or I could conduct an interview on the roof? Why not reception, or the canteen, or the bloody broom cupboard, Kat? If her brief's any good, he'll be screaming "entrapment" before you've finished the caution.'

Kat could try to dodge the inquisition. Spin Linda a line about needing her suspect to be relaxed. Gave it all the consideration it merited. Five milliseconds. Went for the truth. The only thing that might save her.

'I knew she was guilty, but I had no evidence you'd be happy with to give me a warrant. So I offered myself as bait. Which she took. And it doesn't meet the threshold for entrapment. It wasn't random virtue-testing. It was targeted at a person who I strongly suspected had committed multiple linked homicides. And the opportunity I gave her to commit a crime was unexceptional. Anyone would have done it. If turning my back on her was an exceptional incitement to murder, then the exceptionality was all in the mind of the suspect.'

Linda's breathing wasn't laboured. Not as such. But it was loud.

'Nice speech, Kat. Been on the DoJ website, have we?'

'For an hour, Ma'am,' Kat said.

Was she in the clear? Or did Linda have a copy of *Blackstone's Statutes on Evidence* beneath her desk that she was preparing to hurl at Kat.

'She pushed you off?'

'Yes.'

'Yet here you are. Alive.'

'Yep.'

'Did you bounce? Did you have a bungee cord concealed in your knickers? Are you merely masquerading as a DS in my unit while on secondment from the circus?'

Kat, perhaps unwisely, grinned.

'Not funny, Kat,' Linda barked.

'Sorry, Ma'am. I fell on to HR's green roof.'

Linda's mouth dropped open.

'You chose that side of the roof on purpose. You *wanted* her to push you off! Jesus, Kat, did you even pause for one second to consider the risks?' She scrunched her fingers into her hair as if to pull it out. 'What were you *thinking*? What if you'd missed your landing? You'd be dead now and I'd be up to my tits in paperwork.' She paused. Was that a trace of a smile? 'Not to mention mourning a talented if incredibly disobedient detective.'

'I'm sorry, Ma-Linda,' Kat said, ashamed at how easily Linda had seen through her lies. 'I wasn't in any danger.'

'No?' Linda steepled her fingers together under her chin. 'Apart from getting my boot so far up your arse you'd need an MOE team to extract it you mean?'

'Ma-Linda, I had to do *something*! I needed to get her before she did it again. I knew it was her, but I couldn't prove it. Now we've got her I can get her to admit the other killings. I've stopped her.'

While Kat defended herself, Linda doodled something on the pad in front of her. Kat craned her neck. Linda swivelled the pad round.

She'd drawn a cat with eight more behind it, dwindling in size. 'Just make sure you nail her to the wall, Kat,' Linda said, finally. 'I'll try to run interference if her brief starts wailing about your unorthodox methods.'

'Thanks, Ma-Linda.'

'Thank me when you get a conviction, Kat. Not before.'

Kat knew a dismissal when she heard one and left Linda's office while the ground beneath her feet was reasonably firm. Linda hadn't backed her over Leah and Fez, but at least, when it really mattered, she'd come through.

Arriving back in MCU she called to Tom. 'How did it go with Ada?'

He came over. 'She asked for a lawyer, but it's going to be a duty solicitor. In her words, "How much do you think an assistant lecturer at a second-rate provincial university actually makes?"'

'Bit rude about our fair seat of learning.'

He shrugged. 'We've got until 1.30 p.m.'

'Right. Grab some gloves. We're going to have a look at Ada's house.'

◆ ◆ ◆

'What are we looking for?' Tom asked, as they donned purple nitrile gloves.

'Trophies linking Ada to her victims would be nice. But anything that shows she had contact with them in the days or weeks before their deaths. Notebooks, pictures, whatever you can find. Something like joint-selfies. Evidence she didn't just know them but was friendly with them.

'Shall I start upstairs?'

'Take the master bedroom first, then work your way through the other rooms. I'll have a poke around in here. If we can't turn anything up by 1.00 p.m., we'll leave it to the CSIs, but I really want something before we talk to her.'

As Tom's feet clumped above her head, Kat didn't immediately start opening drawers and shaking books out. Instead, she sat in an armchair and looked around the room as a visitor might.

Ada could have kept the mementoes of her kills somewhere private, and Kat fervently hoped Tom would discover them before they had to return to Jubilee Place. But what if she decided to keep them on permanent view? What did she want her guests to see? To use as the basis of assumptions they'd make about her?

A shelf to the right of the TV held the usual array of large-format books interspersed with house plants, all glowing with vitality. The shelf above bore an array of trophies for sports. Kat rose from the chair and moved closer to get a better look.

This was a surprise. Ada was quite the athlete to judge from the range of gold and silver figurines. A tennis player served a ball. A netballer took a shot at goal. A rugby player dived over an invisible line for a try. A plaque recorded her participation in a student exchange with the University of California, Santa Cruz. An engraved plaque on a Lucite block proclaimed her Fundraiser of the Year in the BBC Radio Stoke Charity Champions Awards 2024. She'd debated with other universities. Ridden horses to success in dressage events. Won a painting prize and an essay competition. And she'd been the youngest person ever to complete the London Marathon in bare feet.

Was she compensating for having lived her early life in Emily's shadow? It would make sense. Although this was quite the haul. Were they fakes? Things she'd commissioned from a shop or an internet supplier to satisfy her own vanity, lessen her feelings of insecurity?

Kat looked again at the sporting trophies, particularly the netball figurine. That was, after all, her own sport. But it looked to be genuine, right down to the engraved brass plaque screwed to the base. Next to the goal shooter, the rugby player hung poised in mid-air, on his way to the try but forever prevented from landing it. She looked closer. And she smiled. This was it!

She called upstairs, 'Tomski! Get down here!'

Tom clattered down the stairs, doing a more-than-adequate impression of Riley when dinnertime was called.

'What is it? What did you find?'

Kat pointed at the row of trophies.

'Spot the odd man out, Tomski.'

He took a step closer and worked his way along the shelf, reading inscriptions, even picking them up to examine their bases. Finally, he replaced the Lucite fundraising award on the shelf. Turned to Kat.

'I give up. What am I not seeing.'

'The odd *man* out, Tomski?'

He frowned. Then his dark eyebrows lifted. He turned to look at the sports trophies again. Picked up the rugby player.

'You are shitting me!'

'What's Ada doing with a male rugby player trophy?' she asked.

He put the trophy down and his hand went to his pocket, He brought out a dinky red Swiss Army knife and pried out a cross-head screwdriver. Began working on the four small brass screws holding the plaque – *Ada Monk, Woman of the Match* – in place.

It dropped into his palm. He turned the trophy towards Kat. Engraved directly onto the metal base were the words *George Seaton-Clark, Man of the Match.*

'Box them up, Tomski. We'll let Darcy deal with the rest.'

Tom shook his head. 'Her trophies were literally trophies.'

'I think our Ada is acutely aware of the ironies inherent in her lifestyle,' Kat said, removing her gloves. 'She even boasted to me about her master's thesis. It was all about female serial killers.'

'She's a sly one, isn't she? Leaving them in full view like that?'

Kat nodded. Ada Monk was sly, no question. But she was going to have a hard time explaining away her attempted murder of a police officer. Especially since Tom had filmed the whole thing.

Chapter Sixty-Eight

Kat looked into Ada's eyes, striving to see the humanity there somewhere beyond the blank stare she was currently bestowing on Kat.

'Why did you push me off the roof, Ada?'

Silence.

Behind Kat, the uniformed officer cleared her throat. Tom shifted in his chair, causing the fabric of his shirt to whisper against itself. The spools of the tape recorder whined a little on each revolution. It set Kat's teeth on edge. Ada smiled. Her lips parted with a quiet click.

'Isn't it obvious?'

'Why don't you spell it out for me, Ada? Pretend I'm a bit hard of thinking.'

'I thought you wanted me to.'

Of all the answers Kat had been expecting, this was not among them. What was Ada playing at?

'You thought I wanted you to try to murder me?'

'No, silly! I assumed it was a test of some kind. You said you liked to vet potential friendly witnesses. I imagined you'd made the necessary arrangements.' Ada's expression flickered. The innocent stare vanished for a split-second, to be replaced by something altogether nastier. 'Which you had, of course. What did you use? Cardboard boxes. A trampoline? Gym mats?'

'It was purely my good fortune there was a green roof a few feet lower down, Ada.'

'Bollocks,' Ada said. But, weirdly, she was smiling. Did she, on some level, respect Kat for having caught her out?

The solicitor cleared his throat. 'It appears that you entrapped my client into committing a crime, DS Ballantyne. Any evidence so gathered would be inadmissible in court.'

Kat turned him to him. Didn't miss a beat. 'You can take that up with my colleagues in the Crown Prosecution Service. I'm sure they'll be satisfied my actions were reasonable, proportionate and unexceptional. It's not as if I'd lugged a pile of crashmats up there from the station gym. In any case, that's not what I want to talk about.'

'What *do* you want to talk about, Kat?' Ada asked, with a smile. 'I came here to help, after all.'

'Tell me about the trophies, Ada.'

'What trophies?'

'Well, how about the rugby trophy in your sitting room?'

'What about it?'

'It was awarded to George Seaton-Clark. Why did you take it and have a new plaque made?'

'I told George I'd never won anything for sports. He gave it to me.'

Kat switched track. No sense asking Ada about the others.

'I'm going to read you a list of names, Ada, and I want you to listen very carefully. Tell me if any of them mean anything to you?'

Ada nodded. Sat up straight on the hard-backed chair. The gesture reminded Kat of Tom's way of readying himself to answer one of her questions.

'Ask away,' she said. 'I'll do my best.'

Kat picked up a sheet from the file with the list of Ada's victims on it. Without preamble, she read them aloud. Before the interview, she'd briefed Tom to watch Ada closely. After each name, she looked straight at Ada.

Ada frowned throughout Kat's reading. When Kat put the sheet of paper down, she shook her head.

'I'm sorry, Kat. They meant nothing to me.'

Meant? Not *mean*? A Freudian slip revealing a psychopath's callous disregard for her victims, a knowing taunt, or just some fussily precise grammar, as in *the names on the list you just read meant nothing to me*?

Kat drew the corners of her mouth down. Then she bit her lip. Shook her head. Quite the pantomime of the human emotion entitled 'severe disappointment'.

She put on a brave face. Smiled at Ada.

'That's OK, Ada. Oh, I almost forgot. I have one other name.' No paper this time. She stared into Ada's expressionless eyes. 'Emily Siddle.'

The name worked like a pair of Taser barbs.

Ada reared back, and before she could stop it, hostility twisted her usually pleasant, bland features into something that erected the short hairs on the back of Kat's neck. Then it was gone.

Ada shook her head. 'Sorry. No.'

'No? Only, when you attempted to murder me, I distinctly heard you scream, "I hate you, Em!" That's right, isn't it, DC Gray?'

'I heard it myself. And I captured it on video, too.'

'Sounds like you were expecting it, DC Gray,' the solicitor said. 'That speaks to entrapment.'

'I was taking a selfie for a young friend of mine who's thinking of joining the police,' Tom said smoothly. 'It was pure luck I had my phone out when your client attempted to murder my boss.'

'I was lost in the moment,' Ada said. 'And you say I screamed "Em"?' She turned to her solicitor. 'That could mean anything, couldn't it?'

The young woman nodded. 'It's hardly conclusive, DS Ballantyne. Perhaps we could move on?'

Despite her youth, she seemed in control of herself and her material. Kat was impressed. But not dismayed. This had a way to run yet.

'It took me a while, Ada, but when I looked into your past, I found the answer I'd been looking for. Why you murder your victims the way you do. It's how you killed Emily, isn't it?'

Ada furrowed her brow. 'Who's Emily?'

'Your older sister.'

'I told you, I don't have one.'

'I thought you did. I checked your family history.'

'Well, you checked it wrong. I'm an only child. As I told you in my office.'

Kat checked a document in her folder. 'You're sure?'

Ada made a 'well, duh!' face. Cross eyes and slack jaw. 'I think I'd have remembered something like an overachieving older sister called Emily.'

Kat rolled her eyes. 'Ada, I am so, so sorry. What must you think of me?' She slapped herself on the forehead. 'What a dummy I've been! Talk about a loser, eh, Ada? A massive loser who never achieved anything and always had to live in her sister's shadow.'

Ada's eyes flashed dangerously again. Kat could feel the desire to kill radiating off the psychopath opposite her like a hot gas cloud.

Kat had brought a messenger bag into the interview room with her. Black leather. A Christmas present from her parents a few years back. Not really practical for work, although every time she used it she marvelled at the soft leather and beautifully finished stitched seams.

Now she reached down and unsnapped the magnetic catch holding the flap secure. She unzipped the main compartment and reached inside.

Chapter Sixty-Nine

Owing to the awkward angle, Kat had to use both hands to lift the heavy, leather-bound photo album out of her bag.

She let it fall onto the table with a loud thud. Ada jumped. Finally, she'd lost her composure. Worse was to come.

'I borrowed this from your mum, Ada. Deborah Siddle *is* your mum, right?'

Ada went for an easy-going smile. Her lips twisted upwards as if hoisted into place by wires. But her eyes were as cold and dead as those of a shark. 'I've never heard of her. My name is Monk.'

'Monk is the name you go by professionally,' Kat said. 'But you never got round to changing it officially, did you? You're Ada Siddle. Please don't bother denying it. We have payroll records from Middlehampton University confirming it.'

'So what? It's a common-enough name.'

'It really isn't, Ada. But let's move on. I thought we could take a look at a few photos.'

'DS Ballantyne, how is this relevant?' the solicitor asked.

She was doing a good job, given the lack of time to prepare, but Kat could see that even she was curious about the album. Time to reveal all, then.

Kat opened the first page.

Pointed to a photo showing Emily Siddle, aged five, wearing a pink tutu, a gap-toothed grin and holding a delicate silver trophy of a pirouetting ballerina.

'Your sister started young, didn't she, Ada? I don't suppose you remember this, do you? You were only one at the time.'

Ada glanced at the photo then back up at Kat.

'No idea what you're talking about.'

'Really? How about this one?'

Kat flipped through to another page marked with a Post-it.

Emily Siddle, aged fourteen, in football kit, holding aloft a trophy almost as big as her head.

'She captained the school's under-16s to victory in the Hertfordshire schools league. Such an amazing athlete, wasn't she? She won player of the year, too. Shall we look at that photo, too?'

Kat turned the page. Here was Emily again, shaking hands with a middle-aged woman who was handing her a gold trophy in the form of a footballer in mid strike, arms outspread for balance.

Ada clamped her lips together. Looked at her solicitor. 'I don't have to look at this, do I?'

'Yes, Ada,' Kat said. 'Yes, you do. How about this one?'

Emily caught mid-jump astride a horse called, according to the handwritten caption, 'Monty'.

'She's sixteen there. Just two years left to live. Obviously she didn't know that then. Look at how she's smiling, even in the middle of winning yet another cup for showjumping. She was just such an all-rounder, wasn't she, Ada?'

Ada's hands were clenching and unclenching. The colour had drained from her face. She looked up at Kat.

'Yes. She was. Whoever' – she drew in a slow, shuddering breath – 'she was.'

Kat smiled. 'Come on, Ada, you know exactly who Emily Siddle was. She was your fantastically talented, smart, brave, athletically gifted older sister, wasn't she? The one your parents showered with more love, admiration and affection than she could handle. Much more than she needed. So much love, when they could easily have spared a little for you. I can sympathise, you know. I have an older sister, too. My mum and dad think the sun shines out of her rear end. There have been times, if I'm honest, when I wouldn't have minded seeing her fall off a car park roof. And there you were – poor ignored, awkward little Ada. Living in Emily the golden child's shadow.'

Ada's hands had unclenched, but only enough to allow her fingernails to scratch uselessly at the unyielding plastic laminate table.

She shook her head. 'No.'

'No? You were happy in her shadow? Is that what you're telling me? While perfect Emily went around picking up prizes and trophies as if they were hers by right, you had to struggle even to get noticed?' Inspiration struck Kat. She widened her eyes. 'I bet your dad built the treehouse for Emily, didn't he? What did he call it, "Emily's Palace"? Something like that? A reward for all her hard work? I bet she loved it. "Oh, thank you, Daddy. I love you so much!"'

Tom spoke for the first time, deepening his voice a touch. The line he'd worked out with Kat ahead of the interview.

'I love you too, Em. Much more than Ada. You're our golden child.'

Ada's fists slammed down on the table. A disjointed double bang that made her solicitor jump. Something happened to Ada's facial muscles. They seemed to slacken then all contract at once, sending her mouth into a terrifying rictus, teeth bared all the way back to her molars.

'Shut up! Shut up!' she screamed. 'Hard work? That's a joke! She never worked for anything. And it was Emily's Castle, not palace. She invited me up there to play but it was all, "Oh, Ada, look what Dad made me. Isn't it great? Now I'll have somewhere to bring my friends." Like she didn't already have a massive room twice as big as mine.' She snatched a breath. Colour returned to her cheeks. She rocked back in her chair, her chest rising and falling. Eyeballed Kat. 'I needed to make her stop. You don't know what it's like to live life in the shadow of someone else. Never being seen. I hated it!'

Kat closed the photo album. She looked at Ada, who was sitting quietly, every trace of her outburst of seconds earlier vanished. Her face was impassive, her breathing regular.

'Ada, did you kill your sister, Emily Siddle?'

'You don't have to answer that,' the lawyer said quickly.

'But I want to,' she said, looking straight at Kat. Then she nodded. 'And you've earned this.' A small pause. Then: 'Yes, I did.'

'Because she had everything you didn't?'

Ada quirked her mouth to one side. 'No. Because she killed our neighbour's puppy and made sure I got the blame.'

Kat frantically recalibrated what she'd thought she knew about Ada's childhood. 'Your mother said you did it.'

'Of course the bitch did,' Ada said with a curled lip. 'She believed every word that came out of Emily's mouth. Well, guess what, Kat? My mum was an idiot. She was blinded by all the prizes Emily won, all the gold stars she got.' Ada sneered. 'You want to know the truth? She liked to hide it, but my perfect sister had a sadistic side-hustle going on. She used to bully the little kids on the street, get them to eat worms, flash their underpants at passing cars. She showed me how to hurt them so it wouldn't leave marks. I liked it, I don't mind admitting it. It made me feel good. Only, every time someone went crying to their mummy, guess who got smacked so hard she couldn't sit down? Who got her pocket money stopped and her TV privileges suspended? Perfect fucking Emily, or sad little loser Ada?

'And then, this one day, she came home all covered in blood. Smiling. Said I was going to be in so much trouble. They found Tommy and I got the blame. Then she was all, "Don't be cross, Ada. It doesn't matter if you get into trouble, everybody expects it. Come and play in my castle." So I went up there, and when she turned her back on me, I pushed her out.'

Ada sat back, her chest rising and falling evenly, as if she'd just recited a poem instead of a horrific account of childhood abuse.

Kat took a moment to compose herself.

'Did you kill Nicole Bagshaw?'

Ada's eyes flicked up to the ceiling.

'Hmm. Middlehampton College. Sixth form council president. Great golfer. Yes.'

'Poppy Arbuthnot?'

'Liverpool John Moores. First year. Crazy good netballer. Yes.'

Kat read out two more names, got a mini-CV and a 'yes' for each.

'This one's been puzzling me, Ada,' Kat said, turning over a sheet of paper. 'Norman Pettifer. According to our records, you lived next door to Norman in Sheffield. But he was a ninety-one-year-old man. He served his country, did his National Service in Korea, but he didn't really fit the profile of your other victims. Was that you as well? Did you kill Norman?'

Ada wrinkled her nose. Chuckled. It sent a shiver down Kat's spine.

'It's a bit of a funny story, actually. I was never much good at making friends with other students, but Norman and I just hit it off. I started running little errands for him. Shopping, a bit of laundry, getting him his lottery ticket when he'd forgotten.

'Then, one day, we were having a cup of tea together – Norman always called it a "brew". His army days, I suppose. Anyway, where was I, yes!' She clapped her hands together. 'This one time, we were discussing pensions. There must have been something on the news, and dear old Norman said – and Kat, I swear I remember his words as if it were yesterday – "It doesn't matter what Boris does to the economy, I'm all right, Ada. My money's upstairs in an ammunition box." It sounded so unlikely, I asked him what he meant, thinking he might have some cash or something. He told me to go and have a look under his bed.

'So I went upstairs, and got down on my hands and knees and looked under the bed. Guess what? There it was. Just like he said. An old green metal ammunition box complete with white stencilling on it. I dragged it out, and by the way, it was really heavy. *Super*-heavy! I unsnapped the catches and opened the lid. And it was full of gold coins. Hundreds of them. "Pretty, aren't they?" Norman said. He'd followed me upstairs and was standing in the doorway of his bedroom. So I said they were and how about I made him a cup of tea?

'He turned to go downstairs, and when he reached the top step I pushed him down. It took me ages to take all the coins next door. Had to make loads of trips. Probably ten. Then I called the ambulance. Norman didn't need the gold, but I was young. I needed somewhere to live. It's how I bought my cottage. Norman wouldn't have minded.'

Kat stared at the cold-blooded psychopath before her. Until that point, she'd managed to hang on to a shred of compassion for Ada. Not for the murderous young woman she'd turned into, but the lonely, unloved child she'd once been. But the matter-of-fact way she'd just described murdering Norman Pettifer for his life savings put a torch to that shred and reduced it to ashes.

'How about Elodie Johns? Did you murder her, too?'

'Hold on, I need to get dear old Norman out of my head. Elodie. Oh, yes! My co-worker at the Department of Trade.

All-round wonder girl and right royal pain in the arse. Yep, killed her, too.'

Kat moved on to the next four girls on her list. Sneha Ashok. Felicity Wise. Dalilah Muhammad. Rebecca Poole.

Ada admitted to their murders with as much interest as if she were agreeing with Kat on places she'd visited on her holidays.

'Rosie Duggan,' Kat said.

Ada's casual demeanour changed. 'No.'

'I beg your pardon, Ada. Are you telling me you didn't kill Rosie Duggan?'

'No. That was Ethan, as you told me.'

'So you didn't collect his DNA and plant it on Rosie's body?'

'Absolutely not. I was at home when he killed her.'

'You're sure?'

'I think I'd remember.'

'My client has shown no difficulty in admitting to the other murders,' the solicitor said, showing admirable poise given she was sitting next to a self-confessed serial killer. 'Can we take it she is also telling the truth here and move on?'

The lawyer had a point. Ada had admitted immediately to murdering ten human beings, yet she had vehemently denied killing a puppy. What reason did Kat have to doubt that Ada was also telling the truth when she denied killing Rosie? With a sinking feeling, she realised that despite all her emotional flip-flopping over Ethan, her gut pulling her one way as her rational copper's brain tugged her the other, he might still be guilty of murder.

'Did you push George Seaton-Clark from the roof of Halliwell House on the night of the vigil for Rosie Duggan?'

'I did, yes. That one was definitely mine.'

'Why?'

'Why what, Kat?'

'Why did you murder George Seaton-Clark? Every other one of your victims, including Rosie Duggan—'

'Who, for the record,' Ada said, turning to address the tape recorder as if it were a living thing, 'I deny murdering.'

'The girls you *do* admit to murdering were all killed on May sixth. The date you murdered your older sister. Yet you killed George Seaton-Clark a week later, on May thirteenth. I'm curious as to why.'

'Isn't it obvious? Ethan broke my pattern. He denied me the chance to round off the year with another goody two-shoes taken off the board. I thought I could wait until next year, but it wasn't working. I was really on edge. My mental health was suffering. And what with all the fuss everyone was making about Rosie, I sort of told myself, "Ada, you need to practise self-care. How can you expect others to love you if you don't love yourself?"'

'And that's why you murdered George?' Kat asked, nauseated by Ada casually spouting self-help mantras to excuse the cold-blooded murder of a teenager.

'That's right.'

'Why him?'

'Oh, the usual story, I'm afraid. I overheard him before one of my lectures, boasting about winning the student union presidency, and then he started rabbiting on about Rosie Duggan. He said, "What kind of loser murders beautiful young girls with everything to live for? They're worth everything; he's worth nothing."' She paused, smiled at Kat and then at her solicitor. 'Can't you see, Kat? He deserved it. So I killed him. And it worked. I felt whole again. Ready to face the world.'

Kat felt like screaming that the only thing Ada would be facing was a short trial and a long – hopefully whole-life – sentence somewhere with very high walls.

She closed her folder.

'Interview suspended.'

Chapter Seventy

That night, Kat took Tom out for a celebratory drink.

Pinot Grigio for her, a Guinness Zero for him.

They clinked glasses. The alcohol hit Kat's stomach with a welcome release of tension.

'We did it, Tomski.'

He wiped pale foam from his top lip.

'We did.'

'You've been brilliant, you know? Every step of the way. Honestly, that was some of the best detective work I've ever seen. People skills, research, digging up facts from all over, interviewing. You smashed it, mate.'

Tom blushed, but he was smiling, too. 'Thanks, Kat. I'll take that. You're turning into a not-bad mentor as well. Although I probably won't follow you off a roof.'

'Cheeky sod!' She took a sip of her wine. 'So, you and Clare?'

He looked at her. Was that a half-smile she saw playing on his lips?

'What about us?'

'Oh, come on, Tomski! Stop being so bloody coy. Have you asked her out yet?'

'Me? No.'

Her heart sank. Just when she'd thought everything was looking up for her bagman. 'Why not? Don't you like her?'

The silence drew out. He drank some Guinness. 'I think she's great. But I can't ask her out, Kat.'

'Why not, for God's sake?'

'Because *she* asked *me*. This being 2026, it would appear she has – oh, what's that word again?' He looked at the pub ceiling for a second then back at her, a huge grin on his face. 'Oh, yes! Agency. Clare has *agency*. We're having dinner tomorrow night.'

Her mouth dropped open. Then she slapped him, hard, on the shoulder, though she was smiling.

'You absolute sod!'

Tom's grin slipped then vanished altogether.

'Kat, can I say something else? And please let me get to the end or I'll probably start crying.'

She put her glass down.

'Go on then, Tomski. Don't keep me in suspense.'

Her heart sank. He was going to tell her he'd got his next posting through. He was back on the fast-track, handbrake off, roaring away from her, up to the Met, or West Midlands. Somewhere they put the Bambis where they could really shine.

'It really meant a lot to me, you inviting me round for dinner the other night. Just sitting with you, Van and Riley. It's been a long time since I had that sort of connection. Just being part of a family. With Mum and Dad running pubs, I always had to spend a fair amount of time on my own. Seeing Rosie Duggan's parents in their pub brought it all back to me.

'And, I don't know, just chatting with Riley, telling him about my life, answering his questions about drinking and girlfriends, well, it made me realise I'm all right as I am. Yes, I was in a coma, which my neurologist keeps telling me is a serious brain injury. But I feel OK. Not the person I was before, but not a worse version, either.'

Kat wiped away the tears that were running down her cheeks. 'Now look what you've done, you nitwit!' she said before rounding the table and crouching to throw her arms around him. 'Come here.'

Chapter Seventy-One

It was hard to stand straight against the force of the wind pushing her ever closer to the edge of the platform. Fear fogged her brain as she looked down, over the edge, at the town laid out like a model hundreds of feet below her. So high she was looking at the Bramalls, the Eels' London Road ground, the town hall, her house in Stocks Green, through wisps of grey cloud.

She clutched the spindly radio aerial mounted dead-centre on the circular platform. It snapped off in her hand, sending her perilously close to the edge. Her stomach was a hard knot and she was screaming in terror.

Opposite her, his legs planted two feet apart, Ethan leered at her.

'You thought you could bring me down, Kat. But the only one going down is you!'

He lunged towards her, arms outstretched. She screamed as his palms hit her chest and she flew backwards, arms windmilling, over the edge. The face looking down at her from the edge of the platform was Ada's.

The earth waited for her, ready to smash her bones, snap her joints, destroy her inside and out.

She woke with a huge physical jolt so overpowering she cried out, sure she must have fallen out of bed. Her nightie was soaked with sweat, her throat, her chest, her belly slick with it.

A dark figure stood at the end of the bed. She was paralysed, staring speechless as it took a step closer until a sliver of moonlight piercing the curtains revealed its features.

Ethan stood there, oversized grey prison sweats cloaking his form, reducing him to a pulpy, caterpillar-like mass.

'Not guilty,' he breathed, before disappearing.

She could move again. Panting with terror, she turned her head to the side, and sure enough, it was 3.01 a.m. Beside her Van snored, oblivious. She thought of waking him, asking for a cuddle. But he was working so hard, she didn't want to rob him of his rest. No sense them both being unable to sleep.

She made a promise to herself. Or to Van, really. Now the case was over, she'd make him his favourite meal at the weekend, open a nice bottle of wine and then sit down with him after dinner for a proper conversation. She'd ask him how she could support him more so he didn't feel he had to stay out late at a friend's playing video games to avoid having his ear bent about her latest case.

She lay awake for another hour, trying to get her breathing under control, Ethan's whispered plea echoing through her mind.

Had he really murdered Rosie Duggan? The evidence said he had. Ada had cheerfully confessed to twelve other murders but baulked at Rosie's. His motive had been captured on video. He had access to benzodiazepines, the drug used to render Rosie suggestible and docile. And he had no alibi.

Ethan would have his day in court.

And a jury of his peers would settle the matter.

As she finally drifted into a dreamless sleep, her last conscious thought was a simple one.

It's not my call.

ACKNOWLEDGEMENTS

I want to thank you for buying this book. I hope you enjoyed it.

As an author is only part of the team of people who make a book the best it can be, this is my chance to thank the people on my team.

For their patience, professionalism and support, the fabulous publishing team at Thomas & Mercer, led by Sana Chebaro and Sammia Hamer. I want to thank Sammia specifically for her help in developing Fez Mohammed as a three-dimensional character (and for coming up with his nickname). Also, my wonderful editor, Victoria Pepe, who, as well as having a sure literary touch and the sort of commercial vision that turns books into bestsellers, I count as a friend. My developmental editor, Russel McLean, is a fiction eagle, able to see an entire plot from his vantage point, but with the visual acuity to spot a clunky phrase from half a mile up. And lastly (but not leastly), my copyeditor, Gemma Wain, and proofreader, Jill Sawyer, without whom I am sure many of my authorial glitches would have escaped onto the finished page.

Plus the wonderful marketing team including Rebecca Hills, Jessica Sharples, Hatty Stiles and Nicole Wagner. And Dominic Forbes, who, once again, really smashed the brief with another awesome cover design.

For sharing their knowledge and experience of The Job, former and current police officers Andy Booth, Ross Coombs, Jen Gibbons, Neil Lancaster, Sean Memory, Trevor Morgan, Olly Royston, Chris Saunby, Ty Tapper, Sarah Warner and Sam Yeo.

I volunteer on Laverstock Ward at Salisbury District Hospital. The wonderful staff there have got used to my occasional (and sometimes worrying) questions about aspects of clinical practice.

The members of my Facebook group, The Wolfe Pack, are an incredibly supportive and also helpful bunch of people. Thank you to them, also.

And for being an inspiration and source of love and laughter, and making it all worthwhile, my family: Jo, Rory and Jacob.

Andy Maslen
Salisbury, 2026

If you enjoyed *The Perfect Girl*, why not read another title by Andy Maslen? Turn the page for an exclusive extract from *Shallow Ground*.

SUMMER | PEMBROKESHIRE COAST, WALES

Ford leans out from the limestone rock face halfway up Pen-y-holt sea stack, shaking his forearms to keep the blood flowing. He and Lou have climbed the established routes before. Today, they're attempting a new line he spotted. She was reluctant at first, but she's also competitive and he really wanted to do the climb.

'I'm not sure. It looks too difficult,' she'd said when he suggested it.

'Don't tell me you've lost your bottle?' he said with a grin.

'No, but . . .'

'Well, then. Let's go. Unless you'd rather climb one of the easy ones again?'

She frowned. 'No. Let's do it.'

They scrambled down a gully, hopping across boulders from the cliff to a shallow ledge just above sea level at the bottom of the route. She stands there now, patiently holding his ropes while he climbs. But the going's much harder than he expected. He's wasted a lot of time attempting to navigate a tricky bulge. Below him, Lou plays out rope through a belay device.

He squints against the bright sunshine as a light wind buffets him. Herring gulls wheel around the stack, calling in alarm at this brightly coloured interloper assaulting their territory.

He looks down at Lou and smiles. Her eyes are a piercing blue. He remembers the first time he saw her. He was captivated by those eyes, drawn in, powerless, like an old wooden sailing ship spiralling down into a whirlpool. He paid her a clumsy compliment, which she accepted with more grace than he'd managed.

Lou smiles back up at him now. Even after seven years of marriage, his heart thrills that she should bestow such a radiant expression on him.

Rested, he starts climbing again, trying a different approach to the overhang. He reaches up and to his right for a block. It seems solid enough, but his weight pulls it straight off.

He falls outwards, away from the flat plane of lichen-scabbed limestone, and jerks to a stop at the end of his rope. The force turns him into a human pendulum. He swings inwards, slamming face-first against the rock and gashing his chin. Then out again to dangle above Lou on the ledge.

Ford tries to stay calm as he slowly rotates. His straining fingertips brush the rock face then arc into empty air.

Then he sees two things that frighten him more than the fall.

The rock he dislodged, as large as a microwave, has smashed down on to Lou. She's sitting awkwardly, white-faced, and he can see blood on her leggings. Those sapphire-blue eyes are wide with pain.

And waves are now lapping at the ledge. The tide is on its way in, not out. Somehow, he misread the tide table, or he took too long getting up the first part of the climb. He damns himself for his slowness.

'I can lower you down,' she screams up at him. 'But my leg, I think it's broken.'

She gets him down safely and he kisses her fiercely before crouching by her right leg to assess the damage. There's a sharp lump distending the bloody Lycra, and he knows what it is. Bone.

'It's bad, Lou. I think it's a compound fracture. But if you can stand on your good leg, we can get back the way we came.'

'I can't!' she cries, pain contorting her face. 'Call the coastguard.'

He pulls out his phone, but there's no mobile service down here.

'Shit! There's no signal.'

'You'll have to go for help.'

'I can't leave you, darling.'

A wave crashes over the ledge and douses them both.

Her eyes widen. 'You have to! The tide's coming in.'

He knows she's right. And it's all his fault. He pulled the block off the crag.

'Lou, I—'

She grabs his hand and squeezes so hard it hurts. 'You *have* to.'

Another wave hits. His mouth fills with seawater. He swallows half of it and retches. He looks back the way they came. The boulders they hopped along are awash. There's no way Lou can make it.

He's crying now. He can't do it.

Then she presses the only button she has left. 'If you stay here, we'll *both* die. Then who'll look after Sam?'

Sam is eight and a half. Born two years before they married. He's being entertained by Louisa's parents while they're at Pen-y-holt. Ford knows she's right. He can't leave Sam an orphan. They were meant to be together for all time. But now, time has run out.

'Go!' she screams. 'Before it's too late.'

So he leaves her, checking the gear first so he's sure she can't be swept away. He falls into an eerie calm as he swims across to the cliff and solos out.

At the clifftop, rock gives way to scrubby grass. He pulls out his phone. Four bars. He calls the coastguard, giving them a concise description of the accident, the location and Lou's injury. Then he slumps. The calmness that saved his life has vanished. He is hyperventilating, heaving in great breaths that won't bring enough oxygen to his brain, and sighing them out again.

A wave of nausea rushes through him and sweat flashes out across his skin. The wind chills it, making him shudder with the sudden cold. He lurches to his right and spews out a thin stream of bile on to the grass.

Then his stomach convulses and his breakfast rushes up and out, spattering the sleeve of his jacket. He retches out another splash of stinking yellow liquid and then dry-heaves until, cramping, his guts settle. His view is blurred through a film of tears.

He falls back and lies there for ten more minutes, looking up into the cloudless sky. Odd how realistic this dream is. He could almost believe he just left his wife to drown.

He sobs, a cracked sound that the wind tears away from his lips and disperses into the air. And the dream blackens and reality is here, and it's ugly and painful and true.

He hears a helicopter. Sees its red-and-white form hovering over Pen-y-holt.

Time ceases to have any meaning as he watches the rescue. How long has passed, he doesn't know.

Now a man in a bright orange flying suit is standing in front of him explaining that his wife, Sam's mother, has drowned.

Later, there are questions from the local police. They treat him with compassion, especially as he's Job, like them.

The coroner rules death by misadventure.

But Ford knows the truth.

He killed her. *He* pushed her into trying the climb. *He* dislodged the block that smashed her leg. And *he* left her to drown while he saved his own skin.

SIX YEARS LATER
| SUMMER |
SALISBURY

DAY ONE, 5.00 P.M.

Angie Halpern trudged up the five gritty stone steps to the front door. The shift on the cancer ward had been a long one. Ten hours. It had ended with a patient vomiting on the back of her head. She'd washed it out at work, crying at the thought that it would make her lifeless brown hair flatter still.

Free from the hospital's clutches, she'd collected Kai from Donna, the childminder, and then gone straight to the food bank – again. Bone-tired, her mood hadn't been improved when an elderly woman on the bus told her she looked like she needed to eat more: 'A pretty girl like you shouldn't be that thin.'

And now, here she was, knackered, hungry and with a three-year-old whining and grizzling and dragging on her free hand. Again.

'Kai!' she snapped. 'Let go, or Mummy can't get her keys out.' The little boy stopped crying just long enough to cast a shocked look up into his mother's eyes before resuming, at double the volume.

Fearing what she might do if she didn't get inside, Angie half-turned so he couldn't cling back on to her hand, and dug out her keys. She fumbled one of the bags of groceries, but in a dexterous act of juggling righted it before it spilled the tins, packets and jars all over the steps.

She slotted the brass Yale key home and twisted it in the lock. Elbowing the door open, she nudged Kai with her right knee, encouraging him to precede her into the hallway. Their flat occupied the top floor of the converted Victorian townhouse. Ahead, the stairs, with their patched and stained carpet, beckoned.

'Come on, Kai, in we go,' she said, striving to inject into her voice the tone her own mother called 'jollying along'.

'No!' the little boy said, stamping his booted foot and sticking his pudgy hands on his hips. 'I hate Donna. I hate the foobang. And I. Hate. YOU!'

Feeling tears pricking at the back of her eyes, Angie put the bags down and picked her son up under his arms. She squeezed him, burying her nose in the sweet-smelling angle between his neck and shoulder. How was it possible to love somebody so much and also to wish for them just to shut the hell up? Just for one little minute.

She knew she wasn't the only one with problems. Talking to the other nurses, or chatting late at night online, confirmed it. Everyone reckoned the happily married ones with enough money to last from one month to the next were the exception, not the rule.

'Mummy, you're hurting me!'

'Oh, Jesus! Sorry, darling. Look, come on. Let's just get the shopping upstairs and you can watch a *Thomas* video.'

'I hate *Thomas.*'

'*Thunderbirds*, then.'

'I hate them even more.'

Angie closed her eyes, sighing out a breath like the online mindfulness gurus suggested. 'Then you'll just have to stare out of the bloody window, like I used to. Now, come on!'

He sucked in a huge breath. Angie flinched, but the scream never came. Instead, Kai's scrunched-up eyes opened wide and swivelled sideways. She followed his gaze and found herself facing a good-looking man wearing a smart jacket and trousers. He had a kind smile.

'I'm sorry,' the man said in a quiet voice. 'I couldn't help seeing your little boy's . . . he's tired, I suppose. You left the door open and as I was coming to this address anyway . . .' He tailed off, looking embarrassed, eyes downcast.

'You were coming *here*?' she asked.

He looked up at her again. 'Yes,' he said, smiling. 'I was looking for Angela Halpern.'

'That's me.' She paused, frowning, as she tried to place him. 'Do I know you?'

'Mummee!' Kai hissed from her waist, where he was clutching her.

'Quiet, darling, please.'

The man smiled. 'Would you like a hand with your bags? I see you have your hands full with the little fellow there.' Then he squatted down, so that his face was at the same level as Kai's. 'Hello. My name's Harvey. What's yours?'

'Kai. Are you a policeman?'

Harvey laughed, a warm, soft-edged sound. 'No. I'm not a policeman.'

'Mummy's a nurse. At the hospital. Do you work there?'

'Me? Funnily enough, I do.'

'Are you a nurse?'

'No. But I do help people. Which I think is a bit of a coincidence. Do you know that word?'

The little boy shook his head.

'It's just a word grown-ups use when two things happen that are the same. Kai,' he said, dropping his voice to a conspiratorial whisper, 'do you want to know a secret?'

Kai nodded, smiling and wiping his nose on his sleeve.

'There's a big hospital in London called Bart's. And I think it rhymes with' – he paused and looked left and right – 'farts.'

Kai squawked with laughter.

Harvey stood, knees popping. 'I hope that was OK. The naughty word. It usually seems to make them laugh.'

Angie smiled. She felt relief that this helpful stranger hadn't seen fit to judge her. To tut, roll his eyes or give any of the dozens of subtle signals the free-and-easy brigade found to diminish her. 'It's fine, really. You said you'd come to see me?'

'Oh, yes, of course, sorry. I'm from the food bank. The Purcell Foundation?' he said. 'They've asked me to visit a few of our customers, to find out what they think about the quality of the service. I was hoping you'd have ten minutes for a chat. If it's not a good time, I can come back.'

Angie sighed. Then she shook her head. 'No, it's fine . . . Harvey, did you say your name was?'

He nodded.

'Give me a hand with the bags and I'll put the kettle on. I picked up some teabags this afternoon, so we can christen the packet.'

'Let me take those,' he said, bending down and snaking his fingers through the loops in the carrier-bag handles. 'Where to, madam?' he added in a jokey tone.

'We're on the third floor, I'm afraid.'

Harvey smiled. 'Not to worry, I'm in good shape.'

Reaching the top of the stairs, Angie elbowed the light switch and then unlocked the door, while Harvey kept up a string of tall tales for Kai.

'And then the chief doctor said' – he adopted a deep voice – '"No, no, that's never going to work. You need to use a hosepipe!"'

Kai's laughter echoed off the bare, painted walls of the stairwell.

'Here we are,' Angie said, pushing the door open. 'The kitchen's at the end of the hall.'

She stood aside, watching Harvey negotiate the cluttered hallway and deposit the shopping bags on her pine kitchen table. She followed him, noticing the scuff marks on the walls, the sticky fat spatters behind the hob, and feeling a lump in her throat.

'Kai, why don't you go and watch telly?' she asked her son, steering him out of the kitchen and towards the sitting room.

'A film?' he asked.

She glanced up at the clock. Five to six. 'It's almost teatime.'

'Pleeease?'

She smiled. 'OK. But you come when I call you for tea. Pasta and red sauce, your favourite.'

'Yummy.'

She turned back to Harvey, who was unloading the groceries on to the table. A sob swelled in her throat. She choked it back.

He frowned. 'Is everything all right, Angela?'

The noise from the TV was loud, even from the other room. She turned away so this stranger wouldn't see her crying. It didn't matter that he was a colleague, of sorts. He could see what she'd been reduced to, and that was enough.

'Yes, yes, sorry. It's just, you know, the food bank. I never thought my life would turn out like this. Then I lost my husband and things just got on top of me.'

'Mmm,' he said. 'That was careless of you.'

'What?' She turned round, uncertain of what she'd heard.

He was lifting a tin of baked beans out of the bag. 'I said, it was careless of you. To lose your husband.'

She frowned. Trying to make sense of his remark. The cruel tone. The staring, suddenly dead eyes.

'Look, I don't know what you—'

The tin swung round in a half-circle and crashed against her left temple.

'Oh,' she moaned, grabbing the side of her head and staggering backwards.

Her palm was wet. Her blood was hot. She was half-blind with the pain. Her back met the cooker and she slumped to the ground. He was there in front of her, crouching down, just like he'd done with Kai. Only he wasn't telling jokes any more. And he wasn't smiling.

'Please keep quiet,' he murmured, 'or I'll have to kill Kai as well. Are you expecting anyone?'

'N-nobody,' she whispered, shaking. She could feel the blood running inside the collar of her shirt. And the pain, oh, the pain. It felt as though her brain was pushing her eyes out of their sockets.

He nodded. 'Good.'

Then he encircled her neck with his hands, looked into her eyes and squeezed.

I'm so sorry, Kai. I hope Auntie Cherry looks after you properly when I'm gone. I hope . . .

◆ ◆ ◆

Casting a quick glance towards the kitchen door and the hallway beyond, and reassured by the blaring noise from the TV, Harvey crouched by Angie's inert body and increased the pressure.

Her eyes bulged, and her tongue, darkening already from that natural rosy pink to the colour of raw liver, protruded from between her teeth.

From his jacket he withdrew an empty blood bag. He connected the outlet tube and inserted a razor-tipped trocar into the other end. He placed them to one side and dragged her jeans over her hips, tugging them down past her knees. With the joints free to move, he pushed his hands between her thighs and shoved them apart.

He inserted the needle into her thigh so that it met and travelled a few centimetres up into the right femoral artery. Then he laid the blood bag on the floor and watched as the scarlet blood shot into the clear plastic tube and surged along it.

With a precious litre of blood distending the bag, he capped it off and removed the tube and the trocar. With Angie's heart pumping her remaining blood on to the kitchen floor tiles, he stood and placed the bag inside his jacket. He could feel it through his shirt, warm against his skin. He took her purse out of her bag, found the card he wanted and removed it.

He wandered down the hall and poked his head round the door frame of the sitting room. The boy was sitting cross-legged, two feet from the TV, engrossed in the adventures of a blue cartoon dog.

'Tea's ready, Kai,' he said, in a sing-song tone.

Protesting, but clambering to his feet, the little boy extended a pudgy hand holding the remote and froze the action, then dropped the control to the carpet.

Harvey held out his hand and the boy took it, absently, still staring at the screen.

BLEEDING INK

News from Andy Maslen

Million Copy Bestseller

Did you enjoy this book?

Whatever the type of thriller you enjoy, Andy Maslen has a book (or two) that'll be right up your street. Join Bleeding Ink, Andy's monthly newsletter, and you'll get insider access to:

- A free ebook of Andy's 75 Favourite Stories on page and on screen
- Sneak peeks at upcoming thrillers
- Bonus short stories and behind-the-scenes insights
- Exclusive giveaways for loyal readers
- Monthly musings from the author's desk

+ much more!

It would be a crime to miss out . . .

Join at www.andymaslen.com

ABOUT THE AUTHOR

Photo © 2021, Kin Ho

Andy Maslen was born in Nottingham, England. After leaving university with a degree in psychology, he worked in business for thirty years as a copywriter, while also continuing to write poetry, short stories and novels. In his spare time, he plays blues guitar. He lives in Wiltshire.

Follow the Author on Amazon

If you enjoyed this book, follow Andy Maslen on Amazon to be notified when the author releases a new book!

To do this, please follow these instructions:

Desktop:

1) Search for the author's name on Amazon or in the Amazon App.
2) Click on the author's name to arrive on their Amazon page.
3) Click the 'Follow' button.

Mobile and Tablet:

1) Search for the author's name on Amazon or in the Amazon App.
2) Click on one of the author's books.
3) Click on the author's name to arrive on their Amazon page.
4) Click the 'Follow' button.

Kindle eReader and Kindle App:

If you enjoyed this book on a Kindle eReader or in the Kindle App, you will find the author 'Follow' button after the last page.